MILK RUN

For more information or to leave a comment about this book,
please visit us on the web at:
www.solarclipper.com

Publishers Note:

To my friend, Kay Persichitte.

She guided me from the sidelines,
inspired me by her example,
and asked the questions that brought me here.

The Golden Age of the Solar Clipper

Quarter Share
Half Share
Full Share
Double Share
Captains Share
Owners Share

In Ashes Born
To Fire Called
By Darkness Forged *

Milk Run
Suicide Run
Home Run

South Coast
Cape Grace*

Tanyth Fairport Adventures

Ravenwood
Zypherias Call
The Hermit Of Lammas Wood

* Forthcoming

MILK RUN

NATHAN LOWELL

Durandus

CHAPTER ONE
PORT NEWMAR: 2363, MAY-25

Natalya Regyri watched the teacup topple from her hand and crash to the floor. It felt like slow motion. Something captured by a high-speed camera for her later perusal in forensic dissection. Shards of white and red skittered across the smooth wooden planks as the tea splashed and stained them. Droplets of tea fell into the pool of blood. The man's eyes stared, flat and unresponsive as it spread beneath his head.

"Natalya, what happ—" Zoya's voice cut off with a quick, harsh, indrawn breath.

"He fell," Natalya said, her voice faint, barely a whisper. "I touched him and he fell."

Margaret Newmar appeared at Natalya's elbow as if risen from between the planks of her studio. "What have you done?" Margaret's voice echoed in Natalya's ears.

"I broke your cup."

Margaret snorted a disbelieving laugh. She grasped Natalya's upper arm and pulled her back from the fluids expanding across the floor. "Not the cup, dear girl." Shouldering her way in front of Natalya, she reached down and placed two of her ancient fingers against the side of Purvis's neck. She waited only a moment before pulling her hand back. Not really long enough to tell, was it? She glanced up at Zoya. "Get her out of here. Wait outside." Her voice came sharp. Used to giving commands. Used to being obeyed.

"Yes, ma'am," Zoya said and took Natalya's wrist. "Come on, Nats." She tugged and Natalya felt herself being led, a balloon on a string bouncing across the floor.

"I broke her cup."

Zoya extended her arm to take her friend's shoulders and pushed her along.

Outside the tai chi studio, night cloaked the campus. The revelry of graduation had faded, the graduates themselves off to begin their new adventures. Natalya and Zoya should have been among them, but when Margaret Newmar—founding family Margaret Newmar, *Sifu* Margaret Newmar—singled you out to have one last cup of tea, you went. Natalya went. Zoya went.

They'd found the honor had extended to a wider family of Newmar associates and students. Senior captains, sharp-faced women with hard eyes. Solid men with flat bellies and cold faces. Students like Andrew Purvis. Purvis the Pervert. The one man no woman ever wanted to be stuck in a room alone with.

The one man sprawled now on the smooth, wooden planks of the tai chi studio, a pool of blood spreading under his head, his eyes staring—the shattered remains of Margaret Newmar's antique bone china teacup strewn beside him. The one man who'd been alone with Natalya in the tiny galley at the rear of the studio.

"What happened, Nats?" Zoya's face floated in the darkness, a pale moon suspended above her dress blacks, her eyes dark as the night.

"I touched him. I didn't even push him. I wanted to get to the sink and he stood in the way." Natalya's voice felt like it came from someone else. She couldn't speak on her own. Someone else must have been talking.

"You touched him," Zoya repeated.

"A hand on his chest to keep him from grabbing me."

Zoya shook her head. "How did he fall?"

"I touched him. He just fell backward."

The door opened. Margaret Newmar stood silhouetted in the light for a moment before stepping out to join them. Her silk dress glowed yellow in the starlight, her back stiff, her face a mask. "Is your ship ready to go?"

Natalya shook her head once to try to make sense of the words. "My ship?"

"The *Peregrine*? Is it ready to go?"

The non sequitur made Natalya's head spin. "Yes, but what about—"

"His name isn't Purvis. He's not a student."

"Of course he's a student. He was in my Orbital Mechanics class." Natalya glanced at Zoya for confirmation.

Ms. Newmar shook her head. "That was his cover. His name was Michael Gavin."

"His cover?"

"He was undercover. Trade Investigation Commission."

Zoya's eyes went wide. "He's TIC?"

"*Was* TIC," Newmar said with emphasis on the first word. She looked at Natalya. "And you killed him."

"But I just touched him. He fell down." Natalya shook her head. "I couldn't have killed him. I couldn't."

Margaret's expression shifted to something unreadable. Her lips pressed into a line and the shadows around her eyes deepened. "Between you and me and Ms. Usoko here, I don't think you did. I have no idea what happened in that room." She shook her head slowly from side to side. "Unfortunately, one of those senior captains in there was his boss. As far as he's concerned, Gavin couldn't have killed himself and you were the only one with him." Her sigh was barely audible over the quiet whispering of the night wind in the leaves above them.

"But I didn't."

"But you did file a grievance against him," Margaret said.

Natalya's stomach turned cold. "Yes. Second year. He was—"

Sifu Newmar held up one graceful hand, a white bird fluttering in the night. "I know what he was. You have a motive. You have an opportunity. You're trained in three different forms of unarmed combat." She paused to sigh again and smile sadly. "You're the best fighter we've graduated in half a century."

"But I don't want to be a fighter. It's just an exercise."

"I know. You're also one of the best engineers we've graduated in decades, but that's all moot right now, my dear." She paused and her face tightened again. "You killed an undercover TIC agent with his boss in the next room. What do you think will happen?"

The night seemed to spin around her. Her head felt like somebody had pulled her brain out of her ears and replaced it with wet clay. She couldn't think. She could barely breathe.

"Is your ship ready to go?" Margaret repeated.

Natalya struggled for a breath. "I just need to get my grav-trunk and get aboard. I planned on leaving tomorrow."

Margaret looked at Zoya. "What did you see tonight?"

Zoya shook her head. "Not a thing."

Their hostess's smile looked a bit thin. "Work on that answer."

Zoya's eyes grew wider still. "You think I'm responsible somehow?"

Margaret shook her head. "I don't think either of you is responsible. What I think doesn't matter." She nodded at the door. "They're going to go sub-orbital in about two more minutes. If I were you, I'd be burning for the Burleson limit right now."

Natalya tried to speak but couldn't get her mouth to move.

Zoya took a half step forward. "But where could we go? If we dock anywhere ..." She shrugged. "They're not going to just let us walk away."

"Where's your tablet?" Margaret asked.

Zoya pulled it out of the holster, the pale light of the screen casting her face in a blue-white glow.

Margaret's fingers flashed on her own device and Zoya's machine bipped. "File for anywhere. Someplace in Ciroda, maybe. I just sent you the coordinates you need to get to and your contact's name. Don't tell anybody where you're going. It's out of TIC jurisdiction but don't linger."

Zoya looked at her screen. "Wait, you mean me, too?"

Margaret gave a tired chuckle. "Unless you want to spend the next ten stanyers trying to explain why your roommate killed an undercover TIC agent."

Natalya heard a man's voice raised inside the studio and Margaret glanced over her shoulder.

"I can give you about half a stan. Maybe."

Natalya's face felt hot and her head didn't seem to want to stay solidly on her shoulders. The night kept zooming around her.

The scream of a shuttle coming in for a nighttime landing at the campus spaceport cut across the sky.

"There's your ride. They'll turn that bird around and you need to be on it when it leaves."

Zoya stashed her tablet and nodded. "Thank you, ma'am."

Margaret shook her head. "I'm not doing you any favors, but at least you'll not spend the rest of your lives in prison."

"But I didn't do it." Natalya's voice sounded like a whisper to her own ears.

Ms. Newmar patted her shoulder. "You know it and I know it, but this is TIC. They're not going to rest until somebody pays. Right now, that somebody looks a lot like you." She leaned in close to Natalya's face. "There's nothing you can do here except sacrifice yourself on their altar of hubris. You and Ms. Usoko here get on that shuttle, take your ship, and disappear fast."

Zoya took Natalya's arm and gave a little tug. "Come on, Nats. She's right. We have to be on that shuttle."

Natalya let herself be towed and stumbled along the darkened path. "I didn't do it."

Zoya sighed. "I know, Nats. I know."

CHAPTER TWO
PORT NEWMAR: 2363, MAY-25

They squeaked onto the shuttle just before the doors closed, still wearing their dress blacks and earning grins from the cadet crew. A sour-faced second mate shot them an angry glance and a pair of astrogation rankers glanced back from the front of the cabin as they buckled in.

"Why are we doing this?" Natalya asked, leaning into Zoya to speak over the noise of the engines and the rumbling of the tires on the tarmac.

Zoya glanced around before answering. "There's nothing keeping us here, is there? Let's talk about it when we get aboard."

"But I didn't do anything."

Zoya patted Natalya's forearm where it rested on the seat divider. "Later, Nats."

The shuttle turned onto the runway and immediately kicked in the afterburners. The low roar cut out any conversation as the acceleration pressed them back into the padded seats.

Natalya sighed and gazed out at the academy campus rushing past the port. She'd arrived with such hope. Her head still felt stuffed with wet clay but her thoughts began to cut channels in it. She'd done nothing wrong. Purvis or Gavin or whatever his name was couldn't be dead. He'd just fallen down. She had barely touched him before he collapsed. People didn't die from that.

Did they?

Why run when she'd done nothing wrong? Shouldn't she stay and exonerate herself?

She thought of Margaret Newmar's face. The sadness and certainty she'd seen there. Was it possible TIC would actually charge her with murder?

The bottom dropped out of her world as the ship tilted skyward, shoving her farther back into the seat as they climbed out of the atmosphere while the ship seemed to slow the higher they climbed. In what seemed only moments, she saw the horizon curve from a flat line to the gently arching limb of the planet. The sky, already dark, turned crystalline when the stars no longer flickered through air and became hard-edged jewels. The shuttle raced around the planet, into the light from the primary, and back into darkness again, always climbing to catch the orbital.

Natalya's thoughts seemed to freeze in her head. Or perhaps they just ran in circles. The image of her cup falling, falling, falling to shatter on the floor. The flat expression on the man's face. The slow spread of blood and the splash of tea. Margaret Newmar's harsh commands. Her insistence that she run.

The suspicion grew that Margaret Newmar knew more than she'd ever said. That the universe that Natalya had grown up believing in was not the one that actually existed. That the evening behind them might be more significant than she suspected. Fear wrapped her gut in cold coils.

"You think they'll let us leave?" Natalya asked, leaning her head close to Zoya's.

Zoya glanced at her. "Depends on whether they know where to look. How soon can we get undocked?"

Natalya shook her head. "We'll need to file a flight plan but once it's on file, they'll let us go. The *Peregrine* is small enough that we won't need a tug or anything."

"So? A few ticks?"

Natalya pondered, her thoughts still slowed and barely tracking. "Yeah. Something like that. Ciroda, she said?"

"Margaret? Yeah. Ciroda. You know anybody in Ciroda?"

"Maybe." Natalya shook her head. "I don't know. Not off-hand."

Zoya patted Natalya's forearm again. "One step at a time."

The sour-faced second mate cast them another impatient look, his brow furrowed in a scowl.

Natalya pushed herself back into her seat as if to hold herself down. As if the seatbelt wasn't keeping her from floating away. What was his problem? Could he smell the blood? She glanced down at her blacks, a bit wilted from a long day that had started so well with a graduation ceremony on the parade ground and ended ... where? She closed her eyes and took a deep breath through her nose, pressing it out slowly through her mouth. She called on her discipline to focus on the imaginary candle in her mind. One flame danced in the dark. She focused on breathing. In. Out. The flame was her life. It burned alone in the dark. In. Out. Her mind grabbed the image and held it. Her training carried her into the place where only the flame mattered. Where other thoughts slipped into the background. Not gone. Waiting to re-emerge. For now, her mind stilled. Her breathing smoothed out. The cold coils in her belly relaxed their hold and warmth filled her body as the heat of the flame filled her mind.

The thump of landing gear locking into the orbital's shuttle bay vibrated in the background of her being. She released the flame, allowing it to fade away before opening her eyes. When she looked, the shuttle seemed clearer than it had when she'd entered. Her hands operated on their own, releasing the seatbelt from long practice.

Zoya looked at her. "Are you all right?"

A laugh struggled against her teeth.

"Sorry. Bad question." Zoya patted her arm.

The shuttle crew came back through the cabin and opened the passenger door. The second mate bundled himself off the ship as soon as the crewman cleared the hatch. The two astrogators stared at Natalya and Zoya. Rank order meant they had to wait for the two new third mates to leave the shuttle.

Zoya nodded at the hatch. "Go ahead. We're gonna need a tick to get our trunks off."

The taller of the two nodded a thank-you and bumped his seat-mate on the shoulder. They hustled down the center aisle while a shuttle crewman released the latches that held the trunks at the back of the cabin. With a friendly nod, he stepped back to let them pass.

"Safe voyage. Sars." He grinned.

Natalya knew him. A third-year. She'd seen him on campus but couldn't remember his name.

Zoya nodded. "Thank you, Mr. Mallory. Good luck with your classes."

Natalya nodded and tried to smile. She didn't trust her voice. She held the memory of her flame, the peace of meditation against the sea of outside influence. The control handle responded to her fingers and the grav-trunk lifted off the deck. She followed Zoya off the ship and into the hurly-burly of the Port Newmar orbital.

Chapter Three
Newmar Orbital: 2363, May-25

Zoya paused in the passage between the shuttle bay and the small craft docks. Most of the foot traffic had gone off toward the main docks or the lifts into the orbital proper. She looked at Natalya. "You hanging in?"

"I still feel like this is a nightmare. I'm going to wake up in my rack in the dorm and it'll be graduation day."

Zoya's sympathetic grin felt good. "Yeah. I'm there. How soon before they lock down the orbital, d'ya think?"

Natalya looked around, taking stock. She blinked her eyes several times and stretched her neck. "Nope. Still here." She returned Zoya's gaze. "Won't be long now, but we're almost at the ship. If we can get out of the docking bay, we'll be free." She sighed. "Still doesn't feel right."

Zoya set off down the passage again. "I know. Not to me either, but Margaret Newmar hasn't gotten to be nine hundred stanyers old by being stupid about the CPJCT."

"She's not nine hundred stanyers old." Natalya felt a laugh forming in her chest. "She can't be a day over five-fifty."

The joke set Zoya off and the stress kept them laughing through the security lock, down the small craft dock, and up to the tiny scout craft resting on its skids at the far end.

"Mercy Maude," Zoya said. "Could you have parked any farther away?"

Natalya just shook her head. "Cheapest slip. Not like I had a lot of spare credits, what with tuition and all." She watched Zoya's gaze take in the ship. "She's not much to look at but she's all mine." She crossed to the lock amidships and keyed in a code to open the outer doors before leading her grav-trunk up the small ramp and into the lock. Zoya stood outside the ship, her grav-trunk behind her. Her gaze kept sweeping the ship. "Come on if you're comin'. We need to leave and you've got the address."

"She's beautiful," Zoya said, jamming herself and the trunk into the lock. "I guess I never really appreciated it before."

Natalya keyed the lock sequence and the outer door closed so the inner could open. "One of the last exploration-class scouts still in service." The door opened and she led the way into the ship proper. She patted the bulkhead as she passed. "Oswald Newmar flew a ship just like this one when he started filing claims in Venitz."

Zoya shook her head. "You sure it's still spaceworthy?"

Natalya grinned at her. "Well, this is a hell of a time to ask. Stash your trunk in there. We need to get out of here." She nodded at a stateroom door and elbowed her way into a compartment across the passage, guiding her grav-trunk through the narrow door and locking it down. "I'll get the engines warming up and file a flight plan for Halpern."

"Why Halpern?" Zoya asked, having difficulty with the narrowness of the small ship's doors and the width of her grav-trunk.

"It's farther away and it's not where Margaret Newmar said to file."

Zoya locked the trunk down and followed Natalya to the cockpit that served as bridge. "Well, she gave us a destination. You thinking of ditching that, too?"

Natalya shook her head. "She never said it out loud. Nobody inside could have overheard."

Zoya stared at Natalya as she dropped her butt into the pilot's couch and started slapping keys. "You're not paranoid or anything, are you?" Zoya asked.

Natalya threw her a smile. "Claustrophobic. Not paranoid."

Zoya looked at the tiny spaces around her. "Claustrophobic? And you fly a scout?"

The ship vibrated and the blowers started a low whispering as the ship's systems came online.

"Once we're out there, there's plenty of room. I've never felt claustrophobic in space." Natalya patted the seat next to her. "Sit. Navigation console. You remember how to lay a course?"

Zoya made a rude sound and dropped into the couch. "Who taught you how to use the Mark Twelve consoles, huh?"

Natalya grinned. "And who taught you orbital mechanics?"

"As if. I knew more about orbital mechanics at twelve than you do now." Zoya keyed the console open and started typing commands. "These aren't Mark Twelves."

Natalya laughed. "No. Fourteens. One of the Plunkett fast packets upgraded. I picked these up for scrap value last spring. Took me all damn summer to get them installed and calibrated."

"Sweet."

"Buckle up," Natalya said, pulling her own harness into place and snapping it down.

Zoya looked up, her eyes wide in surprise. "Already?" She fumbled with her belts for a moment, untwisting them so they'd line up properly.

"No, but any tick now we'll get clearance and I want to be moving before they change their minds."

Zoya pulled out her tablet and slaved it to the console, transferring the coordinates for their jump.

Natalya watched the comms screen for the permission from traffic control to undock. "Come on, come on. How long does it take to let us out?"

Zoya chuckled. "We're not exactly high on their priority list. You remember working there in our third year, don't you?"

"Yeah. I remember." She sighed. "But normally I get buzzed right through."

"I'm guessing that *normally* you don't have a potential TIC problem making every heartbeat feel like a stan."

Natalya snickered.

A yellow warning message popped up.

"Uh oh."

"What?" Zoya asked.

"We're on hold."

"Yellow-hold. Probably just traffic outside," Zoya said.

Natalya took a deep breath and blew it out slowly. "Yeah. Probably."

"As long as it's not red-denied."

Natalya nodded, her eyes not leaving the comms and her hand on the maneuvering controls.

A very long four ticks elapsed before the green-for-go message popped up on the console.

"Yes," Natalya said, stretching the hiss out as she pulled shore-ties and triggered the lockdowns to release.

The ship lifted just off the deck and began floating toward the exit lock. As they approached, the lock's tattletales flipped from yellow to green and Natalya slipped in. Behind them the inner door closed and the orbital's heavy compressors started sucking the atmosphere out of the lock.

Time slowed for Natalya. The wait in the airlock never bothered her, yet she found herself tapping her fingers on the arm of her couch.

Zoya glanced at the pattering digits and smiled.

Natalya forced herself to grip the arm. "I just keep thinking, this would be a good place to keep us locked down until they can figure out how to get to us."

Zoya nodded. "Probably, but the easiest thing is just pump the atmosphere back in and tell us to back out slowly." She nodded at the pressure indicator on the bulkhead outside. "It's almost vacuum now."

A few more heartbeats. The green-for-go light blinked on over the exit door and Natalya goosed the thrusters to push them out of the orbital.

Comms popped a blue informational message for the exit vector to leave the orbital traffic control. Natalya cross-loaded the instruction to helm and followed the guiding signal out of the swirl of ships, cargo handlers, shuttles, and small craft that surrounded Newmar Orbital. The kickers rumbled the spaceframe as they came online and the ship picked up speed.

"There's the delay," Zoya said, nodding out the starboard armorglass port. A massive freighter under tow was still sliding into the dock on their starboard side.

Natalya nodded. "I've got clearance to burn for Burleson as soon as we're clear of the inner markers."

"How far out do we have to go?"

Natalya offered a smile. "Half a day. No more."

Zoya's eyes widened and her jaw dropped. "What?"

"Half a day. We'll be able to make a short jump if we can find a clean spot to jump to within two Burleson units."

"Two units?" Zoya's face clouded. "I thought this was a scout."

"Oh, the ship can jump twelve, fourteen units from clean space. From this mess?" Natalya waved a hand to indicate the space around them. "We'd need to go out at least two or three days before we'd be safe to jump that far. We're so small we can make short jumps just a few stans out of port. Once we get out there, we can jump a long, long way." She glanced over at Zoya. "Where are we going, anyway?"

"Someplace called Dark Knight. It doesn't show on the charts."

"Dark Knight Station?"

"Yeah, you know it?"

"Heard of it. Toe-Hold space. That's what she meant about outside TIC control."

"Margaret Newmar is sending us to Toe-Hold space?"

"Don't look so surprised. Lots of people go there." She shot a smile at Zoya. "That's where this ship came from. My father got it from the Junkyard."

"Really? Somebody junked this?"

Natalya laughed. "No. The Junkyard is a station out near Ciroda. It's a kind of dumping ground for ships, tanks, station parts. All kinds of stuff."

"Junk."

"Well, some of it is. You should have seen the *Peregrine* before she got cleaned up."

"What was wrong with it?"

"Not much that a persistent engineer with a half-decent yard nearby couldn't fix. My father and mother replaced the fusactor. That was the most critical piece. They'd been tinkering on it for stanyers. Finally got it where they wanted it and gave it to me for my eighteenth birthday so I'd have a way to get to the academy."

"Nice birthday present."

"Yeah. Well, they split up. Mom went to be chief engineer for Consolidated Freight and I think Dad's back out in Toe-Hold space. I haven't heard from him since I started at the academy."

"You're my roommate for four stanyers and you never mentioned any of this before?"

"Never came up." She glanced at Zoya. "What do your parents do?"

Zoya's face closed down. "Long story. It's complicated."

They cleared the inner markers and Natalya pushed the throttles forward. The murmuring vibration in the space frame ratcheted up. Natalya looked at Zoya and raised her voice to speak over the noise. "We'll be clear in a couple of ticks and can coast a bit."

"Do you know of any place nearby that we can jump to?" Zoya asked.

"Pull up the waypoint menu on the console. Label is 'Picnic Area.'"

Zoya pulled up the menu and snickered. "Now I know what you did instead of summer cruises."

Natalya pulled the throttles back and the kickers resumed their low grumble. The quiet was a blessing. "Hey, I did my time. I got most of those from other pilots." She grinned. "Lotta old timers around Port Newmar. They remember these scouts and they're more than happy to share what they know."

Zoya laid in the plot and watched the timer start ticking down. "You weren't kidding. At this rate we'll be out of the system in another two stans."

Natalya nodded and slapped the release on her seatbelt. "Want some coffee?"

"You have coffee aboard?" Zoya grinned.

"Yeah. Coffee is just water and beans. We have water and the beans don't have much mass. I don't mind a cup of tea now and again, but when I'm out here, there's just something that makes me want coffee." She lifted her chin. "So? You want a cup?"

"Oh, yes. It's been a long day and I could use it."

"Me, too. I still feel like I've got my head in a bucket or something." Natalya made her way back to the passageway and the tiny galley beyond. "You don't suppose they spiked my tea with something, do you?"

Zoya didn't answer for a few moments.

Natalya stuck her head back around the corner. "What? They didn't, did they?"

Zoya shook her head. "I have a hard time imagining they'd do something like that. To what end? Not like any of them was going to take you home as a plaything. Did you *see* those guys?"

Natalya laughed at the image and went back to fixing the coffee.

"Nats? You might want to come out here."

The high-pitched squeal of a collision alarm filled the tiny space.

Natalya jumped as if she'd been stabbed and threw herself into the couch, her eyes scanning the displays. She slapped the override on the alarm. "Where?"

Zoya pointed to her scanner display. Two blips showed intercept courses. The ships were small and fast. The range markers seemed to be melting away as Natalya looked.

"TIC interceptors?" Natalya asked, not quite believing her eyes.

"That's what the transponders show."

Natalya checked her boards again, double-checking the comms array. "They haven't tried to hail us."

"They're burning like crazy," Zoya said. "They'll catch up with us in a stan."

"Are we sure they're coming for us?"

Zoya shrugged. "No idea. I saw them pop up on the scope just before the alarm spotted them."

Natalya stared at the screen, measuring the angles and velocity in her head. She buckled her seat belt again and reached for the throttle. "Hold on. Let's see if we can learn anything." She pushed the throttle all the way up and the heavy thrusters kicked hard. The noise and vibration practically rattled her teeth, but Natalya watched their velocity increase. Their projected tracks changed on the displays and the intercept courses slowly crept backward to cross behind them.

"Maybe they're going someplace else in a hurry," Zoya said, almost shouting to be heard over the noise.

Natalya squinted at the screen, hoping against hope it wasn't what she thought it was. She kept the throttles up, even as the engineering console showed the strain on the big engines approaching the redline.

For a few ticks, it looked like a false alarm; then the blips shifted on the screen. Their new projected courses intersected with the *Peregrine* in just over a stan.

Zoya looked at Natalya, her face pale in the subdued cockpit lighting.

Natalya sighed. "Looks like they know." She pulled the throttles back enough to keep the engines from burning out and the screaming vibration faded a bit.

"Intercept in seventy-five ticks," Zoya said.

Natalya looked at the navigational plot. "They're going to catch us before we can jump."

"Can you get any more out of the kickers?"

Natalya looked at the engineering displays, flipping through the readouts and trying to find something that might give them an edge. She shook her head. "If I redline them, they can still catch us in time and they're not really broken in that well yet. They might blow."

"Not really the way I want to escape," Zoya said, her eyes bright but her face still pale.

Natalya looked at her comms panel. "No hails."

"Maybe they're not after us?" Zoya's question hung there.

Natalya didn't answer. She just gazed at the displays.

Zoya's fingers started flying over the keys on her console.

Natalya's head snapped around as she tried to figure out what her roommate was doing. "Astronomical data? What are you looking up?"

Zoya shook her head. "Maybe nothing. Maybe the answer. Hush."

A warbling screech filled the cockpit and a computerized voice chanted. "Weapons lock. Weapons lock."

Natalya slapped the keys to silence the alarm and looked at the scanner display. The small icons blinked red. Both ships had target lock on the scout. "The bastards!"

Zoya shook her head. "Hush."

After a tick, Zoya looked at Natalya. "If we shift course we might be able to outrun them."

"Shift how? Why?"

"The system's calculating mean Burleson thresholds for a ship of this class, right?"

Natalya's brain stuttered once but she caught on. "Yes!"

"We have that big gas bag out there, but most of the mass of the system is on the other side of the primary. If we come to this heading and goose it, we can probably outrun the interceptors and jump before they catch on." She pointed to a course laid out on the navigational console. "Hit it."

The small ship twisted and slowly reoriented its trajectory. The interceptors didn't lose lock and didn't slow down. They simply adjusted their courses.

Natalya felt like there wasn't enough air in the ship as she waited for the computer to recalibrate the intercept.

When the displays settled, the distances were too close to call.

"Pull back the throttles," Zoya shouted.

"They'll catch us."

"Maybe not," she said. "And I've got a feeling we'll need that extra boost before we're done. Slow down. Save them for now."

Natalya pulled back so the engines stayed out of the red and tried to gauge the distances and times. The computer said they'd be caught.

"They're not trying to catch us," Zoya said.

"How can you be sure?"

Zoya looked at her. "They didn't lock weapons for practice."

Natalya felt her stomach drop. "Maybe they're just trying to warn us. How soon before they're in firing range?"

"TIC interceptors have paired missile bays. Smart munitions. Kinetic warheads. Ship-to-ship range something over half a million kilometers," Zoya said. "Exact range is classified."

The emergency klaxon screamed and the computer voice said, "Weapons fire. Weapons fire. Weapons fire."

Natalya found the voice oddly calm, given the message. For a brief instant she wondered why they didn't program the voice to make it sound more urgent.

"Punch it!" Zoya said.

Natalya slammed the throttles forward again and slapped the alarm off. The noise from the engines mostly drowned it out anyway.

"Four tracks. Both ships fired two birds," Zoya shouted.

"How soon?"

"Half a stan."

Natalya's fear melted away, leaving a molten anger. How dare they? She'd done nothing wrong. She didn't kill that idiot. Zoya had done nothing at all. And TIC was trying to kill them both. No evidence. No jury. No trial. Just the silent interceptors in space.

"How far are we from Newmar?" Natalya asked.

"Too far," Zoya answered. "By the time this is over we'll be in that gas bag's shadow anyway. Nobody's going to be able to see anything." She sat back in her couch, panting. "This can't be happening."

"It's happening."

"This can't be happening," Zoya said again.

"It's happening, Zee. What do we have?"

"I got nothing, Nats."

"Set up the plot. Prime the Burleson for jump to the Picnic Area."

"You can't jump this close. We're inside the limit."

"Maybe. Maybe not. There's a safety margin built into the systems."

"If we try to jump too close, the drives may take us apart," Zoya said.

"If we don't jump, those missiles *will* take us apart. What gives us better odds?"

Zoya stared for a moment and then her fingers began flying. "You've got engineering."

Natalya flipped to the Burleson control screen and started charging the jump capacitors. "Ten ticks until we can jump."

"Eleven until we're in position," Zoya said. "Nine until the missiles get here. We're not going to make it."

Natalya brought up the engineering overlay and toggled in the maintenance menus. She gritted her teeth and pulled the safety overrides off the engines. "We're going to be damn near dry on fuel before we get out of here, but if we don't get out, fuel won't matter."

The vibration and noise picked up a fraction.

"What'd you do?" Zoya shouted.

"Reset the overrides and goosed the fuel pumps. It's not much but it might be enough."

They watched the computers recalculate courses and trajectories. The missiles missed the velocity shift for a few seconds before coming to a new intercept.

"Ten ticks until they hit us," Zoya shouted. "Just under eleven to the limit. That jink bought us a fraction."

Natalya watched the scanner plot and tried to think of something else they could do. "This isn't right," she said.

"What?"

"This isn't right," she shouted. "Something is just not right here."

"With the ship?" Zoya's eyes grew even wider.

"No. This whole thing. Why are they trying to kill us?"

"You killed a TIC officer. They don't really like that, you know."

"But I didn't. Any competent forensics analysis should prove that."

Zoya pointed at the screen. "They don't look like they believe that."

Natalya looked at Zoya's screen again. The interceptors seemed to be falling back.

"Five ticks, Nats. What can we do?"

Natalya pulled up the Burleson drive overlay. The capacitor had enough charge for a very short jump—barely a bump in the road by interstellar standards, but it might be enough. She slapped keys and dragged the navigation interface onto her console. She zoomed the chart in on the edge of Newmar's boundary. "Check long range. Dead ahead. Push the range all the way up," she shouted. Her fingers kept moving on the keyboard and the navigational computer began the calculations to take her to the point she had marked on the chart.

"Nothing out there for a billion klicks that I can see right now," Zoya shouted. "What are you doing?"

"Saving our asses," she shouted back and punched the jump button.

Nothing seemed to happen but she reached forward and pulled the throttles back to zero. The screaming, roaring vibration chopped off. "Where are the missiles now?"

Zoya looked down at her screen and shook her head. "Gone. Or so far back in relativistic terms we won't see them for another few ticks." She brought her own screen up to a navigational plot and started running her own scans. "You jumped to the edge of the system?"

"About a hundredth of a Burleson unit."

"You could have killed us."

"We were dead if I didn't."

Zoya turned back to look at the scanners. "I can't even see the interceptors, let alone the missiles at this range."

"They're really small targets a very, very long way off."

Zoya looked out the forward ports and adjusted her display. "You jumped into the outbound heavy freighter lane."

"It was the only place I could think of that might be clean enough for us to jump to."

"What if there'd been a ship?" Zoya asked, incredulity leaving her voice squeaky.

"You'd have seen it on long range. They're moving fast by the time they get out here, but you'd have seen where it had been. You didn't see anything. I jumped us. The odds of actually hitting a ship out here are stupidly low. We had a better chance of hitting a stray rock where we were."

They sat there, the tiny ship still racing toward the Deep Dark at a breakneck pace.

"Now what?" Zoya asked.

"How far are we from Dark Knight?"

"Twelve, maybe thirteen BUs."

"So one good jump."

"You weren't joking about the legs on this ship?"

Natalya shook her head. "No. It was built for exploration in the uncharted areas of the Deep Dark. I wouldn't want to jump blind into a system but the old timers used to cross this whole region in a matter of a few days, not months."

Zoya brought up the charts for the Deep Dark around their destination coordinates. "Not much to see."

"The Confederated Planets Joint Committee on Trade doesn't recognize Toe-Hold space on their charts. The station's there."

Zoya looked at Natalya. "How do you know it's there?"

"If Margaret Newmar says that's where it is, that's where it is. When we get there, we can probably get the updated Toe-Hold charts."

Zoya's eyes narrowed. "Probably?"

"Well, we'd need to find somebody there who'd be willing to let us have a set. We'd probably have to pay for it. Somehow." Natalya shrugged.

"Somehow?" Zoya's eyes blinked rapidly. "Somehow? You're not filling me with confidence here."

"Relax. We're going to Toe-Hold space. As long as we don't run up against any of the Iron Mountain trolls, we'll be all right. May have to work for our suppers, that's all."

"Doing what?"

Natalya shrugged a shoulder. "Depends on what needs doing. Mining, probably. Maybe need to take a couple cruises on a freighter. We could probably make a decent living out here just using the gas skimmers on this ship."

"Gas skimmers?"

Natalya sighed. "How do you think these boats kept themselves in volatiles?"

Zoya shook her head. "I guess I never really thought about it."

"Never mind. We need to get back on track and get out of Newmar before TIC realizes where we are. Plot us a new course for a jump to Dark Knight Station. Who did Margaret say to contact?"

"A guy named Verk something. Lemme look it up."

"Verkol Kondur?"

Zoya looked up in surprise. "You know him?"

"Know *of* him." Natalya pursed her lips. "My father used to talk about him once in a while."

"What? Good? Bad?" Zoya chewed her bottom lip. "What?"

Natalya chuckled. "Some of each. He wasn't one of the people Dad warned me about. He either founded or took over Dark Knight. Dad never was clear on it. Interesting that he's Margaret Newmar's contact."

"So, what will we do there?"

"Beats me. Get jobs, probably. Toe-Hold space isn't that different from CPJCT-controlled space." Natalya shook her head. "If you'd plot that course, you could see for yourself."

Zoya bent to her task while Natalya put her ship back together, starting with resetting the overrides. By the time Natalya had satisfied herself that the ship wouldn't fall apart on her, Zoya had the course adjustment plotted.

"Pass it to helm?" Natalya said and took the handles.

"Course passed to helm."

"Course locked." Natalya started the slow burns that would reorient the ship toward a point in space a long, long way out into the Deep Dark. She locked the autopilot down. "We'll be in position in two stans. You want that coffee now?"

Zoya nodded. "Can I ask you a question, Nats?"

Natalya scrambled up out of her couch. "You've never been shy about it before."

Zoya chuckled and looked down at her hands. "You were always going to come out to Toe-Hold space after graduation."

Natalya shrugged and headed for the galley. "That wasn't a question."

"Alone?"

"Yeah. Probably." She finished flash-heating the coffee and took the two cups back to the cockpit. "It's not the kind of place you can just invite people to, you know?"

Zoya sipped the hot liquid and closed her eyes for a moment, the steam rising across her face. "I suppose not," she said after a few moments. "Would you have told me?"

Natalya sipped her coffee and thought about the question. "You really wanted to join TIC, didn't you?"

"Captain Evans made a good case for it." She sighed. "That was before they tried to kill us."

"You know they kept trying to get me to join."

Zoya's eyebrows went up. "Really? You never mentioned it."

"I never considered it. I have the *Peregrine*." Natalya shrugged. They sipped for a few moments. "Are you sorry?"

"For what?"

"That you've been linked with a wanted killer and have to give up all your plans for a career?"

Zoya grinned. "I don't know yet. When I got up this morning, I thought I knew what I wanted."

"Now?"

Zoya shook her head. "I'm beginning to think I never really thought about it. I just did what I was supposed to do. Now? I don't know. I don't know what I want, other than keep flying."

"Better to choose a path you're unsure of than be forced onto a path you don't want."

"Sounds profound. Something your father said?"

Natalya shook her head. "Fortune cookie I got in a great little oriental restaurant over in Dunsany Roads."

Zoya snickered. "How was the food?"

"Fantastic. If we ever get out that way, I'll take you."

"Sounds like a plan."

"Well, one thing at a time." Natalya leaned over to look at the display. "You tired? We've got a couple of stans before we're going to jump again."

Zoya took a deep breath and looked around the cockpit. "I should be. Something about having missiles locked on my ass seems to have given me a second wind."

"Did I ever tell you the time Dad took me out to High Tortuga?"

"Is this a long story?"

"Couple of stans. Why? You going somewhere?"

Zoya grinned and settled into her couch. "What's High Tortuga?"

CHAPTER FOUR
DARK KNIGHT: 2363, MAY 26

The system primary showed as a tiny disk in the distance. Natalya double-checked the navigation displays and tapped a minor course adjustment into the system before engaging the autopilot for a best-time burn to the station. The engines vibrated the ship with a low-pitched growl. "We're a little short. It'll be a day or so before we dock."

Zoya stood and peered through the forward armorglass. "There's nothing out there."

"It's there. Just too far to see without a magnifier or a screen." She pointed to the navigation display. A flashing blip marked a spot out in the Deep Dark. "Long range shows it just fine."

Zoya dropped back into the couch and bit her lip. "Now what?"

"Now we relax and enjoy the ride. Coffee?"

Zoya stifled a yawn and shrugged. "It's that or a nap. I've been up way too long."

"Why don't you go stretch out and get some sleep?"

"You sure? You've been up as long as I have."

Natalya snickered. "I'm still buzzing. Something about being shot at makes me a little hyper. Lemme take the first watch, and you get some sleep if you can. I've got a lot to keep me busy."

Zoya rolled out of her couch and shuffled off the bridge. "Holler if you need me."

Natalya decided she wanted the coffee even if Zoya hadn't. She released her belts and stood for the first time in what felt like days. A glance at the chrono on the bulkhead told her that it had barely been four stans since they'd left Newmar with TIC interceptors shooting up their kicker nozzles. She shook out her arms and twisted her shoulders as she crossed the bridge to the compact galley.

The aromatic coffee beans reminded her of all the times she'd worked on the ship with her father and she wondered what he was doing at that moment. It gave her a small pang of homesickness, knowing she couldn't go home again. Of course, she'd always planned on moving out to Toe-Hold space after graduation. The current circumstances just pushed her timetable up a few days.

She filled a mug with fresh coffee, snapped down the lid, and returned to her couch. A few clicks brought up the communications interfaces. She took a couple of ticks to link up the voice headset. Dark Knight traffic control would want to chat at some point.

She sipped the hot coffee and stared at the slow blink-blink on the long-range scanner. With nothing else to do, her brain replayed the scene in Sifu Newmar's kitchen—Purvis falling, the blood spreading across the floor, the coldness in her hands and face. She'd had trouble putting enough of her thoughts in order to speak, let alone defend herself.

Why had Margaret Newmar been so certain TIC would blame her? She and Purvis had a history but nothing that would add up to her killing him. Certainly not in the middle of the graduation party in a room where everybody knew she'd been alone with him.

She inhaled the warm, dark aroma of coffee and sipped again.

Why then? And why Zoya? She hadn't even been in the room at the time. The only connection Zoya had was being Natalya's roommate for her entire time at the academy. Natalya smiled at the thought that she couldn't have been all that easy to live with. Most of their classmates had played musical roommates over the four stanyers. Some even played musical bunks, but Zoya hadn't seemed interested in any of it. Neither of them had enough spare time to get involved sexually or romantically with any of the other cadets. They'd been well matched for their drives toward graduation. With nearly identical grade point averages and widely disparate backgrounds, they made a good team.

Natalya assumed they had widely disparate backgrounds. Zoya never said much about her family, other than they were back in Dunsany Roads somewhere. Natalya had to admit to herself that she hadn't talked much about her own history either. Forays into Toe-Hold space with her father didn't make suitable conversation for polite company. Particularly when that company had any relationship with CPJCT.

So why was TIC trying to kill them? She leaned forward in her couch and tapped a few keys to replay the log of their encounter with the TIC interceptors. She routed the navigation display to a window on her console and watched. For the longest time, nothing appeared, then the ship jumped to the edge of the system.

Natalya froze the replay and enlarged the window. She added the time stamp and a text readout window beside the navigational display. As she triggered the replay, she leaned forward to watch the actions scroll up the screen. Her commands to change the ship's speed and heading registered, but nothing at all showed on the navigational log. As far as the log showed, it was empty space.

She watched the log recording her system overrides and then the blink of the jump into the outgoing traffic lane. There were no sensor readings at all for the ships, the missile tracks, or the explosions. The logs held no record of missile locks or weapons fire. She watched the recording until all the systems returned to normal, then keyed the window closed.

She leaned back in her seat and gazed out at the Deep Dark around them. The hot coffee grounded her and wafted moist air across her face as she held the cup in both hands in front of her chin. Her mind sorted through the various steps that brought them to knocking on Verkol Kondur's door. She had an idea how the incident might have happened but it would have required somebody from outside the ship to compromise her systems.

She leaned forward again and opened the ship's system log instead of the navigation log. She scrolled back through the encounter time frame. She searched for the command that released the system overrides on the jump drive.

Key not found.

"That can't be right," she muttered.

She reran the search to look for the command to restore the override and found it immediately. Scrolling back, she found no other system log entries after the main system power-up at Newmar Orbital until the entry showing the restored overrides. She scrolled back in the log. The time stamps showed big gaps in time between visits. Few of her visits lately had been more than routine maintenance. She'd been so busy with school and graduation there hadn't been time to take the ship out for a spin. She kept scrolling looking for the last time she'd left the station.

When she found it, the log looked normal. Nothing about the process stood out as odd. System power-up. Engines on standby. Station-ties released. She checked the navigation log entry for the time and saw her request for departure clearance and the subsequent granting of same. The next significant change to the system log came when she'd slaved her tablet to the engineering console displays. She nodded to herself. She'd been tuning the fuel mixture back in engineering and used her tablet to track the minute changes as she made the final adjustments.

She popped the log back to the top, displaying the most current entries, and sat back in her couch. The system log showed nothing between initial power-up and the time she replaced the system overrides.

She'd seen this kind of thing before, but only in training simulations— and the knowledge put a cold seed of doubt in her belly.

A window bipped open on her pilot's console. She sat down and keyed the acknowledgment.

The message opened in a separate window to show a standard docking assignment, an approach protocol string, a frequency designator, and a single line of text. "Welcome to Dark Knight."

"At least I understand this," Natalya said. She keyed the receipt and sat back in her couch.

She transferred the docking protocol to her navigational computer and kicked it on. A countdown timer popped up and started ticking down. Fourteen stans before the automated course corrections. The annotations said they'd dock ten stans later, more or less.

That gave her plenty of time to dig around in the innards of the ship's systems to see if any simulator code still remained. Somebody went to a lot of trouble to convince her to run. She couldn't help but wonder who and why. One thing she knew for sure. Her roommate—her *friend*—had a lot to answer for when she woke up.

CHAPTER FIVE
DARK KNIGHT: 2363, MAY 26

The navigation timer ticked down to zero and the ship's system kicked into the next stage of the course. The plotter showed Natalya the estimated course along with some navigation notes on local traffic control. The ship rumbled as the kickers provided the tiniest bit of thrust to start slowing them. She eyed the readouts and nodded to herself.

"We here already?" Zoya's voice sounded raspy from sleep.

Natalya turned to look at her. "Not quite. We're still looking for a place to park."

"How long was I out?"

"About six stans. Maybe a bit more."

Zoya nodded. "You want to grab a nap? You've got to be knackered."

"I should be but I'm not." She bit down to contain her rage.

"How much longer?"

Natalya double-checked the navigation plot. "About another eight stans before we contact traffic control for an approach vector. It'll be about ten stans after that before we dock."

Zoya blinked several times, stretching her face up and down. "Is there coffee?"

"Galley."

Zoya shuffled into the galley and came out a few ticks later sipping from a covered mug. She yawned once and dropped into her couch. "I may be alive soon."

"We pulled harder time during exams. This is cake. Nobody's going to flunk us out when we dock."

Zoya shot her a sour look. "I'm more worried that somebody will shoot us."

"Why would they?"

"Oh, I don't know. Perhaps the lack of laws?"

Natalya gave her head a small shake. "There are laws. And people to enforce them. Just fewer than we're used to in CPJCT space."

"Really?" Zoya's eyebrows punctuated her skepticism.

"What do you know about Toe-Hold space, Zee?" Natalya pursed her lips and leaned toward Zoya. "I mean really know. You didn't learn about it at the academy. You ever been out here?"

Zoya's face closed down and she lifted her mug to sip before answering. "No. I've never been out here."

"How do you know about it?"

She frowned. "I've heard stories. No laws. No police. Everybody just does what they want and devil take the hindmost." Her voice started strong but faded out the longer she talked.

"So. You really only have a bunch of hearsay and propaganda."

"CPJCT doesn't recognize it. You can't trade here."

Natalya laughed. "Oh, they recognize it all right. They just don't talk about it. You can't file a flight plan to a Toe-Hold station, but they can't stop you from docking."

"That's why you filed for Halpern?"

"Yeah. As far as the Confederated Planets Joint Committee on Trade is concerned, we're flying to Robison in Halpern and they won't notice if we're a bit late. Ships jump through the Deep Dark all the time. You know that."

Zoya nodded. "Yeah. I guess."

"Well, Toe-Hold space is in the Deep Dark. All you need is a set of charts, just the same as you do in CPJCT space. They're not even illegal to own. You just can't tell the CPJCT you're going there."

"Why not?"

"You can't key in the destinations on a CPJCT flight plan. It won't go. They'll error out as invalid."

"You mean literally?"

"Yeah. So, we jump into the dark and go where we want. None of the Toe-Hold stations will show on our manifests or flight logs. We can travel at will out here and nobody will say a word. If we wanted to jump back to CPJCT space, we'd just file an amended flight plan when we dock."

"If ...?"

"As far as we know, we're wanted for murder. That's a good reason for not docking in a CPJCT station in my book." Her immediate anger had cooled while Zoya slept, but began building again as they sat there calmly discussing the situation.

"You are. I'm not."

"No, you're just accessory after the fact."

Zoya's eyes grew large and round. "No. That can't be."

Natalya didn't know if she wanted to scream, smash Zoya's face in, or both. "You were there. You helped me escape. TIC thinks I killed Purvis or Gavin or whatever his name is. You climbed aboard a ship with me when I ran, didn't you? What legal status do you think that conveys?"

Zoya seemed to shrink in on herself and stared at the top of her coffee mug. "I guess I didn't think about it."

Natalya sat back in her couch and stared at Zoya for a few heartbeats, a troubling realization beginning to dawn.

"What?" Zoya asked, glancing at Natalya before looking away again.

"I'm just trying to decide if you're a really good actress or if they just didn't brief you before they sent you out here to bird-dog me." Natalya worked very hard to keep her voice even against the ice-cold ball of betrayal in her gut.

Zoya sat very still, her eyes fixed on the top of her coffee mug while the color leached out of her face.

Natalya took a deep breath and shook her head. "You didn't get any training at all, did you?"

Zoya bit the side of her mouth. She shrugged. "I had a couple weeks."

"Who? TIC?"

She shook her head. "I don't know. I don't think so. They said they were agents for the CPJCD."

"Committee on Defense? Seriously?"

"Commandant Giggone had me sign a nondisclosure and security letter before he'd even let them in the room. They said they were CPJCD. I had no reason to suspect they weren't."

Natalya's anger began to slip away as she considered the implications. "So what can they do to you now that you've told me?"

Zoya choked out a single laugh. "Prison, probably. Specifically, they warned me about disclosure, so that's treason, I guess."

"And they didn't teach you basic craft?"

Zoya hung her head. "I know what you mean by that."

"But you knew those interceptors weren't real, right?"

Zoya bit her lips together and shook her head. "No, I thought they were. You scared the crap out of me when you jumped. You could have killed us."

"What was I supposed to do? Let them blow us up?"

"I don't know. They never told me. They said I'd react more naturally if I didn't know. I just knew they'd let us pass."

"If it's any consolation, you fooled me."

"What gave it away?" Zoya asked after staring straight ahead for several long moments.

"I checked the navigation logs. The only thing they showed was the engine changes and the maneuvering commands. So I dug into the system logs and there's nothing between the time we fired up and when I put the overrides back on the Burleson drive. Things that should have been there were missing. I'm pretty sure the ship didn't skip them, which meant they had to have been erased. It had to have been an elaborate simulation that erased itself after it finished. Nothing else makes sense." Natalya stared at Zoya, trying to get her to look up. "Once I knew it wasn't real, it had to be you. You're the only person who's been on the ship since I installed the Mark Fourteens last summer. The code erased the logs from the time you synced your tablet until it finished running."

"Oh." Zoya all but deflated into a small ball in her couch.

Natalya realized her sense of betrayal no longer centered on Zoya. "Zee, we have a problem."

Zoya nodded without looking at Natalya.

"You realize they set you up, right?"

Zoya looked up, her eyes wide. "Set *me* up?"

"Well, set us both up. In theory I'm here for some reason I don't know. I assume you don't either?"

Zoya's tongue flicked out to moisten her lower lip and her eyebrows drew together in a frown. "Maybe."

"Maybe what? You do or don't know?"

"I don't know why you're here. I'm here because they told me to stick with you and wait for further instructions when we get where we're going."

"Where? Dark Knight Station?"

"I don't know," Zoya said. "They wouldn't tell me. Only that you'd be leaving and I needed to go with you. Somebody would contact me. Somewhere. I'd know it when they did."

"So they wanted you to get caught, but why?"

"Get caught?" Zoya asked.

Natalya huffed in exasperation. "Either they think I'm a complete idiot or they expected I'd twig. Once I knew there was a game in play? You're the only other player here. One look at the logs gave it up. Your hidden masters either didn't think I'd look at them or assumed I would. Right now, I don't know which is more troubling."

Zoya's frown of concentration shifted to lifted eyebrows of surprise. "Why would they want you to?"

Natalya pursed her lips. "I don't know. I suspect so I'd be mad enough to kill you."

Zoya's face clouded and a red flush swept up her neck and across her face. "The bastards."

"Pretty much my thought," Natalya said.

"Are you going to?" Zoya asked.

Natalya let her squirm for a bit before answering. "Probably not. I'm mad as hell, but killing you wouldn't solve anything that I can't solve by dropping you at Dark Knight with a KICK ME sign on your back."

"What do we do?"

Natalya shrugged. "Carry on, I suppose. We've already got bank records out here. When we dock, lay in some supplies. Somebody out here will need a scout ship and we'll get a job."

"Just like that?"

"What else?"

"What about me?" Zoya asked, teeth pulling her lower lip in.

Natalya sighed and sat back in her couch. "That's up to you. I suspect they want me to do something ill-advised and rash because you betrayed my trust."

"I wouldn't blame you if you did." Zoya looked at the deck between the couches. "I probably would."

"No, you wouldn't," Natalya said. "I know you better than that. We've been roomies too long. I think the psy-ops goons didn't plan on me actually thinking about the situation rather than responding to it emotionally and throwing you out the airlock."

Zoya's face paled again and her eyes grew wide.

Natalya chuckled and shook her head, feeling the knot of anger dissolving. "You've been screwed by the people who sent you. I've been screwed by the people who sent you. Seems to me that gives us *more* reason to work together, not less. Besides, I don't much like being manipulated. By anybody. You're not the one pulling the strings."

Zoya offered a tentative smile. "You'd trust me again? After all this?"

Natalya looked up at the overhead and thought about it. Part of her still felt the sting of betrayal but another part found the mystery almost irresistible. "Maybe," she said after more than a few heartbeats. "What did they offer you?"

"They said it was a matter of public safety. If I didn't, a lot of people would die."

Natalya felt her eyebrows climbing into her hairline. "Because of something I was going to do?"

Zoya shook her head. "Not you directly, but something out here in Toe-Hold space."

"What?"

"They didn't say. They just said—"

"That someone would contact you. Yeah. I got that part."

Zoya shrugged.

"So they appealed to your civic duty and you agreed to what, exactly?"

"To go to Toe-Hold space with you and wait for my contact."

"What about Purvis or Gavin or whatever his name was?"

"I was as shocked as you were."

"You know he's not dead, right?"

Zoya blinked. "Of course he's dead. You saw him. Margaret Newmar told you ..." Her voice trailed off.

"And suddenly I'm whisked off to Toe-Hold space with my trusty sidekick?"

Zoya's lips twisted in a wry grimace. "Terribly convenient."

"Yeah. Once the drugs wore off, none of it made any sense unless it was a put-up job."

"Drugs?"

"You don't think I'm normally stupid enough to run from the TIC, do you? On a trumped-up charge based on a bladder of stage blood taped to the back of some jerk's head?"

Zoya chewed on her lower lip for a few moments. "Now what?" she asked, looking across at Natalya.

"Now I'm going to grab a fast shower and crawl into my bunk for a few stans. Can you keep an eye on things while I'm sacked?"

"Really? You'd trust me?"

"No, not really. I thought I knew you better than that. If I just reacted on emotion, I'd toss you out the lock." She stared at Zoya for several long moments. "The reality is, I'd have invited you along if I thought you'd have accepted. I didn't ask because you were so tickled about being recruited into the TIC." Natalya chuckled. "The irony is that it's TIC that's forced you out here with me and you've been screwed over as badly as I have. If not worse. I'm not sure you appreciate that." She paused and ran through the arguments in her head. "Yeah. I think we've covered the basics. We're both screwed. If I were you, I'd be pretty peeved with my unseen masters right now. If I'm wanted for murder, you're an accessory. At least that's the line we've been fed. We've got to be on the same side, because there's really no other side. The alternative is that I'll sneak up on you while you're sleeping, smash your head in with a wrench, and toss your lifeless body out the airlock."

Zoya's eyes grew as big as platters.

Natalya smiled. "That's not much of an alternative for either of us. Besides, I need you for bait. You're my only link to the bastards who set us up and those are the people I want answers from."

Zoya laughed. It was a quiet laugh. More of a low chuckle that kept going. When she stopped, she looked across the bridge at Natalya. "Sleep well."

"Keep your eyes peeled. Wake me if anything comes within ten million klicks."

"Will do."

"That's supposed to be 'aye, aye, Captain.' Didn't you learn anything at that fancy pants academy?"

Zoya gave a sheepish looking shrug. "Apparently not as much as you did."

"Don't sell yourself short, Zee."

"Aye, aye, Captain."

Natalya nodded and turned toward her stateroom, a grin working its way across her lips. "You've got the conn."

After the hot shower, the cool sheets soothed her skin. She lay on her bunk for several ticks wondering if she'd made a mistake in trusting her longtime friend. Sleep took her down before she could make up her mind.

CHAPTER SIX
DARK KNIGHT: 2363, MAY 27

Natalya couldn't be sure if it was the smell of fresh coffee or the shift in the thruster noise that brought her out of the depths. She rolled out of her bunk and into a fresh shipsuit before her eyes focused properly. The aroma drew her to the galley where she found Zoya grinning at her.

"Good morning, Captain." Zoya smirked around a mug of coffee.

"Same to you." Natalya rinsed her mug at the sink and drew off a fresh cup. She took a tentative sip, letting the warm liquid wash the fuzzy morning feeling from her mouth and throat. "And bless you."

"You're welcome. If the navigation notes are right, we're about two stans from handoff to local traffic control. Or what passes for it here."

Natalya nodded and took another healthy slurp. "Voice comms. They'll wanna talk to us before we get too close in case they decide they want to deny docking."

Zoya's eyebrows went up at that. "Deny docking?"

Natalya shrugged and headed for the command couch on the bridge. "Sometimes. Not often. Helps if you're trying to dodge your ex or something."

Zoya trailed along and flopped into the copilot's seat. "Is it likely?"

"Why? You have an ex-boyfriend or girlfriend out here we need to be aware of?" Natalya grinned at Zoya's shocked expression. "Relax. This is just how they do it out here. CPJCT uses automated interfaces and devices to keep people out of the loop. Toe-Hold likes to keep it personal."

Natalya picked up the headset she'd prepped earlier and locked it over her left ear. She watched the navigation alert counter pip down to zero.

A woman's voice spoke from the overhead speaker. "*Peregrine*, this is Dark Knight Control. Over."

"Control, this is *Peregrine*. Over."

"*Peregrine*, state your business at Dark Knight Station. Over."

"Control, food, fuel, and gasses. Over."

"Roger, *Peregrine*. Stand by."

They sat staring at the speaker for several long moments.

"Why are we staring at the overhead? It's not like we can see anything," Zoya said.

Natalya chuckled a little and shrugged. "Habit to look at who's talking, I guess."

"*Peregrine*, Dark Knight Control. Docking permission granted for food, fuel, and gasses. Docking bay four-seven-nine. See the docking agent for extended visa. Over."

"Control, *Peregrine*. Confirm docking permission granted for food, fuel, and gasses at bay four-seven-nine. We'll see the docking agent for extended visa. Thank you, Control. Over."

"Welcome home, *Peregrine*. Control, out."

"*Peregrine*, out."

Natalya toggled the communications array off and glanced over to see Zoya staring at her. "What?"

"What's an extended visa and why are they welcoming you home?"

"We'll be met at the docking bay. One of the station agents will assess our level of threat, whether we have any money, and what we might want to do on the station. If they're happy with our answers, we'll be allowed to leave the ship. If not, we'll stay on the ship and may or may not be given the supplies we need."

"And the 'welcome home' bit?"

"Station records probably show that *Peregrine* has been here before. They looked up that record before replying. Apparently Dad left on good terms the last time he was here."

Zoya looked up at the speaker and then over at Natalya. "And if he hadn't?"

"They'd have denied docking and we'd be left hanging until we found another station."

"Was that a likely thing?"

Natalya shook her head. "Unless it was really egregious and really recent, they'd at least let us dock to see if we could pay for whatever we wanted. They might not want us hanging around, but they'll be happy to take our credits."

"Everybody wants their piece. Even here." Zoya's mouth twisted into a wry grimace.

"At least here, they're up front about it."

"What's to stop them from taking our credits and the ship, too?"

Natalya squelched the urge to sigh. "You know how every system in the CPJCT relies on every other system to keep them going?"

Zoya shrugged. "More or less. I still don't see why more of them aren't self-sufficient."

"They probably could be, but that's irrelevant. Every single operation up there has specialized to the point where they can only survive and maintain their quality of life if they work together."

"That's right out of the Econ 440 seminar. So what?" Zoya asked.

"That's with the entire machinery of the CPJCT and all its minions organizing and orchestrating to make it work. You think it's an accident that everybody has enough fuel, food, parts, and whatever they need to keep going?" Natalya found she had to work hard to keep the exasperation out of her voice.

"Of course not. They have planetary management, logistics oversight, and all the rest to make sure of it." Zoya's brow wrinkled as she appeared to be struggling with some amount of frustration of her own. "What of it?"

"Toe-Hold doesn't."

"What do you mean?" Zoya asked, sitting back in her couch.

"Every Toe-Hold station is on its own. They don't have a central clearinghouse authority. They don't have logistics oversight. Every station operates on its own and does as much as it can for itself." Natalya paused to let that sink in for a few heartbeats.

Zoya's breath seemed to catch for a moment and her eyes grew wide. "But they can't do it all." Her words barely reached across the narrow console between the couches.

"No," Natalya said. "They can't. And they know it. Anybody who thinks they can soon learns otherwise."

Zoya took a sip of her coffee and her gaze focused inward.

"Reputation is everything out here," Natalya said, speaking quietly but needing to make the point before they got to the station and Zoya's ignorance got them into trouble they couldn't get out of. "The stations that behave honorably, who trade fairly, and who treat visitors well survive."

Zoya's gaze met Natalya's. "I get it," she said.

"So, heads up, mouths closed, ears open, and we take care of business. They aren't liars or thieves or crooks or murderers." Natalya smiled at her friend. "At least not any more than we'd find on your average Confederation planet."

Zoya snickered.

"They survive by doing business and whether you can accept it or not, the CPJCT needs Toe-Hold way more than Toe-Hold needs the CPJCT."

"How so?" Zoya's curiosity seemed to be pulling her out of the fear.

"Safety valve. It's where they bleed off all the people who don't fit into the nice, neat, clean boxes. The people who don't want to be just another cog in some industrialist's machine."

"I thought that's what the fleet was for," Zoya said.

Natalya didn't speak. She just lifted an eyebrow and willed her friend to think about what she'd just said.

Zoya's eyes narrowed for a moment and she opened her mouth to speak but stopped. All that came out was a quiet "Oh."

Natalya nodded. "Now let's get busy and figure out what we need from Dark Knight so we can tell them what we want to buy."

"You have credits?" Zoya asked.

Natalya laughed. "I need to check my credit balance, but it should be enough to pay for groceries until we get set up." Natalya glanced at Zoya. "Your handlers didn't give you any contact info?"

Zoya shook her head. "They said a guy would be in touch." She smiled a rueful apology.

"You never know. Maybe somebody will. Maybe I wasn't supposed to find out right away. Maybe they figured I'd be taken in."

Zoya gave a bitter laugh. "I sure was."

"You've really never been in Toe-Hold space?"

"You never once mentioned any of this in all our time together?" Zoya asked.

"I told you. Toe-Hold is not a subject for polite company. I got enough strange looks just for having this ship."

"*Peregrine*, this is Dark Knight Control." The voice from the speaker startled Natalya.

Natalya clicked the comms array back up. "Control, *Peregrine*."

"*Peregrine*, we're sending you an updated navigation squirt for final approach and docking. Please acknowledge receipt. Over."

Natalya checked the transmission queue and found the incoming message. She ported it to the navigation subsystem which reset and accepted the new course and speed. "Acknowledged, Control. Approach and docking to bay one-three-three. Over."

"*Peregrine*, Control. Affirm. One-three-three. Hold at one zero meters from the door for green light. Over."

"Control, *Peregrine*. Roger, hold at one zero meters for green light. Over."

"Thank you, *Peregrine*. Control, out."

Zoya said, "They're polite buggers."

Natalya toggled the comms array off. "Politeness doesn't cost anything. I wonder why they shifted us."

"Is the bay significant?"

Natalya shrugged. She pulled up the navigational notes and found a rough layout of the docking bays. "It's a small craft dock. Probably for system shuttles and maintenance craft. Very close in." She pointed to four-seven-nine. "We *were* being shunted out to the hinterlands."

"Shuttles to where?" Zoya asked, pulling up her own display to get a system chart.

"They're bound to have mining stations out along the belts. Maybe even some refineries."

Zoya zoomed her display in on a gas giant just outside the largest asteroid belt. "Lot of moons there. Suppose they're developing them?"

"I would. Not like they're going to advertise. They're at least skimming that giant for volatiles."

"So why are we paying for gasses?" Zoya asked, her head cocked sideways.

"Because skimming is slow. It's fine if you've no other sources, but it can take a few days to get a full load."

"Could we sell excess gas?" Zoya asked, nibbling her lip.

Natalya thought it over for a couple of heartbeats. "Probably. If we can't find something that pays better."

"What would pay better?"

"I'm planning on doing data couriers. We could fly data across the Western Annex before radio waves could get it out of the sector."

"Huh."

Natalya grinned at her. "You'll see. We'll have opportunities that don't involve jumping drugs, selling our body parts, or slaving in a hot asteroid mine."

Zoya smiled back and gave her a little nod. "I'll take your word for it. At least until somebody contacts me."

Natalya laughed and settled into her couch.

Over the next dozen stans, the station grew in the aft ports. Natalya and Zoya passed the time watching the ship traffic and trying to see as much of Dark Knight Station as they could. What started as a glittery collection of lights resolved into a massive multi-armed collection of galleries, hubs, and gantries. Ships and parts of ships stuck out in all directions. Natalya spotted a huge, mostly rectangular shadow against the backdrop of stars. "Big solar array up there, too."

"I saw that earlier," Zoya said. "You think they're running on solar power? The system primary looks a long way off."

"It's possible. We're in the Goldilocks zone. Rocks and giants outside with one rocky planetesimal inside according to my scans." Natalya shrugged. "Probably more than one source but I wouldn't rule out at least one hefty fusactor in one of those hull sections in there."

The navigation computer kicked into the final approach and began applying heavy deceleration, slowing the ship for final docking. It took nearly a stan before the navigational computers were satisfied and ended the program with a triple beep.

"*Peregrine*, Dark Knight Local. Over."

"Local, *Peregrine*. Over."

"*Peregrine*, we show you on track to one-three-three. Will you need assistance docking?"

"Local, *Peregrine*. Negative. We have one-three-three on visual. Will hold at one zero meters for green light. Over."

"Roger, *Peregrine*. Be advised the management doesn't look kindly on bumping the door. Over."

"Acknowledged, Local. Neither do I. *Peregrine*, out."

"Dark Knight Local, out."

"What was that about?" Zoya asked.

"Just letting us know they've got us on approach and we need to be careful not to scratch their paint."

The ship faced the station and it stretched out for what seemed like kilometers in a snarl of catwalks and tubes. Small craft docking bays lined up along the nearest gantry with blocky numbers painted on the doors and spotlights shining across the pitted surfaces. Some of the numbers looked like they'd been scrubbed off with sand paper and others seemed to be missing parts of the digits.

"Not an idle warning, by the looks," Zoya said, staring at the somewhat battered doors.

Natalya chuckled. "This is pretty good considering. Wait till you see the Junkyard." Her fingers danced across the console's keyboard and the ship twisted to line up with the door marked with one-three-three. "Watch our approach vector, would you, Zee? I'm on Mark One eyeball and don't wanna look away."

Zoya's keys clattered and she began reading out numbers. "One thousand meters. Twenty meters per second delta-vee."

"It looks a lot closer."

"It's huge," Zoya said. "Seven hundred meters."

Natalya punched the thrusters to take a bit of velocity off at one hundred meters and brought the ship to a stop relative to the door at precisely ten meters. A red light strobed above the door, a slow pulse that almost matched her heartbeats. After a few moments, the light turned green and the door slid downward. When it cleared, Natalya moved the ship through an opening that might have handled a freighter.

"Makes me feel really small," Zoya said.

"Makes me wonder if they don't have a smaller dock."

"That, too."

They had to wait for the outer door to close and the inner door to open before they could enter the station proper. They found themselves in a docking bay built for small ships. Several nuzzled up to docking tubes against the bulkhead. Natalya saw a few shuttles, a couple of couriers, a mining support skiff, and a large collection that she couldn't guess about.

"Big door for little ships," Natalya said.

"Maybe they need to let them out all at once or something."

One of the docking tubes started to flash a green light. Natalya took a moment to wipe her palms off on her thighs and gripped the helm control again. She settled the *Peregrine* onto the deck on a big X-marks-the-spot target in front of the tube, rotating the ship so the lock side faced the tube. They watched the tube extend and heard it clamp onto the side of the ship with a soft thunk.

"*Peregrine*, Dark Knight Local. Secure engines. Stand by for port authority. Over."

Natalya started shutting down the navigation systems as she spoke. "Roger, Local. Securing all engines. Standing by for port authority. Over."

Almost immediately the lock-call buzzer echoed in the bridge.

She pulled off her seat belt and nodded to Zoya. "Come on. They'll want eyeballs on both of us."

Zoya followed her down the short corridor to the lock. Natalya opened the inner door and stepped into the lock. She waved Zoya in and closed the inner door. Two men and a woman waited outside the lock. All of them wore simple jump suits with some kind of logo on the left chest. One of the men and the woman wore sidearms, but the man in front had a tablet and a bored expression. Natalya keyed the outer door open and smiled.

The front man nodded, looking back and forth between Zoya and Natalya. "Captain?"

Natalya stepped forward. "I'm the captain and registered owner. Natalya Regyri."

"Welcome to Dark Knight Station, Captain. I'm Thomas Russ. I'm your station liaison. How may we help you?" He smiled and it crinkled at the corners of his eyes.

"This is my crew, Zoya Usoko. We need food, fuel, and gasses. We'd also like freedom of the station. It's our first visit to Dark Knight and we'd like to look around."

Russ's gaze flicked to Zoya and back again. "Of course, Captain. Docking fees are a hundred a day. Shore power is available, but billed at station rates. Tankage connections are available but you'll need to arrange for delivery with the chandlery."

"That's satisfactory," Natalya said. "Do you have a banking terminal handy so we can check our balances before we get too far over our heads here?"

A tightness in the man's face seemed to relax. "Of course, Captain. If you'd follow me? There's a terminal right outside the tube."

The two guards led the parade and Russ waved Natalya and Zoya ahead of him. Natalya keyed the outer door closed before following the guards into the station proper. The corridor inside felt positively roomy after being aboard the scout but fell short of the wide, well-kept promenades on CPJCT orbitals. The guards took up station on either side and Russ pointed to a mundane-looking bank kiosk mounted on the bulkhead across from the docking tube. "I trust this will suffice?"

Natalya nodded and stepped up to the console. She keyed her bank ident and stared into the darkened port. The machine beeped and the screen popped open. She checked her balances and schooled her features to a careful neutral while she queried deposits. Satisfied, she turned to Russ. "Do you need an escrow for our stay?"

Russ shook his head. "That won't be necessary, Captain. Can I ask how long you plan to remain on station?"

"Two or three days at least."

He nodded. "We'd ask that you pay for docking fees in advance. A hundred credits for today's docking."

"Routing?" Natalya asked.

"DKS Services should suffice."

She turned back to the kiosk and transferred five hundred credits to the station. "There's five days. That should do for now."

Russ checked his tablet and nodded. "Thank you, Captain. If you should leave earlier, any unused portion will be returned to your account."

Natalya stepped back and motioned Zoya to the kiosk.

Zoya looked at Natalya and back at the console. "Just like home."

Natalya nodded. "Same credentials."

Zoya looked skeptical but stepped into the kiosk and tapped a few keys. After a brief exchange, she closed the windows and stepped away from the kiosk.

"Now, freedom of the station?" Natalya asked. "It gets a bit cramped in there."

Russ smiled and nodded. "I can only imagine. As for freedom of the station, Mr. Kondur asked if you'd be so kind as to meet him for breakfast at 0700 station time?"

Natalya and Zoya traded glances. Zoya shrugged.

"What time is it now, Mr. Russ?" Natalya asked

"Current station time is 0436, May 27."

"In the meantime?"

"We'd appreciate it if you'd stay aboard until meeting Mr. Kondur. It's only a couple of stans."

Zoya gave Natalya a nod. "I could use a nap."

"Me, too," Natalya said. "Of course, Mr. Russ. Should we expect an escort?"

"Tony Eng heads up the day crew. Someone from his team will be along at 0645, if that's satisfactory?"

"Thank you, yes." Natalya nodded to Russ and led Zoya down the docking tube to the ship, keyed the lock open, and stepped aboard. Neither woman spoke until the outer lock clamped down and the inner door opened.

"That was interesting," Zoya said.

Natalya continued down the passageway into the galley. "I thought so, too. In what way?"

"That kiosk accessed my account from Port Newmar."

Natalya started some water heating and picked a mint tea from the cupboard. "It would be more accurate to say the kiosk at Port Newmar accessed your account here. I told you. High Tortuga runs the banking system for the whole Western Annex. You want tea?"

Zoya shook her head. "I want a shower and a few stans communing with my closed eyelids. What did you find interesting?"

"Verkol Kondur owns this station. He wants to meet us as soon as we dock."

"That's unusual?"

Natalya shrugged. "Might be. I'm guessing he's not available to every rock-knocker and jet jockey who docks here."

"Maybe it's the ship. You said it's rare."

"Possibly." Natalya looked at the overhead and considered for a moment. "Likely, even, but it's not the most interesting thing."

"What would that be?"

"While we were flying in from the jump, somebody transferred fifty thousand credits into my account."

Zoya's eyes widened. "Who?"

Natalya snickered. "That's the question, isn't it? The deposit was made at the Newmar Orbital."

"So after we escaped?"

"We didn't so much escape as got herded."

"Herded?"

"Yep. Somebody wanted us here at Dark Knight Station. Margaret Newmar is the driver but I don't know what her role in this might be. For that matter I don't know why they didn't just hire us to do it. That fifty grand looks suspiciously like a carrot after being chased out of the sector with a stick."

"Or evidence that you've been bought," Zoya said.

Natalya grunted. "Hadn't thought of that. Bought for what?"

"Killing Gavin?"

"But I didn't kill him. He's no more dead than I am."

"He looked dead to me," Zoya said.

Natalya shook her head. "He was supposed to, but we got hustled out of that room real fast and we were off planet before the blood stopped spreading."

Zoya nodded half-heartedly but didn't look convinced.

"Logic with me. You were told to stick with me. That I'd be leaving the planet. Right?"

"Yeah."

"How long ago? Last week? Last month?"

Zoya's gaze shifted for a moment. "Last week, I think. Maybe ten days ago."

Natalya spread her hands in an encompassing gesture. "And voilÃ . Here we are. So, how did we get here?"

The realization washed across Zoya's face like a wave. She stared at Natalya, her lips parted as if to speak but no words came out.

"Exactly. They knew I wouldn't refuse a last hurrah with Sifu Newmar and the invites came out last week."

"My invitation arrived the day after Captain Smith gave me my orders."

"Smith? Really?"

Zoya shrugged. "He made no bones about it being a fake name. The only other two I met went by Jones and Garcia."

"Really? Garcia? Was he Hispanic?"

"She was peaches and cream with flaming red hair, so I'm guessing no. Smith, on the other hand could have been. He had that dreamy, olive-toned skin. Black hair. Gorgeous eyes—"

"Yeah. That's probably more than I needed."

Zoya grinned for a heartbeat before turning toward her stateroom. "I'm gonna try to get some sleep. See you in a couple of stans." She stopped at the door and looked back at Natalya. "We don't need to set a watch or anything, do we?"

Natalya shook her head. "We're good. The ship's too small to hide problems, and the automated alarms pick up everything from low oxygen to armed intruders."

Zoya nodded once. "Good." She gave a wan smile. "It feels like we only graduated a few stans ago. Has it been a full day yet?"

Natalya glanced at the chrono. "Almost two, I think. Sleep well. I'll knock at 0630 if you're not moving."

"Same." Zoya twiddled a few fingers by way of a wave and disappeared into her stateroom.

Natalya poured boiling water over the herbal tea and punched the timer button. She needed to sleep, but she had a lot to think about and not much time to do it in.

Chapter Seven
Dark Knight Station: 2363, May 27

Natalya rose just after 0600 and spent a long five ticks in the shower, letting the hot water splash over her skin and wash some of the tension out of her back. Afterward she put together an outfit of polished black ship boots, the slacks from her dress blacks, and a couple of layers of rust and red topped with her favorite brown leather flight jacket. It wasn't exactly the height of fashion at Port Newmar but it reminded her of her father and had a lot of pockets. She added a periwinkle scarf and smiled at herself in the mirror.

Zoya raised an eyebrow at the outfit. "You expecting it to be cold?"

"Expecting we'll have a lot to do." She eyed Zoya's neatly pressed undress khakis in return. "You look a little too regulation to fit in. Got a pair of jeans?"

"Seriously? You're going out in that and you're going to critique what I wear?"

Natalya sighed. "Your call."

"I've got a couple of shipsuits, but that's about it besides my dress uniforms and a couple of sets of undress khaki," Zoya said. "Never thought I'd need more."

Natalya shrugged. "Well, maybe we can fill in your wardrobe a bit while we're here."

The lock-call chimed at precisely 0645.

"That's our escort. Ready to meet the man?" Natalya asked.

Zoya wiped her palms on the sides of her slacks and nodded.

Natalya keyed the inner lock and Zoya followed her in.

After the lock cycled, the outer hatch opened on a trio of people in Dark Knight utilities.

"Captain Regyri?" the lead man asked.

Natalya stepped forward. "Good morning. You are?"

"I'm the day-crew supervisor, Tony Eng." He gave a little half-bow in lieu of a handshake. "If you'd follow us, we'll see that you get to Mr. Kondur without any problems."

"Of course."

"Ms. Usoko will accompany us?" he asked.

"She will."

"Very good." He turned toward the station and extended a hand. "Right this way."

His guards led the way out of the docking tube while Natalya closed the lock behind them.

The station's light level might have been a bit brighter than earlier, but Natalya couldn't be sure. The air in the passageway lacked the hydraulic tang she had grown used to in CPJCT orbitals, and carried more humidity and an earthy odor.

"Your first time on Dark Knight Station, Captain?" Eng asked.

"Yes. I visited High Tortuga and some of the other stations before. My father took me on a brief tour before I went away to school."

"So you know about the procedures?"

"I'm familiar with the concept of extended visa, yes," she said.

He offered a wide smile that seemed genuine enough to reach his eyes. "That will make things go more smoothly, I'm sure."

"Tell me, does Mr. Kondur vet all new visitors?"

Eng shook his head. "No, usually he leaves that to the shift supervisor." He glanced at her out of the corners of his eyes. "New visitors flying an exploration scout ship? That's unusual enough. New visitors arriving in the *Peregrine*? Yes, he'd want to see you himself."

"You know the *Peregrine*, then?" Zoya asked.

Eng nodded. "I know *of* her. She's a stout ship. Made her share of registrations, she has, and then some. Steve Fick brought her out here back in—gosh, musta been like 2061 or '62. She's two centuries old by now. Doesn't seem possible she's still flyin'."

"I'm not sure how many of her parts are original anymore," Natalya said.

Eng chuckled and shrugged. "Doesn't really matter. She's still the *Peregrine*. She's still flyin'." He cast a glance at Natalya. "If you don't mind me askin', how'd you come to be flyin' her?"

"Gift from my father," Natalya said.

Eng's eyebrows twitched up and down, but he nodded. "Nice gift. You wanna sell her?"

"What? And walk home?" Natalya asked, smiling at the man.

Eng chuckled. "You could buy three ships for what you could get for that one."

Natalya shrugged. "Dunno about that. This one's mine and I think I'll keep it."

"Don't blame ya. I'd keep it, too."

Their rambling walk took them deeper into the station. At one point they crossed an open, brightly lit atrium that went up at least five decks. A fountain splashed noisily in the center and planters full of frilly green plants surrounded it. Natalya watched a couple of teens in station jumpsuits working on a bed of flowers as they passed.

Eng said, "Jamey and Doreen. Good kids. Doreen keeps him in line but he's got the knack for plants. They keep this space shipshape, and we give them a place to live and a meal allotment."

Natalya's gaze lifted to the open area and spotted huge planters filled with flowers and other plants all the way up to the ceiling. It took her a moment to realize what she was looking at. "These are your CO2 scrubbers?"

Eng looked up. "Some of them. We've got some industrial scrubbing units scattered about, but these clean up the air and make it smell good." He took a healthy sniff. "Smell that."

Natalya nodded. "I've been noticing the difference in air quality since I came out of the docking tube."

"Where are their parents?" Zoya asked as they were about to enter a passage on the far side of the atrium. She glanced back at the two teens. "They don't look any older than fifteen or sixteen."

Eng paused and looked over his shoulder. "She's eighteen and he's nineteen. Their parents were killed in the belts a couple stanyers back."

Zoya's face clouded. "Accident?"

Eng sighed. "Claim jumpers. Come on. Mr. Kondur will be happy to tell you anything you need to know."

He led the way down a passage so narrow, it was difficult to walk two abreast. The moist, green air gained a tang of engine lubricants and the bite of some kind of antiseptic. They took two more turns and Eng stepped out into a long gallery. Three stories tall and wide enough for a couple of lorries to drive side-by-side down the center. Moisture in the air masked the space at either end in a gauzy mist.

"Welcome to Main Street," Eng said. "You can find anything you need and some things you didn't know you wanted here."

"Chandlery?" Natalya asked.

"Ship's services are all back near the docks. Anybody can tell you where they are."

"I'm wishing I'd left breadcrumbs. I'll never find my way back," Natalya said.

"Your extended visas have already been approved. You'll be able to access the station's network after your meeting with Mr. Kondur."

"Well, by all means, let's go get some breakfast." Natalya smiled at Eng.

They turned left onto Main Street. Eng led them past clothing stores, drug markets, and bars. One store front featured scantily clad men and women lounging behind the armorglass displays. Natalya returned their smiles but didn't stop.

Eventually Eng pushed through the front door of what appeared to be a bar. The light level dropped far enough that Natalya found herself blinking and trying to see what lurked in the gloom. It had that yeasty, beery smell of a good brew house and none of the stale beer and vomit that typically pinched her nose in dark bars.

"This way," Eng said and led them to a large corner booth.

A round table filled the corner and a curved banquette worked around the wall. A beefy man in Dark Knight Station livery leaned against the wall near the end of the bench seating. He appeared to be giving more attention to his manicure than the room around him. Natalya didn't believe it for a moment.

"Mr. Kondur, your guests. Captain Regyri and Ms. Usoko," Eng said and stepped back.

Kondur leaned his elbows on the edge of the table and nodded to Eng before turning his gaze to Natalya. "Welcome to Dark Knight Station. Please have a seat." He waved a hand at the banquette, then motioned at somebody across the restaurant. "Martin will bring us some coffee."

Natalya slipped into the booth and scooted over to give Zoya room to join her. "Thank you, Mr. Kondur. We're glad to be here."

Kondur's attention focused on Zoya for a moment before returning to search Natalya's face. "Well, one of you is, at any rate." He smiled. His close-cropped mustache and goatee seemed to move about his face as his lips moved.

A server in a white apron brought a tray of coffee cups, utensils, and a carafe to the table. He scattered them around and nodded to Kondur before slipping back into the shadowy interior of the dining room.

Natalya looked around but Eng and his two colleagues had disappeared while she'd been distracted.

"Tony has other duties," Kondur said. He slopped a bit of creamer into his cup, added three sugars, and topped it off with coffee from the carafe. He slid the carafe across the table to them. "Try it. I think you'll like it. I import the green beans and roast them here. Makes a big difference." He lowered his muzzle into his cup and took a slurping sip while Natalya and Zoya filled their mugs.

Natalya held her cup up to her nose and took a deep whiff. The dark, nutty aroma struck her olfactory system like a belt of Scotch to her stomach and she immediately grabbed a taste. The hot liquid nearly burned her mouth but the flavors exploded and slipped down her throat.

"Good, huh?" Kondur asked. The corners of his eyes crinkled as he grinned across the table.

"Very," Natalya said. "You sell it?"

Kondur's smile stayed fixed on his face as he shook his head. "Can't get enough beans to sell and I'm too self-centered to share."

Natalya took another sip and glanced at Zoya. "Try it, Zee. You'll love it."

Almost reluctantly Zoya lifted the mug to her mouth and took a tiny sip. Her eyes widened momentarily in surprise. She took another sip and nodded. "Very nice. Yes."

"Can I interest you in some actual breakfast? I haven't eaten yet myself and I did invite you."

Natalya nodded. "Breakfast would be great."

"Yes, please."

"You fussy about breakfast food?" Kondur asked, looking back and forth between them.

"I'm not much on fish in the morning," Natalya said. "I'm good with anything else."

"Fish?" Kondur asked, leaning forward a bit. "For breakfast?"

"I tangled with a kippered herring in a past life."

Kondur laughed a little "ha ha ha" that sounded honest. "Don't blame you. Ms. Usoko? Any preferences?"

"I'll eat most things." Zoya stared into her mug, a small frown on her forehead.

Kondur held up his hand with three digits extended. "Martin will bring us some food in a few ticks. In the meantime, why don't you tell me where you're from and why you've graced my humble station with that magnificent antique?"

"The *Peregrine*?" Natalya asked.

"Unless you have some other magnificent antique stashed away?"

"Margaret sent us," Zoya said.

Kondur's eyebrows rose and his head swiveled so his gaze raked to Zoya's face. "Margaret." He made it a simple statement but something in his eyes made Natalya uneasy. "I know a lot of Margarets."

"Newmar." Zoya's voice barely sounded loud enough to reach her coffee mug, but Kondur's eyes flickered at the name.

"I see."

The server brought three platters loaded with eggs, potatoes, sausage, pancakes, and toast. He slapped a small pitcher of syrup onto the table and paused for a moment.

The fingers on Kondur's left hand twitched and the server scuttled back into the kitchen.

"What did Margaret tell you?" Kondur asked after staring at Zoya for a few heartbeats. He picked up his fork and began slicing through the eggs and sausage, mixing them before forking a bite.

Zoya poured a dab of syrup on her pancakes before answering. "Just that we should come here and talk to you. Thank you for inviting us to breakfast." She placed the syrup back on the table where the server had set it.

Kondur sighed and nodded. He looked at Natalya. "Who'd you kill?"

"Me? Nobody."

Kondur paused with his empty fork half way to his plate. His gaze flipped to Zoya and back to Natalya. "Margaret doesn't send me people who haven't killed somebody already. She didn't kill anybody."

Zoya sat up stiffly. "What makes you say that?"

"What? You? Kill somebody? No. You're fleet through and through. Boot third mate. Probably just graduated." Kondur stared hard at Natalya for a moment. "But you? Maybe. That's why I asked." He dug into his breakfast again and watched them from under his eyebrows.

"They think I did," Natalya said after working through half her eggs. "At least they say I did."

Kondur's eyes narrowed. "That explains it." He sopped the loose egg yolk up with a piece of pancake and popped it into his mouth. "Love this guy's pancakes. He always makes 'em thick and fluffy." He leaned back in his seat, pushing his plate away and bracing an arm against the table's edge. "So, what are you going to do now?"

"Re-provision the ship. Look for work." Natalya shrugged. "Pay some dues. Make a life. What else?"

Kondur looked a Zoya. "And you, Fleet? You're a long way from home."

"I'm with her," Zoya said.

"Why are you with her? Inertia?"

Zoya glanced at Natalya before answering. "Maybe. I can't go back so I guess I go forward."

Kondur stared at her while he ran his tongue around inside his mouth and over his teeth. After several heartbeats he said. "How linear." He looked at Natalya. "What kind of work?"

"Courier, maybe. Mining, if I need to."

"You any good in zero?" Kondur asked.

"I get by."

"Shuttles? Ore haulers?"

"I can fly a shuttle," Natalya said.

"Haulers," Zoya said, earning another stare from Kondur.

"Really?" he asked.

Zoya shrugged. "I wasn't always fleet. I grew up between the belts in Margary." She glanced at Natalya. "Not exactly in the curriculum."

"My goodness, Ms. Usoko. We may make a Toe-Holder out of you yet," Kondur said. His tone sounded faintly mocking but Natalya saw something closer to respect in his eyes. Kondur looked at Natalya again. "You say you got the ship from your father?"

"Yep."

"Got title?"

"Yep."

"Wanna sell her?"

"Nope."

He grinned and shrugged. "Can't blame a guy for askin'."

"She's old and she's a little cranky but she's sound and she's mine. Day may come when I need the credit more than the ship, but until then she's got long legs, low overhead, and she's paid for."

Kondur nodded. "Regyri. I knew a Regyri once. Best rock-knocker in the belts. Son of a bitch could smell the ore, I swear." He squinted at Natalya. "He was a pretty good pilot, too. Dominic?"

Natalya shook her head. "Don't know any Dominic Regyri."

"You play close to the vest, eh?" Kondur grinned. "I can respect that. You've got his eyes and a fair slice of his stubborn, too, I bet."

"Who?" Natalya asked, the hair prickling on her arms.

"Your father. Demetri. Who else."

"You know him?" Natalya wasn't sure if she believed him, but it wasn't the first time somebody had commented about her eyes.

"Yeah. Long time ago we flew together. Did some mining for Mel. Made a few cargo runs for—" Kondur stopped speaking and ran a hand across his mouth. "Well, let's just say we ran a little cargo. He ever take you out in the belts?"

"Once or twice." Natalya shrugged. "I can run a sled but I'm rusty. Not much practice lately."

He nodded. "It comes back fast if you need it." He threw back the rest of his coffee and tapped the table with the empty mug. "I got a job if you want it."

"Doing what?" Natalya asked.

"I need something delivered."

"How big a something?" Natalya asked.

Kondur reached into the sleeve pocket of his jumpsuit with two fingers and pulled out a data chip. "This."

"Do I want to know what's on it?" Natalya asked.

Kondur shook his head. "Probably not. It's just boring data. Nothing to see, but I need it delivered over in Diurnia."

"Where in Diurnia?" Zoya asked, leaning forward over the table.

"Yeah, yeah. I got it. You can't dock at a High Liner station. Ever hear of Odin's Outpost?"

Zoya shook her head but Natalya nodded. "Rinky-dink station halfway between lost and nowhere."

Kondur snickered. "That's your father talkin', but yeah. Combination den of iniquity and gateway to the stars."

"What's in it for us?" Natalya asked, hiding her mouth behind her coffee mug.

"You'll want to top off your tanks. Maybe buy some food?" Kondur asked.

"Maybe."

"All right. I'll give you a chit for the chandlery. Whatever you need for supplies and I'll toss in five kay as sweetener, but you have to leave as soon as you're supplied and I need this in Gunderson's hand in forty-eight stans."

"You don't have couriers to do that for you already?" Zoya asked.

He smiled and nodded. "I do, yes, but nobody's going to be watching you except to admire that shiny old space ship."

"Charts," Natalya said. "I need a set of Toe-Hold charts."

"See Inky at the chandlery. Tell her Bobo sent you." He grinned.

"Visa?"

He nodded. "Half day unlimited. Deliver that chip by the deadline. Come back, might be I've got another little job needs doing and you'll have full visa. Unlimited."

Natalya thought about it. "Deal."

"Pad?" Kondur asked.

Natalya pulled out her tablet and put it on the table beside her plate.

Kondur pulled out a similar unit and pecked a few keys on the screen before sending a near-field message.

Natalya's tablet bipped a receipt.

"Charge what you need to that account. I'll credit half when you file pre-flight and half on delivery with Gunderson's receipt."

"What if we're late?"

"Don't come back."

Natalya nodded. "I can live with that."

"Trick is to not have to," Kondur said, the right side of his mouth curled in a half-smile.

Natalya extended a hand across the table.

Kondur shook her hand and slipped the chip into her palm. "Now scoot. See you next week."

Natalya nudged Zoya and they both slipped off the bench.

"You got somebody to escort us back?" Natalya asked.

"Follow the green arrows," Kondur said. "Your visa is good. Nobody will bother you."

Natalya nodded. "Fair enough. See you next week."

Zoya followed Natalya out of the dive and into the broad passageway that felt blindingly bright in comparison. "Green arrows?" Zoya asked when the door closed behind them.

Natalya pointed her chin at the decking. Somebody had painted green arrowheads every few meters along it. A few of them looked a little scuffed but the path pointed back the way they'd come in.

"Follow the yellow brick road," Zoya said.

"What?"

"Old saying. Let's go find the chandlery."

The Main Street passageway had plenty of room for them to walk side-by-side and still allowed the other early morning travelers and revelers to walk—or stagger, as the case may be. The arrows took a turn back through the narrow passage to the atrium. The gardeners had gone, but the airy space had filled up with people sitting at small tables scattered around the area. Some chatted, some just sat quietly. A few left and more arrived. Almost all of them had drink containers or finger foods.

"Now we know where to take our coffee in the morning," Zoya said.

"If we were going to be here in the morning," Natalya said.

Zoya nodded. "Why Bobo?"

"What?"

"Kondur. Inky. Bobo? Remember?" Zoya asked.

Natalya shrugged. "Might be some kind of Toe-Hold slang. It was something my mother used to call my father when he did something stupid."

"That something he did often?"

"Often enough. Probably why they split up."

"So why'd you take only five kay?"

The path led them back into a dim passageway. Natalya didn't answer until the passing foot traffic had cleared.

"He doesn't know what we need for supplies." She grinned at Zoya.

"What are you thinking?"

"He said whatever we need," Natalya said.

"Nats. You've got that look."

"Let's see what the chandlery can supply in the way of galley supplies, shall we?"

"You wouldn't."

Natalya tsked. "For two kilos of that coffee? I most certainly would."

"I don't think that's what he had in mind."

"It's a test. I suspect there's a credit limit on this account number. Food, fuel, water, volatiles. Coffee is food. He knows it. I bet he's watching to see if we take any. That's why he only offered five kay and why I accepted it."

Zoya sighed and shook her head. "You're gonna get us killed."

Natalya laughed. "Maybe someday. Not today." She quickened her pace. "Come on. Time flies and so should we."

The green arrowheads led them back to the docking section. "Now where?" Zoya asked, as they stood outside their docking tube. "Logically, the chandlery shouldn't be far from the docks."

Natalya looked down the long gallery in each direction. "Logically, it's not far from the large ship docks. Freighters, mining tenders, and bulk haulers would not be docking here." She waved a hand at the small ship bay.

"I'd buy that."

"Also logically, they're not going to run down here with a fuel dolly or a water hauler to top our tanks. Come on. I bet we're overthinking it." She led the way onto the ship.

Zoya laughed. "Of course."

Natalya dropped into the pilot couch and brought up the station network on her console. The menu listed chandlery services first. A few keystrokes and Kondur's account number got them tied to tankage. Natalya ordered water, volatiles, and gasses be topped up.

"That's that, but what about food?" Zoya asked.

"I wanna do that in person. We need to go there anyway to find Inky. I'm also going to run a spares inventory to get a shopping list." She twisted her mouth into a wry smile. "We may not have the regulation quantity of all the spares we're supposed to have."

"What regs?" Zoya asked.

Natalya laughed. "Let's just say, prudence might suggest we have a few more scrubber filters and a couple extra potable water filters."

"You're going to charge them to Kondur?"

"If I can."

Zoya laughed. "All right. Where's the chandlery?"

Natalya pulled up the chandlery's contact page, which showed a handy station map with blinking yellow lights tracing a line from where they sat on the ship, down the long corridor, around a bend, and into a passageway so wide it looked like a six-lane road.

"They build things big here," Zoya said.

"They probably need them wide to carry supplies and goods. You're used to orbitals where every storefront and shop on the promenades has a service door in the back with heavy lifts in the core." Natalya checked the engineering readouts to make sure the tanks were getting filled before closing the screens.

"That was fast," Zoya said.

"I should have figured they'd have tied on the tankage connections with the shore-ties. It's what we did in every other port." Natalya shook her head. "We need to get moving and I don't know where we're going without the charts."

When they stepped out of the docking tube, Zoya pointed to the deck. "Yellow."

Natalya blinked. A line of scuffed, faded, and dirt-smudged yellow arrows pointed the path toward the chandlery. "Were they there all along?"

Zoya shrugged. "I'm guessing yes, but they're so worn and grubby, we didn't notice."

Natalya gave a short laugh and struck off along the gallery. The moist, green smell faded away to something slightly more astringent. It tickled Natalya's nose with familiarity but she couldn't quite place it. They turned the corner and found the large craft docks. The stink of hydraulic fluid and antiseptic cleaners masked the homier smells of plants and soil.

"I'll say one thing for this station," Zoya said. "The docks aren't freezing."

Natalya nodded. "I'm not sure what the difference is. They're even using the same ten-meter docking rings." She pointed at the nearest lock.

"That could have come right out of any orbital I've ever seen," Zoya said. "Even the tattletale readouts are the same."

Natalya walked over to the nearest one and peered at it. "Not quite."

Zoya looked to where the screen should have shown the vessel. All it said was "Occupied."

Foot and vehicle traffic kept them close to the bulkhead as they made the final leg to the chandlery. The yellow markers led them into a massive warehouse space with a service counter across the front. The smell of packaging and cleaners mixed with the slimy aromas of lubricants and sealants.

"Must be the place," Natalya said.

Zoya chuckled. "What makes you think so?"

Natalya pointed up. The word "Chandlery" had been painted in two-meter-tall letters in an eye-searing yellow. "I bet it glows in the dark."

Zoya glanced up at the lighting panels in the overhead. "I don't think it ever gets dark here."

"Good point." Natalya said and headed for the counter. "Let's see what they have for packaged food."

Spacers lined the service bar two deep, but the crew behind the counter was fast. Natalya barely had a chance to check out the bouncers and enforcers lounging around before a short, wiry guy with just a fringe of gray around his bald pate waved them forward.

"What cha need?" he asked.

"Need to replenish food."

"You want individual meals or you gonna cook?" The man's voice seemed just a pitch too high for his frame, but it cut through the background noise without him having to yell.

"Individual meals. Frozen, if you got it."

He gave a judicious nod. "Frozen we got. Biggest freezer in the universe just outside the lock." He smiled at his own joke. "Any preferences?"

Natalya looked at Zoya, who shook her head.

"I've got six empty cubes in my freezer. Mix and match the meals," Natalya said.

The old man's fingers rattled a tattoo on the keys and he looked up at Natalya. "Payment?"

Natalya pulled up her tablet and displayed Kondur's account number. "Charge it to this account."

The old man flashed a scanner at it, then consulted his screen with a nod. "Anything else?"

"Coffee."

A tiny hint of a smile brushed the man's mouth and he arched an eyebrow. "Kondur's blend isn't for sale."

Natalya grinned at him. "Can't blame a girl for tryin'. Got anything good?"

"You like something earthy like Sulawesi?"

"I prefer something brighter. Like Caturra."

He nodded. "I have a nice Arabasti. Light city roast in five-kilo vacuum tubs."

"How much?"

He grinned. "What do you care? Kondur's paying."

"Gimme two."

He laughed outright at that. "You two gonna drink ten kilos of Arabasti?"

Natalya thought for a moment. "How much are they?"

"A hundred twenty a tub."

"I'll give you a kilocred for ten. Separate order."

"You two are off that scout, right?" he asked.

Natalya glanced at Zoya. "So?"

He nodded and winked. "Let's finish your replenishment order and we'll talk." He punched a few more buttons. "Anything besides the food and coffee?"

"Charts? I need an update."

He pointed to a door off to the side of the counter. "Through there. Down the hall. Cartography. She'll help you. Anything else?"

Again Natalya glanced at Zoya, who again shook her head.

"We're good," Natalya said.

He tapped that screen closed and opened a new one. "Now? You wanted some coffee?"

"Ten tubs." Natalya said.

"Yes, Captain. I can give you a nice discount on ten tubs." He offered the tab showing a thousand credits on the total and ten tubs of Arabasti.

She thumbed the tab. "Could you have that delivered to the *Peregrine* with my other order?"

He nodded again. "You bet, Cap. Anything else I can help you with today?"

"Thanks, no. You've been a great help."

"My pleasure." He looked over Natalya's shoulder and said, "I can help who's next."

Natalya and Zoya took the cue and went in search of the cartography office.

"What are you going to do with fifty kilos of coffee?" Zoya asked.

"Sell it, I hope." Natalya grinned over her shoulder at Zoya. "Or we're never going to run out of fresh brewed."

"Why coffee?"

Natalya shook her head. "Dunno. Because it was there. Maybe this Outpost we're going to needs some. Maybe we carry it around until we turn a profit on it."

"Where are you going to store it?"

"Under my bunk if I need to, but I think there's room in the utility closet."

Zoya shook her head but she had an amused smile on her lips.

Chapter Nine
Dark Knight Station: 2363, May 27

A narrow passage led them deeper into the station. The scent of industrial soap wafted in the air, a bit too floral and a bit too sharp. Natalya heard voices behind some of the partitions but nothing she could make out. One of the overhead lights buzzed as they walked under it, the sound fading behind as they walked deeper.

"How far is it, do you think?" Zoya asked.

"Feels like we're almost back at Main Street, doesn't it?"

Zoya gave a short laugh. "Much further and I'll be looking for Margaret Newmar."

They stopped outside the first door they came to. A small, hand-painted sign at eye-level read "You made it."

"What the ...?" Zoya muttered.

Natalya stepped back, looked at the door, and laughed.

"What's so funny?"

"The door is the sign."

Zoya blinked and shook her head. "I don't—oh."

What had looked like whorls and patterns up close resolved itself into a sweeping map with the letters spelling out "Cartography" in the rivers and mountains.

Zoya smiled but the frown remained. "We could have walked right by without spotting it."

Natalya shot her a look. "I think that's the point."

"Heck of a way to run a business."

"You're not thinking like a Toe-Holder," Natalya said and tried the knob. The door opened at her touch and they stepped into a fairyland.

When the door swung closed behind them, it left them standing in shadowed darkness. Brightly colored maps—each with its own spotlight—decorated the bulkheads. Some had elaborate frames, a few no frame at all. A fanciful orrery with more than a dozen planets on ovals of silver wire floated without apparent support, its primary a glowing and shifting golden ball. Aromatic smoke wafted from somewhere. A deep-throated chanting filled the space and vibrated Natalya's diaphragm yet never resolved enough for her to make out whether the sounds were voices, instruments, digital constructions, or all of the above.

Beside her, Zoya said "Wow."

Natalya drifted toward the nearest bulkhead to peer at the chart displayed there. "This one's St. Cloud. I've been there. Gorgeous place. Great beaches."

"I've visited," Zoya said. "This one's Port Newmar. It's a much fancier version of the charts we used on the academy cutter."

The sound faded into the background as they moved languidly from chart to chart along the walls. Natalya felt her heartbeats slowing to match the dull thumps of some deep bass drum.

"Can I help you?"

The woman's rich alto blended so well with the chorus of voices and instruments that it didn't register with Natalya right away. She looked toward the counter that spanned the back of the compartment and blinked her eyes several times. She felt as if she might be waking from a dream. "I hope so," she said, her voice sticky in her throat. "We need charts."

The woman behind the counter all but glowed. Her skin reflected the dim light as if she stood in a spotlight of her own. Even her hair glowed white and lustrous. She wore a halter top with straps that disappeared behind her neck over a lacy under-blouse that traced patterns down her arms to the wrist. She smiled. "You've come to the right place."

"We're looking for Inky," Natalya said.

"You've found Inge Sonjasdottir. Some find it amusing to call me Inky." She held her arms out in an odd pose and spun gracefully in place. What Natalya had seen as a lacy top were intricate and colorful tattoos. Her entire torso appeared to be covered, the patterns disappearing under her top and down her back to her waistband.

Natalya found herself leaning over the narrow counter to see more closely. "That's amazing."

Inge smiled. "That's several decades of work, but you need charts."

"Bobo sent us," Zoya said, her voice blurting in the soft sounds of gongs and tinkling chimes.

Inge froze. Her gaze sought Zoya's face and she stared. Hard. "Bobo? Is he here?" she asked after several moments.

Natalya shared a glance with Zoya before answering. "Yes. Where else would he be?"

The woman's face could have been carved from marble. "Who are you and why are you here?"

Natalya held up her hands, palm out. "Easy. We need an astrogation update for Toe-Hold space. Verkol Kondur sent us over and told us to say Bobo sent us."

Her face, so smooth and cold, seemed to melt. "Why would he do that?" She looked like she might cry.

"Who's Bobo?" Zoya asked.

"Oh, nobody." Inge shook her head and waved her hands in front of her face as if to bat away the incense. "It was a pet name for somebody I haven't seen in decades."

Natalya stiffened. "Demetri Regyri."

Inge stared at Natalya. "Yes, but how did you know?"

"I'm his daughter."

"Natalya, of course." Her voice barely registered over the temple gong sounds still rumbling in the background. "How is he?"

"Fine, I think. I haven't seen him for a while. He's back here in Toe-Hold space somewhere."

"And you're flying his old *Peregrine*?" she asked.

Natalya nodded.

"I heard that a scout had docked. I had no idea it was Demetri's ship."

"Mine now. He gave it to me when I went away to school."

Inge's eyes narrowed a bit and she tilted her head a few degrees to the left. She looked back and forth between Zoya and Natalya. "Port Newmar?"

Natalya shrugged. "It's a good school."

"Yes, it is." Inge smiled. She pulled a data chip from under the counter, holding it out to Natalya. "Toe-Hold updates."

Natalya took the drive and tucked into a sleeve pocket. "Thanks. What do I owe you?"

Inge shook her head. "Nothing. Updates are free. Just let me know if you find anything that needs changing."

"Nothing?" Natalya asked. "How can you stay in business?"

Inge's gaze swept the gallery of charts around the wall before she looked back at Natalya. "What do you think my business is?"

Natalya laughed at herself. "Of course. I should have seen it."

"Sometimes we look too hard and miss the obvious," Inge said. "It happens."

"You said this was an update," Zoya said. "We didn't see any Toe-Hold stations on our navigation systems."

Inge shrugged. "*Peregrine* has a full set. Or at least she did."

"I know we must have had them," Natalya said. "I remember using them now that you mention it."

"It's not likely he threw them away," Inge said. "They're probably just suppressed because you were flying in CPJCT space and didn't need them. Demetri had a pass phrase that he used all the time. Something about love."

"The important thing is to be in love with something," Natalya said.

Inge nodded. "Yes, that's it." Her focus turned inward for a moment and a gentle memory seemed to stir her face. "I always teased him about it because it sounded cold and distant. I thought it should be someone, not something."

Natalya laughed. "I asked him the same thing once. He just shook his head and changed the subject."

"Yes," Inge said. "That's Demetri. Try rebooting the navigation system with that as pass phrase. If that chip is mounted, the update cycle should trigger."

Natalya nodded. "Thanks. I'll poke about and see what I can find."

"Is there anything else I can help you with?" Inge asked.

"Thank you, Inge. It was nice to meet somebody who knows my father from before."

Inge smiled. "And lovely to meet you both. Call again. Any time."

Natalya led Zoya back into the cramped passageway and blinked in the brighter lights.

"That was different," Zoya said as they walked back toward the chandlery.

"At least." Natalya sighed. "Makes me wonder what my old man was up to here before he got old."

"You really want to know?" Zoya asked, a laugh in her voice.

Natalya shrugged. "I don't know. Maybe not." She paused before pushing the door open and looked back at Zoya. "She seemed nice."

Zoya shook her head. "She seemed a little weird to me."

"Those two things aren't mutually exclusive, are they?"

"I guess not. She's really talented, though. Those charts are works of real art."

"They are that." Natalya pushed through the door and they headed out of the chandlery, back down the long walk to the ship. "We should be almost tanked up by now and they should deliver our replenishment order shortly. Let's see if we can get the navigation updates done before that."

"Anything else we need to do before we leave?"

"Nothing I know of."

"No flight plans?"

"Nope. And given the job for Kondur, it's just as well," Natalya said.

CHAPTER TEN
DARK KNIGHT STATION: 2363, MAY 27

Natalya rebooted the navigation system with her father's favorite phrase. "That's disappointing," Natalya said.

Zoya looked over her shoulder to see "Incorrect entry. Try again." flashing on the screen. "We know one thing," she said. "At least there is one. Any idea what it might be?"

Natalya pondered for a moment before typing "Natalya."

The error message returned.

"Can you look it up from the backside?" Zoya asked.

Natalya shook her head. "Already looked. Encrypted and we don't have time to crack it."

"Are you sure it's something you know?"

"Not really. I didn't make up my mind to come to Toe-Hold space until last stanyer. He might not have realized I'd want the charts."

"How long did he have the ship?"

"Not sure. I know he had it before I was born."

"So he brought it back from Toe-Hold space before that. What's your mother's name?"

Natalya typed "Charlotte."

The error message returned.

"Suppose we can get a full chart load from Inge?" Zoya asked.

"Probably, but if it loads it over the old one, it might just stay hidden." Natalya bit her lip and pondered. "What did Inge say her last name was?"

"Sonnysdottir?"

Natalya shook her head. "Close." She typed "Inge Sonjasdottir."

The system ruminated for a moment before redisplaying the error message.

Natalya groaned. "It shouldn't be this hard."

Zoya sighed. "I'm stumped. Suppose it's just Inge?"

Natalya tried it with no luck.

The lock-call chimed.

"That'll be our delivery," Natalya said. "Would you get it?"

"Sure thing. Where do you want the extra coffee?"

"Just put it in my stateroom for the moment. We'll sort it out later."

"Aye, aye." Zoya headed for the lock.

Natalya pulled up the station net and found Inge Sonjasdottir's contact. She fired off a message and then checked the status on the tankage before going aft. She found two stacks of coffee tubs, a few cases of foodstuffs, a case of spare parts, and Zoya thumbing the receipt for the goods.

"We got it all?"

Zoya nodded. "Everything we ordered and then some. When did you order parts?"

"While we were looking up the chandlery. I kicked a spares inventory update and tagged the replenishment to the tankage." She grabbed a case of food and headed aft to the walk-in. "Gimme a hand with this and we'll be ready to rumble as soon as I figure out how to unlock the Toe-Hold database."

Zoya followed her with another case of frozen food. "You know, I can cook. A little."

Natalya looked over her shoulder. "I can, too, but realistically, we can be almost anywhere in the Western Annex in less than three standard days. Most places less than one. I just wanted food we could grab and eat until we get docked." Natalya pulled the latch on the walk-in and dropped the case on an empty shelf.

Zoya looked around. "You think you got enough?"

Natalya chuckled. "Well, CPJCT regs said I needed ninety days' worth. It's a good habit to get into and I was a bit short." She surveyed the shelves. "I'll need to rotate some of this stock. Something to do while we're underway."

They stowed the remaining food and Natalya stacked the extra coffee in her stateroom before securing the spare parts in the engineering cubby.

When Natalya got back to the cockpit, a message flashed in her queue. "I hope she had another idea." She popped open the message.

Zoya stuck her head around the corner from the galley. "Anything?"

"Just one. Kristiana. With a K."

Natalya rebooted the system with the new key and the refresh kicked in. "That was it."

"Really? Who's Kristiana?"

"I'll ask as soon as I get this update started." Natalya kicked the update process and watched the data spooling out. While she waited, she sent a message back to Inge. *Thanks. That was it. Who's Kristiana?*

Zoya came out of the galley and handed Natalya a fresh cup of coffee. "We good to go?"

"We still have a bit of tankage," Natalya said with a glance at the status. "Maybe half a stan before we can leave."

"What do we do now?"

Natalya sipped a bit of coffee before climbing out of the couch. "Now, I stow the spares and update the inventories. Wanna help?"

Zoya gave her a very clear look expressing exactly how much she wanted to help, but said, "Sure. Why not?"

They ambled aft. With both of them working, the stowage and inventory updates took less than the half a stan. Zoya took the excess packing materials to the lock. "Leave it here or dump it in space?"

"Keep space empty. I'm sure they can recycle it here. Kondur's not one to let material go to waste. I thought I saw a bin just down the passage from the docking tube."

Zoya nodded. "Be right back." She stepped into the lock and triggered the cycle.

Natalya finished her coffee and stacked the cup in the sanitizer rack. The engineering console beeped as she sat back in her couch. She smiled and started laying in the course for Odin's.

The lock-call chimed and she chuckled when she remembered Zoya didn't have the access code. She trotted back down the passageway to the lock and keyed the outer door. She was halfway back to her seat when Zoya spoke.

"Uh, Nats? We may have a problem."

Natalya turned around and saw Inge standing behind Zoya in the passageway.

The woman's skin glowed in the lights from the overhead, and Nats could swear her tattoos writhed on her white skin. She stared at Natalya, her pink eyes giving her an otherworldly appearance.

"Inge? What is it? We're just about to shove off."

"I know. It seems I have business with Bjorn. Please. Take me with you."

"Bjorn?"

"Gunderson. He runs Odin's Outpost."

Natalya felt her mind skip a beat or two. "We're not exactly set up for passenger service."

Inge smiled and the overhead lights picked up the wrinkles at the corners of her mouth and eyes. That smile made her look much, much older than Natalya had first assumed. "I've slept in the navigation couch before." She held up a small satchel. "I travel light. I don't eat much. And you need to be there in less than thirty-six stans now if you're going to fulfill your contract with Kondur."

Natalya glanced at Zoya who shrugged in return.

"All right, then. You want some coffee? I need to get us out of the docking bay and burning for the Deep Dark."

"I'm fine," Inge said. "Please. Continue with your preparations."

Natalya grinned. "Fair enough," she said.

Inge's whole body appeared to relax at once.

Natalya climbed back into the pilot's couch. "Find a place to sit. I'm requesting clearance to undock in about five ticks."

Inge followed Zoya into the cockpit and pulled down a jump seat from its stored position in the aft bulkhead.

Natalya buckled her harness and typed a request to undock. She finished laying in the course and waved Zoya into the navigation couch. "Double-check me, please?"

The comms screen flashed with permission to undock. Natalya pulled the lock releases to unlatch the docking tube. The quiet thunks preceded a brief flickering of the cabin lighting.

Zoya said, "Undocked. We're running on ship's power."

Natalya nodded and drew more power from the fusactor. She slipped on her headset and keyed the traffic control frequency. "Dark Knight Local, *Peregrine*."

"*Peregrine*, Local. Go ahead."

"We are unlatched and ready to depart, Local."

"Roger, *Peregrine*. Hold one."

"Local, *Peregrine*. Roger. Hold one."

They sat for just a few heartbeats before the outer door began sliding open.

"*Peregrine*, Local. You are clear to depart. Use local lane alpha-two for departure. Over."

"Local, *Peregrine*. Roger. Clear to depart on lane alpha-two. Over."

Natalya goosed the maneuvering rockets a bit to get them off the deck and moving toward the open door. As she cleared the station, her nav plotter laid a track on the console labeled alpha-two.

"*Peregrine*, Local. You are on the beam. Contact Dark Knight Control when you clear the local markers. Over."

"Roger, Local."

"Dark Knight Local, out."

"*Peregrine*, out."

"This course looks fine, Nats," Zoya said. "We're about four stans from the first jump point."

Natalya looked aft to where Inge sat strapped into the jump seat. "So, you've been aboard before?"

"Indeed, I have. You've done a wonderful job refurbishing it, but it's still the *Peregrine*. It brings back so many memories."

Natalya checked her boards. "We're clear of station traffic. You can unbuckle if you want."

"How long until we reach the outer markers?" Inge asked.

"Another stan or so," Natalya said.

Zoya turned to Inge. "If you don't mind my asking, why do you need to get to Odin's so fast?"

Natalya turned to say something to Zoya but Inge held up a hand. "I need to talk to him about my daughter. Family business. I'm sure you understand."

Zoya shrugged. "Sure. No problem."

Inge released her harness and folded the jump seat back into the bulkhead. "Can I make some coffee for you? Tea perhaps?"

Natalya nodded and smiled. "Thanks. That would be lovely."

Inge slipped into the galley and started rustling about. "Do you have enough coffee for the trip?" Her voice carried the lilt of amusement.

"Should get us most of the way there. I've got some spare tubs in my stateroom," Natalya said.

Inge's low chuckle reached them even over the sound of the kickers.

"That was rude," Natalya said, leaning closer to Zoya to speak softly. "You don't ask people's business."

Zoya scowled and her lips pressed together for a moment before she spoke. "We don't know who she is or what she's doing here. She could be drugging our coffee right now so she can steal the ship."

Natalya glanced at the passageway and weighed Zoya's fears. "It's possible."

Zoya's eyes went wide with shock.

"But not probable." Natalya shook her head. "We don't know that she could fly the ship even if she got control. She's a well-known fixture at the station and she's a talented artist."

"We don't know that." Zoya stared at Natalya. "All we know is what she's told us."

Natalya shook her head. "No, we know a lot more than that. She and Kondur both knew my father. She's flown on this ship before. Simplest answer is she flew with my father. That's enough for me."

"How do you take your coffee?" Inge asked from the galley.

"Black for me," Natalya said.

"None for me, thanks," Zoya said. She sighed and nodded. "I'll take your word for it, but this is just reckless."

"Like jumping out of Port Newmar wasn't?"

Zoya sighed again and shook her head. "I'm going to catch up on some sleep while it's quiet. Wake me for the jump?"

Natalya checked the plot. "You don't need to get up for this one. Get a solid six. We can make a couple of jumps before we need to let the capacitors recharge a bit. You can take the next watch."

"Fair enough." Zoya pushed past Inge in the passageway as she slipped into her stateroom.

Inge brought Natalya a mug of coffee and slid into the navigator's couch with her own. "Will she be all right?"

Natalya took a sip and let the rich brew roll around on her tongue, so hot it nearly burned. She swallowed and nodded. "She's not used to Toe-Hold space."

"And you are?"

She thought about that for a few heartbeats. "Not really, but at least I've been introduced to it. My father took me on a few short jaunts growing up and a grand tour for my sixteenth birthday. He always said CPJCT was the real danger."

Inge blew on her coffee before sipping. "He might have been right."

Natalya nodded. "Zoya's afraid we're going to get mugged and killed, and the ship stolen."

"You're not?"

Natalya sipped her coffee and gave it serious thought. "No. Well, yeah. Anything's possible. Sure, it could happen. It's probably more likely that we'd get the ship stolen here, but I'm not sure how much more likely than in Confederation-controlled space." She paused. "I've got friends who've been mugged in Port Newmar. Friends who've been killed. Accident and misadventure don't respect politics." She glanced over at Inge.

"Your father must be proud of you."

Natalya chuckled. "Maybe. I'm not sure what he'd think if he knew I was herded out of Port Newmar by TIC interceptors."

"Does it matter? Were you planning on working your way up the chain of command in a Confederated merchant fleet?"

"No, I was actually planning on coming out here after graduation. I just didn't expect to be bringing a crew."

"Will she settle down?"

"I think so. It's funny. We've been roommates for four stanyers. The academy is tough and put us both through the wringer."

Inge nodded but said nothing.

"We never talked."

"Never?"

"Oh, about homework, assignments. The instructors. Summer cruises. We always just talked about the academy. It was all-consuming."

"But nothing about your pasts."

"Yeah. She knew I had a ship. I spent every weekend I could get away on the orbital working on her. Cleaning, polishing. It took me one whole weekend to paint the engine room and it's not much bigger than a closet."

"You never invited her along?"

Natalya shook her head. "Never considered it."

"Any idea why?"

Natalya sipped more coffee and let her gaze rest on the navigation plot. "The *Peregrine* was my escape. It helped keep me sane."

"It was a connection to your father."

Natalya nodded without looking over. "Yeah. That, too. I guess I didn't want to share it."

"How about now?"

Natalya grinned at Inge. "Now? Just being out here in Toe-Hold space is a connection to him. The ship is freedom. We can go where we need to. If I could be sure I wouldn't get arrested, the ship would be the perfect courier between Toe-Hold and Confederation ports."

"Why would you get arrested? You mean for smuggling?"

"They said I killed a TIC agent on graduation night. CPJCT doesn't really approve of that."

Inge's eyes grew wide. "Really? How long ago was that?"

Natalya looked at the console. "About three days."

Inge started a quiet laugh. "So, in less than a week, you've escaped from TIC, made contact with Verkol Kondur, and got a job. With your academy roommate as—what? Observer?"

"I think of her as my wing man."

Inge settled into the couch and took a few sips from her own mug. "I'm not going to steal your ship." Her voice barely reached Natalya's ears.

"Were you planning on it?" Natalya asked.

Inge wrinkled her nose. "No. I really do need to see Bjorn about Kristiana. Kondur said you were going that way so I thought I'd thumb a ride. Why didn't you charge me for passage, by the way?"

Natalya took a moment to process the question. "I honestly don't know. I probably should have, but you're like family. It just didn't seem right."

Inge gave Natalya a strange, penetrating look. "Like family?"

"Well, you knew my father. You have pet names for each other. This was some time ago, right?"

"Yes. Before you were born."

"So, you were more than just friends. You've sailed on the *Peregrine* before." Natalya looked a little sideways at Inge. "Any friend of my father's is a friend of mine. I don't make money off friends."

"How do you know we were friends? We may not have parted amicably."

Natalya shrugged. "Possible. Not probable."

The navigation display beeped as they cleared the outer markers. Natalya triggered the computed burn to put them onto the course for Odin's and sat back, listening to the small whooshes of the maneuvering jets. The kickers came online with a low growl and pushed them along the vector, gaining velocity with each passing heartbeat. She looked out at the shards of light all around.

"It's beautiful out here, isn't it," Inge said.

"It is."

After a long, comfortable pause, Inge asked, "What did she do?"

"To be dragged out here?"

Inge smiled and shook her head. "I was thinking about before. You spent your down time here on the ship. What did she do? Did she have a circle of friends that will miss her?"

Natalya sighed and shrugged. "I don't know. Studied. She spent time in town, I know." She shook her head. "I suspect some of that time was spent on extra training."

"Must have been lonely for her," Inge said. "What about you?"

"I never thought about it. *Peregrine* seemed enough." Natalya felt a chuckle bubble up from her chest. "After all the forced togetherness in school, I really needed to get away to recharge."

"And now here you are, jammed in a ship built for two with an extra stranger." Inge's eyes practically twinkled.

"It won't be for long and there's always the staterooms." Natalya nodded toward the passageway. "If you want to nap, you can use mine. This is too short a run for me to get much sleep."

"How long do you think?"

"I've plotted it at just over twenty-three stans from now."

"That long?" Inge's pale eyebrows lifted toward the overhead. "How many jumps?"

"Ten. We can make three jumps back to back, but then we need to recharge the jump capacitors for five stans and I'm allowing for one stan between for course verification and corrections."

Inge pursed her lips. "Odin's about a hundred Burleson units. You're only jumping ten at a time?"

"Yeah. The accumulated jump errors make me nervous. At ten, we're going to be as much as a whole unit off, one way or the other. Any longer and it's a big distance to make up if we're short."

"It's also a big bonus if we're not." Inge cast a sidelong glance at Natalya. "It's your ship, Captain. I'm just the supercargo." She tilted her coffee cup and drained it.

Natalya bit her lip and pondered. "You would recommend what?"

"When your father rebuilt the engineering spaces, did he put in smaller jump drives?"

"No. She's still got the Origami M9s. They're actually the M9As. They're a bit more stable and can recharge slightly faster."

"Do you mind a little backseat piloting?" Inge asked.

"You've got something in mind?"

Inge nodded. "Your father always made a short jump first so he could jump longer. He liked to stretch her legs."

"Yeah. He taught me that, too." Natalya pulled up her course plot. "I didn't do it here. I'm just running out an extra couple of stans so I can get the first jump in as a ten."

"May I?" Inge nodded at the console in front of her.

"Sure."

Inge put her cup down and flashed through to the navigation sandbox before Natalya could blink. She plopped down some points, shifted them to where she wanted them, then linked them in as a course. "There," she said. "Look that over."

Natalya cloned the workspace onto her console and traced the route. "Of course," she said, nodding at the results. "We're far enough out to jump four units now."

"That saves two stans right off the top and that leaves only eight jumps at twelve."

Natalya nodded. "Only two extended recharge periods instead of three."

"If the M9As recharge faster, you'll probably be able to carve some time off those numbers, too."

Natalya nodded. "Lemme run it against the model."

"Of course, Captain."

Five ticks of furious testing later, Natalya nodded again and replaced the old plot with the new one. She brought up the engineering controls and prepped the Burleson drives. While they spun up, she smiled at Inge. "Thanks. That'll save us a few stans."

Inge smiled back. "You don't get to be an expert in interstellar cartography without learning a bit about plotting and navigation. Nice consoles, by the way. Upgraded recently?"

"Got them last stanyer for scrap value when a fast packet upgraded their systems suite. Had to upgrade the backbone and system plane, too, but it was worth it."

The console flashed a green light on her engineering display. "I'm showing on course now," Natalya said. "Verify?"

Inge pulled down the sandbox and pulled up the navigation readouts. "Six sigma. Green."

Natalya punched the button to bend space and the tiny ship jumped into the Deep Dark, leaving the sprawling station far behind.

CHAPTER ELEVEN
ODIN'S OUTPOST: 2363, MAY 28

Natalya squinted at the long-range scanner and tried to make sense out of the returns coming back from Odin's Outpost. "What am I looking at?"

Inge leaned over the back of Natalya's couch to get a better look. "That's Odin's. It's a relatively new station compared to Dark Knight. Bjorn started it when he got stranded out here without a Burleson drive."

"From this range it looks like a collection of hulls and containers," Zoya said, tilting her head sideways as she stared at her screen.

"It will look the same from close up," Inge said, a smile coloring her words with amusement. "It's a gateway station. A lot like Dark Knight. CPJCT turns a blind eye to it and it gets a lot of fast packet traffic because it's midway between four different systems. I suspect we'll see one or two fleet haulers transit before we dock."

"What do they do here? There's nothing around," Natalya asked.

"Publicly they run a casino and prostitution operation. They do a good business in tourism, oddly enough."

"Tourism?" Zoya asked, turning wide eyes on Inge. "What's to see?"

Inge shrugged. "Gambling and prostitution, mostly. There are those who want the thrill from participating in the illicit activities without permanently giving up their comfortable lives."

"What do they really do here?" Natalya asked.

"Cargo transfer node. It's a handy place to stash containers of cargo until they can be smuggled into CPJCT space."

Zoya coughed. "That's impossible."

Inge looked at her with a raised eyebrow. "What? Stashing containers?"

"No. Smuggling them into CPJCT space."

Inge gave a low laugh.

"No, it's impossible. You can't even unload a cargo if it doesn't have the right codes proving provenance," Zoya said.

"Hence the need to stash them here until that provenance can be established," Inge said. "The very fact that nobody believes it's possible is the greatest advantage."

Zoya's jaw hinged a couple of times but no words came out of her mouth. Eventually she managed "Seriously?"

Inge nodded. "Sure. There are several ways to get people and goods in and out of CPJCT space."

"Out?" Zoya asked.

"Oh, yes. People are easy. You're looking at one way now."

"Odin's."

"Packet comes out with twenty registered passengers and three stowaways. Eventually, they return with twenty registered passengers."

"Bob goes out as blond. Bob comes back with gray hair?" Natalya looked at Inge.

"Sometimes," Inge said.

"How does new-Bob and old-Bob work? How can he even thumb a restaurant tab?" Zoya asked.

Inge shook her head. "Can't be giving all our secrets to Fleet, now can we?"

Zoya's mouth twisted into a grimace.

"Sometimes Bob just disappears from his house and shows up on a labor manifest to a mining colony." Inge shrugged. "High Tortuga masks his bank account activity at Star Shine Station or at Mel's or wherever he wants to go. As far as anybody in CPJCT space knows, he's just off-grid at a mining colony."

"So why doesn't CPJCT close it down?" Zoya asked. Her brow furrowed in a scowl. "They must know what's going on."

"What? Odin's?" Inge asked.

"Yes. This close to Confederated space and getting as much traffic as you say? TIC must know about it."

Inge smiled. "Of course. There are TIC agents on the station."

"Why don't they do something?"

Inge shook her head. "Do what? All of Toe-Hold space is outside of CPJCT jurisdiction. They are bound by the laws they've created. It's who they are. They can no more violate those laws here in Toe-Hold space than they can in Dunsany Roads, and the first problem is that none of these stations are under CPJCT jurisdiction."

"Then what are they doing here?" Zoya asked. The red flushed up her neck and across her face and ears.

"Mostly observing. Some of them use the station as a base for their own black ops."

Zoya shook her head as if to rattle something loose. "Wait. Black ops? I thought you said they're outside their jurisdiction."

"Say you're TIC and you want to know what's going on in Toe-Hold space. Maybe you've heard Iron Mountain's pressing into Tellicheri and want to make sure they're not encroaching. Legally, you can't do anything to those thugs as long as they're not breaking CPJCT regs in CPJCT space, but that doesn't mean having intelligence on who they are, what they're doing, and where they're doing it isn't of tactical advantage." Inge spread her hands. "They can't enforce CPJCT regulations here but there's no law that says they can't be here. There's no Toe-Hold jurisdiction to enforce an embargo against them."

Zoya looked at Natalya, who shrugged in return. "I've been trying to tell you. Toe-Hold space isn't what you think."

"I'm still having trouble with the concept," Zoya said. "Why aren't people just killing each other left and right?"

Inge sighed. "Unfortunately, many do. Some stations have pretty lax station enforcement. They're not the more successful ones because the risk isn't worth it."

"What's Iron Mountain?" Zoya asked after a few heartbeats. "That's the second time I've heard that name."

"Station up in the northern rim, just this side of Tellicheri. The woman who established the station—Empress Nicole—saw her chance to recreate the world in her preferred image," Inge said. "Anybody who didn't agree got shown to the Empress's Freezer," Inge said. "Their frozen corpses are said to be decorating the outside of the station as a warning."

"Why hasn't somebody done something?" Zoya asked.

"Who? What?" Inge said. "Their station. Their rules. Just because they're psychopaths doesn't give us the right to toss them into space. They leave us alone, for the most part. We leave them alone. They rely mostly on smuggling goods and people in and out of Tellicheri because almost nobody will trade with them on this side of the line."

"Why not?"

"They also make a habit of raiding neighboring stations and poaching their belts," Inge said.

"You just let them get away with it?" Zoya asked.

Inge shook her head. "First rule. Your house, your rules. Somebody comes into your house and breaks your rules, they pay. Iron

Mountain knows that and some of their people are fine with robbery and murder as long as it's not against their own."

"That's just not right," Zoya said.

"You're hung up on a set of rules that don't exist here. You need to get over that," Inge said. "As long as they keep it in their own system, nobody here has the right to interfere. That's the first rule. Your house, your rules. Leave your house and you need to be ready to play by new rules."

"What if you don't like the rules in your house?" Zoya asked.

Inge sighed and looked down. "That can be a bit of a problem. Most places are easy to leave. Even Iron Mountain doesn't care who comes or who goes. The empress ran a very well-disciplined station and I've heard nothing to contradict that now that she's gone."

"As long as you rape and pillage off the station, it's all right?" Zoya asked.

"Yes. That's largely the case."

"That's just wrong," Zoya said, practically shouting.

"I agree," Inge said. "What would you have us do?"

"Stop them."

"How do you suggest we do that?" Inge asked.

Zoya stared at Inge for several long moments. The longer she stared the more she frowned. Finally, she seemed to deflate. "I don't know."

"Think about it," Inge said. "Maybe there's a way we haven't thought of yet. They're a problem—at least in part—because they are pariahs. There's little they can do to harm their reputation because it's already so bad. Repairing that would make life easier for all of us. I don't see that happening any time soon."

Natalya smiled at Zoya. "Laws are funny things. The more you have, the more you need. You know there are more CPJCT regulations about food safety than addressing violent crimes?"

Zoya blinked. "I never thought about it." She looked at Inge. "Who does the arbitration when there's a dispute?"

Inge smiled. "Now you're thinking. Depends on who's got the dispute. Neighbors get the station holder or a proxy. Stations can ask a neighboring station they both agree on. If it gets ugly, they can take it to arbitration at High Tortuga."

"That sounds unwieldy."

"It can be," Inge said. "It's also a pain, so people figure out their own solutions more often than not."

Zoya shook her head. "It's all messed up in my head."

"Remember three things. Right, wrong, and the law. One of those things doesn't belong," Inge said.

"That makes no sense," Zoya said.

"Makes perfect sense. Didn't you pay attention in philosophy class?" Natalya asked.

"Right and wrong are moral concepts," Inge said. "The law is a human construction."

Zoya looked back and forth between Natalya and Inge. "So, some ambiguity between the moral concepts but the construction aims to reduce ambiguity?"

Natalya smiled. "You *were* paying attention."

Natalya's comms display popped up a navigation advisory and she queued the command strings into the autopilot. "Looks like we'll be docked in five stans." She checked the chrono and nodded. "Leaves half a day to get to Gunderson."

Inge smiled. "It's a small station. He won't be too hard to find."

Natalya felt a little tickle of chill up her spine. "You just had to say that, didn't you?"

"Sorry." Inge patted the back of Natalya's couch. "He's expecting you. He'll probably meet you at the dock."

Natalya shot a side-eyed glance at Inge. "Is he expecting you?"

Inge's smile lit up her face. "No. That's why I asked for a ride."

Chapter Twelve
Odin's Outpost: 2363, May 28

The lock's tattletale turned green and Natalya popped the seal. A waft of warm air from station-side washed into the *Peregrine,* bringing the aromas of cooking food, many humans, and—if she wasn't mistaken—a recent electrical fire. She felt her eyebrows rise at the last.

The iron-haired woman on the other side of the lock wore a stock shipsuit with an O-O logo on the left breast, a sidearm on her right thigh, and one arched eyebrow. "Don't look so surprised," she said. "I greet a lot of newcomers to the Outpost."

Natalya shook her head and laughed. "Sorry. It was the smell of burning electronics." She stuck out a hand. "Natalya Regyri."

The woman shot a disgusted look down the docks to her left. "Some people shouldn't be allowed in space. At least they didn't burn down the station." She looked back at Natalya and shook her hand. "Nancy Gunderson. Bjorn's first—and last—mate." She smiled and winked.

"I've got a chip for him. I was told to put it in his hands. Do you know where I can find him? It won't take but a moment."

"He was up to his armpits in damage control foam the last I saw him." Nancy nodded toward the station behind her. "Let's go see if he's cleaned up any." Her gaze flicked over Natalya's shoulder and she froze.

"Hello, Nancy." Inge's voice sounded calm enough.

"Inge. We weren't expecting you."

"I dare say." Inge stood at the edge of the lock. "May I come aboard?"

Nancy glanced at Natalya, then back at Inge. "Anybody else aboard, Captain?" she asked.

"I've one crew. Zoya Usoko."

Nancy smiled and her eyebrows flickered briefly up and down. "Must have been a cozy trip with three of you."

"Wasn't bad," Natalya said. "We left Dark Knight yesterday."

Nancy pursed her lips and looked at the deck. "Well, you're all welcome to debark. Mind your p's and q's. No firearms. Pay your bills. Try not to kill anybody while you're here."

Natalya heard a gasp from inside the ship and closed her eyes with a deep sigh.

Nancy chuckled. "Come on. Let's go see the boss."

"Glad to see you haven't lost your sense of humor, Nancy," Inge said.

Nancy glanced at Inge. "Kristiana's gonna be thrilled to see you, too." She started down the docking gallery.

Natalya stepped out and turned to look at Zoya. "Zee? It was a joke. Sorta."

Zoya brushed her palms down the front of her shipsuit. "Shouldn't somebody stay with the ship?"

"You can if you want to, but it's not actually necessary."

Nancy stopped and looked back. "Is there a problem?"

Zoya stepped out of the lock and gave an apologetic shrug.

Natalya slapped the lock-close and punched some keys on the pad. "All secure. See?"

Inge smiled and touched Zoya's shoulder. "You'll be fine. Bjorn's ex-Fleet. He still runs a pretty tight operation here. He's a good guy."

Nancy laughed.

Inge nodded down the gallery. "Let's not keep the boss waiting, huh?"

The short trek through the small craft docking gallery took them past a scorched docking tube where sooty workers spread black ash around with mops and brooms. Nancy gave all of them the stink-eye as she strode past. The half-dozen crew kept their heads down and didn't make eye contact. The reek of burned circuit board wasn't entirely masked by the cloying lemon-and-fart scent of fire foam.

"That coulda been nasty," Inge said as they passed.

"It's nasty enough," Nancy said, biting off her words. "Third time in two months."

"Same ship?" Inge asked.

"Same outfit. Different ships. Some renegade group nobody ever heard of trying to set up shop spinward of the Junkyard. They keep using us as a staging area and personnel dump." Nancy shook her head. "Seems like every third ship has a problem. Last time it was a melted scrubber. The stench cut into our food sales."

"Not like you can open a window," Natalya said.

Nancy chuckled. "Well, you can, but that's got problems of its own. Took us three weeks to scrub the funk out." She led them deeper into the station, leaving the smells of melted electronics and hydraulic fluid behind but taking them closer to cooking food.

Zoya's stomach growled loudly.

Inge glanced back at her. "You hungry?"

Color flooded the back of Zoya's neck. "Apparently. Whatever that is, it smells delicious."

"We'll treat ourselves to a decent meal before we head back, Zee." Natalya grinned. "Then it's back to the frozen ones."

"At least we have good coffee," Zoya said.

"Coffee?" Nancy stopped in the middle of the passage. "*Good* coffee?"

Natalya glanced at Zoya. "Yeah. Need some?"

Nancy grinned. "Business first. Then we need to talk. I'd kill for a decent cup."

As they got deeper into the station, the sound of beeping and bells ringing filled the corridor. Nancy paused at a wide doorway and let them look in at the people and machines filling the compartment. "Casino. Card tables in the back." She smiled at Zoya. "No, they're not rigged. We make enough off them without it."

They made a couple of fast turns and found themselves at an airtight hatch with a pair of beefy types standing outside.

"He in there?" Nancy asked.

The guy on the right nodded. "Last ten ticks or so."

Nancy punched a few digits on a keypad and pressed her thumb to the sensor. The latches thunked and she pushed the hatch open. "Let's get this over with." She stepped through the hatch and into a room that looked like the airlock on a freighter. She laughed at Zoya's expression. "This part of the station is the original *Wanderer*. Everything else got added on since we've been here."

"This is the ship that stranded you here?" Natalya asked, reaching out to stroke the metalwork.

"Yeah. After months of being stuck in here and thinking we were gonna die, I didn't know if I'd be able to live here." She keyed the inner door open. "After the crew left and it was just Bjorn and me, it wasn't so bad. We knew we weren't lost. Now, with all the changes and additions, it's nice to have a place that's just ours, you know?"

They followed Nancy into what would have been the mess deck on a tractor. The crew tables had been cleared out and the space set up as a combination office/dining room with a table for eight and a six-screen display suite showing different views around the station. A barrel-chested man with a fuzz of white hair lounged in an overstuffed chair, hammering away on a keyboard. "Gimme a tick. Be right with ya." His gravelly voice seemed to come from somewhere near his navel.

After rattling keys for a tick, he banged the keyboard's enter key extra hard and spun his chair, leaping to his feet. "There," he said. "Inge, lovely to see you. You'll have to talk to Kristiana yourself. I did what I could to dissuade her but she's her mother's daughter." He grinned ruefully and turned his one good eye toward Natalya. "Captain Regyri, welcome to Odin's Outpost. How can I help you?"

Natalya blinked at his rapid fire onslaught and tried not to stare at the eye patch. "We've a data chip for you, Captain."

He reached out a hand, palm up.

Natalya dropped the chip into it and Zoya stepped forward with her tablet out. "If you'd thumb the receipt, Captain?"

He held the chip up to the light as if he could read it in silhouette. "Hang on," he said and turned to slot it into his desk. A screen popped up, which he erased almost instantly. "Right, then." He pressed his thumb on Zoya's tablet and nodded. "Thanks. Anything else?"

"Thank you, Captain. We'll grab a meal and head back to Dark Knight," Natalya said.

Gunderson nodded and reached into a sleeve pocket. He pulled out several small cards and held them out. "Here. Give these to any of the service staff. They'll cover your meals."

Natalya took the chits. "Thank you. Very kind."

He waved her thanks aside. "Thanks for getting this to me. Least I can do is give you a good meal before sending you out."

"Bjorn? Don't you have something you need to send back to Verkol?" Nancy asked.

Gunderson opened his mouth as if to speak but closed it again after glancing at Inge. "Maybe so, maybe no." He scratched his jaw line with a fingertip before looking at Natalya again. "I might have a little package for you to take back, if you're willing, Captain."

"Always happy to make a living," Natalya said.

Gunderson grinned. "Heh. Yeah. Been there. I'll know within two stans. Can you hang around that long?"

"No problems, Captain."

"Thanks." He nodded to Nancy and flopped back into his chair, turning back to his displays.

Nancy waved them back to the lock and they retraced their steps back into the station proper. "As you've probably figured out, Kristiana's not on station."

Inge grunted. "Figured as much. Bjorn let her go?"

Nancy cast a grin over her shoulder. "Actually, no. She snuck onto an outbound freighter before we knew she'd gone. We just found out while you were on final."

"Mel's Place?" Inge asked.

"Bound for The Ranch, we think. *City of Krakow.* Left half a day ago."

"What's she going to do at Bar None?" Inge asked. "I thought she wanted to be a rock-knocker."

Nancy chuckled. "Well, I suspect she's going to try to grab a ride to Mel's from there. She may have to shovel some to get enough credit for passage but she seemed pretty determined."

Inge grunted again. "I suppose she's got to make her own mistakes sometime."

"Don't we all," Nancy said. "Don't we all."

"You still interested in that coffee?" Natalya asked.

Nancy's eyes fairly danced. "Oh, yeah. You want to eat first?"

Natalya shared a glance with Zoya, who shrugged in reply. "Let's go get a cuppa and see if we can do some business. We've got time."

Nancy led them back through the station, not even glancing at the damaged docking tube.

At the ship, Natalya keyed the lock open and led the way to the galley. "This is going to be cozy," she said.

Inge passed the galley and sat down in the navigation couch while Zoya stood in the open door of her stateroom. Natalya fired up the coffee maker. After a few ticks the aroma of fresh coffee filled the small space.

Nancy's eyes all but rolled back in her head and she took a deep inhale. "Oh, stars, that's the real thing, isn't it?"

"You bet. It's one of the Arabasti varietals. Not sure which one based on the generic labeling, but it's the real thing." Natalya drew a mug and handed it to Nancy. "Anybody else want one?"

"I'll wait for dinner," Zoya said. "Or whatever meal it is."

"Yeah. I'll hold off for now," Inge said. "Thanks."

Natalya pulled a half cup for herself and took an appreciative slurp while watching Nancy over the rim of her cup.

The older woman drew a deep lungful of the aromatic steam off the top of her mug, then took a sip, rolling it around on her tongue. "Oh, my." She sighed. "That's delightful." She took another sip and nodded. "You said you might have some of this to sell?"

"Fifty kilos," Natalya said, then took a sip off her mug. "Ten five-kilo tubs."

"How much you want for it?"

"How much would you give me?" Natalya asked.

Nancy chuckled. "I'll take all ten at a hundred credits each."

"I paid more than that," Natalya said. "Three hundred each."

Nancy sipped her coffee, closing her eyes as she did so. "That's why we can't have nice things. One-fifty."

"Two-fifty," Natalya said.

"Two?"

"Deal," Natalya said and stuck out a hand.

"Deal," Nancy said and they shook on it. "Now where did you stash ten tubs of coffee in this motorized closet?"

"Engineering. You want to arrange a dolly before we hump it out of here?"

Nancy pulled out a tablet and nodded. "Good idea. First I want to finish this cup of ambrosia."

Zoya rolled her eyes behind Nancy's back but Natalya knew exactly what she meant.

Chapter Thirteen
Odin's Outpost: 2363, May 29

Zoya did not look pleased. She flung herself into the navigator's couch and propped a leg over the console. "When Gunderson said a couple of stans, I thought he meant a couple of stans yesterday."

Natalya shrugged and continued scanning the astrogation updates from Inge's disk. "Happens. Not like we're on a schedule, and he's waived docking fees. You got a hot date waiting at Dark Knight?"

The lock-call buzzed and Natalya scooted down the short passageway. Peeking out the port, she saw Inge peeking back. She punched the cycle button and opened the heavy door. "Didn't expect to find you here."

Inge sighed. "Didn't expect to be heading back so soon."

"Kristiana?"

"Yeah. She's halfway across Toe-Hold space by now. Unless you feel like making a run to Bar None, there's not much I can do about it."

Natalya led the way back into the cockpit.

Zoya looked up from the couch and grimaced. "You're back."

Natalya slapped the back of Zoya's couch. "Manners matter."

"No. She's right. I know it's a terrible imposition. The next scheduled packet is a Plunkett's run next week." She looked like the name tasted sour.

"Something wrong with Plunkett?" Zoya asked, her pique apparently forgotten.

"Most of their people are decent. They've got a lot of mom-and-pop pairs keeping the books balanced by running tourists and would-be high-rollers in and out of Toe-Hold."

"I hear a but," Natalya said, handing Inge a cup of coffee.

"Thanks," Inge said and sipped before answering. "I had a run-in with one of their skippers over an update a couple of stanyers ago. He claimed the update infected his system and wanted me to spring for a replacement."

"Ouch," Natalya said.

"Hard to give out free updates if the customers want indemnity for being jackasses," Inge said.

"What'd you do?" Zoya asked.

"Offered him a full diagnostic overhaul on his systems."

Zoya blinked a couple of times. "Did he accept?" she asked.

Inge grinned into her coffee mug. "Nope. Seems he didn't want me looking at the supposed damage."

"Any idea why?" Natalya asked.

Inge shrugged. "Beyond not having any damage that could have been caused by an astrogation update?"

Natalya chuckled. "Yeah, that."

"Scuttlebutt said he had some old BOE databases on there and didn't want anybody to see the data."

Zoya sat up at that. "Board of Exploration? Why would that matter?"

"Eldorado," Natalya said. "Lost colonies and missed opportunities."

Inge nodded. "You may be surprised to learn that some individuals out here think that there are vast riches hidden in the stars." Her eyes fairly twinkled.

Zoya hmphed. "Or not. I thought those were just rumors and pipe dreams."

"Probably so," Inge said. "But there are enough people out here ready to take a flyer on a get-rich-quick scheme."

"The only people getting rich are the ones selling the scheme," Natalya said.

Inge stared into her mug and kept very quiet.

"What?" Natalya asked, catching the older woman's eye. "You don't think so?"

"Your father might disagree with you."

"Dad?" Natalya felt her breath leave her in the single syllable.

Inge looked up with a faint smile. "Yes. Your father—Demetri Regyri—always claimed there was more out there between the systems than the old explorers ever reported."

Natalya scoffed. "My father is the most practical, pragmatic guy who ever jumped."

"Yes. I remember," Inge said, her gaze focused elsewhere for a moment. "He never talked about what's really out in the Deep Dark?"

"Well, sure. Old pilot tales. Long on possibilities and low on actualization."

Inge pursed her lips. "You might wonder why that practical and pragmatic father of yours would share them with his daughter."

"Oh, pfft. Entertainment while we worked."

Inge stared into her mug for a moment before draining it. "Sure," she said.

Natalya opened her mouth to say something else but the lock-call buzzed again.

"Finally," Zoya said.

Natalya went back down the passageway and found Gunderson himself outside the lock. "My day is filled with wonder, Captain," she said as the door opened.

Whatever he was about to say stopped at his teeth and his eyebrows rose. After a moment he said, "I've been called many things, but 'wonder' was never one."

Natalya laughed. "I don't know, Captain. You saw the value in setting up shop in the Deep Dark. That's a wonder all by itself."

Gunderson rubbed the back of his neck and grinned. "Maybe so, maybe no. The old *Wanderer* wasn't going any further and necessity won out."

"Well, come in, come in. There's coffee if you'd like a cup." Natalya ushered him into the ship and closed the lock behind him. "It's getting to be pretty crowded but there's room for one more."

He chuckled when he saw Inge. "Mornin', Inky. You twistin' arms here?"

She smiled at him. "Good morning, yourself. I know when I'm beat. I'm just trying to get a ride back to Dark Knight."

"'Zat so?" Gunderson looked around at the faces in the room. "I figured you'd be headin' for The Ranch."

Inge looked into her coffee cup and shrugged. "It was foolish for me to come out here. I thought I could talk some sense into her."

Gunderson sniffed. "That's real coffee?"

Natalya dragged another cup out of the galley and handed it to him. "Yep. And I sold a bunch to Nancy last night so this one's on the house."

He took a sip and sighed. "Yeah. That's the stuff." He took another sip and smiled. "Beer and coffee. Two things you gotta have good water to make. Seems like we been trying to make water taste good as long as we been drinkin' it, eh?"

"You need beer?" Zoya asked.

Gunderson shook his head. "We got beer. Brew it ourselves. You mighta had some last night."

Zoya shook her head. "Not a beer drinker."

"It's easy to make, doesn't take up a lot of time or space, and we're the only bar for a million kilometers in any direction."

"Captive audience, eh?" Natalya said, toasting him with her mug.

He shook his head. "Let's just say it's only one of the many features that makes Odin's Outpost a tourist destination."

Inge snickered. "It's the only destination in this part of the Deep Dark, you old pirate."

Gunderson pursed his lips and grunted. "Never was a pirate. Don't plan to start." He turned to Natalya. "Sorry it took so long. You're going straight back to Dark Knight?"

Natalya nodded. "Soon as you give the word, we can pull out and bend space."

Gunderson rubbed the back of his neck again. "Willing to take something back for me?" He glanced at Inge. "Besides her?"

Inge snorted.

"That's what we waited for," Zoya said, a bit of acid in her tone.

"Yeah, yeah. Sorry about that. I thought we'd be ready before this." Gunderson took a solid pull off the coffee cup.

Natalya shot a quelling look at Zoya. "It's nothing, Captain. Thanks for your hospitality." She paused for a couple of heartbeats. "If I could ask, what is it that you want us to take back?"

"A lock box. Goes direct to Kondur, just like that chip came direct to me."

Natalya nodded. "Seems fair. Terms?"

"What'd he pay you for the chip?" he asked.

"Enough. What are you offering for the return run?"

He grinned and shrugged. "Fifty kay and I'll cover your fuel bill. Already waived your docking fees. Half now. Half on delivery."

"Any deadline?" Zoya asked.

"Soon as you can. Sometime this week would be good."

Natalya stuck out a hand. "Deal."

Inge nearly choked on her coffee and held up a hand while she cleared her pipes. "I'm all right. Just inhaled wrong."

Gunderson shook Natalya's hand and glared at Inge. "I'll send Nancy over with the box in half a stan."

"You don't want a surety bond?" Inge asked, one eyebrow rising slightly.

Gunderson looked at the deck and shook his head. "Not from these ladies. Tortuga covered it."

Inge's other eyebrow lifted. "Good to know." Her tone made it sound like maybe it wasn't actually that good.

"Yeah, well." Gunderson drained his mug and handed it back to Natalya. "Thanks for the coffee. I better get Nancy movin' on this so you can head back." He started down the passageway, Natalya close behind.

"Anything in particular I need to worry about with this shipment, Captain?" Natalya's voice barely reached the deck but Gunderson heard it and glanced back at her.

"Nothing unusual. My usual courier is delayed on the far side of Toe-Hold. If you're going right back to Dark Knight, you can save me the hassle." He paused at the lock.

"You're being pretty trusting."

He looked into her eyes. "Not so much. I've got a bond in case you scarper with the box. Tampering with it will likely be the last thing you'd ever do, but I suspect you knew that."

She nodded. "Yeah. I'm familiar with the routine."

"Your ole man taught you well," he said. A tired smile reached all the way to his eyes.

"You know my father?"

"Demetri?" He nodded toward the bridge. "Everybody knows Demetri Regyri."

Natalya keyed the lock open. "How *well* does she know him?"

"I bet she knows him better than he knows himself." His smile warmed toward Natalya. "Probably better than his own daughter."

"I doubt that," Natalya said.

He started down the short ramp and stopped halfway to the deck to look back at her. "You know where he is now?"

Natalya felt a pang of alarm. "Not exactly. Somewhere here in Toe-Hold space, last I heard."

He nodded toward the bridge again. "She knows." He waved and stepped off the ramp. "I'll get Nancy over here with the box. You'll be able to leave in half a stan."

Natalya watched him stride off into the station without a backward glance. She keyed the lock closed again and stood there for a few moments. Random thoughts chased themselves around her skull without making a great deal of sense. She'd covered half of Toe-Hold space in a few days and still was no closer to figuring out why Margaret Newmar had drugged her, staged a theatrical murder, and chased her into the Deep Dark.

A nagging feeling that she might never know started tugging on her hind brain. It wasn't a comfortable feeling, and she felt pretty sure it wouldn't go away any time soon.

Chapter Fourteen
Dark Knight Station: 2363, June 2

Natalya and Zoya found Kondur in his booth at the bar on Main Street. He smiled at their approach.

"Nice to see you again," he said. "You have something for me?"

Natalya nodded as she slid onto the end of the bench across from him. "We do. How would you like to handle it?"

"You can deliver it here, if you like. Nobody'll think twice about it."

Natalya nodded to Zoya, who pulled the small box from the messenger bag hanging from her shoulder. She placed the box on the table and put her tablet on the top.

Kondur grinned at her and thumbed the tablet before sliding the box off the table and handing it to the beef beside him.

"You don't want to check it?" Zoya asked, sounding more curious than surprised.

"What for?" Kondur spread his hands out. "You didn't tamper with it. I've every confidence that it contains what it's supposed to. If not, then I'll have somebody visit Bjorn." He looked at Natalya. "Coffee, Captain?"

She smiled at him. "Thanks. I could use a cup."

Kondur waved a hand and mugs appeared as if from thin air, followed shortly by a thermal carafe. He topped the mugs and held his up in a toast. "To business."

Natalya lifted her mug and clinked china to china. "To business."

Zoya followed suit, albeit somewhat less enthusiastically.

Kondur took a solid pull from the cup and smacked his lips. "So, tell me, Captain. Now that you've stocked up with spare parts and gotten a couple of runs under your belt, what do you fancy next?" He winked at her.

"Last time we were here you mentioned there might be something else."

"So I did. So I did." He sipped some coffee and gave them each a considering glance. "As it happens, I need some people I can trust."

"You think you can trust us?" Zoya asked.

"No," Kondur said, giving a little shake of his head. He nodded at Natalya. "Her, sure. You? I don't know yet."

"What's the deal?" Natalya asked, cutting off whatever Zoya might have been thinking about saying.

"Well, I've got a ship that needs some hands for a run out to Dunsany."

"We're not exactly crew material," Zoya said, a sour look on her face.

Kondur pursed his lips. "How about officer material?"

"Officers?" Zoya asked.

He nodded. "I need a third mate and an engineer." He looked back and forth between them. "I assume you graduated before being framed for murder?"

"What's the job?" Natalya asked.

"I've got a Barbell running a can into Siren. Needs enough hands to fill out the crew roster and I'm just old-school enough that I kinda like to have people who know what they're doing when I can get them."

"Not exactly what we signed up for," Natalya said.

Kondur shrugged. "Just thought I'd ask. Something to do while you're making connections." He shrugged again. "Pay's good."

"How good?" Natalya asked.

"Fifty kay. Each."

"Shares?" Natalya asked.

He snorted. "For hire. One run. Round trip to Siren and back. This ain't no High Liner operation here."

"How long?"

"Twelve weeks, plus or minus. Most of it'll be in Siren's gravity well."

"Siren? That's a Confederation port. We have this problem with TIC," Zoya said.

Kondur shook his head. "Won't be a problem. I just need bodies to fill out the rosters. You'll never see the docks."

Natalya sipped her coffee and thought about it.

Zoya nudged her with an elbow.

Natalya shook her head. "Not exactly what we're about, Mr. Kondur."

"Understood." He shrugged. "Offer's open. Ship's not leaving for a few days. Worst case I find a couple of rock-knockers to pretend for a few weeks."

"Thanks," Natalya said, draining her cup. "And thanks for the coffee. We probably better get on with our day and let you get on with yours."

She slipped out of the booth with Zoya close behind.

"Any time," Kondur said. "Good luck and safe voyage."

Natalya led the way out of the pub and onto the wide thoroughfare.

"That was disappointing," Zoya said as they strolled along looking in the windows.

Natalya shrugged. "Not exactly what I was expecting, but it's not a bad offer. Chance to find our way in the Deep Dark. Probably make some good contacts out of it, too."

Zoya stopped and put a hand on Natalya's upper arm. "You're not thinking about taking it."

"We could do worse. That would be a nice paycheck for basically ninety days' work."

"What about the *Peregrine*?"

"She'd be safe enough here. I'd owe him docking fees, but maybe we could work out a deal."

"I thought you were the free spirit out to see the universe," Zoya said.

Natalya laughed and started walking again. "I can see a lot more of it when I've got the credits we need for fuel."

"We could skim it."

Natalya glanced at Zoya. "We could. I haven't ruled that out. We could probably earn a week or two of docking fees that way."

"What's the holdup, then?"

Natalya sighed. "We can't get contracts while we're out there sucking gas. We turned down Kondur's job, which means he's not going to be thinking of us for the next one."

"But it's not what we do."

Natalya shook her head. "You don't get it. He's the big fish here. It's his pond. We'll have better luck doing what he wants rather than what we want."

"Then why'd you turn it down?"

"If I'd wanted to be an engineering third, I'd have signed up at Port Newmar."

They walked several meters in silence before Zoya spoke again. "So what do we do?"

"Well," Natalya said. "You've still not made contact with whomever it was who's supposed to contact you, right?"

"Right."

"I think we hang out for a while. See the sights, such as they are. See what kinds of jobs we might do here that won't tie us up for three months." Natalya glanced at her friend. "Maybe your spook will show. We're not exactly broke."

Zoya didn't look convinced but she shrugged and walked along.

"Meanwhile, I need to get that fuel coupling looked at by somebody who knows about them."

"Fuel coupling?"

"Yeah. It started overheating while we were on final approach to the station here."

"That doesn't sound good."

"It usually means the lining is giving out."

"I thought the engines had just been rebuilt."

"Yeah, and they're still barely broken in, but the fuel coupling isn't part of the engine rack, exactly." Natalya sighed. "I pushed the envelope pretty hard trying to evade those phantom TIC interceptors."

"You think you damaged it?"

"I don't know. That's why I want to get somebody in here with the right tools to look before we need to get underway again."

"What's the worst that could happen?"

Natalya snorted. "I really wish you hadn't asked that."

Natalya stared at the toad-faced yard manager. "You want what?"

He pulled a red handkerchief out of a pocket in his coverall and wiped the sweat off his brow. "I don't *want* anything, missy. You got a problem with that fuel coupling. I don't think they even make them anymore."

She felt her molars grind together in frustration. "I know there's a problem. I'm the one who diagnosed it."

"Then you know you're taking your life in your hands to get underway in that antique unless you get it fixed."

"Yes. The operative word there is 'fixed.' I didn't say anything about 'replaced.'"

"Look, I'm tellin' you. You can't fix it. It's too far gone. That throat lining is down to metal and I don't have the tools, materials, or even the know-how to reline it. That would take a ceramic fab shop and somebody who likes restoring old ships."

"So you want to charge me two hundred thousand credits to replace it?"

"Lady, I can't fix the old one. What I got is a replacement. It's not new. It's not even the right model, but it'll do the job."

Natalya turned and stalked three steps away from the impossible little creep, running her hands around her neck and trying to think of a way out. "You're asking more than the ship is worth," she said, turning her head to talk over her left shoulder.

He snorted. "I'm sure that ship's worth a whole lot more than two hundred kay."

"Even with a bum fuel coupling?"

"Oh, yeah. Somebody with the right connections and some time could slide that into a shop in Dree. They *make* those couplings there. Probably do a nice business in refurbing old ones."

"Even with an antique like this?"

He grinned. The sight didn't make Natalya feel any better. "They'd probably toss in a relined main rocket nozzle just for the braggin' rights."

"But I'd have to sneak it into Dree and I don't dare undock it the way it is."

Toad-face pursed his lips and nodded, wiping his brow again with the red rag. "You know that much anyway. It's more sense than most have."

She sighed and mentally counted the credits in her account one last time. "This is extortion, you know."

"Extortion is such a nasty word. I prefer to think of it in economic terms. Supply and demand. I got the only supply in a billion kilometers so I get to demand what I want for it."

"I'll have to get back to you," she said. "Gimme a day or two to finagle the finance."

He nodded. "You want my advice?"

She turned to look at him. "You gonna charge me for it?"

"Pfft. No need to get snarkish." He jerked his chin toward the ship. "Sell it. Get what you can for it. You could probably get enough to grab a modern courier right out of the yards and not have to put up with old crap breaking down and giving out." He paused as if to gauge her reaction, his head tilted to one side. "You got lucky this time. Another few days and you might not have made it back to breathable air. Old ships like this one, well, they're a rich guy's game. Somebody startin' out can't support the habit."

Natalya felt her molars grinding and had to force herself to relax her jaw. "Not an option." She pulled in a deep breath and blew it out through her nose. "Gimme a couple of days to figure something out."

He shrugged. "No skin off my hide. Not like I get a lot of call for replacement parts for antiques." He scowled at her for a moment before saying, "Price will be the same."

"I wouldn't expect anything else," Natalya said.

Kondur smiled when Natalya slid into the booth. "Twice in the same day? To what do I owe this rare treat?" he asked.

She shrugged. "Seems I need the credits. *Peregrine* needs repairs that I can't cover. If that job's still open?"

He nodded. "It is. Will your lovely companion be joining you aboard? I still need a third mate. Where is she, by the way?"

"She will. She's grabbing a bit of sleep while she can."

"Prudent," Kondur said.

"I've got a couple of questions about the job."

"Ask."

"Docking for the *Peregrine* for twelve weeks will add up. Is there someplace I can park her that's less than a hundred a day?"

"Permanent party docks are on the other side of the station. See Russ or Eng in the dock master's office and get a berth assignment. They're not exactly convenient, but they're cheap. Three hundred a month. Shore-ties for power, water, and air at station rates. You can arrange a fuel tender to top off your tanks for a fee."

"I won't be using much fuel." She paused a moment before asking, "What's security like?"

Kondur smiled. "Nobody will touch her. I'll see to it."

"That seems generous."

He shook his head. "Looking out for an asset I hope to use later."

"Me or the ship?"

He chuckled. "Both, of course."

She nodded and granted him the point. "Fair enough. How'd you know I was an engineer?"

"Natalya Regyri. Class of '63. Top ten in the class. Top engineering student. Top-rated martial artist. Natural-born shuttle pilot. Even attracted TIC recruiters who became frustrated by your unwillingness to join their merry band."

Natalya felt her eyes widen. "That's pretty specific."

"I try to stay informed when strangers come to call. Demetri's daughter rates even higher."

"Zoya?"

"Ms. Usoko is an interesting case. Top ten in the class. Medium marks for a deck officer, but strong showing in her leadership index. Recruited to Trade Investigation last February. Currently on assignment."

Natalya blinked. "Meaning here with me."

Kondur nodded.

"That doesn't bother you?" she asked.

He laughed. "If I had a problem with TIC on station, I'd have to fire half the staff. They have no jurisdiction here and I occasionally find them useful."

"And you have your own people in their pockets, too, I take it?"

"I'm a simple businessman, Ms. Regyri. Long ago I found it prudent to know what people were saying about me."

"Is it going to be a problem for Zoya to be on this run to Siren?"

"If it were, I wouldn't have offered it. At least a third of the crew are probably TIC informants."

"So where do we go from here?"

"Get your ship settled. Report to dock twenty. Captain's Tommy Trask. He'll be expecting you sometime during day watch on the seventh."

"Fair enough." Natalya slipped out of the booth, not knowing why she felt like things might be breaking her way. She needed to visit a certain toad-faced yard man, then break the good news to Zoya. She laughed quietly to herself. "I just hope she thinks it's good news," she said under her breath.

Chapter Fifteen
Dark Knight Station: 2363, June 7

Natalya led Zoya along the large ship docks until they stood in front of number twenty. She glanced at Zoya before pushing the call button.

"I still don't know about leaving the *Peregrine* unattended," Zoya said.

"Not like we got a lot of choice. We need to get her repaired and we need credits to make that happen." She shrugged. "Kondur's word is fine with me."

"You didn't get it in writing."

"No." Natalya sighed. "I didn't."

"Will you get enough from this run to pay for the repair?"

"No, but the fuel coupling is a common part. I can probably buy one in Siren for a couple kay."

"Why's he charging so much?"

Natalya looked at Zoya. "He's got the only part in a billion klicks. I can't fly the *Peregrine* without it. He's gonna be pissed if I come back with my own and install it myself."

"He just cost himself a repair job?" Zoya asked.

"By being greedy. I'd have paid him to do it for ten kay. Maybe even twenty. Two hundred?" She winced. "Not with an option like this available."

The lock clamps thunked and the heavy door rose to reveal a spacer in a relatively clean shipsuit showing shiny new able-spacer pips on the collar. He stood inside with his hands on his hips and stared hard at Natalya before giving Zoya a deliberate up-and-down gaze. "Yeah?" he asked.

"We're here to see Captain Trask," Natalya said. "Mr. Kondur sent us."

The spacer's attitude relaxed a bit and he nodded his head into the ship. "Come on, then." He led them into the ship and up to officer country where he knocked on the cabin door.

"What?" The voice sounded muffled.

"Kondur's new people are here, Skip."

Silence greeted that statement for several heartbeats. Long enough for Natalya to glance at Zoya.

Zoya rolled her eyes and shrugged.

A sharp thump vibrated the deck under their feet and the cabin door swung open, snatched from the inside by a wild-eyed man with a patchy gray beard and a wispy gray pony-tail. His collar held gold stars but his shipsuit looked like he'd slept in it for a week. "Kondur?"

Natalya nodded. "Said you needed an engineering third and a third mate. He sent us."

He looked each of them up and down with a sour expression. "Couldn't find real ones, huh?"

Natalya shrugged. "We're the ones he sent, so, I guess not."

He shot her a glance that might have had some approval behind it, although Natalya couldn't quite tell. He stepped back from the door, holding it open for them. "Well, don't just stand there. Come on in and report." He looked at the rating. "Don't you have brow watch, Helms?"

"Yeah." He nodded to Natalya and Zoya before flipping his middle finger at the captain where he couldn't see it as he shambled down the passageway the way they'd come in.

Natalya suppressed her grin and stepped through the door to the cabin.

The cabin looked barely lived in. A grav-trunk stood in the middle of the deck and the only sign that somebody lived there was a small, framed image on the desk.

"So, Kondur sent you. You know anything about engines?" Trask asked, scowling at Natalya.

"Some. I fly an Explorer Scout and do most of my own maintenance."

That earned her a double-take and a short nod before he turned to Zoya. "What about you? You ever stood a real watch on a real ship?"

"Started running ore haulers when I was twelve," Zoya said.

His eyebrows shot up. "When you say 'running ore haulers' that means what?"

"It means I brought in a few hundred thousand cubic meters of ore from the belts in Margary in a big damn ship."

"By yourself?"

She tsked. "Of course not. I had a crew of four."

"And they followed a twelve-year-old?"

"They followed the owner's granddaughter." Ice wouldn't have melted in her mouth.

He rubbed the palm of one hand across his lips and squinted his eyes a little. "Yeah. I can see that." He paused for a moment. "You know your way around systems?"

"I can run a backup. You still running Mark Twelve consoles?" Zoya asked.

"Hell if I know. I press the buttons. They do the work."

She smiled. "Good enough."

He nodded a few times, his gaze going back and forth between them. Finally, he stuck out a hand. "Thomas Trask."

Natalya shook his hand and noticed the calluses across the palm. "Natalya Regyri."

He offered his hand to Zoya.

She shook it and nodded. "Zoya Usoko."

His eyes widened just a bit at that. "Margary. Usoko Mining?"

"My grandparents' company."

"Why the hell are you out here?" The words seemed to boil out of him before he gave them any thought.

Zoya jerked a thumb at Natalya. "She brought me."

He focused on Natalya. "Regyri. I know that name."

"Seems like everybody does," she said.

"You flew that scout in here, right? You're Demetri's what? Daughter?"

She nodded.

His face lit up. "I'll be damned. Where's he at now?"

"Somewhere out here in Toe-Hold space. I lost track when he split with my mother."

The captain nodded. "Ah. Makes sense. He gave you the scout?"

"Yeah."

"Never thought he'd part with that. What's he flying these days?"

"No idea. Haven't seen him for a couple of stanyers. Thumbing a ride as far as I know."

The captain's wheezy laugh filled the cabin. "I doubt that. He's got a hidey-hole out here somewhere. He's not gonna let anybody else fly him to it."

Natalya smiled but glanced at Zoya, whose expression had gone blank.

"So, what's the drill here, Skipper?" Natalya asked.

He nodded them into chairs and plopped himself behind the desk. "Kondur's trading a can of ore for a can of white oil."

"In Siren?" Zoya asked.

The old guy's gaze flipped to her. "He told you that?"

They both nodded.

"Huh. Well, yeah. Siren. We've got a supplier there who can handle cargo for us."

"White oil?" Natalya asked.

"It's a class of food-grade lubricant," Zoya said.

Trask grinned and nodded. "You'd know. We use a lot of it in the hydroponics farms."

"Gramps used it for the same purpose." She smiled back at him. "Just not two hundred metric kilotons at a time."

"Kondur'll split it up. He usually buys a can, uses half and sells the rest around Toe-Hold."

"You know a lot about his operation?" Natalya asked.

"Naw. Mostly I run his mining tender fleet but about once a stanyer he taps me to fly this old brick somewhere and swap cans."

"Barbells are the backbone," Zoya said.

Trask snorted. "Barbells are the best way we have to get stuff in and out of High Liner stations."

"Really?" Natalya asked.

The captain ran a palm across his lips again. "Yeah. Well, stick around and you'll see for yourself." He nodded at the door. "You didn't bring any luggage?"

"Mr. Kondur just said to report and you'd fill us in," Natalya said.

"Albee's portside now. He'll be back for lunch mess. We're planning on pulling out of here tomorrow at 0800. Go get your trunks and get settled by dinner time." He offered each of them a glare. "Can do?"

"Consider it done, Skipper," Natalya said.

"You know your way around a Barbell?" he asked.

"We both spent time on them. Not a lot but I can find my way down the spine."

Trask nodded. "Summer cruise?"

"Does it show?" Natalya asked.

Trask shook his head. "Not on you." He nodded at Zoya. "Fleet runs deep."

It only took a few ticks for them to exit the ship. Helms even smiled at them as they left.

"What is it with people and fleet?" Zoya asked.

Natalya took a moment to look at her friend. "You're basically wearing undress khakis."

Zoya looked down at herself as they walked along the docks. "It makes sense."

"To you, sure." Natalya lifted her chin. "Look around. You see anybody else in khakis?"

The few people in view wore a variety of outfits. Some wore beige station overalls while most sported more flamboyant looks that made Natalya's outfit of black slacks, polished ship boots, and reds and browns on top seem positively drab.

"Who dresses like that?" Zoya asked, leaning in close to Natalya.

Natalya smiled back. "Turn that around." She waved a hand at Zoya's outfit. "Who dresses like *that*?"

Zoya looked down and then around at the people on the docks. "Ah."

"Come on. Let's find you something other than academy wear."

"And where do we do that?"

"Main Street, of course."

"Wait." Zoya stopped in her tracks and put a hand on Natalya's arm. "I've seen some of those clothes. I wouldn't be caught dead in those outfits."

Natalya grinned. "That's sorta the idea."

Zoya blinked. "What?"

"To not be caught dead." Natalya looked down at Zoya's clothes again. "This might come as a shock, but being called fleet isn't exactly a compliment. It's a good way to get picked out of a crowd for all the wrong reasons."

Zoya looked around again and swallowed hard. "I guess I never thought of it that way."

"You just need to find something other than the uniform shirt. Maybe a nice jacket and a few tops that aren't brown."

"You're wearing brown," Zoya said.

Natalya looked down at her layered tops of red, brown, and a flash of white under an old-style pilot's jacket. "Yes," she said, grinning up at her friend. "But I'm wearing it with style."

They both laughed and Natalya grabbed Zoya by the upper arm. "Come on, bunkie. We need to find your inner Toe-Hold. You didn't wear khakis when you piloted those barges at twelve, did you?"

Color flooded up Zoya's neck and across her cheeks.

Natalya felt her eyes bug out as she realized the truth. "Oh, no. You didn't."

"It was what all the cool kids wore."

Natalya laughed again and picked up her pace. "Come on. We'll get you fixed up."

Zoya dragged back for a few steps and then caught up. "All right, but I'm not tossing these."

"You shouldn't," Natalya said. "We'll need them when we get to Siren."

"You don't think we're going to be going ashore, do you?"

Natalya shrugged. "No idea, but we'll need to look the part and be believable when we get there or the whole game is up."

"You have such a way of making me feel assured."

"Look at the bright side. You haven't been mugged, stabbed, raped, or murdered since making that jump from Port Newmar."

"Yet," Zoya said with a frown on her face. "Yet."

Natalya laughed again. "Fair enough. Yet. Now let's get a move on before you make any more of a spectacle of yourself here on the docks."

CHAPTER SIXTEEN
DARK KNIGHT STATION: 2363, JUNE 7

They returned to the ship at 1400 with Zoya looking a little less fleet in a mauve sweater and a black bolero over her khaki slacks. "I wonder where they'll put me," Natalya said as they stopped at the lock.

"Why?"

"Barbells don't usually rate an engineering third. We usually go onto the larger mixed freight or tankers for seasoning."

"I hadn't thought of that."

"You'll have a stateroom in officer country, but it's even odds whether I'll pull engineering berthing or not."

The lock levered up and a whip-thin man with a severe buzz cut and a narrow fringe of dark hair along his upper lip scowled down at them. He wore a maroon shipsuit with gold piping and first-mate pips on his collar tabs. The effect left Natalya blinking in astonishment.

"About time. Which one's Usoko?"

Zoya nodded. "That would be me."

"Stow that gear and get your butt up to the bridge. We need the system backup done. Ay-sap." He turned and stomped into the ship.

Natalya looked at Zoya. "Pleasant enough chap."

Zoya caught her lower lip in her teeth. "Suppose it'll occur to him that we both need system credentials before we can do anything?"

Natalya shrugged and started up the ramp just as a snarly male voice echoed out of the lock.

"Sometime today, ladies."

Zoya chuckled and Natalya bit back her own laugh.

"You know," Natalya said. "Twelve weeks of this could get real old."

Zoya nodded. "I know, but you have to admit. It's a picture."

"Oh, yeah."

They slid into the lock and dropped their trunks on the deck. Helms stood behind the watchstander's desk and looked at them.

"Mass allotments?" Zoya prompted.

"Huh?" he said.

The maroon avenger stuck his head out of the passageway. "Ladies. This isn't some High Liner fleet operation. Get your crap settled. We got work to do here." He disappeared back down the passageway.

Natalya looked at Helms. "That the first mate? Alden, is it?"

"Albee. John Albee."

Natalya grinned. "He always in this good a mood?"

Helms grinned back. "Some days he's a bit cranky. Today's a good day. He always gets excited when we get underway."

"Any idea where he wants me to live?"

"Supercargo stateroom in officer country, most likely." He jerked his thumb in the direction of the passageway. "Straight in, first ladder up."

Natalya nodded. "Not my first Barbell, but thanks."

Zoya led the way down the passageway with Natalya on her heels. Behind her she heard Helms mutter, "This should be interestin'."

They maneuvered up the ladders to officer country and found the staterooms designated for third mate and supercargo at the end of the passage.

"Cozy," Zoya said. "We share the head."

"Bigger bunks than the *Peregrine*." Natalya locked her trunk down in the alcove and peeked into the head. "Could use a good scrub, but I've stayed in worse."

Zoya looked in from the other side. "Yeah, well. We'll probably have time once we get underway." She sighed. "Probably better get up to the bridge. Wish me luck."

"Good luck."

Zoya ducked back into her stateroom and closed the door on her side.

Natalya shook her head and wondered what to do next.

A tap on the outer door turned her around and she found a shortish fellow wearing pristine undress khakis with chief engineer insignia at the collar. He smiled at her. "Hi. Regyri, right?"

"Yes. You are?"

"Steve Pritchard. Chief engineer this trip." He stuck out a hand and Natalya shook it.

"Natalya Regyri. I'm apparently your engineering third officer."

He beamed. "Yes, yes. Excellent." His expression sobered almost immediately. "So, tell me. Are you really an engineering officer?"

"Yes," Natalya said. A little alarm bell went off in her head. "Are you?"

"Oh, gracious, no. I'm just playing the part of the chief engineer for this trip. I'm really a mining sled jockey normally. This is just so exciting."

"I see. I think."

Pritchard grinned at her. "I don't mind telling you, I was very nervous about this whole deal but Mr. Kondur told me I just had to be here and wear the insignia. Did I put them on correctly? I had to go by a tiny diagram and I wasn't sure."

Natalya nodded. "They look fine, Chief."

"Good, good. Well, I should let you get to work."

"What would you like me to do?"

Pritchard stared at her for a moment. "Do? Why, engineer, of course. Whatever they do on a ship like this. This is huge, isn't it? My mining sled would fit on the mess deck here. It's amazing. Anyway. I'm sure you have a lot of things to look into before we get underway tomorrow so I'll leave you to it." He gave a little wave and started back down the passage.

"Wait. I need credentials to access the ship's systems."

"Oh, just use mine. Pritchard, welcome aboard."

"Thanks, but I need more than your name."

He laughed. "No, that's my ShipNet login. Pritchard. Password welcome aboard. Two words, actually, but they told me it was all right. It's easy to remember."

Natalya gave her head a little shake to clear it. "Yes. Yes, it's easy to remember. Thank you, Chief. I'll get right on that engineering thing."

He gave her a wide smile with too many teeth showing. "Excellent. I knew Mr. Kondur wouldn't let us down."

"Indeed." Natalya felt a little breathless and watched as the ersatz chief of engineering disappeared into a stateroom leaving a whiffy cloud of cologne behind him. Or mouthwash. It was hard to tell. After a moment or two while she weighed her options, she strode down the short passageway and knocked on the cabin's door.

"What?" The captain's voice didn't sound any better the second time she heard it.

"It's Regyri, Captain. Have you a moment?"

The door jerked open again and Captain Trask raised his eyebrows at her. "Well?"

"I've met the chief engineer."

He barked a single laugh. "Pritchard? Now you know why I asked if you'd ever done any actual engineering."

"He's serious."

"Yeah. Don't look for any help or guidance from him. Did he give you system access?"

"He gave me his system access."

The captain barked again. "Last name, welcome aboard. Change it when you get in there. You should have full access. If not, see Usoko to get you set up."

"Zoya?"

The captain nodded. "She's up on the bridge with Albee now. It'll probably kill him to give her access but he hates doing backups more. She any good with systems?"

Natalya nodded. "Yes, Captain. She's very good."

"But you're better?"

Natalya shrugged. "Maybe."

Trask looked up and down the passageway and then leaned over to Natalya and spoke quietly. "Just between you, me, and possibly Usoko, we've got maybe ten people in the whole crew who know which end of the ship goes first. Me. You. Possibly Usoko. Our navigator is top notch, thank the furies. You'll meet Charlie at dinner in the wardroom."

"What about Mr. Albee?"

Trask shook his head. "He'll play the part as if he knows what's happening. He gives you or Usoko any guff, just ignore him. He's got no real authority except the suit and his voice. We'll be on a normal three-watch deck rotation as soon as we get underway and we won't see him except for meals."

"Can I ask a question, Captain?"

Trask grinned. "I'd be disappointed if you didn't, Ms. Regyri."

"Isn't this—I don't know—dangerous?"

He snorted. "Depends on what you mean by dangerous. Yeah. We got a few loose nuts aboard. The ratings aren't all that bad. Most of them have made at least one trip before. You've got a couple of actual engineering crew. Pearson and Solomon are solid. The new environmental guy—Knowles—came in from Kondur's environmental section so he knows which side of the scrubber has slime. We've been taking on tankage and gasses for the last two days so I'm pretty sure we got enough juice to get us to Siren and back." He paused and gave her a sheepish look. "I'd appreciate it if you'd double-check me on that."

Natalya stared at him.

"Yeah. I know," he said . "You wanna bail on it?"

A whole crate of "what could go wrong" ran through Natalya's head. Any sane person would leave this catastrophe waiting to happen far, far behind. "I need the credits."

"You could die," he said.

"So could you. Why are you here?"

"Because the other nine months of the year I'm a key-pressing nobody keeping a fleet of mining tenders running in and out of the belts." He glanced up the ladder toward the bridge. "I used to do this all the time. Every day. A long time back." He looked her square in the eyes and shook his head. "This is the only chance I have to do it again, even if only for a few weeks out of the stanyer." He sighed. "There's worse things than dying."

Natalya read something in the old man's eyes. She'd seen hints of it in her father's eyes, stanyers past and systems away. She remembered seeing it and not knowing what it meant. "Well, let's see about not dying anyway."

He smiled a crooked smile that reached his sad eyes. "I like the way you think, Regyri. You run into any trouble. Need anything. Anything. You see me. Clear?"

"Clear, Skipper."

"Good. Now go make sure we aren't going to blow up when we light off the kickers, huh?"

"Aye, aye, sar." She turned away as he closed the door in her face. She thought it over for a few heartbeats. Her father's voice echoed in her head. "Don't leave port unless you're sure you can get back," she said to herself and headed for the spine. First priority: check fuel, water, air, and spares.

Chapter Seventeen
Dark Knight Station: 2363, June 7

In the aft nacelle, she found the door to the chief engineer's office unlocked and took advantage of the console there to do a fast survey of the ship's logistical status. She had to run a damp rag over the keyboard to get the dust off it and promised herself to give the whole office a fast swab as soon as they got underway.

The console gave her complete access to the ship's systems using Pritchard's credentials, so she gave herself access to only those functions required by her job and reset his password to keep him out of the system. She'd ask Zoya to set up a dummy account for him so he could have access to communications and alerts but for the moment, she didn't trust him enough not to make an honest mistake that could kill them all.

She cross logged to her own account and checked the tankage. The tanks all showed nearly full and she thanked the captain's forethought in getting those taken care of. A quick survey of the spares inventory showed it to be complete, but she slaved her tablet to the console and made a fast trip to the spares storage to spot-check things like scrubber and potable water filters. They'd be underway six weeks before docking again; that was plenty of time for them to suffocate in their own emissions.

Coming out of the spares closet, she ran into one of the crew trying to enter.

"Sorry," she said, nearly bouncing off him. "Didn't realize anybody else was around." She had to look up rather a long way to find his smiling face.

"You're Regyri, right?" he asked.

"I am. You are?"

He held out a hand. "Paul Knowles. I pass for a spec-one environmental. I take it you're the real engineering chief?"

She took the hand and grinned. "Actually just an engineering third officer, but apparently I'll be doing double duty."

"Mr. Pritchard means well. He won't give you any trouble."

"You sound like you've done this before?"

"My second trip. First one was a bit hairy, but I got used to living in terror. Mr. Kondur promised we'd have a real engineer in the crew this time."

"The captain said you work in station environmental?"

"Yeah. Huge operation compared to here. Everything's so compact." He looked down the length of the engine room. "This whole thing would fit in one of my precipitation tanks."

"You know how to work it?"

He grinned down at her. "Oh, yeah. Masters in environmental systems from New Farnouk. Grew up on slime. My parents ran the environmental section over at High Tortuga and I came to work for Mr. Kondur—must be ten, twelve stanyers now."

"You know any of the rest of the crew?"

"You met the skipper. Albee is a bit of a pompous twerp but he stands his watches. Second mate, Charlie Blanchard. Great guy. He'll be the one you go to if you can't get to the captain."

"Good to know."

"I don't know much about the power and propulsion people but Val wears spec-three environmental tabs. She's good people. Works for me on the station most of the year. You'll meet her when we get underway. She's in port until morning finishing up a few tasks for me."

"Watch standers?"

"A couple of enginemen and wipers. I don't know them but they showed up on my roster."

"Speaking of which, do we have watch schedules?"

He snorted. "Did you make any?"

"No."

"There's your answer. Roster's on the system, but we aren't much for watch standing. Have you logged in yet?"

"Barely. I've only been aboard a couple of stans and it feels like much longer."

"Well, Environmental Section is ready to sail. I was just double-checking the spares status."

"Yeah. Me, too."

"Well, Ms. Regyri. You'll be my boss for the next twelve weeks or so. I look forward to working with you."

She smiled. "Thanks. I'm beginning to feel a little better about the whole thing."

"Are you supposed to confess that to crew?" His eyes twinkled.

"Probably not, but we're all in the same boat here. Literally."

"Amen to that."

"Let me know if you spot anything problematic. I don't know what I can do about it, but at least I can take it to the captain."

"Of course, sar." He grimaced. "Sar? It's really sar?"

"So they tell me. Don't get hung up on it. My ego's not so fragile I need to assert my authority every time you speak to me."

"Thanks. I'm not really a spacer."

"You'll get the hang of it." She sighed. "I better go find the rosters and cobble up a watch rotation."

"Good luck with that. Charlie might have some insight there. He's been doing this awhile now." He checked his tablet. "It's almost 1700 already. He should be back aboard by now. You might find him on the mess deck."

"Mess deck? Not the wardroom?"

"He's a people person. No people in the wardroom this time of day."

Natalya nodded. "Thanks for the tip."

"Any time. I should probably get cleaned up for dinner. See you around the engine room." He turned away from the spares closet and climbed up the ladder heading to the spine.

She watched him go and turned back to the engine room. It wasn't in terrible condition, at least not to the eye. She wandered around the machinery. The covers all seemed to be in place. The decks had more dirt that she'd have liked but she didn't see any obvious hazards. The big Burleson drives—one on either side of the bay—dominated the space, their dark green cases gleaming in the overheads. On a hunch she crossed to the nearer unit and pulled up the diagnostic interface on it. She'd need these beasts tomorrow, but she'd rest easier knowing they would work when called on. Since that wasn't an option, she settled for overnight testing. With a few clicks, she triggered a diagnostic routine that would run through the night. In the morning, she'd have her answer. She crossed the wide space to the second drive and started the same diagnostic.

Satisfied, she climbed the ladder to the office and killed the overheads. Safety lighting came on, casting the whole engine room in a ruddy glow. She headed down the spine toward her stateroom and a shower. She'd done what she knew to do, and hoped it would be enough.

CHAPTER EIGHTEEN
DARK KNIGHT STATION: 2363, JUNE 7

Natalya found Zoya in her stateroom. "What's the uniform of the day? Do you know?"

"Apparently it's that god-awful musical-theater maroon and gold." Zoya pulled a set of undress khakis from her trunk. "I'm going with this and hoping I don't get blinded by the splendor that is the amazingly horrible Maroon Avenger."

"Since I don't have a set of maroon shipsuits, I'll have to go with undress khakis, too." Natalya paused at the door to the head. "You know this is madness, right?"

"Which part?" Zoya asked, looking up from her trunk. "The part where we're getting underway without enough crew? Or the part that we're going to try to sneak this ship into a Confederation port?"

"The part where at least some of the officers are only playing the part of actual skilled officers and don't really understand what's happening."

"Wait. The officers? I had my doubts about the crew but the officers? Do any of them know what they're doing?"

"I don't really know. I'm pretty sure the skipper is on the up and up. At least was at one point. He misses it so he puts on the captain's hat once a stanyer."

"He seems nice enough, if a bit grumpy." She sighed and looked up at the overhead. "I'm not sure about Albee. He seems like he has something of a handle on it, but other than barking about the backups, he didn't seem overly concerned with basic things like food and fuel for the trip."

"I checked the tankage. We've got enough fuel, water, and air. They're topped off. I'm running a high-level diagnostic on the Burlesons overnight. I'll know in the morning if they're more likely to bend space or break the ship."

"That would be good to know," Zoya said. "I thought there was a chief engineer."

"We have someone in a chief engineer's uniform who is flat-out enjoying the role of chief engineer but who is quite delighted to have an actual engineering officer aboard for this trip."

Zoya's jaw dropped.

"Yes. Chief Pritchard isn't actually an engineering officer. Mr. Albee isn't actually a first mate. They're just playing the roles."

"How did you find this out?"

"I had a short chat with Captain Trask and another with an environmental expert wearing a spec-one disguise."

"What the—?"

"This is apparently their normal mode of operation. The second mate is apparently a good guy who actually knows astronavigation and can plot a course. You're the third mate and you're more qualified than the first."

"What're you going to do in engineering?"

"I've already usurped control of engineering systems. Which reminds me. I need you to give Mr. Pritchard guest access to ShipNet so he can get messages and use the entertainment system."

"You what?" Zoya's eyes practically bugged out of their sockets.

"He had full system access to the operational controls for the entire ship. He had everything in the engine room along with personnel jackets. He even had access to the helm and bridge controls."

Zoya lowered herself to her bunk and stared at the deck. "Mercy Maude."

Natalya watched her for a few ticks. "If it's any consolation, most of the crew apparently knows what they're doing."

Zoya chuckled. "That would explain Helms's apparent disrespect for everybody in a management role. Why are they doing this?"

"No idea. Something to do with the smuggling operation maybe?"

"You'd think they'd want the ship to get there and back again all in one piece."

Natalya nodded. "I was thinking about that. In reality? What's the downside for Kondur and company if the ship doesn't make it?"

"What do you mean, downside? He's out a ship and crew."

"The ship, maybe. Crew?" Natalya sighed. "Honestly, I'm not sure he's too concerned about losing this crew. Might be he's done this before and lost ships. Are these the only people desperate enough to take the trip?"

"I don't know that I'm that desperate," Zoya said.

Natalya sat on the bunk beside her. "I am."

Zoya turned her head to stare.

"I am," Natalya said again. "I need to get the *Peregrine* repaired and this trip can make it happen."

"We have to make it back first."

Natalya glanced at Zoya out of the corners of her eyes. "I was thinking about that."

"Thinking what? I'm thinking we need to grab our trunks and run." Zoya's face had grown pale.

"Assuming the ship is in reasonable repair, what are the chances we won't make it back?"

"Given the state of the crew? What makes you think it's in reasonable repair?"

"The engine room doesn't show any sign of neglect. The systems records looked adequate if not top shelf. You remember that summer cruise from hell?"

"Yeah. Bunk bunnies and crap food."

"That engine room was a shambles. In retrospect I'm surprised the orbital allowed it to dock, let alone the academy approving it for summer cruise."

"What's your point?"

"Barbells are pretty forgiving. Redundant systems. Solid navigation. Over-engineered environmentals. There's a reason they're called bricks. Beyond the shape."

Zoya pursed her lips and her gaze focused elsewhere. "Having one can makes for fewer moving parts and adds a huge amount of stability."

"She's got kickers and massive sail generators. You can take a Barbell anywhere."

"What are you saying?" Zoya asked.

"I'm saying we can do this."

Zoya caught her bottom lip between her teeth and squinted at Natalya. "Seriously? You're suggesting we set sail in this death-trap?"

"That's the thing," Natalya said, turning to face Zoya. "The ship looks like it's actually decent. The crew? Maybe not so much. If we can keep them from killing us, the ship should make it."

"You're out of your mind."

"You've known that for at least a couple of weeks now."

"We'd be violating I don't know how many regs."

Natalya grinned. "Not out here, we're not. When we get to Siren? Yeah. Regs will be the last things we're going to worry about."

Zoya's head shook back and forth. "No, I suppose not getting arrested on a trumped-up murder charge will matter more."

"Or not getting caught with an illegal can of ore."

Zoya snorted. "I suppose, on balance, having fewer than the regulation numbers of crew in appropriate ratings falls a bit short on that score."

"You'll do it?" Natalya asked. "I can't ask you to but we've come this far."

Zoya kept shaking her head. "This is nuts."

"Yeah."

"Can you run the engine room? You're only a boot third. We only graduated—what? Two weeks ago? It's an awful lot to bite off."

Natalya took a deep breath and asked herself the same question. "I don't know. I've been running the *Peregrine* for stanyers now. Same principles."

"Other than the sails and keel."

"True, but the Burlesons are the same. Just bigger. Kickers are kickers. *Peregrine's* are actually oversized for a small ship. Environmental is plug-and-play on *Peregrine*, but we've got an honest-to-Maude environmental expert to keep us out of trouble there." Natalya hated to admit it to herself but the idea of running the entire engineering department on the ship gave her more of a thrill than it should have.

"We'll each get fifty thousand if we succeed," Zoya said. "Won't be able to spend it if we fail." She looked Natalya in the eyes. "What are the odds?"

Natalya shook her head. "I've no idea. The ship part? I think we're actually in better shape than we might think. It's a solid ship. As long as the crew doesn't sabotage us—and as long as Blanchard can actually plot a course—we could almost make the whole trip on autopilot."

"As long as we don't run into anything unexpected."

"There's that."

Zoya frowned and stared at the undress uniform in her hands for several long moments. "Let's go see what the wardroom looks like. Maybe scope out Blanchard to see if he has a clue."

"You'll do it?" Natalya asked.

Zoya shook her head. "I don't know yet. Let's get some due diligence on this and see what we can learn. It doesn't make sense that Kondur would risk a ship without some expectation that it would pay off."

Natalya grinned. "You're thinking like a Toe-Holder now."

"I only met the guy a couple of times. Did he strike you as the kind of guy who'd toss a billion credits into the void without some expectation that they'd come back with a few friends?"

"No. He didn't."

"All right, then. Get changed for dinner and let's go see who else we have to play with."

CHAPTER NINETEEN
DARK KNIGHT STATION: 2363, JUNE 7

Natalya and Zoya found themselves nearly the last ones to enter the wardroom. Albee and Pritchard stood near the head of the table, apparently not looking at each other or anybody else in the room. A pleasant-looking older man turned out in neat undress looked up from the coffee mess in the corner and raised a cup in salute as they entered. "You must be our new blood. Charlie Blanchard, second mate. Call me Charlie."

Zoya nodded. "Zoya Usoko, third mate."

"I'm Natalya Regyri, engineering third officer."

"Nice of you to join us finally," Albee said.

Blanchard chuckled. "Easy there, big fella. We'll be underway soon and you'll be able to get that stick out of your ass."

Albee rounded on Blanchard. "That's insubordination, Mr. Blanchard."

Blanchard sipped his coffee and smiled at the now red-faced Albee. "No. Actually that was not insubordination. Insubordination is when I refuse your orders or defy your authority. That was more like disrespect for an officer, or perhaps conduct unbecoming. Under the circumstances, and given your example, just let me assure you that you set a very low bar to get over on that score."

The door opened and another man staggered in. "Sorry I'm late. Got lost in the head." He drew up short, nearly falling into Zoya as he realized she stood in his way. He stared at her face and frowned quizzically. "Do I know you?"

"I'm the new third mate. Zoya Usoko."

"I'm the old luch. Lust. Luck." He sighed. "Drunk." He looked toward the head of the table. "Oh, good. I beat the skipper."

Blanchard said, "Ladies, this is our cargo master, Josh Lyons. Mr. Lyons has the singular privilege of having nothing to do but sign a document on the other end of our little sojourn certifying that the can of ore we're hauling actually came from Margary."

Josh nodded. "Yes. Yes, I do. And it's a darn fine piece of work."

"Did it?" Natalya asked, looking at Blanchard. "Come from Margary?"

"No. As luck would have it, it came from our very own ore-bearing belts here in Dark Knight, but the CPJCT can be such sticklers."

"Stupid process," Josh said. "Hate these trips."

"Why do you do it, then?" Albee asked. "You're a disgrace to the uniform."

Blanchard turned his head and gave Albee's maroon-and-gold shipsuit a long up-and-down stare.

The captain threw the door open and stomped in. "Good. You're here. Let's eat." He bustled his way to the head of the table, jostling Albee out of the way and nearly elbowing Pritchard in the gut in the process. He paused for a moment and then lowered himself into his chair. Everybody else followed suit. As first mate, Albee sat on the captain's right and Pritchard, as nominal engineering chief, on the left. The rest of them found seats in decreasing order of displayed rank.

"Gentlemen—and ladies—welcome aboard, and I look forward to sailing with you." He clinked a fork against his water glass and a steward in white coat and black slacks carried in a tray with cups of soup to begin the evening mess.

He said nothing, simply distributed the soups around the table and took up station just inside the pantry door.

The captain lifted his spoon and took a portion of the soup, lifting it toward his lips and then pausing to watch Albee start to take up his own spoon, only to stop and replace his hand beside the dish. The captain teased him several more times before finally eating the soup on his spoon, freeing Albee—and the rest—to begin their own meals.

Blanchard chuckled and Albee shot him a dark look.

"Don't blame me, John. He just does it because you always fall for it," Blanchard said.

Trask grinned and winked at Blanchard. He looked at Albee. "Didn't I tell you to get a decent set of undress khakis?"

"I have some, Captain, as you ordered."

"Why are you still wearing this, then?" He waved his empty spoon at the shipsuit.

"I'm saving them for when we dock at Siren. The uniform of the day is shipsuit in company colors, Captain."

"Those aren't the company colors."

"They are now, Captain."

The captain sat back in his chair. "Since when?"

"Since I filed them with the CPJCT's corporate registry last voyage."

Trask's eyes narrowed. "Mr. Albee. If I catch you wearing these company colors again, I will exercise my right of summary judgment. Am I clear?"

"Perfectly, Captain."

Trask took a few more spoons of soup before pushing the cup away. "Bray, clear this and bring the main course, if you would?"

The waiting steward stepped forward and placed the cups— some nearly full, only Pritchard's completely empty—on his tray and left the wardroom. He returned almost immediately with a helper who doled out meager portions of some kind of pasta casserole in sauce.

Natalya looked at it and wondered if staying aboard was such a good idea after all.

Blanchard leaned forward to speak to her across the table. "It tastes better than it looks. Try it." He smiled encouragement.

Natalya found herself liking the man in spite of the situation and took a small portion on a fork. She smelled it before tasting and was pleasantly surprised.

It must have shown on her face because Blanchard grinned in response.

Trask looked at Natalya. "You found your way to the engine room all right?"

"Yes, thank you, Captain. Tankage is topped off and I started some diagnostics on the drives to run overnight."

Trask's eyebrows went up. "Diagnostics?"

"Just a last minute check to make sure the Burlesons are up to spec."

"Thank you, Ms. Regyri. Good initiative." The captain looked at Zoya. "I understand you did the backups for us today, Ms. Usoko?"

"Yes, Captain. Systems and comms backed up and verified. We've left a copy here with Mr. Kondur's people."

Trask scowled at Josh who sat slouched over his plate. "I don't suppose you've checked stores, Josh?"

Lyons didn't even look up. "I'm not a grocer."

Trask sighed and looked to the waiting steward. "Mr. Bray, my compliments to Ms. Marah. If you'd have her let me know if there's anything we need by way of stores before we leave tomorrow?"

"Of course, Captain." Bray slipped out of the wardroom.

Trask looked back at Lyons. "Josh, we've talked about this."

"Talk, talk, talk, talk, talk. We're launching into the Deep Dark in a tin brick and I'm risking my neck every time just so you can get a legit signoff on a smuggled cargo. I hate it. You know I hate it. Leave me alone." With that he slammed out of the wardroom, leaving his half-eaten meal on the table, his fork balanced precariously on the edge of the plate.

Blanchard said, "Well, I'm glad we got that out of the way early."

Trask shot him a dark look. "Are you going to be insufferable, Charlie?"

"Have you ever known me to be any other way, Skipper?" His bright smile seemed to carry a certain level of warmth toward the old man.

Trask gave him a small smile in return. "No. No, I haven't."

"I'll get us there as long as the ship holds together," Blanchard said, his voice low.

Trask nodded several times. "I know you will, Charlie. I know you will." He looked at Natalya, then at Zoya. "Welcome aboard," he said.

Zoya looked like she might be going to bolt, but something stiffened in her spine. She glanced across the table at Natalya before speaking. "We'll do our best, Captain."

The old man smiled and he nodded. "I'm counting on it."

Albee sniffed.

"You have a comment, Mr. Albee?" the captain asked, raising an eyebrow at the first mate.

"No, Captain." He pursed his lips and screwed up his face like somebody had waved a dead fish under his nose.

"Good. Get some decent clothes on, John. You look like a movie poster."

"Yes, Captain. Anything else you'd like to criticize in front of the crew?" Albee's face had turned an unfortunate shade of red.

"Many things, John, but I'll spare your delicate sensibilities. See me in the cabin at 1930 and I'll give you a list."

"You need me, Trask," Albee said, his voice a bare growl through his teeth.

The captain turned his head to look the first mate square in the eye. "What I need is a first mate I can count on to run the ship.

Not one that spends all of his time running everybody else into the ground while dressed like a mummer in a burlesque farce."

"You need my name," Albee said. He held up his right thumb. "You need my thumb."

Trask shook his head. "Get your gear and get off my boat."

Albee jerked to his feet. "It's not your boat. It's Kondur's and Kondur hired me."

"I'll call him if I have to." Trask gazed up at Albee's face without standing. "You willing to take the chance of being on the wrong end of that discussion?"

Albee practically vibrated in his outrage. "Listen to me, you crazy old fart. You can't run this ship without me. Nobody will follow a command you give without me to back it up."

"Good-bye, John," Trask said and looked away, reaching for his coffee cup.

Albee sprang on the older man, smashing his head down onto his plate and grabbing for his outstretched arm.

Before she had a chance to think, Natalya launched herself out of her chair, over the table, and took the larger Albee down in one move, cracking his skull against the bulkhead on the way by and pinning his face against the decking by the simple expedient of kneeling on the back of his neck and locking his arm behind his shoulder blade.

It happened in an instant and for several long moments, the blowers provided the only sound.

Captain Trask straightened up and started wiping his dinner off his face with a napkin. He gazed at Albee and then nodded at Natalya. "Thank you, Ms. Regyri. I think you can let him up now."

Natalya released the pressure on Albee's arm and shifted her weight back off his neck. She stood and waited for him to move.

Albee glared at her as he stood. His hands opened and closed, finally ending as fists tight against his side. He didn't take his eyes off Natalya when he spoke. "We're not done, Captain." He spit the word out like a curse. "You'll have to come back here when the trip is over. Think on that while you're gone."

"Mr. Blanchard, would you escort Mr. Albee to his stateroom and assist him in collecting his things. Make sure he leaves the ship."

"Of course, Captain." Blanchard stood and smiled at Albee as if nothing had happened. "Shall we, John?" He held out a hand as if to usher him toward the door.

Albee shoved Blanchard out of his way and kicked the empty chair on his way. He paused at the wardroom door and turned to send a glare at everyone left in the room, stopping with the captain. "See you in hell."

The captain gave him a half-smile that never reached his eyes. "I'll call ahead for a reservation and save you a seat."

Blanchard closed the door on his way out, the latch making a soft click.

Pritchard turned to Natalya, his eyes wide. "I've never seen anybody move that fast."

"I'm a little off my game. Not getting enough sleep lately," Natalya said.

Captain Trask held out a hand. "Thank you. That coulda gotten nasty."

Natalya shook his hand. "You're welcome. Can we not do that again any time soon?"

Trask rubbed his face with his napkin once more. "Yeah. I think I can agree to that."

Zoya said, "So what will you do for a first mate now?"

He turned and leaned an elbow on the table. He looked down at the table cloth for a few moments. "I'll see what Kondur wants to do. It's his show. See if he wants to run with what we have or bring in a new face." He shrugged. "I can stand watch if we need to, but it would be better if we had another first mate. Raises fewer flags on the far end."

"Should I go make sure things are all right with Charlie, Captain?" Pritchard asked.

The captain gave a small laugh. "I think you'd probably better just sit here for a bit until the coast is clear, Steven. Charlie can take care of himself and his section is all aboard if he needs help."

Pritchard settled himself back in his chair, his face slightly pale and his fingers toying with the edge of his napkin. "If you think it's best, Captain."

The captain nodded. "I do, Steven. I do."

"Captain?" Bray asked from the galley door.

"Yes, Bray?"

"Dessert, sar?"

He turned to the steward who stood holding his tray like a shield, his eyes wide and his face pale. "Mr. Bray, I think you can clear. I don't think we'll be having dessert."

CHAPTER TWENTY
DARK KNIGHT STATION: 2363, JUNE 8

Natalya's tablet bipped her awake at 0530. She fumbled it up to her face and then sat up in her bunk, rubbing the sleep from her eyes. The tablet showed her diagnostics had completed with no reportable discrepancies. She scrolled through the details and saw a clean set of readings all the way down. Only tiny discrepancies between the two units showed up. Nothing that would flag the drives as anything but straight up.

She took a moment to scroll through the rest of the engineering status reports and found nothing more serious than a potable water filter tagged for routine replacement by end of day. She forwarded it to Knowles.

The sound of water running in the head convinced her to get up and moving. She wasn't sure if the captain would still try to get underway at 0800 but she wouldn't bet against it. She rummaged in her trunk for a clean set of undress and knocked on the door to the head.

Zoya opened it and peeked out. "Morning. How're the Burleson units?"

"Straight up. I haven't seen better diagnostics since I did that jump drive rotation in third year."

"That's a relief."

Natalya grinned. "Now all we need to worry about are all the other things that could go wrong."

"Breakfast in the wardroom at 0600?"

"That'd be my guess," Natalya said.

"I'll be done in a tick. I can't wait to find out what the captain does about the first mate."

"That makes two of us. With our luck, it'll be somebody who doesn't know which end the fire comes out."

"Fire comes out?" Zoya asked.

Natalya threw a pillow at her.

Zoya chuckled as she pulled the door closed.

A few moments later she was as good as her word. "All yours," she said through the door.

Natalya did the needful and grabbed a fast shower before sliding into fresh khakis. She policed her stateroom, stowing all the loose bits in case they got underway before she had a chance to get back.

In the passageway outside, the smell of fresh baked bread drew her down the ladder to the wardroom. She found Zoya already there with a stunned look on her face and the captain looking pleased with himself over something.

"Good morning, Ms. Regyri. I hope our little unpleasantness didn't interfere with your sleep."

"Good morning, Captain. I slept very well. Thanks."

"Have you the results from your overnight diagnostics?"

"I do. Burlesons are straight up. Shouldn't be a problem."

"I'm relieved but not surprised. Mr. Kondur spends a lot of time and credits to make sure the ship is in tiptop condition before we sail. Wouldn't do to fail a routine safety inspection when we get in close."

The captain stuck his head through the door to the pantry. "Mr. Bray? If you could find us some coffee?"

"Right away, Skipper." Bray's voice echoed back down the passageway, followed only moments later by Bray himself. "Sorry about that, Captain." He flourished a thermal carafe and the captain took his seat at the head of the table, signaling Zoya and Natalya that it was safe to sit. Bray poured the few cups and left the carafe before slipping back out of the wardroom.

Natalya took the seat she'd taken the night before, leaving room for Pritchard at the captain's left hand.

Zoya started to take her seat to the right of Blanchard's but the captain raised a hand. "Sit here, if you'd be so kind, Ms. Usoko?" He indicated the first mate's chair to his right.

She blinked a couple of times, stopped halfway into her chair.

The captain nodded and smiled. "Please," he said.

Zoya took Albee's seat.

The captain smiled and reached over to pat Zoya on the shoulder. "Buck up, Ms. Usoko. You'll be fine."

Zoya seemed to pull herself together and straightened up. "Of course, Captain. It just came as a bit of a surprise."

He chuckled. "Not as much as Albee got, I bet." He glanced at Zoya. "You can have his stateroom if you like."

Zoya shook her head. "Thanks, Captain, but I'll stay where I am."

Trask nodded and glanced at Natalya. "Not a problem."

"What will happen to him?" Zoya asked.

Trask pursed his lips and shook his head. "No idea. He's a good enough line supervisor. He'll probably just go back to the ore plant and pick up his next shift."

"What did he mean that you needed his thumb?"

The captain shrugged. "He seemed to think he'd need to certify the voyage. His identity records have already been sanitized so that they all think he's who we say he is."

"I see," Zoya said. Her expression belied her statement and she looked at Natalya, eyes wide.

Natalya said, "What about the cargo master?"

"Josh?"

"Yes, Captain. He seems a bit—well—disabled."

"We do need Josh. His thumb goes on the final transfer docket. It's a bit of a strain on him. He's been getting worse each trip. I'll ask Mr. Kondur to find us a new cargo chief before we go back again."

Charlie Blanchard breezed through the wardroom door with Pritchard close behind. "Good morning, all. Sorry we're late. Traffic was terrible on the commute this morning." He smiled at Zoya. "I see I have a new boss. Good morning, Ms. Usoko. How may I suck up to you today?" Blanchard winked at Natalya across the table.

The captain chuckled and waved a hand. "Shut up and sit down, Charlie. She's still in shock."

Pritchard edged around the table and took his seat at the captain's left hand. "Good morning, Skipper. Congratulations on the promotion, Ms. Usoko." He practically beamed.

"Good morning, Steven," the captain said.

"Thank you, Mr. Pritchard," Zoya said and nodded at Blanchard. "I'm still not sure why or how I got bumped ahead of Mr. Blanchard."

"Charlie, please. And you got bumped because I turned it down." He shot a look at the captain. "As I always do."

Zoya said, "You people realize—"

The captain placed a hand on her forearm and spoke over her. "We realize that your experience handling the ore haulers in Margary have given you very much more experience than your chronological age might indicate, Ms. Usoko."

Pritchard didn't seem to notice the exchange but Blanchard did and nodded. "Precisely."

The captain looked at Blanchard. "Charlie, we'll need to push the departure back to at least noon. Mr. Kondur is sending a replacement third mate but he's going to be a bit delayed."

"Shall we push it back to 1500? Nothing goes as planned and I'd rather give him some extra time than have to adjust it again."

The captain nodded. "Yeah. Let's do that. I know Mr. Kondur wants this shipment out of here but a couple of stans aren't going to make much difference across twelve weeks."

"Will do, Skipper," Blanchard said. He looked at Zoya. "You need help adjusting the watch schedules?"

"I'm sure I can handle that much."

The captain looked down the table at Natalya. "Engineering is ready to go?"

"I'll have everything on warm standby by 1500, Captain."

"Very good."

Mr. Bray brought in platters of scrambled eggs, bacon, and fried potatoes. "Breakfast is served, sars."

By the time breakfast was over, Zoya looked a little less anxious.

Natalya still had her doubts but for fifty thousand credits and getting her ship back, she was willing to take the chance.

Natalya called a section meeting for 1300 hours, right after lunch. She had the whole engineering crew with the exception of Pritchard assemble at the foot of the ladder in the main engine room. She stood on the ladder where she could address all of them at once.

"Good afternoon, people. I've met a few of you in passing but this is the first time I've been able to meet with you all. In a couple of stans we're going to get underway, and that means we're going to have to start paying very close attention to what's happening back here."

A couple of the ratings near the back rolled their eyes.

"How many of you have real engineering experience? Environmental, power, whatever."

Natalya raised her hand and was gratified to see Knowles and the half-dozen people around him raised theirs. The two near the back that found her welcome so eyeroll-worthy also raised theirs.

"Great. How many have made one of these runs before."

Natalya kept her hand down but most of the people on the floor raised theirs.

"Thanks. That helps. Collie and Pearson?"

Two ratings in neat shipsuits stepped forward. "Thanks. I just wanted to get faces with the names. Solomon?"

"Here." An older woman in the middle of the pack raised a hand.

Natalya nodded to her. "Excellent. You three with Mr. Knowles are my section leads. Let me know if you need anything, day or night. Bip me."

They all nodded.

"I know you don't know me any more than I know you. I'm sure we'll get to know each other better over the next few weeks. Any questions for me?"

One of the eye-rollers in the back stuck his face in the air. "Yeah. I got one."

"Great. Who are you? What section are you in?"

"Mike Town, Propulsion."

"What's your question?"

"Who made you God?"

Solomon turned to face the crewman who seemed to be ignoring her.

"Mr. Town, I am not God. That would be Captain Trask." Her response got a bit of a chuckle. "I'm the only trained engineering officer on this vessel. I'm probably the only person here who's torn down a Burleson drive and put it back together so it ran. The only one who's rerouted fuel ducts around a failed structure to get a ship flying again. Your section leads know their sections but I'm the only one who knows how every one of these machines works, how they work together, how to keep them all running, and how to fix every one of them if it fails. I'm your ticket home if any of this gear goes tits up half way between here and nowhere. But I'm not God." She paused and stared him down. "Does that answer your question, Mr. Town?"

"Where's Steve?" he asked, his jaw stuck out and his arms folded over his chest. "He's your boss. Why isn't he here givin' the orders?"

"Chief Pritchard is in his stateroom," Natalya said. "You are free to check in with him if you like. He gave me my orders, Mr. Town. I am carrying out those orders now."

Solomon cast a glance up at Natalya. "Sorry, boss."

Natalya shook her head. "I'm happy to answer questions. I'm less happy to have to explain the facts of life to spacers, but I don't mind doing it."

Town took a step forward. "You and who's army?"

The crew stepped away, leaving a clear path between Town and Natalya. Only Solomon stood in the way.

"Stand down, Mike. You're out of line," Solomon said. "What's gotten into you?"

Town shook his head and waved her off. "We've been hangin' our asses out here—some of us for stanyers—and she's some prissy newcomer goin' to tell us how to run our shop? We're just going to take it? Those pips are barely out of the box. Gimme a break."

Natalya took the three steps down to the deck in a single hop and strode to stand beside Solomon. "Mr. Town, we've got enough trouble without adding more to it. Do you have any problem with anything I've said or done so far?" She paused. "Anything specific, other than calling you all together so I can see who's who?"

Up close, Town was a bigger guy than Natalya had thought. Apparently he thought she wasn't big enough because he lunged for her and swung a vicious right at her head.

Natalya sidestepped, slapped the fist away, and kicked his legs out from under him. He slammed to the steel deck and slid with the momentum. Natalya turned to face him. "Bad move, Mr. Town. Your balance is way off. You telegraphed that blow. You're angry and not using your head to plan. You also don't know me or what my skill level in hand-to-hand combat is."

Solomon said, "Jeez, I'm sorry, Ms. Regyri. He's not normally like this."

"Think nothing of it, Ms. Solomon." She smiled at the older woman and shrugged. "Sometimes we have to do things the hard way and we all have our own way of learning lessons, don't we."

Solomon blinked at her several times. "I can have him replaced."

Natalya looked at Town who still sprawled on the cold steel. "Oh, for goodness' sakes, get up, Mr. Town." She held out a hand to help him up.

He looked at it like it might be a trap and levered himself up on his own.

"You want to sit this one out, Mr. Town? Stay here on station instead of sailing with us?" she asked.

He scowled and looked at the deck at her feet. "No. I'll go."

Natalya smiled at him. "Good. We'll have more chance to get to know each other, but in the meantime, I think we've all got stuff we need to do. The skipper will be calling navigation stations soon. Let's not keep the man waiting, shall we?"

The group broke up, Knowles leading his environmental team off to Environmental and Collie and Pearson taking a troop of enginemen up the ladder to Propulsion and Grav.

Natalya offered her hand to Town. "No hard feelings?"

"No hard feelings?" Solomon said. "Why are you apologizing to him? He's the turd in the soup here." She looked like she wanted to take Town by the ear and drag him to the woodshed herself.

Natalya place a hand on Solomon's shoulder. "Ms. Solomon, Mr. Town was only saying what half a dozen of the crew were thinking. If he hadn't said something, that thought would have festered and turned nasty later in the voyage. With any luck, we've lanced that boil and we can move on." She looked back at Town. "Isn't that right, Mike?"

He didn't look up but nodded his head. "Probably."

Natalya stuck her hand out again. "Shake. Move on, spacer. We got places to be that don't include here."

He glanced up at her, shook her hand, and then nodded. "Moving on," he said. "Sar."

"Thank you, Mr. Town. I'm sure Ms. Solomon has something for you to do." She glanced at Solomon who nodded. Judging from the look on Solomon's face, Natalya was pretty sure that Town hadn't actually seen the end of it.

Chapter Twenty-two
Dark Knight Station: 2363, June 8

At 1400 Natalya took a tour of engineering. She stopped at the fusactor pair and did a manual check on the status of each before firing them up. Each of them powerful enough to run an orbital, together they powered the generators that kept the various ship's systems in juice. When not otherwise engaged, the power diverted to the capacitor banks that gave the Burleson drives their ability to bend space. She also brought the Burlesons online. It would be stans—perhaps days—before the bridge would call on them, but they'd be ready. Finally, she cross-checked the sail and keel generators. The manual safeties showed as set, and she double-checked the proximity overrides. The ship wouldn't extend her sails this close to a station and the manual safeties assured it.

Finally, she scampered up the ladder to the big kicker engines that would give them their first push out into the dark. There wasn't anything she could actually see or do in the compartment, but she walked around the behemoths, festooned as they were in pipes and tubing. Supercooled coils wrapped critical junctions; the whole assembly looked nothing like the sleek, streamlined rocket engines in the holos. It didn't need to. She found the beauty in the beast in knowing how it worked and why. She couldn't look at the kickers without thinking of the images her father had once shown her of the ancient steam engines that powered the early industry on Earth. Her survey completed, she patted one with the flat of her hand and left the compartment, dogging the airtight door behind her as she left.

She felt a solid warmth around her as she considered what they were about to do. Getting the *Peregrine* underway always gave her a sense of freedom, of possibility. Anything might happen. She smiled to herself as she thought of all the things that might go wrong on this voyage and her heart seemed to beat a little faster at the thought, even as the excitement of taking the huge ship out into the Deep Dark washed over her. It felt good in a way she couldn't explain.

At 1430, Zoya's voice called the crew to navigation stations over the ship's speakers. Natalya's feet carried her to the engineering control room. The captain had the bridge, but the chief engineer had engineering control. She found her power and propulsion crews already in place, mostly skylarking and drinking coffee. They had the consoles fired up and tracking, but little showed on them yet. As the bridge's demands grew, so would their readouts here.

The chatter died down as she entered. Town sat at the main propulsion control terminal; his ears and the back of his neck still showed red a whole stan later. Solomon caught Natalya's eye and gave her a nod. Natalya swung into the engineering chief's chair. Nobody questioned her right to it, although a couple of the ratings cast glances in her direction.

One of the power section spec-threes sat at the main power console. Natalya pulled up her ship's tablet and checked the logs to make sure she knew the correct names. "Mr. Collie?"

The spec-three turned to look at her.

"How stand we for power, Mr. Collie?"

"Fine, sar. Fusactors are online. System is ready to take the load from shore power."

"Thank you, Mr. Collie. Ms. Solomon, propulsion?"

Solomon smiled. "All field generators on safety standby. Kickers are primed and ready for firing."

"Thank you, Ms. Solomon." She keyed her comms and spoke to environmental. "Mr. Knowles, how soggy is the swamp?"

Natalya heard him laugh. "Fine as frogs' fur, sar. All systems up, running, and nominal. We're ready down here."

"Thank you, Mr. Knowles." She scanned the room once more and nodded at the spec-three on gravity. "Ms. Pearson? How's the gravity?"

"Not much outside, sar, but we're stable in the ship."

"Thank you, Ms. Pearson."

She signaled Zoya on the bridge that Engineering was ready to get underway.

"And now, ladies and gentlemen, we wait on the convenience of the captain," she said and settled down in the seat to wait.

After only a few moments, Zoya's voice came over the speakers again. "Standby for undock in ten."

Natalya buckled the seat belt on her chair and noticed which of the crew followed suit. Solomon and her propulsion team all buckled up. Collie seemed busy with Pearson on the next console. Neither of them bothered.

A low thump vibrated the hull. Natalya watched the propulsion systems log the maneuvering thrusters. She felt a tiny slosh of movement before the inertial stabilizers squelched it. Nobody spoke in the room. All eyes remained focused on the tasks in front of them.

Within a few ticks, the kickers rumbled into life just above Natalya's head. Vacuum isolated most of the noise but vibration propagated through the engine mounts and into the ship's frame. Natalya found it comforting, even if it made the armrest on her chair hum under her fingertips.

Natalya's tablet bipped an incoming message from Zoya with a schedule for jumps and their anticipated power needs. She acknowledged and turned to the crew.

"Listen up, my dears. In about half a stan we're going to make a short hop out of the local. We'll adjust course and make another longer jump before we huddle down to recharge and regroup. Any questions?"

Solomon lifted her chin and asked, "No sails?"

"Apparently not. We're going in with kicker velocity and jumping between systems as far as Albert. We're expecting to pop in to Albert's system space in about three days."

Solomon nodded. "That sounds familiar."

The chronometer ticked down for just over half a stan until Zoya's voice sounded on the speakers. "Stand by for jump."

"They're not wasting any time," Solomon said and turned back to the propulsion console.

The kicker vibration faded out for a moment and then the Burlesons jammed space-time into a ball for a split second.

"Status?" Natalya asked.

"Power normal. Full charge in half a stan."

"Propulsion normal. Kickers secured. Burlesons live for jump. Sails and keel on safety standby." Solomon looked up at Natalya. "We've got enough for one more full jump, sar."

"Stand by. Mr. Blanchard will have to confirm our location and velocity."

The Burlesons fired again almost immediately.

"Apparently he liked where we were, sar," Town said.

"Charge time, Ms. Solomon?"

"Full charge in three stans, sar. Enough for another full jump in one."

"Thank you, Ms. Solomon."

"Secure from navigation stations. Resume normal watch rotation." Zoya's voice sounded calm and measured on the speakers.

As soon as she stopped speaking, the speakers clicked again and Trask's gravelly tones filled the room. "Take a nap. Get some food. Charlie's running the numbers and I'm hoping to pick up two full jumps on the next cycle. You've got about four stans to do what you need to. Get to it." The speakers clicked off.

"You heard them," Natalya said. "Which section has the duty?"

Everybody in the room looked at her like she'd just grown a second head.

"Sar? We don't have watch sections," Solomon said.

Natalya felt her eyeballs all but bulge out of their sockets. "What do you mean? Who stands watch while we're underway?"

Everybody in Engineering Control looked at everybody else. Most of them shrugged.

"You don't have watches?" Natalya asked.

"We never have before," Solomon said. "We're just here to monitor during navigation stations."

"How do you know if something goes wrong?"

"What could go wrong?" she asked.

Natalya sighed. "I don't even know where to start." She keyed her comm to Environmental. "Mr. Knowles, please tell me you're keeping a watch down there."

She waited for a few moments. "Mr. Knowles?"

"You looking for me, sar?" Knowles stuck his head into Engineering Control.

"I was just trying to set the watch and Ms. Solomon tells me they don't have watches in engineering."

He shrugged. "Never have before. Why?"

"How do you monitor environmental status?"

He held up his tablet. "Slaved it to the console. It tells me if something goes out of balance."

Natalya sat back in her chair, suddenly aware that the entire room was staring at her. "Thank you, Mr. Knowles. If you have a moment, could we chat in my office?"

"Of course. We're clear until the old man decides to call navigation stations again."

"Ms. Solomon, if you'd care to join us?"

"Sure." Solomon's lips twitched like she might be trying to suppress a grin.

"The rest of you." Natalya paused, at a loss as to what to say. "See you later."

Natalya got up from the chair and beat the rest of the crew out of the control room only by virtue of moving the fastest. She slipped into the chief's office and took the chair behind the desk, bringing up the engineering overview display on her console before looking at Solomon and Knowles standing uncertainly by the door.

"Sorry. Come in. Sit. I need your help."

Knowles grinned and Solomon smiled as they each took a chair.

"Not exactly what you're used to?" Knowles asked.

"No. Nothing close. I'm having heart palpitations at the thought that nobody's on engineering watch."

Solomon's eyes widened slightly. "Really. It's no big deal." She jerked a thumb at Knowles. "He's been the only real environmental guy we've had and it's only his second trip."

"But surely you've had engineering officers before," Natalya said, her hands spread palm down on her desk as if to anchor her sanity.

"Well, sure. Steve's been our chief engineer for, gosh. I don't know. Three or four stanyers now."

"But he has no engineering background."

"Well, no, but he's an officer," Solomon said. "Isn't he?"

Knowles shrugged. "I never talked to him long enough to find out. Last trip he'd cruise through environmental a couple of times a week, ask how things were going, and sniff the air. Once he thought maybe a scrubber was off and would I look into it. That's it."

"Was it?"

Knowles shook his head. "Damn ship is a brick. With this crew we could probably go the whole round trip without changing out scrubber filters."

Natalya felt herself staring and had to look down at her hands. "You wouldn't actually, would you?"

Knowles laughed. "No. We'd be safe enough but the place would get a little whiffy."

Natalya looked up at the smile in his voice. "You're really an environmental systems specialist?"

"You want to see my degrees?"

"No, that's all right. Sorry. I'm just a little gun-shy." She looked at Solomon, who smiled back. "And your experience?"

"I learned propulsion and fields under old Henry. He'd been making the run almost since Kondur started them up a dozen stanyers ago."

"Did he have any formal training?"

"Damned if I know. He had the job and taught it to me so he could retire to Bar None and breed cattle." She paused. "Not personally breed. That is, not with his own—"

Natalya held up a hand. "I get it. Can I ask you some hypotheticals?"

"What? Like a test?" Solomon frowned.

"If you wouldn't mind. It would make me feel better."

Solomon glanced at Knowles and shrugged. "Sure. All right."

"What happens if the sail generator overheats?"

"Safety interlocks shut it down."

"How do you get them up and running again?"

"Wait for them to cool."

"Then what happens?"

"The interlocks reset themselves and we're back in business." Solomon shrugged. "Same thing with the grav keel generators."

"How do you find the cause of overheating?"

Solomon blinked and stared at Natalya. "We've only had it happen once and it was because some hot-shot on the bridge put out too much sail in a high wind. Strain gauges showed he shoulda reefed up a bit, but he thought it was fun."

"Oh." Natalya nodded. "Yeah, that would do it."

"We don't get much sail time, truth be told. We're usually in the Dark between systems. Only time we see them is when we get into a High Liner system like Albert or Siren." She shrugged. "No call for sails here. A little boost with the kicker and we're moving."

"Kicker ever failed?" Natalya asked.

"No," Solomon said shaking her head and looking down. "We had a fuel pump blow out on us once."

"Who fixed it?"

"We were on our way back from making a run. Jumped into Dark Knight and had just turned to decelerate when it went out and we lost the port engine. Fuel couplings kicked out so we didn't spew fuel everywhere. We called Kondur and he sent out a spare and a tech to install it."

"Why doesn't he have techs on the ship?" she asked.

Solomon shrugged. "You'd have to ask him."

Knowles leaned forward in his seat. "May I offer some insight?"

"Of course."

"Kondur's been making these runs once or twice a stanyer for as long as I've known. They were making the runs when I was a kid, before I went away to school. He's no fool but he's also not bound by the same regulations you're probably used to."

"How many ships has he lost?"

"None. He's been running this same ship the whole time."

"For a dozen stanyers?" Natalya felt the wind whoosh out of her in surprise.

"More like twenty," Solomon said. "This is a perk. People sign up for these runs stanyers in advance but it's tough getting the job."

"Why?"

"Why is it tough? Or why do they sign up?" Solomon asked.

"Either. Both."

"Competition. Past crew gets priority as long as they don't screw up. Old Henry had been running fields forever. I'm lucky he took a liking to me," Solomon said.

"He basically passed his berth to you," Natalya said.

"Yeah. In effect."

"Why does everybody want the job?"

"I don't know what you're used to makin', but most of us are gettin' paid enough on this one trip to live comfy for the next stanyer. Anything we do outside is gravy," Solomon said.

Knowles nodded. "That's my excuse. Kondur pays me a good salary to do a job I like, but this is like another whole stanyer's pay for three months playing aboard ship."

"How'd you get aboard?"

"Last guy screwed up. Stunk up the ship so bad Captain Trask wouldn't let him back on. Shipped him back from Dree on a hired packet and made him pay his own passage." Knowles shrugged.

"Ouch." Natalya winced at what must have been a hefty pile of credits.

"Did I pass?" Solomon asked.

"Yes, Ms. Solomon. You passed." Natalya sat back in her seat and looked up at the overhead. "I'm sorry. This flies in the face of everything I've grown up believing to be true."

Knowles grunted. "Yes, well, you ever think why those regulations exist?"

She looked at him, wondering where he was going. "Ship safety?"

"Really? Why?"

"Having people in the loop protects the ship from badly programmed automatic systems."

"How?" he asked, a small smile struggling to reach his lips.

"People see what doesn't make sense but a program can't recognize."

"Fair enough." Knowles crossed one long leg over the other as he sat back. "What happens when one of the environmental systems goes out of balance?"

"The computer flags it and flashes an alert to the watch stander."

"Exactly." He held up his tablet. "I'm the watch stander."

"You can't do it all."

He shrugged. "Why not? I have people I can tap if I need help with something. I can point Val at scrubber maintenance and she can get a couple of the boys to help her swap them out. What purpose does it serve to have somebody sitting there filling out make-work log entries?"

"In case the system goes wrong."

He smiled then. "No, it's to keep the people busy. Without having something to do, some reason to get up in the morning—or in many cases in the middle of the night—there's no reason to do so. The time can weigh heavily."

"You're suggesting that the CPJCT regulations governing ships and crews are so much busy work?" Natalya couldn't believe what she was hearing.

"Not at all. Well, maybe." Knowles shook his head. "I'm actually saying that the regulations are stupid and archaic. The on-board systems are more than capable of doing whatever the average untrained watch stander can do. At least in environmental. Don't you have a saying about the first rule of watch standing or something?"

"If something looks off, tell somebody," Natalya said.

"Precisely. Without me—or somebody with my skillset—aboard, if something went wrong in environmental, who would they tell?"

"I don't know."

"Me, either. Until you came aboard, I don't think Kondur ever put an engineer aboard." He nodded at Solomon. "Melinda here has been trained on the job. She's good at what she does, but if push comes to shove, we'd need to find somebody with the knowledge, skills, tools, and parts to make it go again. We all recognize that and it's why Mr. Kondur pays so well for these trips. We all know the risks, more or less." He shrugged. "Think about it. Catastrophic drive failure will take out the ship before we can respond. No amount of watch standing will help that. Same with fusactors, generators, even the Burlesons. Ever think of what would happen if we jump with one of them out of alignment? Or into an ice field?"

Natalya could think of nothing else to say. "You're right, Mr. Knowles. I hadn't really thought it through."

"Would the ship be safer with a watch set in the engine room?" Knowles shrugged. "I don't really know. I've got the division's main readouts right here on my tablet. I'll get the same warnings, the same alerts, the same notices wherever I am on the ship. Serious ones will wake me even if I'm asleep. Since I am trained in environmental systems, I'm also the one who's best prepared to fix it. I understand the decision to set watches. Or rather, the lack of decision. It's more of a default action. Like your response has been." He grinned at her. "You're the only person aboard who knows how those big chunks of machinery down there work. I mean really knows how they really work. Wouldn't it make most sense for *you* to be watching over the ship's engineering instead of having somebody like Mike Town, who knows what's normal but not what to do about anything that isn't?"

Solomon started to say something but Knowles leaned over to her. "No reflection on you, Mel. Mike knows which end of a wrench to hold, but he's no engineer."

Solomon nodded. "True. I take your point. He's turning into a fair mechanic, I must say."

"When he can control his temper," Knowles said.

"Granted," Solomon said.

"So? Any other questions, Ms. Regyri?"

She sat there, looking back and forth between them for several heartbeats. "No," she said. "You make a strong case. If we had a full roster of trained crew, I might make a different judgment but I see your point and I think you're right about it. All of it." She shrugged. "I'll just have to get used to it."

"Is there anything else, boss?" Knowles asked. "I'd like to grab a shower and a nap before we get called to stations again."

She glanced at the chronometer display on her console. "Yeah, I'm done. Thanks. Both of you. I'm having a bit of culture shock here even when I know the rules here are different."

Knowles smiled. "Knowing they're different and living the differences are two different things."

"You said it, brother," Solomon said.

They rose and Solomon led the way out of the office. Knowles turned back at the door. "You want this open or closed?"

"Open, please." She paused for a heartbeat. "And thanks again."

"Welcome. Sometime you should come see what we're doing in Environmental."

She nodded. "I suspect I'll have plenty of time."

He grinned and left her sitting there staring at the console and wondering if the accumulated stress and sleep deprivation was making her loopy.

Chapter Twenty-three
Deep Dark: 2363, June 10

After two days and six jumps, Natalya had to admit that the system seemed to work. Her tablet bipped her awake in the middle of the night for a tripped circuit breaker that took out the lighting in deck berthing, but that was the most significant issue. Knowles stayed on top of the environmental division, treating it more like a day worker job than a watch.

In reality a couple of days wasn't a lot of time for things to go wrong and they spent so much of that time either at navigation stations, getting ready for navigation stations, or recovering from navigation stations, there really wasn't a lot of time when a normal watch rotation would have mattered.

Natalya crossed paths with Zoya just before breakfast as they both tried to use the shower. Zoya looked like she'd been awake for most of the trip.

"Are you all right?" Natalya asked.

Zoya nodded through a yawn. "I've gotten some naps in but Trask has been on the bridge longer than I have." She shook her head and gave Natalya a rueful grin. "Man's got stamina, I'll give him that."

"When do we jump into Albert?"

"Should be around 0930. After that things should settle in."

"What's the deal, anyway?"

"We're jumping into Albert so we'll have the right vector for Siren. We don't have the kind of velocity that a straight jump in would have, so we're going to use Albert's primary and the sails to pick up a bit of speed and adjust our vector."

"Won't that look odd?" Natalya asked. "I thought the idea was to be low-key."

"Albert's not more than a mining outpost. Their orbital will be on the far side of their primary from where we'll be jumping in. They're not likely to see us at all."

"Blanchard's navigation?"

"Man's got the touch, I've gotta admit it. He's been within two points on every single jump."

"Can he do it when it counts?" Natalya asked. "You and I both know that's mostly luck."

"Yeah, it is, but if anybody can, he can." She yawned again. "We're positioned just right now for a short hop into Albert so even if he's off by five or ten points, we'll be in good shape on the other side of the primary and going in the right direction. You mind if we table this conversation for later? I need to get some of the sleep washed off before breakfast."

Natalya backed out of the small compartment. "Be my guest. I'll grab a quick splash when you're done."

Trask shambled into the wardroom at the stroke of 0600 and took his seat without preamble. Red rimmed his eyes and the bags under them looked like they should have routing tags. He eyed the cargo master's empty chair but said nothing beyond "Let's eat."

Blanchard looked like he'd just joined the crew. If the previous couple of days with their high pressure navigational demands had stressed him in any way, Natalya couldn't see it. Pritchard had spent the last two days amusing himself in the chief engineer's stateroom. He looked as fresh as Blanchard, with a freshly pressed uniform and a smile for everyone at the table.

The captain took the first helpings of eggs and grits and passed the plates to his right. Bray filled cups around the table and stepped back into the galley to return with a basket of fresh biscuits. The meal proceeded in near silence until the first of the food began to settle in. Trask nodded to himself and cleared his throat.

"Any problems?" he asked, looking at Natalya.

"None, Captain," she said.

"Heard you had a little dustup with Mike Town."

"Wind through the sails, Skipper. We both learned something from it."

"He give you any guff since?"

"None. Been sharp on the boards and right on the knob."

He gave her a shallow grin. "Solomon box his ears for you?"

Natalya shrugged. "She might have. I didn't see or hear of it."

Trask nodded and looked at Zoya. "Nice work at the conn, Ms. Usoko. You getting tired yet?"

"Thank you, Captain." She started to say something else but a yawn caught her sideways and she had to laugh. "Just a bit, perhaps."

"We'll be in the Albert system for a couple of days. I want you to take twenty-four hours off. We'll get some of the boys and girls to mind the helm. I'll want a regular bridge watch for Siren. TIC can't see inside the ship, but if they call, we need to be able to give the right answer."

"Aye, aye, Captain. I'll be ready for a bit of sleep."

He looked at Blanchard. "You seem to be hanging on pretty well."

Blanchard smiled. "These first few days running out of the Dark are always challenging. I prepared for it before we left."

Trask snorted. "What'd you do? Sleep for a week?"

Blanchard nodded. "Actually, more like three days. Also played with the kids. Read a little. Let the wife chase me around the house until I caught her." He smiled. "I hit the lock ready to work."

Trask chuckled and shook his head. "Glad you're here, Charlie."

"I'm still glad to be here, Tom."

Trask looked at Pritchard. "You've had it pretty easy this trip, Steven. What you been up to the last couple of days. Haven't seen much of you."

Pritchard smiled and finished chewing the last of his biscuit before answering. "Mostly reading and watching holos in my stateroom. It's rather relaxing being off the line at work."

Trask snorted. "I dare say. Ms. Regyri working out for you, then?"

Pritchard smiled at Natalya. "Well, Captain, I must say she's been a miracle worker. Since she's been aboard, I haven't been awakened once by any engineering issue. Nobody's bothered me. It's been a relief, frankly."

"I'll bet it has," the captain said with a wink at Natalya.

The captain sat back in his chair then and waved his hand at the table. "You can clear this away, Mr. Bray. I think we're done except for the coffee."

"Aye, aye, Captain."

"If we're done here, I think I'd like to try to grab a short nap, if that's all right, Captain?" Zoya said.

"Of course, Ms. Usoko. See you on the bridge at 0900."

"Thank you, Captain." She stood and nodded around the table before heading for the door.

Natalya started to follow her but the captain caught her eye and lifted his chin in a kind of reverse nod. "Hang in here a few, if you would, Ms. Regyri."

"Of course, Captain." She settled back into her seat and saw the skipper give Blanchard a nod.

"If I might be excused, Captain?" he said.

"Certainly, Charlie. You've earned a bit of a break. Eisley's got the helm up there until we jump into Albert. Take your time."

Blanchard nodded, smiled at Natalya, and made his exit.

The captain looked at Pritchard. He didn't say anything. Simply raised an eyebrow.

"Oh, yes." Pritchard folded his napkin and placed it beside his coffee cup. "I'll just go do something, shall I?"

Trask grinned at him. "Try not to strain yourself, Steven."

"I'll be careful, Captain." Pritchard smiled at Natalya and scurried out after Blanchard.

Trask sat for a few moments, staring into his coffee cup. A smile flirted with the corners of his mouth. "How are you finding it, Natalya?"

Natalya shrugged. "Not exactly what I expected. It still makes me a little nervous not having a live engineman keeping watch in either central or environmental. It doesn't feel safe to me."

"Any problems?"

"Not really."

"What about Town?"

"He just needed to test me, I think. Solomon took him away and had a few quiet words with him. He's been fine for the last couple of days."

"Pritchard?" he asked, glancing over at her for a moment before staring at the cup again. "You locked him out of the system pretty fast."

"I had Zoya give him a guest profile to keep him from fiddling with the machinery. The original user profile gave him access to do anything he wanted to the ship's systems. He already told me he has no engineering background at all."

"This is his fifth trip. You think he'd start messing with the drives now?" His gaze lifted from the mug and leveled on her.

"No, Skipper. I don't. From a liability standpoint, it seemed a risk that we could avoid by chopping it off at the source. He hasn't mentioned anything to me about it. Is it a problem?"

Trask shook his head. "No, and I think that surprised me more than seeing it happen."

"How so?"

"Pritchard's a bit of an odd duck. He's been with the ship quite a while. He's always been the engineering chief even though he really has no qualifications for it. I expected he'd complain about not being able to see what was going on back there. He hasn't. I'm not sure he's even noticed."

"Captain, can I ask?"

"Why he's chief if he has no qualifications?"

"Yeah."

"His name is clear and validated for Engineering Chief in the CPJCT databases. We'll use that to order spares and tankage when we dock."

Natalya felt her eyeballs try to pop out of her skull in surprise. "I didn't think that was possible."

The captain gave a low chuckle from deep in his chest. "That's what makes it so useful. It's not supposed to be possible. Any more than it's possible for us to be the *Melbourne Maru* out of New Kyoto in Ciroda."

"We changed the transponder code?"

"Yep. It was scrubbed out and reset before we left the station. It'll get changed back when we get home."

"What ship is it normally?"

He chuckled again. "Normal's in your perspective. Between runs, she's the *Folly*. Kondur uses her for running bulk cargo around Toe-Hold space. He's got a regular crew of malingerers and ne'er-do-wells who run it around for him."

"Why don't they make this run?"

"They need a skipper with a clean name and I can't complain. Assuming we get home, I'll make a nice wage for three months of nail-biting." He grinned at her. "TIC keeps an eye on us, but they're never sure who we are or where we're going. I'm pretty sure we've got a couple of TIC people in the crew, but we're not doing anything serious enough to warrant breaking their covers to do something about it."

"Why are they here, then?"

He shrugged a shoulder. "Intel, mostly. They want to know where we are, what we're doing there, and what we're going to do next."

"So, what about the transponder? If they know you can change it, won't that make things harder?"

Trask shrugged his shoulder again. "They already know. They've known for stanyers. It's not illegal out here."

"It will be when we jump into Siren. Even Albert, for that matter."

"And so is trading a can full of rocks without proper provenance."

"How can you do that?"

"Easy. We're not docking at Siren." He paused. "At least, not right away."

"Then how is this going to work?"

He grinned at her like a boy with a frog in his pocket. "Siren's Confederation, but they allow private platforms and stations to set up around the belts. We'll dock at one of them, swap the cans, and move on almost before anybody knows we're moored."

"What about ordering tankage and spares?"

"Once we're buttoned up with the cargo, we'll dock. By then the cargo will be legit. It'll show the correct provenance and routing to go back to Ciroda." He shrugged. "Only thing is, it's not going to Ciroda. We'll take good care of it at Dark Knight."

"So basically they're turning a blind eye," Natalya said.

"Yes. We'll slide in and slide out. Our little birdies will get a chance to go ashore and tweet while we're there, but as long as we don't ring any orbital alarm bells, TIC won't bother us."

"Because it serves their purposes."

"Yes."

Natalya considered the idea. "What purposes?"

The captain didn't answer right away. After a few moments he asked, "How much did your father tell you about Toe-Hold space?"

"He gave me the basic history. How it seeded the area. Did the exploration and tagging so the Bureau of Exploration and, later, the CPJCT knew what systems were commercially viable."

"Did he tell you about closing their ports to us?"

"No."

"It's because they never did."

"Then why all the sneak and hide?"

"What they did was establish a rule that made our operations untenable. CPJCT and their enforcement arm exist to keep the orbitals safe, the credits flowing, and the disruptive influences to a minimum."

"That doesn't answer the question," Natalya said.

"Early on, TIC discovered that their plan had a fatal flaw. People."

"Dad mentioned something about that. Psychopaths and the like."

"So, there's also a mindset that separates those who toe the CPJCT line from the people who itch under the weight of that much regulation. Almost from the beginning TIC recognized the difficulty in keeping a really tight lid on."

"So Toe-Hold became the relief valve," Natalya said. "This I knew, but not how it worked."

"Yep. And it only works if it's clandestine. At least in name."

"That's the part I'm struggling with."

"Think about it for a tick. If it's sanctioned by the authority you're trying to escape, are you going to trust it?"

Natalya sat back in her chair and examined that idea. "So by making it illegal, it filters out those who just want to poke a thumb in society's eye?"

Trask shook his head. "No, those people are why TIC continues. They need a way to manage the people who aren't willing to stand up and move out."

"Then why?"

"You had it a tick ago," the captain said.

"The relief valve."

"What happens when too much pressure builds up in a tank?" he asked.

"The relief valve bleeds off the excess. Vents it into space usually."

"Does it bleed off everything?"

"No, just enough to keep the tank from rupturing."

"Toe-Hold bleeds off the excess social pressure," Trask said.

The logic of it snapped into Natalya's head. "Being illegal means that only those people who are willing to escape by any means possible actually go."

"It's a crude valve but it's worked for a couple of centuries now. Those who just want to burn it down? Those who want to cheat the system? They run into TIC. Those who just want to escape have a path. It's tough enough that you have to really want to escape, but easy enough to do once you've crossed that mental threshold."

"Heroes need villains," Natalya said.

"Yeah. Where'd you hear that?"

"Something my father used to say." She smiled at the memory. "He'd get on these tirades about how both sides held the other up as the villain because they each needed somebody to be against."

"Your ole man is a pretty sharp operator."

After a few heartbeats of silence, Natalya said, "So this little production we're taking into Siren isn't really as risky as it's been sold as."

The captain sipped his coffee before speaking. "Yes and no. CPJCT's systems will examine us closely to make sure we're who we say. They can't allow Toe-Holders to bring in unauthorized cargo or operate counter to their regulations. You're a legit engineering third—doing a great job, by the by."

"Thanks."

"I'm a legit captain, although my Master's license was revoked about two decades ago."

"Nobody will check it?"

"Oh, they'll check but they'll find that the license was reinstated just before I flew our first load into CPJCT space."

"Was it?" Natalya asked.

"The records show it was."

"Do I want to know how?"

He grinned at her. "You know the boys over at High Tortuga run the banks for the whole Western Annex, right?"

"Yep."

"They might have put in a backdoor when they set up the banking system for CPJCT."

Natalya nodded. "I knew they put a lot into that system. Dad took great glee in pointing out that credits earned in Toe-Hold spend just as easily in CPJCT space."

"And vice versa," the captain said.

"So what's keeping you in Toe-Hold space?" she asked. "Couldn't you just pick up where you left off?"

The captain smiled at her. "I probably could."

"Ah," Natalya said.

"You ever wonder why CPJCT requires all these watches?" Trask asked.

"Safety."

"Employment," the captain said. "They need to have a lot of jobs for people to keep them busy and earning so they can pay for the goods and services they use."

"That's basically what Knowles said. But compared to all the people working for the corporations?" Natalya asked. "Fleet's not that big."

Trask shrugged. "I may be a little cynical. Does it really make that much difference to have a person there compared to having your tablet wake you up if something goes wrong?"

"The whole idea gives me hives," Natalya said and rubbed her arms. "I mean, I'm not always awake on the *Peregrine*, but the systems are a lot simpler."

"And you don't have a long way to go to fix whatever's complaining," Trask said with a nod. "I'm still not convinced that this isn't all just make-work."

"Knowles agrees with you. He's covering Environmental from his tablet. What about the bridge?" Natalya asked.

"When we're ballistic—like now—there's not a lot for the bridge crew to do. We're out in the Deep Dark. There's nothing we *can* do if a rock has our name on it. There's nobody else within a few parsecs of us. Mostly it's programmed burns and waiting for the capacitors to charge."

"I get that, Skipper, but what about when we jump into Albert and then to Siren?"

"Yeah, we'll need to keep a minimum watch up there. We'll be under sail so we'll need somebody on the helm. Packets are small enough that the autopilot can handle variations. We're too big for that. Someday maybe they'll get the systems to be responsive enough but for now we still need a hand at the helm. We also need to answer any calls that come in which means one of the officers needs to be there in case it's TIC." He pursed his lips and shrugged. "We usually have somebody on the generators down in engineering while we're under sail. It's mostly superstition, if you ask me."

Natalya kept her mouth shut and her eyes down.

"Why'd you want to come out to the Toe-Holds?" the skipper asked after a few moments.

She glanced up at the sudden conversational course change. "Never considered doing anything else."

"Then why'd you go to Port Newmar?"

"My mother insisted. She and Dad both went so she thought I should." Natalya took a deep breath and blew it out slowly through her nose as she considered. "It was probably a good thing."

"That where you learned to fight?" The captain's eyes twinkled a bit.

"I'll admit that it's where I honed my skill." She shrugged. "It came easy and that made me a target for the more testosterone-poisoned in my classes. I got good and stayed there."

"You're fast. I'll give you that." He tipped his mug and drained the last of the coffee. "Albee never saw you coming."

"That was kinda the point."

"You'll have to watch your back when we get home."

Natalya smiled. "Yeah. It's a habit I got into at the academy."

He nodded and pushed his empty coffee mug away. "You're more than we bargained for, but I'm pretty sure we're getting the best of the deal. Anybody gives you any crap, I've got your back." He peered at her like she should know what he was talking about.

"Thanks, Skipper. I'm still feeling my way and trying not to get too distracted when things aren't always what I think they should be."

"If you can do that, Ms. Regyri, you're head and shoulders above pretty much everybody else on this ship." He grinned. "Myself included."

"Thank you, Captain."

"Thank you, Ms. Regyri. You're dismissed."

She gave him a nod and stood. "Probably better make a run down to the engine room and see if it's still there. We're jumping at 0900?"

"If the capacitors are charged."

"We'll be ready."

Chapter Twenty-four
Albert System: 2363, June 10

The jump into Albert left them on the far side of the system's primary from the orbital and a long way out in the periphery. The captain ordered the sail and keel deployed, and the ship settled in for the first of the long waits as they used the kickers and the sails to eke out a bit more velocity before the final jump into Siren.

Luncheon in the wardroom proved to be a haphazard affair, with the captain taking the first bridge watch and leaving the other officers to fend for themselves. Even the hermit cargo master came out of hiding to join them.

They'd only been underway a couple of days, but Josh Lyons looked a bit worse for wear and smelled like he'd been living in the same uniform the whole time. Luckily he sat far enough away from Natalya that she only got periodic whiffs.

Pritchard turned up his nose at the man, but Blanchard tried to reach out to him.

"Anything we can do to help, Josh?" Blanchard asked.

"Bugger off. All right?" Lyons scowled across the table and grabbed a biscuit from the plate.

"Just asking," Blanchard said, holding up a hand in surrender. "I'm here if you need anything."

Lyons shook his head but didn't offer any further unpleasantness.

"I still don't see how we're going to get up enough velocity to be believable," Zoya said, looking at Blanchard.

Blanchard shrugged. "We'll be a few extra days sliding into Siren. Nothing to be done about it without spending too much time here."

"We've been using the kickers pretty hard," Natalya said. "Our tankage is down about half since leaving Dark Knight Station."

Zoya gave a low whistle. "That's a lot of fuel."

"The sails will give us a bit of a boost. Every little bit helps this far out from the primary," Blanchard said. "We'll angle the fields to give us a bit more angular momentum relative to the resident fireball, but we'll be jumping at about 70 percent of normal velocity."

"Won't that look funny to TIC?" Zoya asked.

Blanchard shook his head. "I'd be surprised if they even noticed. We can delay slowing down so it'll look like we jumped in faster by the time we deploy the sails and settle in for the ride to Moe's."

"The sails are still not going to add much in the way of velocity this far out from the primary and with that kind of angle," Zoya said.

Blanchard smiled at her. "You know we've done this before, right?"

Zoya blushed and focused on her coffee mug. "Sorry. I'm just nervous."

Pritchard said, "Oh, you should have seen me on my first trip. I sweated so much I practically had to burn my uniform to dry it out when we got back."

The image left Natalya trying not to retch. "You seem to have adjusted now, Chief."

"I'm doing my best." He smiled at Natalya. "You've been a godsend. I've always lived in fear that something would happen to the ship and we'd be stuck out here forever."

"We'd not be out here forever," Blanchard said.

Pritchard looked up sharply and tilted his head the tiniest fraction to the left.

"We'd run out of food within a few months," Blanchard said, his face a deadpan mask.

Pritchard's face paled. "You're not helping."

Blanchard smiled. "Sorry, Steve. A small—if ill-considered—joke."

Pritchard nodded, but pushed his plate back and stood. "I think I've had enough. If you'll excuse me?" He didn't wait for a reply but scooted out of the wardroom.

Natalya glanced at Zoya, who shrugged.

"Steve's all right," Blanchard said. "He can let his imagination get away with him sometimes."

"What would you know about that?" Lyons said, his voice low and almost menacing in its intensity.

All eyes turned to him. Natalya had almost forgotten he was there.

"Easy, Josh," Blanchard said.

"Don't patronize me, you bullock. It's dangerous out here. Any little mishap and we're all goners. You know that, right?"

"That's why we try to be careful, Josh."

"One mistake. One slip up. One stray rock on a trajectory from hell and we're dead. We're sailing with a crew of misfits, morons, and malcontents. Who's gonna save our backsides when the devil heats the griddle?" He gripped his fork as if he might lash out with it in his anger. His knuckles turned white from the strain.

"It's always been like this, Josh." Blanchard's voice stayed low and even. One finger looped through the handle on his coffee mug and he sat slouched in his seat as if engaged in a bit of friendly repartee with a shipmate. "Nothing's changed since the last trip."

Lyons groaned and shook his head. "Everything's changed." He jerked to his feet, throwing his silver down on the table so hard it skittered halfway across before coming to rest against the water carafe in the center of the table. "It's impossible." He followed Pritchard out of the wardroom, his footsteps clomping up the ladder to officer country.

Blanchard gave a small sigh. He lifted his coffee mug in a toast. "And then there were three."

"Is he going to be all right?" Zoya asked.

"No," Blanchard said. "With any luck, he won't do anything foolish before we dock. Beyond that, we just have to keep an eye on him and hope for the best."

"Lemme guess. He's got a clean record with CPJCT," Natalya said.

"All we need is his thumb," Blanchard said. He paused and looked up at the overhead. "We'll need to get somebody else for the next trip, I'm afraid."

Zoya slumped in her seat and fiddled with the knife beside her plate. "It is a risky business," she said.

"Not you, too," Natalya said.

Zoya shook her head and gave them a small smile. "No. I've been sailing as long as I can remember. I don't have any intention of stopping any time soon."

Blanchard nodded. "But you've seen it go wrong."

"Oh, yes. That I have." Zoya's focus turned inward and she pressed her lips together as if to keep the words from spilling out.

Natalya nodded at the empty chair beside Blanchard. "I thought we were getting a third mate."

Blanchard shrugged a shoulder. "Kondur couldn't find anybody who could step in on a few stans' notice. The nearest body was out in the belts and the skipper didn't want to wait for him to come in."

"I hope that doesn't bite him in the butt," Zoya said, shifting in her seat. "I don't know that I'm ready to be first mate."

Blanchard smiled at her. "You're better than Albee ever was. Just keep doin' what you're doin' and it'll be fine."

"How long before we jump into Siren?" Natalya asked.

"A week, I think," Blanchard said. "Then four or five weeks before we dock at Moe's."

Natalya nodded, the schedule ticking along in her head. "Good. I've got time to do a spares inventory before we jump."

Blanchard grinned. "All this drama and you're thinking about spares?"

"Hey, spares are what will keep us going if it all goes pear-shaped." She grinned. "I'm also going to keep an eye on the engineering watch stander and check in with Knowles to make sure he's got what we need to get home while we're still breathing."

"I like your plan," Blanchard said. "And I'm glad you're aboard." His happy-go-lucky smile crinkled the corners of his eyes.

Chapter Twenty-five
Albert System: 2363, June 22

Natalya took one last tour of the engine room, double-checking the Burleson drives. She patted the dark green casings in passing. They felt warm to the touch, almost like something alive. After the short turnaround jumps they'd pulled coming into Albert from Dark Knight, she felt a little better for letting them cool down properly.

"Touch for luck?" Knowles asked from the foot of the ladder.

She smiled and shrugged. "Maybe something like that. Sometimes you can feel the vibrations if they're off a little."

"Something you learned at the academy?"

She gave a short laugh. "My father. Before I went to Port Newmar. They laughed at me for the superstition." She reached out and stroked the case again. She imagined she could feel the whole ship around her like a living thing even if the whole idea was too fanciful for words.

He smiled in return. "Did you ever diagnose a drive that way?"

"No." She shook her head. "My father did. Or at least he said he did."

"Seriously?" His eyes widened just a touch.

"We were jumping back to Valar from Dunsany Roads in the *Peregrine*. Made about three jumps and had the fourth one scheduled up, but he pulled the nav plot and went aft to engineering. He laid his hand on the drive and stood there for what seemed like forever. Probably three or four ticks."

"How old were you?"

"Thirteen? Fourteen? Something like that."

"What'd he do then?"

"Just nodded and grinned at me. Said, 'Yeah. She's out of alignment.' He got out his toolbox and we pulled the cover and spent the next stan and a half realigning the coils."

"Alone in the Deep Dark?" Knowles shook his head. "That takes some serious gonads."

"It's not that much different than doing it in a dock," Natalya said.

"Except there's nobody there to bail you out if you mess it up."

She snorted. "Nobody to pick up the pieces if you jump into a rock, either."

He nodded and made a stroke in the air with his forefinger. "Good point."

"How are we in the swamp?" she asked.

He gave a short shrug. "Good. Gasses are fine. Nobody's started a fire so the particulates are actually down a bit from when we left."

"There was a fire?"

"No." He ran a hand down the ladder's safety rail. "Dust. Surprising how much of it accumulates when the ship's not in use. Even in a vacuum."

"Having people aboard helps that?"

"Having the scrubbers running hard and having people actually cleaning the surfaces helps that."

Natalya looked around. "I suppose it does. I didn't realize other people were cleaning."

"Captain Trask likes to keep a neat ship."

"Busy hands," Natalya said.

"Oh, you know the captain?" He grinned.

The overhead speakers clicked and Zoya's voice echoed around the engine room. "All hands to navigation stations. All hands to navigation stations."

"Speaking of the captain. I think he wants to jump this afternoon," Natalya said.

Knowles hopped off the ladder and headed for the environmental sections. "Seems like. See you after."

Natalya waved and ran up the ladder, slid into Engineering Control and plopped into her seat. "Everybody here?"

Solomon sighed. "Almost. Ms. Pearson had a last moment trip to the head."

A clattering of footsteps in the passageway heralded the arrival of the slightly flushed Pearson. "Sorry, sar." She put a hand on her stomach. "It couldn't be helped."

"Rather there than here, Ms. Pearson. Let's get on with it," Natalya said and waved the woman into her seat.

"Now everybody's here," Solomon said.

"Power ready?" Natalya asked.

"We're loaded for bear," Collie said.

"Grav?"

Pearson made a fast scan of her console and nodded. "Grav ready."

"Propulsion?"

Solomon looked over Town's shoulder and nodded. "Ready to go, sar. Burlesons are charged. Safety interlocks on. Waiting for the bridge request."

"They're probably having a tea party," Natalya said. "They'll get to us when they're ready."

The crew laughed. Some a bit dutifully, but the tension in the room dialed back a notch.

A window popped up on Town's console. "Bridge requests Burleson control."

"Pull the safety interlocks, Mr. Town," Natalya said.

He tapped a few keys and a red warning showed on his screen. "Interlocks off. Bridge has control."

Natalya made a big show of pulling out her seat belt and strapping in.

Solomon looked at her, one eyebrow raised. "You expecting heavy weather?"

"Just taking precautions."

A countdown timer popped on the main engineering display.

"Burleson's engaged," Town said.

"Seems like we're going somewhere," Solomon said, still standing behind his shoulder.

The timer zeroed and the capacitors discharged, bending the fabric of space-time for a few heartbeats while the ship slid through the hole into Siren.

"Time to recharge, Mr. Town?"

Town slapped a few keys and shook his head. "Reporting six stans."

Solomon leaned over his shoulder. "Wonder where we jumped to."

Natalya shook her head. "Sometimes you just jump long," she said. "At least we're not planning on jumping again anytime soon."

After a couple of ticks, Zoya's voice drifted out of the speakers. "Secure from navigation stations. Set normal watch."

"Thank you, people," Natalya said. "We're in TIC country now. Stay alert and keep the logs up to date with the current stuff."

"What? Not the made-up stuff we filled them with already?" Solomon asked, a cheeky grin on her face.

"Exactly not that," Natalya said, grinning back. "If we get a safety boarding, we don't want them to see anything too outrageous."

Solomon flashed a fancy-dress-party salute. "Aye, aye, sar."

Natalya chuckled. "Maybe best to keep that low-key until you're ready to do it right."

Solomon shrugged.

Natalya pulled the latch on her seat belt and left them sorting out the watch rota for Siren. She'd posted one already with copies to Knowles and Solomon. She wondered if either of the two had looked at them.

In the meantime, she headed for the wardroom. Zoya had the bridge watch, but she hoped to bump into Blanchard when he came down for coffee.

Natalya found Chef Marah had worked her magic on some fancy cookies. A tidy plate waited for her in the center of the wardroom table alongside a thermal carafe of coffee, the warm smell of vanilla mingling with the dark coffee aroma. Nobody else had appeared so she grabbed a mug and poured some for herself, debating on whether to respect rank order and wait for Captain Trask, or grab a cookie before anybody arrived.

Just as her willpower weakened, voices in the passageway warned her of Captain Trask's imminent arrival. He smiled at her when he came through the door. "You made good time up the spine, Ms. Regyri."

"I heard there were cookies and didn't want to miss them."

Blanchard followed the captain into the wardroom and Pritchard sauntered in behind him. With few preliminaries, Trask took his seat and the rest followed suit. The captain started the carafe around the table in one direction and the plate of cookies in the other, after helping himself to each first. "So. Comments?" he asked, looking at Blanchard.

"I'm surprised," Blanchard said. "You almost never jump exactly where you want."

Trask nodded and sipped his coffee before answering. "I'd call it damn fine navigation."

Blanchard sighed and shook his head. "Luck. All it is."

"I'll take luck," the captain said with a wink at Pritchard. "How about you, Steven? You not averse to a bit of good luck?"

Pritchard nibbled on the edge of a cookie and nodded. "You bet, Captain. Mostly I have bad luck so any good luck that comes my way—well—I just look at it as a down payment on balancing the karmic scales."

Trask laughed. "Good luck with getting those leveled out. Most people want them tipped firmly in their own favor."

"So true, Captain. So true," Pritchard said, addressing his cookie with small, rabbity bites.

"You, Ms. Regyri?" Trask asked. "Luck work for you?"

"I'll take it when I can get it. Luck favors the prepared, but all the preparation in the world won't save you if luck goes against you."

Trask shot a glance at Blanchard. "We seem to have sailed with a bunch of philosophers, Charlie."

Blanchard swallowed a sip of coffee before responding. "Takes one to know one, Skip."

Trask chuckled and nodded. "Guilty, I suppose." He looked at Natalya again. "Your father's words?"

"Yes, sar."

"Sounds like him." The captain stared at her for several heartbeats as if trying to read something on her forehead.

Natalya finished off her cookie and washed it down with the coffee while he continued his perusal. "Do I have grease on my face, Captain?" she asked.

He smiled and shook his head. "No. Perhaps you'd stop by the cabin when you're done here?"

"Of course, Captain." Natalya felt a cold chill down her back.

Trask grinned. "Nothing bad. You're not in trouble."

"Was I that obvious?"

"It was the worried frown and shudder, I think," Blanchard said over his coffee mug.

"Just want to touch base," the captain said. "But I need to cut the party short and get my official reports ready in case we're boarded." He stood. "You all enjoy the cookies." He snagged a couple more off the plate. "Except these two. They're coming with me." He shambled out of the wardroom already nibbling.

"Anyone care to bet they don't last as far as the cabin?" Pritchard asked.

Blanchard laughed. "Sucker bet."

Natalya ate another cookie, washing the sweetness down with a healthy swig of coffee. She glanced at Pritchard out of the corner of her eyes before looking at Blanchard. "So, it was a good jump?"

Blanchard nodded. "Almost never see them so close to the mark." He took a bite and examined the cookie as if he'd never seen one before. "Anything unusual about it from your end?"

"Used about half again as much power as I would have expected. Three BUs isn't that far with the legs this girl has."

"I wondered about that," Blanchard said. "I saw the capacitor drain on the astrogation console."

Natalya nodded and snagged another cookie from the plate. "These things are deadly."

Pritchard nodded and took a couple more for himself.

Natalya felt Blanchard's gaze on her but didn't look up. "I should probably go make sure the boys and girls aren't fighting in the back," she said. She popped the last bit of cookie into her mouth and drained her coffee mug.

"Is that likely?" Pritchard asked, his eyes wide in surprise.

Natalya stood. "Not likely, no. I left them trying to sort out their watches and it's probably time I went down to arbitrate the results." She smiled at Pritchard. "Unless you wanna come down and do it?"

He laughed and took a big bite out of a cookie.

Blanchard gave her a little salute with his index finger. His expression looked like a cross between amusement and sympathy.

She found engineering central in good order. A young woman wearing a regulation shipsuit with wiper insignia at the collars looked up as she entered. "Everything all right?"

The woman nodded. "Yep."

Natalya tried to put a name with the face and failed. "I'm sorry. Have we met?"

"I was at the launch briefing but no, not officially. I'm Elizabeth Reisine. Everybody calls me ER."

Natalya stuck out a hand. "Natalya Regyri. Call me whatever you like unless there's CPJCT people in hearing."

Reisine's eyes widened in surprise, but she shook Natalya's hand. "What should I call you if they are?"

"The preferred mode when on duty is 'sar.'"

ER grinned. "I figgered that much."

"Ms. Regyri is usually safe when people can hear. So you're really a wiper?" Natalya asked.

"As I understand it, you only need somebody to hire you and give you the title," Reisine said. "That would make me a wiper."

Natalya leaned a shoulder against the door jamb and crossed her arms. She felt herself warming to the woman. "That would, indeed. You know the first duty of an engineering watch stander?"

"If I don't know what I'm seeing, call somebody."

"Perfect. Who told you that?"

"Mel."

Natalya couldn't place the name at first. "Oh, Ms. Solomon."

"Yep. She's my boss."

"Did she tell you who to call?"

"You. She said you're the only one who would know how to fix it if it went wrong."

"And you believed her?"

Reisine shrugged. "No reason not to. I know nobody else aboard has the skills—or knowledge, for that matter. You're the most likely. Mike Town speaks highly of you."

Natalya felt her eyebrows rise at that revelation. "Does he, now."

"You coulda kicked him," she said with a small shrug. "A lot of people would have."

"Not my style."

"You moved pretty fast." Reisine shrugged. "Usually the new guy has to prove something."

"I made the only point I needed to."

Reisine's head wobbled back and forth for a moment and her gaze sought the overhead while she ruminated visibly. "I can see that." She paused and glanced up at Natalya. "Can I ask a question?"

"Sure."

"Can you really fix it?"

"Fix what?"

Reisine's shoulders rose and fell. "Whatever's broken."

"In theory. It'll depend on what's broken and how badly. I'm not going to try to mend a broken arm."

Reisine snickered. "I was thinking more about the engines and stuff."

"I can fix most of the stuff in engineering, assuming we've got the parts and the tools. Some things we need to be docked for. Others would need a dry dock. Flushing the fusactors needs some specialized gear that only makes sense when docked, even though it's not that big a deal when you have the gear."

Reisine nodded. "I get it. No big with the right tools and damn near impossible without them."

"Precisely. I know how to do it, but getting it done while we're out here under sail would be challenging. We could vent the core, but getting it refilled again?" Natalya shook her head. "Not going to happen."

"I can see that." Reisine nodded. "Thanks. Sar."

Natalya grinned and then straightened as if stabbed. "Crap. I was supposed to stop at the cabin."

"You in trouble already?" Reisine asked.

"I wasn't," Natalya said over her shoulder as she bolted for the spine.

She knocked on the door just a few heartbeats later.

"Yeah. Come in."

She opened the door and stepped into the cabin.

Trask sat at his desk, glancing up from his screen for a moment. "Oh, Regyri. Good. I need a couple of ticks to finish this. Have a seat." He nodded to the visitor's chair. He returned his attention to the screen and after a bit of scrolling and a few keystrokes, closed it down. "Now," he said, and looked at her, his hands folded one on the other in front of him. "Can you pass a TIC safety inspection?"

"Me personally?"

He chuckled. "Well, yes, but I was thinking more about the engineering department."

"Depends on how deep in the weeds they get. I don't know that the logs will stand up to any kind of scrutiny but the spaces themselves, sure."

"So we've got the requisite number of fire extinguishers and emergency suits?"

Natalya got a sinking feeling in her gut. "I don't know. I haven't checked them."

"Might wanna get on that. Whatever we need, get it in a replenishment order."

"And hope we don't need it if it's missing?" she asked.

"That, too." Trask shrugged. "Not like we can buy them until we dock. They might gig us for not checking before we left Margary."

"Margary?"

"That's where they think we're coming from."

She gave her head a vigorous shake. "Of course. Sorry, not thinking."

His smile reached the corners of his eyes. "You're doing great. I'm glad Verkol got you two on the team. Sailing without an engineer is a bit like swinging from a trapeze without a net. We made too many trips with Pritchard. He's comfortable in the role, but paper-thin in a pinch."

Natalya sighed. "I don't get it. Why are we flying so close to disaster?"

Trask tapped the top of his desk with the tips of his fingers. "First, we're not that close. The ship got a full engineering assessment before we left. We didn't count on finding an engineer."

Natalya opened her mouth to speak but Trask held up a hand.

"Lemme finish. This is a milk run for us. It's relatively short, relatively clean, and we're not hauling anything actually illegal on either end. We've made longer, more difficult passages under worse conditions. That's probably why Albee thought he could play games and get away with them."

Natalya sat back in her chair. "Why'd you—" She bit down on her next phrase. "Sorry. Because he was what you had."

"Yeah. The long and the short of it. He has a clean thumb and all the right marks in his personnel jacket at CPJCT." Trask shrugged. "Verkol pays the freight. He says sail, we sail."

"Would he do more if he had better crews?" she asked.

Trask sat very still for several moments, his gaze focused inward and his mouth slightly open as if to speak. He came back from his mental walkabout and tilted his head. "How do you mean?"

"He makes a run every stanyer, you said."

"Yeah. We put together a run about that often."

"Why not run them all the time?"

Trask shook his head. "Honestly? I don't know."

"What's this ship doing the rest of the year? Who's her crew? What are they doing now?"

Trask looked down at his hands, now flattened palms-down on his desk. "I always thought she was flying around Toe-Hold space and that the crew got a nice three-month vacation." He looked up. "Why do you ask?"

Natalya shrugged. "Something Knowles said. The ship was dusty. Like nobody'd been aboard."

Trask's eyebrows rose. "Dusty? In a vacuum?"

"Particulates. I'm not an environmental specialist but he claims they pile up if nobody's around to clean and dust."

"That seems odd."

"Does to me, too, but he's got the degree in it. I'm not going to question him," Natalya said.

Trask pursed his lips and frowned. "So, assume he's right. The ship's idle for over half the stanyer."

"You're the captain," she said. "You know how expensive ships are. They need to be earning their keep."

He gave a half nod. "Granted. You thinking of teaching granny how to suck eggs?"

"Not at all. Just trying to figure out the dynamic of this whole thing. It feels odd."

"That's just fleet talking."

Natalya considered that for a few heartbeats. "Maybe."

Trask gave her a little nod. "What would you do differently?"

"If it were my call?"

He nodded again.

"I know there are good experienced hands out there in the High Line. I've seen them on the stations. Talked to them. Most of them don't even know that Toe-Hold space is out here. They've just been brought up where it wasn't mentioned in polite company."

"Like Zoya?" Trask asked, a smile playing at the corners of his mouth.

She shrugged. "Like Zoya. At least she knew it was there, but she's been spoon-fed the wild frontier story. She's having a bit of culture shock."

"So, you think you could recruit a full crew for us?" Trask said, the corners of his eyes crinkled in amusement.

"It would take time, but yeah."

"Who would you hire?"

Natalya took a couple of deep breaths and let them out slowly, considering the problem before speaking. "The idea is to blend in, right?"

"Blend in?"

"We want to look just like any other Barbell. Crew needs to look like fleet, act like fleet."

Trask made a face. "There's fleet and there's fleet. A lot of the family and co-op outfits don't look a lot different than we do."

"Granted, but is the *Melbourne Maru* registered to a family or co-op?"

Trask blew out a breath. "No. Not as such."

"And even if it were, code enforcement looks at things like consistency in the crew. They'll look at general maintenance and overall demeanor."

"Consistency in the crew?" Trask's eyebrows met over his nose. "Like what?"

"Oh, shipsuits, speech. Is everybody in a clean suit? Do all the crew use 'sar' or at least show a consistent level of shipboard protocol?"

"We don't," Trask said. "Never bothered before."

"How often have you been boarded?"

Trask's gaze went to the overhead and he took a long moment. "Four, maybe five times."

"Been boarded while Pritchard was with you?"

Trask nodded his head. "Albee was here for the last one, too. Why?"

"TIC would spot him as a ringer."

Trask sat up at that. "Pritchard? I admit he's not the sharpest wrench in the toolbox, but really?"

Natalya held up her hands, palms out and fingers spread.

"Oh," Trask said.

"You don't get to make chief engineering officer without getting your hands dirty. Or cut. Or callused. I'm only a third officer, but I've got my share of scars. Even allowing for his lack of theoretical knowledge, he's just too clean."

Trask shrugged and shook his head. "I don't know. That seems a bit judgmental."

Natalya felt the heat rising at the back of her neck and forced herself to take a few breaths. "I'll grant you there are some out there with lily-white hands and smooth skin. For the most part, they fly desks. How they got the rank? Beats me. Engineering is hands-on. Hot metal, broken bolts, stripped threads, and ripped plates. I'm not saying that's the only way—there might be others—but it's the only way I know."

"And you think TIC safety inspectors would look at his hands?"

Natalya sat back in her seat and thought about it. "All right. Maybe not. It's the first thing I look at, but I'm not TIC."

"So who else would you hire?" Trask asked again.

"A real spec-one in propulsion. Mel Solomon is good but she's working on OJT."

"If she could pass the test, would you hire her?"

Natalya's brain box reset. "Solomon? Spec-one propulsion test?"

"Yeah. Would you hire her?"

"Sure. She's got great management skills. She's like the engineering division mom as near as I can see."

"Here's what I want," Trask said. "Give them a chance. What you want is a crew that works together, right?"

"Well, yes, but they have to look the part in order to slide by a TIC boarding team."

"What will that take?" Trask asked. "Shipsuits aside. Gypsy operation. Who would you need?"

"I'm just a boot engineering third," Natalya said.

"You're the one in here trying to convince me to do this full time." He shrugged. "So, sell me. What would it take?"

She sighed. "Marah's cooking is great. I assume she'll mix up the menu a little as we go along. It's going to be a long slog into Siren and another one out."

"Marah runs one of Verkol's restaurants. Her two messmates—Bray and Solomon—work with her."

"I didn't realize there was another Solomon aboard. Son?"

"Brother. Don't change the subject."

"A cargo master. Ship's rated for one but Mr. Lyons seems a bit stressed."

"He doesn't sail well. He's only in it for the paycheck and he spends most of it on his anesthesia of choice." Trask nodded. "Cargo master on a Barbell isn't the most challenging of jobs. One can per trip. Bet wrong and the whole ship hates you for not turning a profit."

"Bet right and they love you," Natalya said.

"Odds are a'gin' ya over the long haul unless you're lucky, gifted, and fast. Our Mr. Lyons had a lot of bad luck over his relatively short career." Trask shook his head. "Kondur picks the cargoes and makes all the arrangements. Cargo master is just for show and signs the documents for delivery and pickup."

"First mate," Natalya said. "Nothing against Zoya but she's just out of the academy. Just like me."

"She's good," Trask said. "It comes natural to her, but you're right. She deserves a little time in grade to work through the rough edges."

"Chief engineer. A real one."

"I thought you were the engineering genius."

"I'm straight aces on the little ships. *Peregrine* has been my second home since I was twelve. I know her systems inside and out. My academy work focused on small ships and small ship systems. Those behemoths you've got leashed back there? I know how they all work. I can do the routine maintenance on them. I can run the diagnostics, but I'm no engineering genius to get them working if they break down."

"You talk a good game." Trask's face gave nothing away.

"Talk's talk. I try not to let my mouth write any checks my butt can't cover."

"Engineering. Crew. Knowles?"

"I've been nothing but impressed with him. Knows his kit and doesn't feel the need to take it on parade. I've swung though the swamp a couple of times in the last few days. It's always spot on. He's tracking his filter and scrubbers. He's even got some kind of contraption to monitor the acidity in the scrubber sluice."

"What's that do for him?"

"Says it tells him if the algae are healthy." Natalya shrugged. "Knowles is playing on a whole different field than any environmental tech I've ever seen."

"Kondur wouldn't like to lose him from the station's life support crew."

"Don't blame him."

"What about Collie on power?"

"Complete cypher. Haven't interacted with him other than the navigation stations. He seems to know what he's doing on the console. Beyond that? I've gotten no read from him."

"What about you?"

"What about me? I'm out of my depth, don't fancy command, but I'm the *de facto* department head on a ship I'm really only qualified to stand watches on."

Trask nodded. "Give yourself some credit."

Natalya shrugged. "I'm trying to be realistic."

"Fair enough." Trask paused for a moment and pursed his lips. "Where'd all that power go?"

"No idea."

"What are you doin' to find out?"

"Mostly talking to you at the moment. It had to go somewhere. I suspect it bled out onto the hull."

"How would you be able to tell?"

"Hull sensors might have picked up an RF spike." She shook her head. "It's a long shot, but possible. None of the sensors got fried, did they?"

Trask gave her a lopsided grin. "You're engineering. You tell me."

"Nothing threw an alarm, but I haven't had a chance to dig into the data yet. I only just found out the jump was a normal length from Blanchard."

"Charlie say anything to you about it?"

"Just noted that he'd seen it on his bridge displays and that it seemed out of line."

Trask nodded. "Your thoughts?"

"I agree with him. Seems out of line. We had solid by-the-numbers jumps all the way through the Deep Dark. Now, our first jump inside Confederation space and we're bleeding capacitor charge." She shook her head. "Something ain't right."

Trask nodded again. "So, you've got four and half weeks to figure it out. We'll be parked in Siren Orbital by then, so you'll be able to order anything you need to fix it."

"Assuming I can find it."

"I got faith," Task said.

"In me?"

He laughed. "In Kondur. He wouldn't have sent you two High Liners on this trip if he hadn't thought you'd both do the job. Now git. You got problems to solve and I got reports to write."

"I'd think being a smuggler you'd have fewer reports, not more."

He laughed. "I've got more and they have to be perfect just in case somebody actually reads one. Now, scoot!" He flexed his fingers over his desk as if flicking away imaginary dust on the surface.

Natalya scooted.

Chapter Twenty-seven
Siren System: 2363, June 23

Natalya had her head in a Burleson drive when Knowles found her. "You sure you're supposed to take that apart?" he asked, a silly grin pasted on his face and a cup of coffee in his hand.

Natalya looked up at him and grimaced. "Something ain't right. We burned way too much capacitor for a short jump."

"Find anything?" He nodded at the spaghetti of boards and busses inside the casing.

She bit her lip and shook her head. "Nothing yet. I ran a deep probe overnight. Nada."

"And nothing on the voodoo you do? The laying on of hands?"

She gave him a hard stare. "You making fun of me?"

He held up his free hand, palm out. "Not at all. I actually believe you in that regard. Once you know what it feels like when it's working, I really do believe that we humans can detect some kinds of variations." He shrugged. "Nothing on the molecular level, but still."

Natalya reached for the cover and started putting the drive back together. "It felt fine," she said. "Diagnostics are clean and there's nothing obviously out of place in the casing."

"Man, I hate these kinds of problems."

She ratcheted the last bolt down and gave them all an extra tap to snug them up. "Me, too. Time to check elsewhere in the chain."

"Good strategy. You need an extra head to bounce ideas off?"

She shrugged. "I'm not out of ideas yet, but I'll keep you in mind. How're things in the swamp?"

"Everything still squishing that supposed to squish. Gas mixes are good. Returns don't show any additives that shouldn't be there."

She powered the Burleson unit back up and waited for it to finish booting before speaking. "Can I ask why you do this?"

"Do what? These so-called smuggling runs or the whole environmental thing?"

"These trips."

He shrugged. "Dark Knight has a huge environmental plant. It's so big, I don't get my hands wet or dirty that often because I need a crew of thirty to keep up with it." He looked around the engine room and up at the overhead. "Here? I get a chance to get down in the mud and tinker."

"Like with the scrubber sluice?"

"Well, that's something we do at the station. I was surprised when I came out here and found ships don't monitor that."

"Any theories?"

"It's a tiny improvement. When you've got ten acres of algae matrix, even a tiny improvement gives you a lot of scrubbing leverage. With ten square meters, that extra improvement is only about a million molecules."

"I can see that. Why do it, then?"

"It's a useful predictor of air quality and the overall health of the algae matrix."

"So a bellwether?"

"In a manner of speaking, yeah."

She pondered for a moment. "You ever think about doing this full time?"

He got a sheepish grin. "Actually, I fantasize about it all the time between trips. We no sooner get back and I start looking forward to going again."

"Why don't you?"

He shrugged. "Too comfy. Pay's too good where I am. I get mad money from this, but the station still pays my bills."

Natalya nodded. "I can see that. One of the advantages of just starting out, I guess."

"No psychological inertia?"

"Something like that. I need to get my ship fixed so I can get back to what I wanted to do."

"Which was?"

"Fast packet courier trade around Toe-Hold space."

"Not much room on those Scouts. You bunking up?"

"Mostly planning on data and small-mass, high-value cargoes that need to go a long way."

He pursed his lips and frowned a little. "Can you make a living at that?"

"Maybe," she said. "My overhead is low and the *Peregrine* has long legs. I can cross almost the whole Western Annex in a couple of days by jumping through the Deep Dark." She looked at the Burleson unit. "Where would power get eaten up?"

Knowles shook his head. "If it were me, I'd be looking at the downstream components."

She glanced about, mentally tracing the power flows. "Any particular reason?"

He shrugged. "All my systems have feedback control loops. If they're not getting enough water, they tell the pumps to send more. Capacitors are like a big tank. If you used more than expected, what would have told the drive to use more?"

"Throttle, for one," she said.

"Was there any activity on the throttle at the time period?"

She shook her head. "None. Typically there isn't during the actual jump."

"So, downstream you have—what? Emitters on the hull?"

"Yeah. A couple of big ones in the outward facing curves of her nose."

He shrugged. "If they're out of whack, could that cause it?"

"Yeah, but ..." Natalya's voice tapered off as she considered.

Knowles grinned. "My work here is done." He flourished his coffee cup by way of a wave and strolled off toward environmental.

"Thank you," Natalya said.

He waved his hand but didn't turn around or stop.

Natalya pulled up the ship's schematic on her tablet and began tracing the emitter bus network that carried the massive jolts of energy around the ship. She pocketed the socket wrench and ran up the ladder to her office to get a plate tool. The schematic showed a lot of places to look, and not all of them would be easy to get to. She considered getting Solomon to help since she held the lead slot in that group, but stopped short of asking. If she was right, she'd find out soon enough. If not, then she wouldn't have a witness to failure. The thought made her laugh.

Three stans later—covered in grease, sweat, and dirt from crawling around in the inspection tunnels in engineering—she felt like giving it up as a bad job. She'd bashed a knuckle on a sharp edge and the sweat from her hands stung in the abrasion. She lay there on the deck and took a breather. The air in the tunnels carried a metallic tang along with a higher than normal level of humidity. Together it made for an unpleasant experience that had her shipsuit sticking to her in places where it shouldn't and restricting her movements.

Her tablet bipped with the first piece of good news she'd had all morning. A diagnostic routine had tripped a warning on a bus control coupling in the spine. She wriggled back out of the tunnel and secured the inspection hatch.

It wasn't much, but it was something.

Her grubby appearance earned her more than a couple of strange looks as she clambered up the ladder toward the spine.

"What have you been into?" Solomon asked as they crossed paths outside Engineering Control.

"Inspection tunnels. Trying to find out where the extra power went during that last jump. And why we needed it to begin with."

"You noticed that, did you?" Solomon asked.

"Kinda hard to miss."

"Find anything yet?"

"Nothing I can put a cause to. Drives check out. I've had a system diagnostic running for the last three stans and it's finally pinged me."

"Need a hand?"

"I got it." She grimaced. "Although if this doesn't pan out, I'm not looking forward to continuing my tour of the inner workings of the Barbell."

Solomon laughed and waved as she headed up the spine toward the bow.

Natalya stopped by the head on the way and rinsed the worst of the grime off her hands and face. She'd need a shower before she'd be able to go to the wardroom for lunch, but first she wanted a look at that bus coupling.

She fired up her tablet and followed the map laid out on her screen. About two-thirds of the way toward the bow, she found the inspection hatch and pulled it. Looking around with a pen light, she saw the problem a split second before the evidence met her nose. As she surveyed the damage, she got a cold knot in the pit of her stomach. Being careful not to touch anything, she levered the hatch closed and rubbed her hands on the thighs of her shipsuit before heading forward to find the captain.

The captain peered into the hatch. "What am I looking at?"

"Emitter bus coupling for the Burleson drives. This one channels most of the energy from the drives aft to the emitters forward."

"That's not supposed to look like that, is it?"

"No, Captain. It's not. That one's almost burned through."

"That what caused the power drain?"

"I believe so. There's a feedback circuit to keep the Burlesons from cutting out too soon. If the bus coupling doesn't have enough juice, it tells the drive to give more."

"You think the extra juice killed this one?"

"No, Captain. I think it was on its way out, when it called for help. I think it must have lasted long enough to complete the jump into Siren but that's where it all stopped."

"Recommendations?"

She nodded at the crispy coupling in the overhead. "That'll have to be replaced. We can do it when we get to Siren but we can't jump again until it's replaced."

"What's the end game here, Ms. Regyri?"

"I don't know, Captain. If this had failed even one jump earlier, we'd have been pretty badly stuck."

He sighed. "We'd have been in Albert, at least." He looked at the coupling again. "You think it's deliberate?"

"It's possible. It's also possible that it's not up to handling the load those oversized Origamis are punching through it over time. I'd have to check the specs on that unit to be sure."

"Odd time for it to happen," Trask said.

Natalya gazed up at the burned unit. "Maybe." She looked at Trask. "Or maybe the ship doesn't get used as much as we think."

Trask sighed and glanced at her before looking back into the inspection hatch. "Can you fix it?"

"Should be able to." Natalya shrugged. "It'll be a while before we need it again."

"Make it a priority, if you would, Ms. Regyri. I don't like not being able to jump."

"Aye, aye, Skipper," she said. "Don't blame ya."

Chapter Twenty-eight
Siren System: 2363, June 23

Natalya returned to engineering and pulled up the spares inventory. Emitter bus couplings showed up right where she expected them to be. The system identified a full complement of a dozen on hand. She scrolled through the pages to see what had been used and what had been aboard the longest. Nothing jumped out at her. None of the items that might have had a limited shelf life, like algae cartridges for the scrubbers, showed even marginal dates. The normal consumables, like water and fuel filters, all looked fine.

On a whim, she pulled up the bus replacement protocol to see if it held any gotchas. The procedure looked familiar. She'd never done a live one herself, but they'd been given instruction on it during her third-year Burleson drive rotation. Emitter bus couplers, capacitor charge fuses, even emitter array maintenance. She remembered that last one vividly. The emitters needed to be on the outside of the hull with an airtight bushing that provided the signal from inside the ship. The array itself consisted of a cross-hatched set of parallel emitters simply plugged into the emitter housing on the hull with a zero-gee fitting. Maintenance consisted of walking—or jetting—over to them outside the ship and replacing the emitter with a new one. Woe be to the cadet who stepped out without locking down her safety line.

She'd never been in any danger. She had more hours of EVA than the instructors, but they'd acted like she'd stabbed her own suit and bled out. She sighed and kept digging.

The procedure itself seemed simple enough. Pull the old one out. Plug the new one in. Use the coupling balance tool to bring both ends of the bus into proper alignment. The process shouldn't take more than a few ticks. She kicked herself on that and mentally added a couple of stans.

As long as the drives were off line, the replacement could be done underway.

"Good enough," she said to herself, and headed for the spares locker.

She flipped the light on, scanning the shelves for the bus couplers. As she did so, something kept nagging at her attention. She was about to give up when she realized most of the parts bins were empty or nearly so. She pulled out her tablet and accessed the spares inventory. She added a quick sort by location and put her hand on the bin that should have held a dozen pristine bus couplers.

What she found was a collection of half a dozen bent pieces of metal covered in some kind of oily grease.

The cold knot in her stomach came back full force. She tamped it down and started spot-checking the various bins against what was in the system. A good deal of it matched, but mostly spares with a low unit cost. Anything of value wasn't just missing. It had been replaced with a similar mass of metal—or in one case, bottles of water. Burleson bus connectors would have been worth twelve thousand credits. The case of spare water filters wouldn't have been worth twelve.

She left the spares locker and dropped down to the environmental department. She found Sheddon and Eloranta changing out scrubber cartridges. "Seen Mr. Knowles lately?" she asked.

Sheddon looked up and wiped the end of his nose with the back of his wrist. "He's off until 1800. Might find him in engineering berthing."

Eloranta shook her head. "He was headed for the mess deck for coffee. Maybe half a stan ago. If he got involved in reading, he's probably still there."

Sheddon grinned. "True. I'd try the mess deck first."

"Anything we can help with?" Eloranta asked.

"You got plenty of cartridges for that sucker?" Natalya asked.

Eloranta shrugged and looked at Sheddon.

"Three cases in the spares locker. We just opened a fresh case for this." He waved a mucky hand at the open scrubber.

"I'm putting together a replenishment order for when we dock. If you think of anything, lemme know?"

"Aye, aye," Eloranta said with a crooked grin.

Natalya found Knowles leaning against a bulkhead on the mess deck, his tablet open to dense text and an empty cup in his hand. "Did you drink it already or haven't you filled it yet?" she asked.

He looked up at her and blinked a couple of times as if reorienting his reality. "Oh. No. Not filled."

"Interesting reading?"

He hefted the tablet as if weighing it in his hand. "Interesting research in some new higher-yield algae. They produce almost twice as much oxygen for the same amount of carbon dioxide absorption."

"What's the down side?"

"What to do with excess oxygen in closed ecosystems."

Natalya felt her eyebrows climbing her forehead. "Is that a problem?"

"Can be. Half the reason we use the algae in the scrubbers is to pull the carbon dioxide out. I'd like to see something that can take twice as much carbon dioxide for the same amount of oxygen exchanged. That would be more useful, I think." He shrugged. "We've got some very good mixes now with exchange at near-parity. We only supplement the mix with the barest whiff of oxygen. If we used these strains, we'd have to figure out a way to keep the oxygen levels under control. We just haven't faced that before."

Natalya gave him a wry smile. "Cut down the number of scrubbers?"

"Possibly. I'd like to see how that scaled." He looked up at her. "Sorry," he said, flipping the screen off. "You didn't hunt me down to ask me about algae."

"Spares."

His eyebrows raised slightly. "Spares?"

"You noticed anything odd in the spares locker?"

He shrugged a shoulder. "No. I only go in there for filters and cartridges and we've only just had to change out the scrubber."

"I saw. Sheddon and Elantora were up to their elbows in it."

"Eloranta," he said.

Natalya winced. "Sorry. I'm usually better with names."

"It's an odd one and she gets a lot of strange takes on it."

"Got a minute?"

"You're the boss."

Natalya took him back to engineering and led him into the spares locker. She pulled out her tablet. "What's a part you might need? Other than the consumables."

He scratched his chin and pursed his lips. "Eight-centimeter stainless valve."

Natalya entered it into the inventory. "System says we have six. Bin D-12-6."

He shrugged. "Six is probably enough. We don't break that many of them."

"Do me a favor and look in D-12-6."

He scanned the racks until he found the right bin. He pulled it open and peered inside. He frowned. "Did you say D or B."

"D as in delta."

He checked the label again and shrugged. "That looks like scrap metal."

"Any idea how much six of those valves would mass?"

His eyes widened a bit and he blinked. He hefted the bin a couple of times. "Not offhand."

"They valuable?"

"Eh, maybe a hundred credits each. They're precision-machined to medical tolerances."

"Gimme a cheap part. Something plastic."

"Ten-millimeter neoprene hose."

She consulted her tablet. "Bin Charlie-15-23. A ten-meter roll."

"Sounds right," he said. He rummaged around for a bit and pulled open a bin. "Looks like this one is here."

"What's it cost?"

"Probably four credits for the roll."

"So, cheap, lightweight stuff and things we might notice right away?"

Knowles nodded. "Consumables like the filters and scrubber cartridges. There's some filter papers and titration reagents we use to test water. Some cheap chemicals we use to suppress biological activity in gray water tanks."

"We'd need to run a full inventory, but I'd guess anything with a significant value has been replaced with dross."

"Anything we'd be unlikely to notice," Knowles said. "We test all the waters about three times a week with this." He pulled out a bin near the door. It contained row upon row of brown plastic bottles, all lying on their side with the label up. "Phenol red. It's for testing water's acidity. We don't use much of it at a time, but we use it a lot and it's not always easy to come by in commercial quantities in Toe-Hold space."

"Expensive?"

Knowles shrugged. "This bin's probably a couple thousand credits worth."

"But you'd notice if it were missing."

He nodded. "Most definitely."

"Will you use all that this trip?"

"This trip? Doubtful. Probably only a half-dozen bottles. Depends on how long we're out."

Natalya reached into the bin and pulled out the top bottle and held it up to the light. "This is the stuff?"

"We can check it by running some water tests with it, but it should be."

She pulled the bin out and flipped it over so the bottles rolled across the deck.

"What the—?" Knowles said jumping back from the scattering containers.

Natalya corralled them with her feet until they rolled more or less together in a line across the deck. "Notice anything?"

"What? They're bottles of phenol red."

"Really?"

Knowles frowned and leaned down, his head turning slowly as his gaze picked out each of the two dozen bottles spread out in the light. "What are you seeing that I'm not?"

Natalya held up the original bottle. "This was the top one." She nodded at the lineup. "About a third of them have a different colored bottle."

"That's not unusual. Different supplier has a different batch of bottles. Those might be a different shipment. Leftover stock that didn't get rotated. Or the new stock that got rotated to the bottom."

"Care to place a little wager?" she asked.

Knowles's eyes narrowed as he looked at the bottles on the deck again. "No, but we can check it fast enough." He snagged one of the odd-colored bottles from the deck and set it aside. Natalya helped him reload the bin.

They took the two bottles down to the small lab Knowles used in the environmental services department. Knowles drew one sample of water from a vat and split it between two beakers.

"This should be relatively neutral," Knowles said. "The reagent should show a yellowy-orange color in both."

He used a clear pipette to dip a measured amount from the first bottle and held it up to the light. "This looks all right. Good color and consistency." He released it into the sample water beaker and they watched as the swirling liquid turned a delicate yellow-orange. "Looks about right. Very close to what we tested it at yesterday. High six, low seven maybe."

"So that's what you'd expect to see?"

"Well, depending on the sample either more yellow or more orange all the way up to fuchsia."

He pulled a clean pipette and sampled the second bottle. He held the sample up to the light. "This doesn't look right. Color's too pink and the consistency is too loose." He released the pipette into the other water sample and the watched as the pink liquid swirled around in the beaker.

Knowles stared at the two beakers and then lifted the offending bottle to look at it more closely. He sniffed it before screwing the lid back on. "Not phenol red. The opaque bottle masked the contents. I can't tell what it is without more tests, but it's not phenol red."

"Water and food coloring," Natalya said.

Knowles hefted the bottle as if weighing it in his hand. "Might be. Why do you say that?"

"Cheap dross. Easy to come by. Impossible to trace."

Knowles grinned at that. "If that's the case, we've just caught a break."

"How do you figure?"

"Because water isn't just water. Every station, every ship. Every source is different. It's stupidly difficult to match waters at the molecular level."

"I thought it was all hydrogen dioxide."

"Wrong numbers of atoms. It would be dihydrogen monoxide. It's more commonly hydrogen hydroxide because of the atomic bonding, but that's just the basic pure chemical. What we think of as water generally contains soluble chemicals from piping, pumps, even microscopic levels of common contaminants. They're like a fingerprint for water."

"You think you can find the source?"

Knowles frowned and screwed his mouth around a little like he was tasting something interesting but wasn't sure if it was good or bad. "Maybe," he said.

"Maybe?"

"I can tell you if the water came from the ship. Or from Dark Knight. I can tell you if it came from someplace else, but without a sample from a known location, we're left with a fingerprint with no record behind it."

Natalya frowned at the pink water swirling slowly in the beaker. "So, maybe five hundred credits' worth of chemicals?"

Knowles took a deep breath and let it out slowly. "Maybe that amount."

"This didn't happen overnight," Natalya said. "And it wasn't somebody random."

Knowles looked at her, frowning. "No, that took a lot of time and somebody who knew what to take and what to hide." He paused, scratching his cheek. "How much do you think they got?"

"Replacement cost for us will be tens of thousands if the scope is anything like I think it is." She shook her head. "Maybe hundreds of thousands." A sudden thought made her start.

"What?" Knowles asked.

"Maybe a lot more," she said and ran up the ladder to the spares locker again. She opened the tool closet, flipped on the light, and stopped dead in her tracks.

Knowles bumped into her and braced himself on the door frame to lean into the closet. "That seems kind of sparse," he said.

Natalya sighed. "If you didn't know what was supposed to be in here, it would look fine." She pointed to a shelf just above eye level. "That's where I'd look to find the coil alignment meter and tools." She pointed to the space beside it. "Burleson bus coupling balancing tools." She pointed to a lower shelf near the middle. "Fusactor test equipment."

Knowles frowned. "Well, that's where you'd look but you're used to fleet ships. Maybe they're all just stowed someplace else."

Natalya slumped against the bulkhead. "That might be worse, in a way."

"How so?"

"Somebody with enough engineering knowledge to know what those tools do moved them from the place where they'd need to be for somebody who needed them to find them. Does anybody aboard have that kind of knowledge?"

"Besides you?" Knowles asked.

She chuckled. "Yeah. Besides me."

"Solomon, maybe. She trained with an old engineer."

Natalya considered that, letting her gaze scan the nearly empty closet. "Solomon's propulsion. Some of the missing tools, sure. Burleson drives. Even some fuel mix adjustment tools for the kickers." She shook her head. "Then who took the power tools? That fusactor test equipment would only be useful for somebody who knew how to use it and when." She looked at Knowles. "You brought your own tools with you, I bet."

"Of course. And my own crew."

"I've got my own tools, too, but they're just a basic set. Nothing like the specialist tools that should be stored here and belong to the ship."

"How much is missing?"

Natalya shook her head and sighed. "Hundreds of thousands."

Knowles gave a low whistle. "That'll eat into shares."

Natalya looked at him and started to laugh. "Yeah. It will indeed."

"What'll you do now?"

"First, notify the captain. Second, get a valid inventory of the spares locker so we can replenish what's been stolen when we get to Siren."

"Third?"

"Pray nothing happens between now and then that needs a part or a tool that's missing," she said.

Knowles looked around the tool closet and then the row upon row of bins and storage cabinets in the spares locker. "I'd put that prayer first," he said.

CHAPTER TWENTY-NINE
SIREN SYSTEM: 2363, JUNE 23

The spares locker seemed too small a space for the enormity Natalya and the captain considered. "Who'd do this?" Trask asked.

"Who *could* do it?" Natalya asked. "Somebody who knows enough about the ship and what it's doing. Somebody with enough knowledge of the engineering division to pull it off."

"How long do you think it's been like that?"

"Without being spotted?" Natalya shuddered. "No way to know. The only reason I twigged was because of the emitter bus coupling. I went to get the replacement and found all this."

"How long must it have taken?" Trask asked.

"I've been asking myself that same question. It's going to take us days, maybe weeks to get a final and accurate inventory in here. Even allowing for some rudimentary inventory filtering to take only things that were worth taking, it must have taken months."

"That long?"

"They stole parts and replaced them with similar masses of scrap. They probably worried that somebody might be able to tell if the ship was missing a few tons of mass."

"Tons?" Trask said, his gaze sweeping the rows of storage.

"Probably. Crew mass allotments are calculated pretty carefully in CPJCT space."

Trask snorted.

"Yeah, I know. It gets lost in the rounding errors on tankage alone to say nothing of the food stores."

Trask's eyes widened at that. "You don't suppose?"

Natalya bit her lip. "Aren't food stocks supposed to be rotated?"

"They're *supposed* to be but I'm going to sleep better if Marah can prove that they have been," Trask said. He cast a final scan around the room. "What do you need to get this straightened out?"

Natalya considered for a moment. "Somebody we can trust to help with the inventory. Once I know what's missing, generating a replenishment order when we dock at Siren should be easy, if expensive."

"You're not going to be able to keep this under wraps, you know?"

She sighed. "Probably not, but I'd like to keep the interference to a minimum."

He laughed. "Can't blame you there. What about Pritchard?"

"Pritchard?" Natalya shook her head. "Uh. No."

"He's not doing anything else at the moment."

"Let me just say, the thought of being cheek by jowl with him for days at a time leaves me less than enthusiastic." She shook her head. "I'd rather Josh Lyons."

Trask opened his mouth as if to speak but closed it again before anything came out. He looked at her with a slight tilt to his head. "Really?"

She shrugged. "He's actually a cargo master?"

"Yeah. I think he was with Sullivan over in Halpern before he came out to Dark Knight." Trask frowned. "He's rather disagreeable."

"I think he's probably just carrying too much baggage and can't seem to drink it away."

"You want me to ask him?" Trask asked.

"You two have a history, I take it?"

Trask shrugged. "Not as such. I keep putting him on the mission rosters and he keeps coming. More than half his mass allotment is liquid."

"He's probably going to run a little low by the time we reach— where was it? Joe's?"

"Moe's. Moe's Mining."

Natalya raised an eyebrow. "Seriously."

"Yeah. Not terribly catchy but she flies under the CPJCT radar." Trask grinned. "If she didn't have us making the runs in with cheap ore, she'd probably go belly up."

"So Kondur uses her to feed goods into the system."

"And siphon off cargoes that we need but don't want to account for." Trask shrugged. "Honestly, it's a shell game and I think TIC does it on purpose to justify their existence." He paused for a few heartbeats. "So you want me to talk to Lyons?"

Natalya shook her head. "Lemme try him."

"Suit yourself," Trask said. "You got a fallback position?"

"I'll get one of the wipers."

"How do you know they're not in on it?"

"I don't," she said. "I don't *know* you're not in on it, but you're the captain so I'm pretty screwed if you are in any case."

He laughed. "I like you, Regyri. Remind me of your father."

"I come by it honestly."

"That you do, lass." He sighed. "I better go talk to Marah and see what's in her pantries." He shambled toward the locker's door and stopped at the jamb to look back. "Good work on this." He waved a hand around the room.

"Thanks, Skipper. We'll get it straightened out soon."

Trask nodded, pursing his lips but not speaking. When he left, the spares locker seemed a lot larger for not having him in it.

Natalya pulled out her tablet and sent a bip to Lyons via Ship-Net. She didn't think he'd answer, but at least she'd give him warning that she was coming.

Natalya knocked on the door. A polite two raps with a single knuckle. When nobody answered, she said, "Chief Lyons?"

"Go away," he said. It sounded like he was just on the other side of the panel.

"Chief, I need your help."

"Yeah, right. Go. Away."

"Chief? Could we at least talk about it face to face instead of face to door?"

Lyons snatched open the door and thrust his pallid, sweaty face out of the darkness on the other side. "Here's my face saying 'Go away.' Is that better?"

Natalya planted her feet and stared into the man's red-rimmed eyes. "Not really, no."

He closed his eyes and his lips pressed into a thin line. "I outrank you. Go away."

"I know that, Chief. I need your help."

He reached for the door jamb with his free hand and almost missed it. "I'm not in any condition to help you."

"You enunciate pretty clearly when you want to, Chief. I do need your help."

He sighed and rolled his eyes. "You're not going to leave me alone. What is it?"

"I've got an inventory problem."

He blinked at her as if trying to process whatever it was she'd just said. "You're engineering."

"I've still got an inventory problem. I need your help."

"You keep saying that."

"It's still true and you keep telling me you can't help me but you don't even know what the problem is."

He fell against the edge of the frame, propping himself on a shoulder. "All right, Ms. Whoever You Are. Tell me so I can tell you I can't help you."

Natalya lowered her voice. "It's Regyri, Chief. Natalya Regyri. I'm engineering third and apparently the only real engineer on the ship."

"All right. That's who you are, but why is your inventory my problem."

"Because unless we get it straightened out soon, we all might die."

Lyons scoffed and shook his head. One shake and he winced before holding very still. "We're all going to die, Ms. Regyri. Some sooner than others."

"I'm aware of that, Chief, but I'd like mine to be later rather than sooner if that's all the same to you."

He sighed and blinked up at the overhead light. "Come in. Keep your voice down, please. I'm planning on having a hangover."

"You're not having one now?"

He shrugged. "That might be why the light's so bright out here." He turned and shuffled back into his stateroom.

Natalya stepped into the dimness and held her breath for a moment, almost afraid of what she'd inhale. She realized she wouldn't be able to talk without breathing and took a tentative sniff. Other than a bit of stuffiness and some rather ripe clothing, it wasn't as bad as she feared.

Lyons lowered himself onto his bunk and waved at the chair. "Spill. I've got a date in a few ticks and don't wanna be late."

"Somebody's stripped the spares locker of everything of value."

One ruddy eye pried itself open and peered out at her. "Engineering spares?"

"Yes, Chief. They replaced it with useless crap that massed about the same as the missing parts."

The eye closed. "That's inane."

"Insane?" she asked.

"No, Ms. Regyri. In. Ane. As in incredibly silly. Stupid. Might even be puerile, now that I think of it and depending on what they replaced the parts with."

"Scrap metal and colored water as nearly as I've been able to tell, Chief."

"Oh, for the love of all that's holy in your world, stop calling me chief." He leaned forward on his elbows and grabbed his temples with his hands. "Mr. Lyons will do but if that's too formal for you, Josh. Better yet, just tell me what you want from me."

"You're the cargo master. You know inventory management. I've got to take an inventory of the whole damn locker and you're the resident expert on how to do that effectively."

He scrubbed his face with his hands and blew out a breath. "Start on one end. Go through it all, bin by bin. Count what's there. Mark it on your tablet. It's not brain science."

"I like this plan, Mr. Lyons. Would it work better with a couple of people? One to look and count and the other to mark?"

He moaned a little. "Just scan the bin label with your tablet. It'll pull up the record and tell you what's supposed to be there. Correct it and scan the next."

"So you'll help me, then?"

Lyons lifted his head up and stared at her. "At what point did I even suggest that might be an option?"

"You're clearly the expert at this, Mr. Lyons. I never would have thought to scan the label with my tablet."

"Were you raised under a rock?"

"In one, mostly."

"In a rock."

"Asteroid station in Valar up in Tellicheri."

He closed his eyes and lowered his face into his hands again. After several moments he asked, "Are you still here?"

"Yes."

"What do you really want?" he asked, speaking into his hands.

"Somebody to verify that the counts are valid. I could cheat them myself without an auditor."

He sighed. "You've never scanned a bin label but you know about inventory audits." He lifted his head again, looking for all the world like it weighed twenty kilos. "Who are you?"

"Engineering third officer."

"Barbells aren't rated for engineering thirds."

"Depends on who's doing the rating. We're not in the High Line anymore."

He blinked each eye individually and then together. "I thought we'd jumped to Siren."

She smiled. "Now you know why I need an unimpeachable auditor to oversee this." She gave him a few heartbeats to ponder. "So. Are you going to sit here in this squalid dump feeling sorry for yourself, Mr. Lyons? Or will you come help me save the ship?"

Her question poked a laugh out of him. "You're going to save the ship with a spares inventory? How does that work?"

"It works by getting the tools and spares we need to keep the ship from blowing up the next time we try to jump."

His eyes widened for a moment. Natalya thought it was mostly a stretching exercise because he didn't seem surprised. "Why jump if it'll blow up?" he asked after several moments.

"Well, it might not blow up. It'll be less likely if we have the replacement emitter bus coupling that should be in the spares locker. But isn't."

He heaved a huge sigh and pressed the heels of his hands into his eye sockets. "You're going to go through every possible disaster which might be caused by a missing spare part, aren't you?"

"If I need to."

"Squalid dump?" he asked.

"Hyperbole. It's not that bad. Certainly better than I expected."

"Why me?"

"I trust you."

He lowered his hands and peered at her. "What could I possibly have done to you to deserve that?"

"Well, you're not Pritchard. You're not part of the engineering crew at all, in fact. That means it's not likely you had a hand in the pilferage." She shrugged. "You're also the only member of the crew who hasn't been all hail and well met since Albee tried to break Captain Trask's face on a dinner plate."

The beginnings of a smile seemed to tease Lyons's lips for a moment. "I heard he got booted off the ship. I didn't know why."

"You left the dinner mess just a few ticks too early."

"We've been underway a week?"

"Yes. Jumped into Siren a couple days ago."

He sat, apparently lost in thought, so long Natalya began to suspect he'd fallen asleep. "You wouldn't happen to have an analgesic on you?" he asked.

"I know where to get one."

"I could use a couple."

"I can get them for you."

He sighed. "Yes, Ms. Regyri. Please." He blinked and sat up a little straighter, then winced.

"And maybe a nice cup of coffee to wash them down?"

"You're going to be like this?" he asked.

"Just trying to be helpful."

"Spare me. Please. Just ... let me dig myself out for a few ticks?" He turned his bleary, bloodshot eyes on her and waited.

"I'll just get those tabs for you." She rose and started for the door.

"Yes, please, Ms. Regyri. I would like a cup of coffee to wash them down. Just a splash of milk, if you would be so kind."

She grinned. "Be right back."

She slipped out of Lyons's stateroom and almost plowed into Steve Pritchard in the passageway outside. The cloud of mouth-washy cologne nearly gagged her. His eyebrows tried to scale Mount Forehead before he got his features under control.

"I heard you'd braved the Lyons den," he said, clearly amused at his own cleverness. "I could scarcely believe it."

"Now you know," Natalya said and sidled past him toward the ladder down to the galley.

"May I ask?"

She turned to find Pritchard close on her heels. "Ask what?"

"What you're doing in Lyons's stateroom?"

He seemed just a bit too busybody for her taste.

"You can ask."

"What were you doing in Lyons's stateroom?"

"Well, we were just having a little chat about this and that. You know, how people do."

"Ms. Regyri." He smiled in a way that made her want a shower. "You don't expect me to believe that, do you?"

"You've found me out. We were having wild monkey sex on his desk and rolling around in the empty bottles under his bunk."

Pritchard's face turned a darling shade of pink. "Well, I never."

"You should try it sometime," Natalya said. "Now, if you'll excuse me? I've got an errand to run." She waved her fingers in a stupid, flirty gesture. "Tootles."

She left him spluttering in the passage outside of the cabin and snickered all the way to the first aid dispensary outside the ward-room.

CHAPTER THIRTY
SIREN SYSTEM: 2363, JUNE 23

When Natalya led Josh Lyons down the spine and through engineering she felt a little like the drum major in a very short parade. Everybody along the way stopped to gawk. To their credit, nobody commented on the cargo master's appearance (rumpled and all but bleeding from his eyes) or his demeanor (something between grumpy and stabby).

She also had to give Lyons credit. Once she got the analgesics into him along with most of a cup of coffee, he never balked.

Before they got to the spares locker, Solomon fell in step with Natalya with a cautious glance behind her at Lyons. "Something up, boss?"

"Spares inventory. Mr. Lyons is going to help me run an audit."

"You need a hand?" she asked, grabbing another glance behind her.

"You've got watchstanding duties," Natalya said. "Besides, I'd feel better getting somebody outside the department as an external auditor."

Solomon leaned in close and lowered her voice. "Can he see straight?"

"No, but I can hear just fine, Ms. Solomon," Lyons said.

Color rose up her neck and over her ears. "Sorry. No offense."

"None taken, Ms. Solomon," Lyons said.

"We've got it, Ms. Solomon. You've got other duties." Natalya shot a pointed look back up the ladder toward Engineering Control and the small cluster of hands peering down at them.

"You're the boss," she said and went back up the ladder.

"You handled that well. You've had experience working with crews?"

Natalya shook her head. "Not so much. Mostly just me and my father on an exploration scout, but I did well at Port Newmar."

"Not exactly the same."

"No," she agreed. "I just do my best and hope it's enough."

He snorted. "Sometimes it's not."

She stopped at the door to the spares locker and looked at him. "Sometimes."

He shrugged.

She opened the door and flipped on the light. "Here we are. Home away from home away from home for the next couple of days."

Lyons's head swiveled left to right and occasionally tracked up and down. He sighed. "I see why you wanted help. You sure Ms. Solomon wouldn't be an asset?"

Natalya shook her head. "Calculated assessment. Could be wrong."

"You think she's involved?"

"Let's just say, I don't want anybody casting aspersions on our process."

He peered at her through narrowed eyes. "You think Kondur's going to be looking for a scapegoat?"

"Depending on how much damage he takes to his bank account, he's going to be looking for a least a few pounds of flesh."

"You don't seem worried that it'll be yours."

"You're pretty observant when you want to be. Where shall we start?"

He surveyed the room again and blew out a long, slow breath. "At the beginning, I suppose. How are they numbered?"

"Section, shelf, bin." She turned toward the far corner. "Alpha-one-one. Over here."

"Well, sooner started, sooner I can get back to wallowing in my own filth," Lyons said.

After a bit of bumbling, Natalya handed Lyons her tablet so he could scan the label and she could count.

"You're a better choice," Lyons said. "I can't tell scrap metal from legit parts."

So they began—section by section, row by row, bin by bin.

After two stans, Natalya called a halt at Delta-four-six. "I'm getting punchy. I don't know how you're doing it."

Lyons looked a bit better than when they started. Some of the inflammation around his eyes had either gone down or was being masked by the lighting. His hands had all but stopped shaking as they worked. She saw a tiny tremor as he keyed in the last number.

"Grit and ignorance," he said, looking up. "I could use a bit of a break before we start making errors we don't catch."

"It's almost time for dinner mess. Will you be joining us tonight?"

He handed her tablet back and stared at the deck for a few moments. "Not tonight, no," he said. "Maybe tomorrow." He looked up at her and smiled. "Wouldn't want too much shock to shipboard culture all at once."

"You're not going to drink your dinner, are you?"

He smiled and shrugged. "What if I do? My business."

"Until morning, when I need your help for another full day of fun and festivities." She raised her eyebrows in question. "Am I going to have to allow time for you to sober up?"

"No," he said. "I am rather exhausted from a week of drunken revelry. I think I'll just have Ms. Marah send a tray and turn in early."

Natalya smiled. "Probably the right choice. I know I'm going to be hitting the rack as soon as I can. It's been a rugged couple of days."

"Of all the functions involved in cargo handling, I find inventories to be the absolute biggest drain."

"On your energy?" she asked.

"On my will to live," Lyons said.

"Sorry, this is probably not your favorite thing to do."

He shook his head. "Actually feel better tonight than I have all trip. I'm rather surprised."

She slapped the light switch, closing and locking the door. "Any idea why?"

"It's either the coffee or the meds," he said, not looking at her.

"Uh huh." She said. "That's your story?'

"That's my story."

"Works for me." She nodded her head at the ladder. "Come on. You're welcome to wallow in your filth, but after crawling through those bins all afternoon, I want a shower."

Lyons fell into step and they climbed the ladder. "I can understand that." He lifted his left arm and gave himself a quick sniff. "Sorry, I seem to be a bit whiffy. In that closed space, too." He grimaced. "Sorry."

She shook her head and turned down the spine. "No apologies necessary. I'm the one who shanghaied you into the job. Least I can do is put up with a little whiffiness."

Chapter Thirty-one
Siren System: 2363, June 26

Natalya slammed the bin marked O-27-56 closed. "That's the one we've been looking for all week."

Lyons stood up from the utility cart he'd been perched on and shook out his shoulders. "Last one?"

"Yep."

"How's it look?"

Natalya winced.

"That bad?"

"You're the one who's been putting in all the zeroes. What do you think?"

He shook his head. "To be honest, I stopped paying attention to what had numbers and what didn't about half past day two."

"I'll be able to get a solid read on it now," Natalya said. "I've been looking at the total spares value every evening and the number keeps going down and down and down. I'll have the exact figure when I run the replenishment order against the Siren databases, but it's going to be ugly. Into the six figures. Maybe as much as half a mill."

Lyons's eyes fairly bulged at the number. "Merciful Maude. That's a lot of parts."

"Literally. It's metric tons. Maybe as much as a hundred."

"How can anybody steal that much from a ship?"

"That's the question. How did they get that much off the ship? How did they know what to take? There are some really expensive items here, but we'd have noticed right away if they'd been missing."

"Without an engineer?" Lyons asked.

Natalya started to nod, but stopped. "Maybe. I'll have to look more closely. Some of the oxygen filtration media. It gets used a lot but it also has a shelf life of only a few months. It has to be ordered fresh regularly."

Lyons nodded. "So, while it's expensive, somebody would have noticed."

"It would also be hard to move with only a partial shelf life. If I were looking to make the most profit with the least risk, that's the stuff I'd leave."

"I don't envy you the task of sorting it all out," Lyons said.

"Thanks." Natalya paused for a moment. "And thanks for helping me out."

Lyons handed her tablet back and shrugged. He ran a hand across the back of his neck and looked at his boots. "I should probably thank you for dragging me out."

"You're welcome?"

He snorted and held out his hands. They trembled like a badly tuned fan. "Not as bad as yesterday. Having something to do helped."

"You didn't dive back into the bottle when you left here?"

Lyons sighed. "That first night? I had a couple shots but it was the end of the bottle."

"Last one?"

He shook his head. "No. I've still got half a case."

Natalya felt her eyebrows rise. "How much did you bring aboard?"

His mouth twisted into a grimace. "Just the one case."

Natalya did the math in her head. "Yikes."

"It's not that much taken across the whole week. A fifth a day." He lowered his gaze to his boots again. "Really long days."

"I'm not judging," Natalya said.

He looked up at her with a half-smile on his face. "Yeah."

"Can I ask ...?"

"I'd rather you didn't. I'm working hard not to remember it. Any more than I have to."

"How's that working out?" She gave him a smile and a wink.

He laughed. "About as well as you might expect."

"I asked Blanchard."

"What'd he say?"

"He said to ask you. It's not his story."

"Huh." He held out his right hand and watched it shake for a while.

"What will you do tomorrow?"

"Probably sweat a lot. Try to sleep."

"What do you do when you're not aboard ship?" Natalya asked. "You don't have to answer if you don't want to."

"I run logistics for Dark Knight Mining and Manufacturing."

"Challenging job?"

"Can be. When one of the mining fleets gets hit, that's the worst."

"Gets hit by what?"

"Belt rats. Iron Mountain thugs figure it's easier and more fun to take the ore than mine their own."

"Happen often?"

"No, thank Maude." He sighed. "Once a stanyer maybe. Everybody going out figures it'll be somebody else. Or not this trip. Or whatever rationale you tell yourself." He shrugged. "Most of the time, they're right."

"How many fleets does Kondur run?"

Lyons bit his lips together and shook his head. "That's probably information that you're not in the loop for."

"A lot?"

"A lot. That's all I'm saying."

Natalya thought about it for a long tick. "That's why it's so hard to defend. Targets are too spread out. Strikes are too spread out."

"In a nutshell," Lyons said. "I don't know if they do it so randomly to throw us off or if it's all they can manage. For that matter, even why they do it."

"Well, there's the value of the ore," Natalya said.

"Which is not inconsiderable, but that's a long way to haul ore."

"All the way back to Iron Mountain?"

"Yeah. It's a long haul for a bulk hauler to get all the way up there from a belt in Dark Knight."

"A bulk hauler like this one?"

Lyons nodded. "Two hundred metric tons, even with as long legs as she has, it would take a while. You can't just skip across the pond in a straight line like we did to Albert." He paused. "We did go to Albert first, didn't we?"

"Yeah."

"Well, there's a messy bit of dark out there between Dark Knight and Iron Mountain. Lots of random rocks. Lots of gas. Protostars lighting off at weird moments. You can't fly through it, even ballistic. You never know if you're going to jump into a rock that wasn't there before. Or into a gravity well you can't jump out of. Assuming you survive jumping in to begin with."

"What if they're not going to Iron Mountain?" Natalya asked. "My father always claimed that Iron Mountain got blamed for a lot of stuff they didn't do. Made it easy for people to make the odd smash-and-grab knowing Iron Mountain would take the heat."

Lyons shrugged. "That would change things, but doesn't change the frequency of hits."

"Yet."

Lyons raised an eyebrow.

"If they're just setting up the operation? Maybe they haven't been in a position to hit more than once a year until now."

"Possible," he said. "The last hit was just a couple months back. They shouldn't hit again until this time next stanyer. Plus or minus a few weeks."

"So if they strike in less than a stanyer?"

"Depends. How much less? A few weeks, even a couple of months, aren't significant."

Natalya gave a little sideways nod of the head. "Granted." She raised her eyebrows. "So what *are* you going to do tomorrow?"

"Read any good books lately?"

"I have a couple I can loan you, if that's the question."

His gaze seemed to focus somewhere on the far bulkhead. "I used to like to read. Used to read a lot."

"What happened?"

He bit his lip and shrugged. "I stopped."

The captain reviewed the report on his console and sighed. "How in the name of all that's holy did somebody do this?"

"Physically, you mean?" Natalya asked.

"Yeah. Greed and desperation make common cause, but this must have been a huge amount of work to pull off."

"It's tons of parts. It either took a lot of time or it wasn't one person."

"Could one person have done it?" Trask asked. "Whoever masterminded this had to know a lot about the ship and how she flies. Does any single person have that kind of knowledge?"

Natalya shrugged. "I don't, but I'm the new kid. I passed my environmental classes so I know what has to be done, but Knowles is operating on a completely different level down there."

Trask snorted. "He operates on a completely different level wherever he is."

"Not surprised."

"You got Josh Lyons out of his stateroom to help. I'm impressed."

"Wasn't as hard as I thought. I hit him when he was weak."

"Drunk?"

"No. Nearly sober. I just pestered him until he had no choice but to choke the life out of me or get on board."

Trask frowned at her. "How was he to work with?"

"Pretty good, actually. Once I got him up and moving in the morning, he hardly ever complained. We just plowed through the locker, one bin at a time. He knows his inventory."

"I almost swallowed my fork when he came into the wardroom for lunch the other day."

Natalya grinned. "He was nervous and still kinda shaky. I don't know if he kept any lunch down but he's been eating regularly again."

Trask cocked his head to the side. "Again?"

"Yeah. He wasn't eating much, if at all. Then when I got in the way of his bottle, he had a little withdrawal. I wasn't sure he was actually going to stay upright the first day but once we got beyond that, he's been getting stronger ever since. Hands hardly shake at all now."

"His? Or yours?" the captain asked with a nod at the console. "That's a hefty chunk of change to replace."

Natalya sniffed. "Not like I'd be able to do anything about it." A stray thought pinged a nerve. "We will be able to replace it, won't we?"

Trask eyed the list again. "Siren should have most of this. Confederation systems like to keep things lined up proper."

"I was thinking more of the credits involved. That's going to be a deep cut."

"Kondur will probably make it good through a blind account at High Tortuga. He's not going to be happy about it."

"Don't blame him."

Trask sucked his teeth for a few heartbeats, his face turned to the console but his mind clearly elsewhere. "You said you thought the ship was idle."

Natalya had to scramble to remember the conversation. "Knowles said something about the particulate count being off for a ship that had been in service all along."

"So somebody could have had access while the ship was docked."

"Makes sense."

"Not really." Trask chewed his lip. "Caretaker crews make a living by being trustworthy. They'd not be doing anything like this. It would be too easy to trace back to them."

"How long do you think this has been going on?"

Trask sighed. "That's the hell of it. I can't be sure. We might have been flying without significant spares for a long, long time. Without an engineer, we'd never have known."

"When was the last time you sailed with a real engineer?"

"Pritchard's been with us so long, I don't remember. I'm not sure if the guy before him was really an engineer or not. Seems like he might have been, but that's still at least almost half a dozen stanyers. There was a guy trained in propulsion systems for a time."

"The guy who trained Solomon?" Natalya asked.

"Yeah. Henry something. Something Henry. Don't know that I ever heard anybody call him anything but Henry, now that I think of it. Old guy. Retired and left the slot to Solomon."

"So, we're back to who has the knowledge to be able to do this."

"Yep. I have no idea. I certainly wouldn't. An engineering chief could probably take a pretty good shot at it. The problem is that they'd have to know that we weren't flying with somebody who'd catch them out."

"Wouldn't they know you were smuggling?"

Trask boomed a great laugh. "Lass, everybody in Toe-Hold space is smuggling, one way or another. It's just part of the culture."

"But I mean, how many people know you're not flying with a qualified crew?"

Trask shrugged. "Depends on what you mean by qualified. A lot of spacers out here don't bother with CPJCT credentials. Your old man must have told you that."

"He did, but I guess I didn't think that all the way through."

"You were always bound for the academy, I suspect."

"Yeah. My mother insisted that I get an education before I hared off to the backside of the beyond."

"So, you and Usoko are Newmar grads. I am. Lyons is. Blanchard isn't."

"He's not? He certainly seems like an academy grad. How'd he get started?"

Trask shook his head. "Apparently, he's been plotting courses since he was a kid. Learned on his parents' ship and just kept at it. He's a good navigator. One of the best."

"He seems nice enough."

The captain humphed. "As long as you're on his good list. Don't get on his bad list."

"He has a bad list?"

"Albee was number one on it." Trask rubbed a hand across his mouth. "I shoulda paid more attention to that." He nodded at his console. "Which of these are priorities?"

"All of them if we get boarded."

He snorted. "I got that, but we have a couple of problems. First, Kondur may not want to pay for parts here that he might be able to get cheaper there."

"It'll be real expensive if we get boarded and they confiscate the ship because we don't have the appropriate spares aboard."

"Tell me something I don't know. I appreciate that's important to you but the probabilities run against you." He held up his right forefinger. "We'd have to be boarded *after* we leave Siren. If we're boarded before then, we have the excuse of getting to Siren to replace the missing spares. It takes a lot of red tape to tie up a freighter. They'll let that slide." He held up a second finger. "They'd have to notice the discrepancy in spares. That's not very likely. Sure they check, but they don't check very far beyond immediate consumables."

"Like scrubber filters," Natalya said.

"And water filters. They're more concerned that we have proper gasses and fuel tankage and that we're not irradiating the crew." Trask held up a third finger. "Assuming both of those unlikely events happen, they have to decide it's serious enough to roll out a really big ball of red tape to keep us from harming ourselves. They *can* do it, but will they? Odds are they'll give us a warning and a writeup rather than trying to get us to kill our outbound velocity and dock up again."

Natalya pondered that for several heartbeats and nodded. "Makes sense, Skipper."

He gave her a wry smile with one eyebrow raised. "Thanks for believing I might actually know more about this than you do."

Natalya felt her face get hot and she looked down at her hands. "Sorry, Skipper."

"No hoo-hoo. Only way you learn is by asking. If I thought you were over the line, you'd be scrubbing the deck in the engine room." He smiled at her.

"Thanks," she said. "What was the other problem?"

"What other problem?"

"You said we might have a couple of problems."

"Oh, yeah. The other problem is that Kondur might want to see for himself before he starts replacing stuff."

"That's assuming we make it back."

Trask chuckled. "That's always a consideration. Spotting that bus coupling malfunction probably saved our asses." He stared into Natalya's face. "We *all* have you to thank for that, not just Kondur. He'll know and remember it." He nodded at his console again. "So what's on this list that you couldn't fix even if we had it?"

Natalya brought the list up on her tablet and they dug in. By the time dinner mess came around, they'd whittled the list down to immediate priorities, a handful of nice-to-haves, and a big pile of wouldn't-helps.

"You know there's another problem I didn't think of," the captain said as he led Natalya to the wardroom.

"I thought the two you had were pretty good."

"What happens if a freighter docks and places a replenishment order for almost a whole ship's worth of spares in a single whack?" he asked.

"The chandlery celebrates?"

"I think it more likely that TIC spots the transaction records."

"Why would they do that if they know the spares will be aboard?"

"They might like to know where the credits came from, but they probably already know that. They might like to know who's on the ship that can drop so much in a single order. I suspect that they already know that, too. Or will, as soon as we dock and the little birds start singing."

"I'm missing the point," Natalya said. "I bet it's something obvious."

"A ship docks with almost bingo spares and commits to several hundred thousand credits to replace them. Seems to me TIC might want to have a look inside that ship and maybe a good look at the crew and officers to see if anybody's on their watch lists."

"Are there?"

"What? People aboard who are on their watch lists? Probably. I suspect you and Ms. Usoko might be."

"We didn't kill anybody."

He stopped in the passageway and looked back at her. "That's a good habit to have. Try to keep it if you can. I don't think you're what TIC will be most interested in."

"What then?"

"I suspect they'd want to see if the rest of the ship was in as bad a shape as a full spares replenishment would suggest."

"If we have TIC informers on board, wouldn't they already know?"

Trask nodded and turned toward the wardroom again. "Yeah, but nothing like getting up-close and personal with a Mark One eyeball to tell you what you want to know."

"And the goal is to attract as little attention as possible," Natalya said.

"Point, Regyri."

Captain Trask looked around the wardroom over the remains of breakfast. He smiled a little when he looked at Lyons and gave the man a short nod. "I'm planning on going to navigation stations around 0930. I don't know what kind of reception we'll get at the dock, but Moe doesn't take kindly to strangers."

Blanchard and Pritchard both offered chuckles while Lyons stared into his coffee cup.

"If we stay on plan, we'll dock just before lunch. Will you be able to sign off, Joshua?" Trask asked, looking directly at Lyons.

"Yeah. Should be. Assuming they've got our can ready to go, we could be out of there in as little time as it takes their people to swap them."

"Good. I'll alert Moe and we'll try to get out again this afternoon." He looked at Blanchard. "Transit to Siren Orbital?"

"Maybe a week. We've matched orbit with Moe's now but the orbital is inside us so we'll have to dig into the primary gravity well a bit more."

"All right then." Trask looked at Natalya. "You've got that replenishment order ready?"

"Yes, Captain."

"Good. When we get secured from navigation stations, forward it to the orbital via Moe's link. And stay on ship's power. We'll top off tanks after we get to Siren."

"Will do."

Trask looked around the table. "Anybody got anything else?"

"I'm very much looking forward to visiting the orbital again," Pritchard said.

"We'll have a couple of days' liberty, Steven. You'll have your visit. Anybody with ship's business?" Trask asked.

Nobody spoke for a few heartbeats.

"Let's get at it." Trask pushed back from the table and left the wardroom.

Pritchard followed him out.

"What was that about Moe and strangers?" Natalya asked.

Blanchard shook his head. "Nothing much. Moe has had some run ins with TIC and the CPJCT inspectors. She's not happy when they're visiting."

"Whew," Natalya said. "I thought the skipper meant we were the strangers."

Lyons said, "Moe's good people."

Blanchard's eyebrows flickered in response. "There aren't many."

"No, there aren't," Lyons said, pushing his coffee cup back from the edge of the table. "See you after we dock." He left without so much as a backward glance.

"That was unusual," Blanchard said. "You're a good influence on him."

"Me?" Natalya shook her head. "Personally, I think he's just bored."

Blanchard stared into his coffee mug. "Did he tell you his story?"

"Nope."

"Huh."

"That's it?" Natalya asked.

Blanchard shrugged. "Josh has always had problems on these runs. He manages logistics for Kondur between."

"That much he told me."

"If the story's true, the man's bloody brilliant with keeping ships, stations, and outposts all supplied with what they need. You have to be a juggler to keep all those balls in the air."

"Why wouldn't it be true?"

"I've only ever seen him on the annual run. He's always a mess." Blanchard shrugged and looked at Natalya. "Always was, anyway. That conversation was the longest civil exchange he and I have had in three stanyers."

"What is there for him to do?"

Blanchard shook his head. "What is there for any of us to do? We're actors on a mobile stage. The play's been written and we're slotted into our roles."

"You don't believe that."

"I do."

"How can you? You're plotting our course."

Blanchard shook his head. "I'm just fiddling the numbers to get us where Kondur wants us to be when he wants us to be there. I'm good at that, but it's just mechanics. Time, distance, velocity. The only uncertainty is when we jump and even that's relatively small."

Natalya shook her head. "I think you're just jaded. You've done it so long, it's second nature, like using a fork. The rest of us poor mortals can barely get the food into our mouths."

"Maybe," Blanchard said. After a few heartbeats he said, "Your friend Zoya is a piece of work."

"How so?"

"She's smart enough. Even capable enough. She could step into the second mate's slot and handle the navigation without any problem."

"So?"

"So everything else pushes her off-balance."

"She's a bit rigid. It's one thing to know Toe-Hold space is out there, but to run your face into its bulkheads puts a different spin on things."

"I've seen armor plating that's less rigid than she is," Blanchard said, a smile making it into almost a joke. "What do they teach about Toe-Hold space in the academy?"

"Basic history. Accurate as far as it goes, I think."

"How would you know?"

"I spent most of my formative stanyers with my father. He's been banging around the Western Annex for decades. He'd take me to places and tell me their stories. Stories I was required to validate, by the way. He's a stickler for accuracy, too."

"Where'd he take you?"

Natalya cradled her mug between her palms and thought back. "High Tortuga was fun. Mel's place was ... interesting."

"How long ago were you at Mel's?"

"I don't remember. Ten stanyers, probably. It was one of the early trips."

"Interesting how?"

"It was like a hive. People buzzing around. Everybody had some kind of deal going, something they'd be able to cash in on. Everywhere you looked, any time of day, people. To me it was crazy."

"You didn't find that at Dark Knight?"

"I haven't spent that much time on station there. There's a certain air of busy-ness, but nothing like the roiling waters at Mel's."

"What was your favorite?"

"High Tortuga. Their systems amazed me. If you could think of a way to look at data, they could make their system render that view."

Bray stuck his head in from the galley. "Sars? May I clear? Diana wants to get the cleanup done before we dock."

Natalya stood immediately. "I'm done. Thank you, Mr. Bray."

Blanchard waved him in. "Have at it. I should go make sure we're still on the approach track anyway."

Natalya followed him out of the wardroom as Bray started piling dirty dishes in a tray.

The ship docked at Moe's Mining at mid-morning. Natalya kept the kickers hot, but safed the sails and keel generators just as a matter of routine. By 1100, the ship was snugged in and waiting for the cargo swap.

Natalya's tablet bipped with a summons to the cabin. She found the door open and all the officers inside.

"Good, Regyri. Come in," Trask said waving her into the crowded cabin. "We've a bit of a problem."

Natalya looked around at all the faces. Zoya looked slightly baffled. Blanchard looked like a particularly well-fed cat, but that was his normal expression. Lyons looked as dour as ever. Pritchard looked ever so slightly bemused, like a kid who's just opened his birthday present and found it to be underwear.

"The issue is TIC," Trask said. "They're here on the station."

"That is unexpected," Pritchard said. "Will they want to inspect us?" His face had a pale and waxy sheen.

"Moe is keeping them busy for now, but we'll want to do whatever we can to move on quickly." Trask looked at Lyons. "How soon before they've swapped the cans?"

"At least another stan. Probably two."

"Anything we can do to light a rocket under them?" Trask asked.

"Nothing I can do, no," Lyons said. "Moe's good. She'll want to cover us as much as she can."

Zoya said, "I have a suggestion."

Trask nodded to her. "I'm listening."

"Invite their command team for lunch."

Pritchard made a short retching sound, but Blanchard's smile widened.

Trask cocked his head to one side a bit as if to shake a loose piece into place in his skull. "Invite them for lunch?"

"It was just an idea."

"I'm not saying it's a bad one. Tell me why."

Zoya looked around at everybody once before facing Trask again. "If we sneak in, dump the can, and scoot, who knows what they'll think. Maybe that we have something to hide." She shrugged.

Lyons looked up at her. "Brilliant."

Pritchard moved as if to step back. His face had gone pasty white and his hands fluttered like birds. "That's madness."

Trask shook his head slowly. "No. Lyons is right. It's brilliant." He looked at Lyons. "Get Moe on the line. Ask her how many in their command team. Unless they're expecting trouble, they'll only have a couple."

Lyons nodded, pulling his tablet out even before the captain finished speaking.

Trask looked to Natalya. "Can you carry the engineering section?"

"Of course."

"Hey, wait," Pritchard said. "I'm the chief engineer here."

Trask frowned at him. "You're barely able to keep from pissing yourself. Stay out of the way."

"Captain, I really must object," Pritchard said, drawing himself up. "You need me—"

"I need you to follow orders," Trask said, cutting Pritchard off in mid-wheeze. "Right now, we need to present our little performance of 'just one of the gang' to a TIC command field agent or two. What I need you to do is retire to your stateroom with a serious migraine."

Zoya shook her head. "Skipper?"

"Hit me," Trask said.

"Migraine might be grounds for medical discharge. Not physically qualified. We need something less permanently debilitating."

"Suggestions?"

Zoya looked to Natalya. "Nats? Something engine-y?"

Natalya closed her eyes and focused. "Burns," she said. "Got too close to an overheated generator bus and the auto-doc put him on an isolation protocol against infection." She opened her eyes to find Trask staring at her.

"Did you just make that up?" he asked.

"No, Captain. I've actually seen it. Wasn't even that bad a burn. Normally the auto-doc would keep you in the pod until the pseudo-skin closed over the wound but it's not required. As in the case of an officer who might need to be consulted but who shouldn't be up and around people generally."

Trask nodded. "Can you jigger the auto-doc to show that?"

"Sorry, Skipper," Natalya said. "Beyond me."

"I can," Blanchard said. "System interface should let me into it to add a bit of a record, sealed for patient privacy, of course."

"Of course," Trask said dryly. "I'll add a log record to that effect as well."

"I could get into the auto-doc and you could seal me in," Pritchard said.

Trask looked at him with the kind of odd regard one might have for a boot that had suddenly presented one with a weather report. "Unfortunately, I suspect even a TIC field agent would be able to see that you were perfectly well in the readouts, Steven. Maybe just stay in your stateroom?"

Pritchard opened his mouth as if to speak but the captain cut him off.

"It's for the good of the ship, Steven. We need to sell this and right now, you're not on your game, are you?"

Pritchard sighed. "Perhaps not."

"Then would you please help us by playing your role?" Trask asked, his earlier impatience seemingly evaporating into the air. "It's for the good of the ship."

Pritchard straightened his tunic, rubbing his palms down the breast as if to smooth the fabric. "Of course. Good of the ship." He looked up, bird bright and nodded. "Of course, Captain. Shall I go now and prepare?"

"I think that might be best. We'll have one of the stewards bring you a tray. How's that sound?"

"Very nice, Captain. Thank you." He looked around at the others. "If you'll excuse me, I must retire to my stateroom."

"We'll send someone to fetch you when the coast is clear," Trask said.

"Yes. Quite appropriate," Pritchard said. With that, he sailed out of the cabin, head high and striding purposefully as if he'd not nearly wet himself over the prospect of having Trade Investigation Commission agents aboard the ship.

"Moe says they've only got one special agent, Captain." Lyons looked up from his tablet. "Might be politic to invite her second as well."

Trask nodded and keyed a note into his console, slapping the enter key with a snap. "Note to Ms. Marah. I'll go down and talk to her when we break." He looked at Blanchard. "Auto-doc?"

"Aye," Blanchard said.

Trask turned to Zoya. "Can you organize a brow watch and messenger? Somebody shipshape and Bristol fashion for the front door?"

"Spec Two Eisley for the watch?"

"Rebecca? Yes, she'll be perfect."

"How about Wazu for messenger?" Zoya asked.

"He needs a haircut. Davis?"

"Perfect, Captain. I happen to know he's got a fresh shipsuit."

Trask gave a short chortle. "Do I want to know how you know that, Ms. Usoko?"

"He came to watch smelly. I made him go change. It took him two tries, but he finally found a fresh suit."

"You're a hard task master, Ms. Usoko. No question." Trask's lips twitched a little.

Lyons asked, "You want me to do anything special, Captain?"

Trask looked at him and ran his fingers over his mouth. "Just keep up your end of the conversation?"

"My end, Captain?"

"Just smile a little and stop being a mope," Natalya said. "Don't sit there hunched over the table like somebody's going to steal your food."

Trask's eyes went wide and even Blanchard flinched.

Lyons looked at Natalya, his head tilted a bit to the right and twisted slightly away from her. "A mope."

"Yes. A mope."

A smile broke across Lyons's face like the sunrise from planetary orbit, a hint of the star at the edge of atmosphere and then a brilliant flare of light. "I think I can do that. You can poke me if I seem to be falling back onto hard times, all right?"

Natalya nodded. "Done." She looked at the captain. "Anything else, Skipper? I'd like to run a mop through my hair and give the engine room a good combing if we're going to have guests."

Trask started chuckling and just waved a ham-size hand in dismissal. "Go to," he said. "Go to."

Chapter Thirty-four
Moe's Mining: 2363, July 23

Diana Marah outdid herself on short notice. Natalya admired the buffet spread that included Marah's signature curried chicken and a chickpea dish she called *msabbaha*. A covered bowl of rice waited at the end along with some fresh rounds of flat bread. The scent of cumin and sweet curry made Natalya's mouth swim.

"Is everything ready?" Zoya asked.

"I think so." Natalya shrugged. "Close enough at any rate. When are they arriving?"

Lyons waved his tablet. "Any minute now. Moe says they've just left the office."

Blanchard slipped into the wardroom just ahead of the captain. "Relax. They're just people."

"People who could lock us up if they wanted to," Trask said. "No pressure."

Lyons glanced at Trask and shook his head.

"Something, Mr. Lyons?" the captain asked.

"No, Captain. Just admiring your aplomb."

Trask grinned and stood over the buffet, surveying it from one end to the other as if trying to decide where to begin. "Fruit cobbler for dessert, I heard."

Mr. Bray stuck his head in from the pantry. "Yes, sar. Don't say anything but I heard the ice cream maker going earlier as well."

"Excellent, Mr. Bray. My compliments to Ms. Marah. I'll deliver them myself when this is over."

A three-rap knock on the door warned them just before Spacer Apprentice Jason Davis opened it. "Your guests have arrived, Captain." He looked every inch the proud spacer apprentice as he stood at attention at the door.

"Welcome, welcome," Trask said. "Come in, come in."

Two TIC agents wearing black jumpsuit uniforms entered. The first, an older woman with a prodigious smile, reached for the captain's outstretched hand. "Captain Trask, I'm Special Agent Paula Rewers. Thank you for your kind invitation."

Trask gave a little bow over Rewers's handshake. "Agent. Thank you for coming. It's always a treat to find new people to invite aboard."

"May I present my second in command, Agent Michael Hardwall?"

Hardwall took a step forward and smiled. "Captain."

"Welcome, Agent Hardwall."

"Thank you, Captain. We don't get invited aboard many vessels."

Trask laughed. "I dare say. We're happy to have you." He waved a hand at the buffet like a stage magician introducing his lovely assistant. "Our chef loves the opportunity to cook for new people and I hope you'll find something to enjoy." He ushered Special Agent Rewers to the head of the line. "Normally captain's privilege, but hospitality rules today. If you'd start down the line, Ms. Rewers?"

"Paula," she said.

"Paula," the captain repeated. "Thomas, although Tom works well. Only my late wife called me Thomas. Generally when I was in the soup." He smiled as he squired Ms. Rewers along.

Lyons caught Natalya's eye and grinned.

Zoya stepped forward to greet Hardwall. "Agent Hardwall, I'm Zoya Usoko. May I introduce Second Mate Charles Blanchard?"

"Charlie, please," Blanchard said, reaching to shake Hardwall's hand.

"Today I'll be Michael," Hardwall said. "Nice to meet you, Charlie."

"Our cargo master, Josh Lyons," Zoya said.

Josh stepped up with a smile and a quick handshake. "Welcome aboard, Michael. Today I'll be Queen of the May."

"No, Mr. Lyons," the captain said from the end of the buffet. "That's Ms. Usoko's name today. You can be Queen of the May tomorrow."

Lyons snapped his fingers in a theatrical gesture of disappointment. "Some days are like that," he said with another nod at Hardwall.

"Last but not least, Natalya Regyri, engineering officer," Zoya said.

Hardwall tilted his head. "Regyri. I know that name."

Natalya's stomach clenched and a cold streak slipped down her spine. "Do you?"

Hardwall's eyes narrowed but he wasn't looking at Natalya. His focus rested somewhere in the middle ground. "Charlotte Regyri?"

Natalya's mind did a flip. "You know my mother?"

Hardwall smiled. "Indeed, I do. It's been ages since I've seen her. How is she?"

"Doing well, the last I heard. An engineering chief for Consolidated Freight."

"And here you are in engineering as well. Wrench doesn't fall far from the machine."

"I come by it honestly," Natalya said.

"If you people are through, this food is not getting any warmer." Trask waved the crew forward.

Blanchard stepped aside for Hardwall to precede him and the rest followed in rank order.

In a matter of a few ticks everyone had food and found seats. Special Agent Rewers took the place of honor at the foot of the table, opposite the captain, with Mr. Hardwall to her right. Bray came in with both coffee and tea, serving around the table before making a discreet exit back through the pantry.

Trask raised his mug. "To good profits and safe voyages."

"Hear, hear," Rewers said.

After the toast, the company settled down to address the food. Natalya became so absorbed in her meal that she almost missed the opening salvo.

"You've an interesting crew, Captain," Hardwall said.

"Thank you, Mr. Hardwall. They get us there and back again."

"No first mate?" Hardwall asked.

Trask glanced at Zoya. "Ms. Usoko here has proven to be most capable."

"You're barely out of the academy, aren't you?" Hardwall said, looking at Zoya.

"I grew up running ore haulers for my family's business over in Margary," she said. "At least this crew doesn't have to tiptoe around the owner's granddaughter." She smiled at him.

"Usoko Mining?" Rewers asked.

"My grandparent's company."

Rewers nodded. "You left to join the merchant fleet?"

"My parents will run the company for decades. There's little enough for a number three daughter to aspire to there." Zoya shrugged. "I thought to try my wings on my own for a while. I can always go back with a great education and some decent experience behind me."

"And how are you finding it?" Hardwall asked, glancing around at the wardroom.

"I'm quite enjoying it."

Hardwall looked back at the captain. "I'm sure Ms. Usoko is quite skilled but regulations require you to have a licensed first mate."

"We have two aboard, Mr. Hardwall." Trask shrugged. "Neither of us are being paid for that position."

Hardwall's eyebrows shot up. "You're the captain. Of course you're licensed as first mate. Who else?"

Blanchard tipped his head. "That would be me."

"You're the second mate and astrogator."

"Yes," Blanchard said. "That's true."

Trask sighed and glanced at Rewers before staring at Hardwall. "We had a bit of a blowout with our first mate just before we left. He thought he was indispensable. He wasn't. Perhaps we'll find somebody to take the berth, or maybe Ms. Usoko here will prove to be so effective, I'll keep her on until she grows into it. In the meantime, Mr. Hardwall, the regulations only require the ship have a licensed first mate. We do. There is nothing in the regulations that requires us to actually pay a first mate."

"Who's handling the watches?" Hardwall asked.

"I'm perfectly capable of standing bridge watch, Mr. Hardwall."

Hardwall started to speak again, but Rewers touched his forearm and his mouth closed with an audible click. "Your chief engineer isn't with us?" She glanced at Natalya with a slight shrug.

"Mr. Pritchard is currently recovering from a nasty burn. He's in his stateroom if you'd like to disturb him," the captain said.

"A burn?" Rewers asked. "Nothing serious, I hope?"

"He got too close to a hot keel generator. Clumsy accident. Quite painful, but nothing life-threatening. He's upright and able to take nourishment," Trask said. "By rights, he should be in the auto-doc until the pseudo-skin has a chance to close the wound, but he gets claustrophobic in small spaces. The auto-doc allowed a quarantine procedure to reduce the chance of infection while it heals."

"That sounds serious. Will he need additional care?" Rewers asked.

"He's uncomfortable but visiting the auto-doc regularly for updates and medications to help manage the process. His prognosis is excellent," Trask said, a smile returning to his face.

"We'll be docking at Siren Orbital in a few days," Lyons said. "If he needs additional care, we'll have an opportunity there."

"In the meantime, Ms. Regyri? You're running the department?" Hardwall asked.

"There's not much to it. The watch schedule has been posted. The ship's in good repair other than a faulty generator bus coupling, which we'll get repaired at Siren. Even if Mr. Pritchard were up and about, he wouldn't be trying to do this himself with the facilities at Siren to call on." Natalya shrugged and took a forkful of *msabbaha*.

"I don't suppose you'd object to a safety inspection since we're here?" Hardwall asked.

Trask shrugged. "Not in the least. I'd ask that you make it fast, if you're going to. Moe's promised that our new can will be locked in by the time lunch is over."

Rewers gave her head a small shake. "That won't be necessary, Captain. We understand you've got places to go, people to meet."

Hardwall sat back in his seat and let the matter drop without another comment.

The rest of the luncheon passed without difficulty. The buffet line got scraped down to metal. They had another round of tea and coffee before Bray returned with a tray full of small dishes containing individual cobblers topped with vanilla ice cream.

"Mind the dishes, sars. They're hot from the oven."

Hardwall, for all his initial confrontation, proved to be a witty and clever dining companion. Natalya still didn't trust him, but Rewers appeared to have him under control.

Promptly at 1300 hours, Rewers smiled at Captain Trask. "This has been lovely, Thomas. We probably won't be seeing you in Siren, but when you get back this way again, it'll be our treat on station. If we might be excused? We have more work to do and your can is probably in position for your departure."

Trask stood and nodded. "Of course, of course. Let me walk you out."

The whole table stood as Rewers and Hardwall prepared to leave.

"Thank you for coming," Lyons said. "We don't often get the chance to sit down with Trade Investigation and just visit."

"Yes, thank you," Zoya said with a warm smile at Hardwall. "It was lovely to get to know you."

Trask nodded to Bray, who'd stuck his head in from the pantry. "You can clear, Mr. Bray. We're all done here."

Bray nodded and started to clear away the dirty dishes as Trask ushered Special Agent Rewers out into the passage.

Hardwall paused and looked at Zoya. "If you'd walk with me, Ms. Usoko? I think I owe you an apology."

Zoya glanced at Blanchard who gave a small shrug. "Of course, Mr. Hardwall, but you don't owe me anything." She followed the small party out of the wardroom and down the passage, leaving everybody else standing there with nothing to say.

Natalya looked at Lyons. "That didn't hurt much, did it?"

Lyons shook his head and sighed. "I'll give you that."

"Did Moe's crew get the can swapped?" Blanchard asked.

"Yeah. I got a ping just before dessert. We're ready to fly as soon as the ole man is ready to go."

Trask stuck his head in the wardroom door. "You people need to clear out of there so Mr. Bray can work. We've got a bus to catch. Move it."

Natalya chuckled and headed for her stateroom to change into something other than her best khakis. She had just zipped up her working shipsuit when Zoya knocked on the door to the head.

"You there?"

Natalya opened the door. "Yup. What'd Hardwall want?"

Zoya held out a hand, palm up. A thumb drive glinted in the bright lights from the overhead. "He slipped me this while the captain and Rewers were saying their fond farewells."

"Hardwall was your contact?" Natalya shook her head quickly a couple of times to see if she might rattle some sense into it.

"So it would seem. How he knew to find me here, now? They clearly know more about what's going on with this ship than Captain Trask believes."

Natalya ruffled fingers through her cropped hair. "Maybe," she said. "He's said some things the last few days that make me think he believes they know exactly who we are and what we're doing here."

"Then what's with all the smuggling talk, about not getting caught? If they know already, what's the big deal?"

Natalya shook her head. "Right hand, left hand, maybe."

"Plausible deniability?" Zoya asked.

"Deny to whom?"

"What's the relationship between TIC and CPJCT?"

"You think TIC is keeping it out of CPJCT's oversight?" Natalya asked.

"You're the expert in Toe-Holds," Zoya said. "You tell me."

Natalya spun the ideas around in her head but nothing jelled. "We need to get ready to dust off here. See you after dinner?"

Zoya's gaze unfocused for a few heartbeats. "I pass off the watch to the skipper at 1800. He'll have it until midnight when Blanchard comes on." She nodded. "After dinner." She closed the door and Natalya scooted down the spine in time to take her seat before Zoya's voice on the announcer called the ship to navigation stations.

CHAPTER THIRTY-FIVE
SIREN SYSTEM: 2363, JULY 23

After the dinner mess, Natalya and Zoya retired to Zoya's stateroom to examine the chip.

"Are you going to just plug it into your tablet?" Natalya asked.

Zoya frowned at the chip. "There could be anything on it."

"If it's compromised, whatever's on that chip can get directly into the ship's systems."

Zoya nodded but shrugged. "Why would TIC give us a compromised chip?"

"Maybe to get remote access to the ship?"

Zoya snorted. "They already know more than I'm comfortable with."

"So? I thought they were on your side?"

"So did I," Zoya said, her voice low and her brow still furrowed.

"If we had the *Peregrine*, we could use her sandbox to look at the chip without exposing the network."

"I wonder if Blanchard can help us," Zoya said.

Natalya felt her eyebrows rising. "Would you trust him?"

"Do we have a choice?"

"We need a story."

"We *need* a standalone chip reader," Zoya said.

Natalya grinned. "Duh."

"What?" Zoya asked.

"Ship's library."

"It's on ShipNet. What are you getting at?"

Natalya shook her head. "I bet it's not. I'll bet you credits to crescent rolls that the ship has some readers dedicated to 'private time' displays."

"Wha—?" Zoya's voice choked off and her eyes got wide. "Oh, 'private time.' Like when somebody's brought a bit of entertainment media aboard? Something not for general consumption?"

"Yes, exactly."

Zoya's face took on a bit of a ruddy glow. "How would we find such a unit?"

"We ask for one. Who's the morale officer?"

Zoya's lips crumpled into a wry grin. "Not CPJCT, remember. Ancillary duties are going to be sketchy."

"We ask Blanchard. He's in charge of systems. Logically that includes keeping digital freeloaders from hitching a ride on our Ship-Net every time some horny spacer plugs in for some sexy time without partner."

A ruddy glow crept up the back of Zoya's neck and over her ears.

"My goodness, Zee. You aren't that naÃ⁻ve are you?"

Zoya chewed on her response for a while. "Sheltered childhood," she said after more than a few heartbeats. She didn't look up at Natalya.

Natalya reached over and patted Zoya's forearm. "I'll ask Blanchard. Who knows? We might get some loaners, too."

"Ew. Loaners? Really?"

Natalya twiddled the fingers on her left hand and waggled her eyebrows. "South paw rules."

Zoya swatted her on the shoulder. "I didn't need to know that."

Natalya laughed. "Sorry, bunkie. We're learning so much more about each other now that we're not sharing a room."

"Spare me the details, all right?"

"Skipper's got the watch?" Natalya asked.

"He relieved me at 1745."

"Just like real fleet," Natalya said.

"He's old guard. Not sure why he's out here with the riff-raff."

"So Blanchard is off. I'll go knock on his door."

"Won't you be embarrassed?"

Natalya shook her head. "Why? It's not like I'm doing anything illegal. They don't even have a nonfraternization policy on this ship. Who knows how many bunk bunnies are breeding down in the crews' quarters."

Zoya sighed. "Now you're trying too hard."

Natalya stood and shrugged. "Can't blame a girl for tryin'."

"You are trying. I'll give you that."

Natalya laughed and headed out the door. "Be right back."

It took Natalya just a few steps to knock on Blanchard's door. He opened it almost immediately. "Natalya? I didn't expect you here. Problem?"

Natalya shook her head. "Do we have such a thing as a firewalled reader aboard?"

He nodded. "Yeah. Several. I wish more people would use them. Why?"

"Can I get one?"

His eyebrows shot up. "Lemme guess. It's for a friend?"

"No. It's for me. She can get her own."

"Wardroom pantry. Cabinet under the coffee maker."

"Do I need to sign for it or anything?"

"There's a log book to thumb. You might be the first one to use it."

"That loose?"

Blanchard shrugged and grinned. "Not exactly a high-demand item. I have to keep scrubbers running on the ship's systems non-stop."

"Lotta activity?"

"Not so much yet. After we leave Siren Orbital, it'll be a free-for-all."

"Can't you firewall the tablets?"

"I can. It's not like I can make anybody use them." Blanchard shrugged. "As soon as I protect one, somebody buys a new one and links into the ship. That's why things will get a little spongy after Siren. At least half the crew will upgrade their tablets." He glanced up and down the passageway. "Anything else?"

Natalya shook her head again. "Thanks."

"Have a nice evening," Blanchard said and closed his door.

Natalya thought about Blanchard's problem all the way to the wardroom. She found the cabinet and pulled a reader from the rack. As soon as she did, a pop-up tablet offered her a thumb tab. She pressed her thumb to the pad and it beeped once before withdrawing.

She stood there for a moment, staring into the cabinet.

Chef Marah stuck her head in from the galley door. "Oh, Ms. Regyri, isn't it?"

"Good evening, Chef. I didn't disturb you, did I?"

She shook her head and smiled. "No. Just finishing the evening cleanup and heard the beep. It's not normal to have people in here after hours. Is there something you need?"

"No, I'm just getting a reader."

"Your tablet broken?" she asked.

"Just wanted a sandbox to play in."

"I believe you're the first person I've ever seen take one of those."

"Really?"

"I have to make sure everything is shipshape in here. I'm always checking to make sure things are where they need to be while we're underway. I don't think I've ever seen one out of the rack."

"I was just marveling that they weren't all gone," Natalya said.

"Who'd want them?"

"Good question, Ms. Marah."

Natalya took the reader back to Zoya. "We may have been looking at this parts issue wrong," she said.

Zoya tilted her head. "How so?"

"I've been operating on the assumption that somebody's just skimming to augment their income."

"Reasonable."

"Blanchard sent me down to the wardroom pantry for this." She held up the reader. "There's a whole rack of them in a recharging frame in there."

Zoya frowned for a moment and then her eyes snapped wide open. "That doesn't make sense."

Natalya bit her lip and shrugged. "It might if the person doing the pilfering didn't know about the readers."

"That's possible. We didn't know about them."

"Yeah, but we're the new kids. There's probably an encyclopedia full of information about this ship we don't know."

"You think it's something else?" Zoya asked.

"What if it's somebody who specifically wants Barbell parts?"

"That makes sense. Barbells are the most common bulk hauler," Zoya said. "What makes you think Barbell parts instead of general spares?"

"I'm not sure. There's not that much that's specific to Barbells. The tools could all be used on any ship. The bus connectors that triggered this whole thing aren't exactly universal, but they're cross-compatible with a lot of the larger ships."

"Any unique Barbell spares?"

"Scrubber cartridges. Larger ships and most of the Manchester-built hulls use algae in a nutrient matrix. Barbells use a particular shape of cartridge to filter out airborne contaminants."

"We didn't lose any of those?" Zoya asked.

"No, but they're cheap—relatively speaking—and we'd have noticed pretty fast since they're one of the regularly consumed parts."

"What about Burleson spares? We've got some heavy drives back there."

"True, but any high-end jumper would have very similar drives. They're almost all plug-and-play parts. Other than the calibration and power circuits, the drives all use the same parts."

"So what you're saying is that these are easily disposed of."

"To anybody with a large ship, yeah. I can't use these parts in the *Peregrine*, for example. They're just the wrong size."

"But you think that it's not just random pilferage," Zoya said.

"It makes more sense if whoever took this stuff already had a buyer lined up. Less possibility that they'd get caught with the goods."

"And you're jumping to this conclusion because nobody stole the firewalled readers." Zoya's eyebrows rose.

Natalya felt the heat rise on her neck. "That's a bit of a stretch, isn't it?"

Zoya shrugged. "Interesting hypothesis, but I think we'd be wise to keep the possibilities open. The readers aren't exactly a solid data point. And speaking of readers?" She held out her hand.

Natalya gave her the unit and shrugged. "Sorry. Got carried away."

Zoya plugged the chip and frowned at the screen.

"What is it?" Natalya asked.

"Bank deposit."

"That's all?"

"That's all," Zoya said.

"Are you rich yet?"

"Twenty thousand."

"Any orders?"

"Just the deposit." Zoya turned the tablet around to show Natalya.

"What do they think they're getting for this?"

Zoya shook her head. "No idea. I hate surprises."

"Maybe we'll run into Hardwall at Siren and you can ask."

"You think so?"

Natalya shook her head. "No. Not really. If he's really TIC, he'll keep a low profile in station."

"But if he's Rewers's gopher? Won't he have to be out and about?"

"Probably no more than Rewers herself."

"You think he's not TIC?"

"No, I think he is TIC. I just wonder where he really falls on the chain of command."

Captain Trask's face turned an alarming shade of red. "They want what?"

Blanchard held up a hand, palm out. "Just the messenger, Skipper."

"At least they're waiting until we dock," Lyons said.

Pritchard smirked. "Guess my hiding didn't work out so well."

"You going to be all right now?" Trask asked, arching an eyebrow at Pritchard. "I wasn't sure you weren't going to have a heart attack at Moe's."

"Here we've got a legal cargo," Pritchard said. "There's nothing for them to find now."

Lyons snorted and pushed his dinner plate back from the edge of the table.

"Something you want to say, Josh?" Pritchard asked.

Lyons looked up at the overhead and took a couple of deep breaths. "No, Mr. Pritchard. There's nothing I want to say." He glanced at Natalya. "I'm not being a mope."

She grinned at him.

"If we're done with the drama for the moment, is there anything we need to do before we dock in the morning?" Trask asked, looking around the table.

Blanchard pursed his lips and shook his head. "I think we're as clean as we're likely to be."

"I can discharge a couple of fire extinguishers," Natalya said. "Nothing major, just something they can find and write us up for."

Pritchard turned to her, his jaw flapping, but no words came out of his mouth for several heartbeats. "You'll *what*?" His voice squeaked on the last word.

Natalya sighed. "If they don't find anything, they'll dig. Everybody has something. If we give them something easy, they're less likely to go poking about where they might find something serious."

Pritchard blanched. "What could they find?"

"I thought you were good with them coming aboard now," Trask said. "You've done this drill before, Steven. What's got you so spooked this trip?"

Pritchard drew himself up in his chair. "I am not spooked, Captain. I'm aghast that Ms. Regyri would consider lowering the operational standards of the ship in such a cavalier way."

"Uh huh," Trask said, casting him a sour look. "What's your biggest concern, Ms. Regyri?"

"I don't want them looking too closely at the Burleson drives."

Trask frowned for a moment. "Is there something wrong with them?"

Natalya shook her head. "Not as such. They're too big for a stock Barbell. They're Class T's where normally we'd have Class O's."

"Ah," Trask said. "I see your point. If they ask, just tell them it's your first trip with us and they should ask me. I can probably come up with a cover if we need it, but I'd rather not try to use it."

"That's it?" Pritchard asked.

"What's it, Steven?" Trask asked.

"You're not going to say something about discharging fire extinguishers?"

Trask pursed his lips and nodded slowly. "I wasn't going to, no, but now that you mention it," he looked at Natalya. "There's one at the foot of the bridge ladder. It's a backup in case of fire in the data closet. That would be a good one to hit. Also one in the spine around frame sixty-five."

Natalya nodded. "I know the one you mean. Should I pop one in crew berthing as well?"

"No, but see if Ms. Marah can expend one of her small ones from the galley and red tag it for replacement when we dock."

Natalya grinned. "Nice touch."

"Not my first circus," Trask said with a wink.

Pritchard's expression of horror almost made Natalya laugh. Almost. "Captain, I must protest. This is highly irregular."

"Thank you, Mr. Pritchard. Protest noted. You'll pardon me if I don't log it until after we leave Siren?" Trask stared at Pritchard. "Is there anything else you'd like to bring to my attention?"

Something in the captain's expression made Pritchard back down. He sighed and deflated like a week-old balloon on the exhale. "No, Captain. Nothing else."

"Good," Trask said. "Then let's clear out of here so Mr. Bray can clear away the dinner mess, shall we?" He stood and ambled out of the wardroom, leaving Pritchard scowling at his empty plate and Lyons shaking his head.

"Something funny, Josh?" Blanchard asked.

Lyons looked across the table and grinned. "All this time and I never realized how much fun I was missing."

Blanchard gave a small chuckle. "Blame her," he said, jerking his thumb at Natalya.

Lyons glanced at Natalya. "Thank you, Ms. Regyri."

There was more behind the simple thank-you than a light-hearted comment. Natalya grinned. "Don't get all sappy on me now. That's worse than moping," she said.

"All right, people. Let's move on, shall we?" Blanchard stood and poked his head into the pantry. "You can clear now, Mr. Bray. Thank you."

Bray's voice came from the galley end of the pantry. "Aye, aye, Mr. Blanchard. Have a good night."

Blanchard nodded at Natalya and gave a little snort when he looked at Pritchard, still glaring at his plate, his brow furrowed. "I've got the mid so I'll see you in the morning," he said to nobody in particular and left the wardroom.

Natalya stood and followed him out, Lyons on her heels.

"Speaking of mope," he said. "I never knew Mr. Pritchard had such a flair for the dramatic."

Natalya shrugged. "I don't think he can help it. Something ain't right with that man's head."

Lyons stopped and looked at Natalya. "What makes you say that?"

"I don't know," she said and shrugged again. "He's like a twelve-year-old playing dress up in Daddy's work clothes. He's so self-conscious about playing the role of chief engineer, I don't think he realizes that he's terrible at it."

Lyons frowned, looking down at his boots for a few heartbeats before nodding. "I can see that." He glanced up at Natalya from under his eyebrows without raising his head. "What do you say about me?"

"Generally that you're a nice guy," Natalya said without hesitation.

"You don't think there's something wrong with me?" The earnestness in his eyes almost took her breath away.

"No, Mr. Lyons. I think you've got some kind of issues that probably need professional treatment, but honestly? I think I do, too. So does Zoya." She snorted. "Especially Zoya, but no. Not like Pritchard. Even drunk you're more self-aware than he is."

They separated at the passage to officer country, Lyons heading toward his stateroom with a wave and Natalya heading for engineering. They'd be docking in the morning and she wanted her ducks all quacking in the same direction when they did.

Docking felt like coming home. Natalya ran through the power changeover and assured the station-ties connected solidly for all the tankage. She keyed the fuel, gasses, and water replenishment before the captain secured from navigation stations. The spares order had already been forwarded from Moe's.

She sat back in her chair and watched as her crew secured their terminals, shutting down the systems they no longer needed, putting the fusactors on ready standby. The sail and keel generators had been secured and set to safety before the tug picked them up and guided them into the docking ring. Natalya had shut down the Burlesons herself. On the one hand, TIC seemed to know all about the ship. On the other hand, having to wait for the Burlesons to spin up would take time. If the safety inspection was simply a *pro forma* exercise in bureaucracy, the inspection crew might not want to take that time. If it was more, then the Burleson drives weren't their biggest problem.

That made her think of Pritchard. His behavior at Moe's left a lot of unanswered questions. His subsequent turnaround on undergoing inspection at Siren made even less sense.

"All hands secure from navigation stations. Secure from navigation stations." Zoya's voice sounded calm and smooth on the squawker.

Engineering central went silent for several heartbeats.

"No liberty?" Town asked, looking at Natalya

"Well, this is a Confederation port. They'll have to run Customs in first. The captain will need to clear up the issue of the safety inspection before he can do much."

"We won't need to be aboard for that, will we?" Solomon asked.

Natalya shrugged. "No idea. Might be a good plan to set up a port-side watch rotation for the engineering space. Simple fire-watch rotation."

"Is that necessary?" Collie asked.

"Necessary, probably not. Useful camouflage for the inspection? Certainly."

Solomon grinned at Collie. "You've done the Visual Site Inspection before. What's your beef?"

"VSI is tedious and boring."

"Cheer up," Solomon said. "It's only for a couple of days. You'll only have one watch before we're out of here again."

"Mr. Knowles can probably add to our merry band as well," Natalya said, rising from her station and stretching her back. "Once the TIC people are satisfied, the captain will probably relax ship doctrine, but for the meantime, do us all a favor and pretend you're actually CPJCT qualified, yeah?"

Everybody nodded and Ms. Solomon winked at Natalya.

Solomon tapped Reisine's shoulder. "Go get gussied up, dearie. We'll put you on watch first in case they decide to come in right after Customs is done."

Reisine looked down at her shipsuit. "What's wrong with this?"

Solomon pulled on her own collar tabs and held up her left arm showing the Spec-One Fields insignia. "You've got a spec-three set, don't you?"

Reisine nodded. "You know I do. You made me buy it."

"Go get into costume, dearie. Your audience could appear any moment."

Reisine sighed but stood and scuffed out of Engineering Control.

Solomon looked around at the others. "You've all got about three ticks to get yourselves out of here and into engineering berthing, unless you're looking for some day work."

Natalya snickered when they took less than two ticks to vacate the area. "You've got a talent for this, Ms. Solomon. You ever consider the academy?"

Solomon's laugh bounced off the bulkheads. "I'm way too old and set in my ways to be going there. Besides, I don't have that pristine a background that I could fake my way in." She shook her head. "No, dearie. I'm Toe-Hold through and through."

Natalya shrugged. "You never know. You're not that old. I had classmates in their thirties."

"I don't know that I'd want to do this full time," Solomon said, sitting down at the propulsion console. "One quarter a stanyer I get to come out and play." She shook her head. "It's enough for me. Any more and it would get tedious, I think."

"What do you do between runs?"

"Third shift supervisor at Dark Knight Gamma."

"Gamma?"

"Ore processing terminal. I make sure the boys and girls don't get their hands or feet in the crushers or smelters."

Natalya felt her eyebrows rise. "Is it that dangerous?"

Solomon shook her head. "Not really. We just have to keep the machinery going. The barges bring the raw ore in and load our bunkers. We keep the rocks moving all safe and sound in the booth. Don't even need exosuits most days."

"You got a family?"

"My brother and his wife work there. They've got a couple kids, my nephews. Hellions but good lads."

"Parents?"

Solomon's mouth twisted and she looked down at her hands. "Lost Dad—a couple of stanyers ago. He worked one of the barges. Mom works for Kondur now. Easy job in the office. Clean. Pays good. You know?"

"That must have been rough."

Solomon shrugged without looking up. "Everybody dies eventually. Every day's a risk. Until you run out of days." She shrugged again.

"You were close to him?"

Solomon's grimace reshaped into a wry grin. "Hated the ole bastard."

Her response startled a short laugh out of Natalya.

"Growin' up, I always thought he wanted to run my life. Had to do this. Couldn't do that." She bit her lip and took a couple of shaky breaths. "When Andi and Rick had the kids, he changed. Or maybe I changed. Having the little ones around can do that." Her eyes glistened and she looked down at the deck. "The kids are just so funny and clever and dumb all at the same time. He doted on them. Spent most of his downtime playing with them. Taking them places around the station." She chuckled. "You never know whether one of them will stick a leg into the grinder to see if it really will chew it off or maybe step outside without a suit to see if they'd really freeze to death before they could get back in."

Natalya laughed. "They're not that bad, are they?"

"No. Hellions, but not stupid." She sighed. "They miss him, too. When the *Starduster's* beacon went out, Kondur sent a ship right away. Standard procedure. Usually it's a matter of going out and hauling them back in. Happens half a dozen times a stanyer."

"Really?"

"Having the beacon go out, that's not normal. Engine failure. Jammed mining bore. Even one time I remember, one of the mining barges got squeezed between two rocks and couldn't get out." She sighed again. "Most of the skippers we got out there worked up through the ranks and know their way around the belts. Even at that, we lose a crew about once every other stanyer."

"My father was a rock-knocker but he never talked about it much."

"Not much to talk about. Find a rock. Eat the rock. Dump the rock."

Natalya laughed. "Sounds singularly unappetizing."

Solomon sniffed one more time and shook her head as if to dislodge loose ideas. "Anyway. When Kondur's people got out there, they found the cracked-open hull and a dozen corpse-sicles."

"Nasty."

"Yeah, and that wasn't something anybody'd do on the spur of the moment. You don't rip open a mining barge and grab the ore unless you've got one hell of a can opener and something to catch the rocks in. Damned Iron Mountain thugs."

"Iron Mountain? Seriously?" Natalya asked, remembering Lyons's earlier comments.

"If not Iron Mountain, who would do that?"

Natalya shrugged. "Hard telling. There's a whole lot of nothing out here and only half of it's been mapped."

Solomon snorted. "And somebody'll try to sell you the charts to the uncharted bits for the price of a few drinks at the nearest bar."

Natalya laughed and looked up as Reisine scooted into the compartment.

"How do I look?" she asked, doing a little pirouette.

"Too fleet," Natalya said, taking in the careful creases and shiny collar pips.

Solomon and Reisine both had the same look of shocked surprise on their faces.

"Can you look too fleet?" Solomon asked.

"We're not running a big hauler. We don't even have everybody in uniform while underway. TIC will see that. There's a lot of leeway, but generally, watch standers and officers look like they try."

Reisine looked down at herself, arms slightly spread away from her body. "What's wrong with this?"

"For a parade ground inspection? Nothing. For a working stiff on watch?" Natalya shook her head. "It's too good."

Reisine looked at Solomon and then back at Natalya. "What do we do?"

"Roll up your sleeves. Just below your elbow. Unbutton a couple of buttons on the blouse," Natalya said, standing to walk around the younger woman.

Reisine rolled the sleeves and unbuttoned. "This isn't too much cleavage?"

"You were showing more before you changed your top." Natalya looked down at her own uniform. "It's no more than I've got showing."

"I suppose," Reisine said.

Natalya tugged one side of the woman's blouse up a bit under her left arm, leaving a little bit of slack so the fabric wasn't pulled down tight, but not so much that it came untucked. "Can you hitch your waistband around about a centimeter so you're not quite so lined up?"

Reisine slipped the trousers a little sideways and frowned. "Doesn't feel right."

"Then slide the top around so your gig line isn't perfect."

"Gig line?"

"The placard on your tunic lines up with the fly on your pants. At parade, you're supposed to have them lined up perfectly or you'll get marked down for it."

Reisine's eyes flashed. "I'd get gigged."

Natalya nodded. "Hence the gig line." Natalya took another walk around Reisine and nodded again. "Better. You're in the uniform, but you're not on parade."

Solomon looked at Reisine and back at Natalya. "Seriously?"

Natalya shrugged. "The point is not to be perfect. Nobody's perfect. Even Saltzmann's engineering crew isn't perfect. Why would they be? They've nothing to prove."

"Saltzmann?" Solomon asked.

Natalya gave a little laugh. "Only the biggest haulers in the Western Annex."

Solomon stood from the console and waved Reisine into it. "Get settled. They'll be here before you know it."

Natalya grabbed a couple of red tags from the bin. "Time to make the ship look just a little sloppy," she said with a nod to Reisine. "Stay calm and keep your head in the console when they come through."

"Aye, aye, boss," Reisine said.

Solomon snorted. "I better get myself under cover before they get here." She gave Natalya a wave as she headed forward up the spine.

Natalya red-tagged the Burleson drive with a handwritten note about the bus coupling. She eyed the fire extinguisher and decided against making it look too shoddy. She thought of the spares inventory and hoped the inspection team would be aboard before the replenishment order hit the orbital's system.

On her way past, she stuck her head into Environmental and spotted Knowles working at his lab. "Hey," she said.

He looked up with a grin. "Hey, yourself." He held up a vial. "We can cross Siren off the list."

"The list?"

"The list of places where that bogus phenol red came from."

"You found out already?"

"I profiled the source on the way in. Just had to grab an uncontaminated sample from the station's supply before it mixed with our potable tankage."

She laughed. "Of course you did. I should have known."

"That leaves every place else in the known universe," he said.

"Along with every place we don't know about," she said.

Knowles nodded and gave a small shrug. "That, too."

Chapter Thirty-eight
Siren Orbital: 2363, August 1

Natalya took a short step ladder and the plate tool down the spine to the generator emitter bus. "Shoulda done this sooner," she grumbled to herself. "Or had somebody else do it." In just a couple of ticks she had the cover off and stood head and shoulders into the inspection port.

She heard voices coming down the spine but didn't think anything of it until Captain Trask stood at her feet, looking up.

"Problems, Ms. Regyri?"

"Just clearing this away for the new emitter coupling. Chandlery says it'll be here this afternoon." She glanced down and saw two people in TIC blacks standing with the skipper. "Oh. I'm sorry. I didn't hear any announcements."

Trask shot a sour look at the elder of the two TIC inspectors. "They suggested I not make one."

Natalya stepped down off the ladder. "I see. Anything you need from me?" She addressed the two agents, looking from one to the other and back.

The younger agent—a woman not that much older than Natalya—consulted a tablet. "You're Regyri?"

"Yep."

The elder agent—a man somewhat younger than Trask, with a furrowed brow and brown hair shot with gray—looked up at the emitter coupling. "That looks like fun."

Natalya glanced up at the half-disassembled unit. "Not so much, really. It took a surge on our jump into Siren. Just trying to clear it away."

"No spares?" he asked.

"We've got a half dozen coming from the chandlery and I'd just as soon use the new parts."

With another look up at the unit, he nodded. "I can understand that. Any idea why it failed?"

"Not offhand. Those don't fail often, but they take a beating during jumps." She shrugged and looked at him. "Maybe when I get it out of there, I'll know more. I'm going with entropy for the moment."

He chuckled and smiled. "Entropy is as good a reason as any."

"Would you like me to accompany you to engineering?" Natalya asked, looking to the captain.

"That won't be necessary," the elder agent said. He held out his hand. "Special Agent Holden Martel, TIC Safety Division."

Natalya shook the man's hand and nodded. "Engineering Third Officer Natalya Regyri," she said. "You probably already knew that." She addressed that to the woman.

She nodded. "Agent Karen Kalquist. We did, actually."

"Nice to meet you both," Natalya said. "If you have no need of my assistance, I'll get back to my demolition work." She shot the TIC agents a grin.

Martel grinned back and waved a hand toward the inspection hatch. "Have at it, Ms. Regyri. If we have any questions, we'll know where to find you."

Trask gave her a small nod and a pat on the shoulder. "Carry on, Ms. Regyri."

Natalya climbed back up the ladder and tried to focus on pulling the coupling. She kept wondering what they were doing in engineering. Wondering if they'd find the spares problem or some other problem she wasn't aware of. Her wrench slipped off the bolt and she bashed a knuckle into the sharp edge of the unit. She swore and stuck the knuckle into her mouth.

By the time she got the next two bolts out, she heard Trask's voice getting nearer. She really wanted to know what had happened but wasn't about to ask.

Trask stopped by the foot of her ladder. "How's it going, Ms. Regyri?"

"Another half stan, unless I keep bashing my knuckles." She held out the battered digit in question. "Stings a bit, but I'll live." She glanced down. The TIC inspectors stood close to the captain, looking up at her.

The two inspectors grinned at each other then looked back up at Natalya.

"Carry on, Ms. Regyri," Trask said and led the two agents away toward the bow.

Natalya groaned to herself and wanted to disappear. What kind of engineer whines about bashed knuckles? Especially after complaining that Pritchard's hands were too clean. She sighed and went back to work on the coupling. Two more bolts and she'd be able to drop it out of the bus inspection port and make room for the new unit.

In typical engineering fashion, the placement of the last bolt required her to practically climb into the inspection port and reach around to the blind side to touch it. With much fumbling and a certain amount of quiet cursing, she finally got the bolt out and the coupling fell into her hand. She took the three steps down to the deck and looked up at the empty slot in the bus array. Some char marred the paint job. The unit in her hand showed significant discoloring, probably from the heat.

She rolled the unit over and checked the part number. It didn't look familiar. She pulled out her tablet to check on the part they ordered. It would be typical for them to have ordered the wrong part because of a screwed-up parts inventory to begin with.

The part on order had a different number. She groaned and headed for the office.

It didn't take her long to pull up the part number in the inventory and look at the specs for both units. The chandlery catalog showed that the unit in her hand cost about a third of the price of the units they'd ordered. "Figures," she muttered and pulled up the operating parameters.

The units on order were for the next generation Burleson Kyoryokuna drives, something you might find on one of the new massive bulk haulers coming out of Manchester. They'd been the talk of the academy for months. Natalya frowned. The unit in her hand had the correct specifications for Class T's. Not exactly a common part in CPJCT-controlled space, but she knew some of the tankers used the heavier drives on a routine basis.

The larger question was who used the Kyoryokunas, and why were they listed as a spare part for a Barbell?

She slapped her terminal closed and bolted for the spine. She hoped the inspection was over and the TIC agents hadn't looked at her replenishment order very closely. It wouldn't take much of an inspection to know that an aging Barbell wouldn't mount next-gen Burlesons. The fallout on that finding could be catastrophic.

Chapter Thirty-nine
Siren Orbital: 2363, August 1

She stopped at the cabin and listened for a few heartbeats. She didn't hear any voices. A quick knock brought Trask to the door. "Ms. Regyri," he said, eyeing the lump of charred metal in her hand. "Come in."

She stepped through the door and glanced around the cabin. "Are they gone?"

"Yep. Engineering was the last stop. We passed with a couple of minor infractions."

"Good news."

He shrugged. "Easily fixed, at any rate." He nodded to one of the visitors' chairs and took his own seat behind the desk. "What's with the part? I assume that's the emitter bus coupling from the spine?"

"Yes, Captain. It's the right size for the class of Burlesons we're running. I don't see any obvious signs of sabotage or anything. Like I said before. Probably just entropy."

He grinned. "Yeah, things break. What's the problem?"

"The chandlery order isn't for this part. It's for a more expensive part. One for ships with the next generation Burleson drive."

Trask appeared to chew on that for a few moments, his jaw working side to side. "Somebody fiddled the spares inventory?"

"I just ordered what was labeled. I didn't check to see that the labels were actually correct."

He shook his head. "Somebody compromised the inventory database so that it looked like the right thing on the surface." His gaze met Natalya's across his desk. "How many more parts are bogus?"

"I don't know, Captain. I came to you as soon as I found out."

He started punching keys on his console. "Read me that part number."

She read it to him and he keyed it.

"That's fixed that. You weren't kidding about the cost difference. Those suckers are expensive."

"Yeah, they are."

He consulted his console again. "The chandlery confirms the change. I've asked them to hold on delivery until we've verified the order." He looked back at Natalya. "Now, what's the best way to find out what else might be wrong?"

Natalya shook her head. "It's hundreds of items. Almost everything on the list costs a lot."

"That's what I'm afraid of," Trask said.

Natalya felt herself staring at him for a long moment before realizing what he had said. She felt an icy trickle of sweat down her back. "You're thinking everything."

Trask's head bobbed once. "How do we find out?"

"Lyons."

"Really?"

"He's the inventory specialist."

"Go see what he says," Trask said.

When Natalya knocked on his door, she got no answer. "Mr. Lyons?"

Blanchard's door opened and Blanchard stuck his head out. "Mr. Lyons is ashore. Something I can help you with, Ms. Regyri?"

Natalya shook her head. "More inventory issues. We'll get it sorted."

"Good luck." Blanchard disappeared back into his stateroom.

Natalya stood there for a moment before heading for the brow. She found an able spacer she didn't recognize lounging behind the desk. "Good afternoon," she said. "I don't believe we've met."

The man looked up from a tablet. "You're that engineer. Reggie?"

She held out a hand. "Natalya Regyri."

He looked at her hand a moment before shaking it. "Aaron Wolk."

"Nice to meet you, Mr. Wolk."

He snorted. "Can I help you? Sar?"

"I'm looking for Mr. Lyons. I heard he went ashore."

Wolk nodded. "Half a stan ago."

"Did he happen to say where he was going?"

He snorted again. "To me? Not likely."

"Thank you, Mr. Wolk. I'll let you get back to your reading."

Natalya turned and started down the passage leading back into the ship.

"He'll probably be back in another stan or so," Wolk said.

She looked at him.

Wolk shrugged. "He never goes ashore for more than a couple of stans at a time. Usually comes back with a load on and a case in tow, if you know what I mean."

"Thank you, Mr. Wolk. Kind of you to share."

He shrugged and settled back into his seat, lifting the tablet up to his face.

Natalya pulled out her own tablet and sent a message to Lyons before climbing the ladder to her stateroom. She paused before entering, then continued past and down the spine to the engineering office. The console there had a bigger screen and the chair had hardly been used. If she was going to grind though the list, at least she'd be comfortable.

It took her only a few moments to bring up the list and sort it in descending order by unit price. The emitter bus couplings weren't near the top of the list. She found them near the bottom of the list and noted the new part number. She nodded to herself and went back to the top.

She spent the better part of a stan working through the actual specifications for the parts, rather than relying on the ship's inventory. She filtered out the tools—like the bus coupling balancing tools and the fusactor test equipment. They represented a few of the top slots but not all. She was more concerned with whether the items coming as spares would even work on the ship.

Every one of the first dozen items were over spec and anywhere from half again to five times more expensive than the actual parts she needed. Some of them would work, but more of them would simply be excess mass. She pulled a comms interface and sent a note to the skipper to tell him of her findings before digging back into the long, long list of parts.

She made it a third of the way down the list before she had to stand and stretch. The muscles in her back and shoulders screamed at her from the tension of being huddled over the console. She checked the chrono and realized that she'd need to move to make it to dinner mess on time.

She hurried down the spine and slid down the ladder to reach the wardroom deck. She found the captain, Pritchard, and Zoya gathered around the head of the table. "Sorry I'm late. I got involved in some inventory issues."

"Again," Zoya said with a grim smile.

"Again," Natalya said.

"Never mind that now," Trask said and waved at the pantry door. "Mr. Bray, I think we're all here now."

Natalya looked around at the empty places.

"Lyons is still ashore. Charlie decided he wanted to eat on station tonight. He's got the duty in the morning. What did you find?" Trask asked, looking at Natalya.

"About what you feared. I'm glad you held the order."

"How long will it take you to fix the discrepancies?"

"At least a couple of days."

Pritchard watched the exchange, his face turning toward each speaker in turn. "Whatever has happened?"

"Spares inventory problem," Natalya said.

Trask stepped in when she took a breath. "Minor inconvenience, Steven. Nothing serious."

Natalya looked at the captain and raised an eyebrow.

Trask looked down at his plate and gave his head a small shake.

Zoya offered her the tiniest of shrugs as Pritchard addressed his dinner.

"As long as it's not a problem," he said.

Natalya took a bite of her fish and cast about for something to talk about. Her head was full of the problem and she had to give it a good shake to think of something else to say.

Trask saved her. "You'll be glad to know the inspection went off without a hitch," he said.

"Oh, excellent," Pritchard said.

"The boarding team was most impressed with you, Ms. Regyri. It's not often they find an engineering third who knows enough about the ship's systems to be doing repairs unsupervised."

Pritchard looked up at that. "You were fixing something? Why wasn't I informed?"

The captain reached over to pat Pritchard on the forearm. "Strictly routine, Steven. Nothing for you to be concerned with."

Trask's soothing words appeared to mollify the man and Pritchard turned back to his dinner again.

Natalya wasn't sure she believed Pritchard, but she glanced at Lyons's empty seat again. "Anybody heard from Mr. Lyons in the last couple of stans?"

Pritchard looked at her. "I believe I heard him getting ready to go ashore just after lunch."

"Does going ashore have a specific sound?" Zoya asked, her head cocked sideways a little.

Pritchard shrugged. "I assumed he was going ashore. There was enough thrashing and banging next door to wake the dead."

Natalya considered Pritchard's words.

"Something wrong, Ms. Regyri?" Trask asked.

Natalya pressed her lips together and cast a sidelong glance at Pritchard. "I don't know, Skipper. I have no reason to suspect there is."

Was it her imagination or did Pritchard's posture relax just a tiny bit?

Trask glanced at Pritchard and gave Natalya a shallow nod. "Perhaps you'd stop by the cabin after dinner mess? We can go over the inspectors' punch list. It shouldn't take long," he said.

"Of course, Captain."

The meal finished up in largely awkward silence, punctuated only by Captain Trask chatting with Zoya about navigation around Toe-Hold space. Natalya couldn't shake the feeling of dread—the feeling that something had gone terribly wrong.

CHAPTER FORTY
SIREN ORBITAL: 2363, AUGUST 1

Trask led the way up to the cabin. "Close that behind you, if you please, Ms. Regyri." He settled behind his desk and pulled a flask out of the bottom drawer. "Sit. We need to talk."

She closed the door and sat across from him. "I'm at your disposal, Captain."

He gave a single, chesty laugh at that—half chuckle, half grunt—and pulled a couple of glasses from the same drawer. A flick of his fingers released the cap on the flask and he dribbled a spare finger of the liquid into each glass. He closed the flask again and replaced it in the drawer. One fat finger chased a glass across the desk toward Natalya and he took the other.

Natalya looked at the glass and then at the captain.

He shrugged. "Rank still has some privilege. Even in Toe-Hold." He nodded at the glass. "Humor me. I hate to drink alone."

She lifted the heavy glass and gave the contents a quick sniff, then a deeper appreciative inhalation. "What is this?"

"It purports to be single-malt Scotch whisky, but it's really just a good counterfeit. Far as I know the real thing only comes from a tiny portion of old Earth and nobody I know goes there anymore."

She took a cautious sip and tasted smoke and an earthy flavor. As the fire slipped over her tongue, she thought maybe some kind of fruit flavor appeared for an instant and disappeared. It warmed all the way down to her stomach and spread. She took a deep breath and let it out slowly. "Holy mother of pearl."

Trask chuckled for real then, his eyes dancing as he took a short sip of his own. "About my only vice these days," he said. "That flask is the last of it so you'll pardon the parsimonious pouring."

"I'm honored," Natalya said. She paused, then looked into his eyes. "Why?"

He stared into his glass for a long moment before taking another small sip. Eventually, he looked across the desk at her. "I trust you."

"Thanks, I think."

He grinned. "You've saved our asses."

"My own, too, don't forget."

"Well, sure, but we've also survived two close calls with TIC thanks to you and Zoya."

She shook her head. "I don't think I can claim any contribution there, Captain. I still don't understand how we can have TIC informants aboard, TIC inspectors, and even TIC special ops agents running through here and still be in danger of getting busted for smuggling."

His eyebrows lifted and he smiled. "So, you caught that, eh?" He smiled and sipped. "Tell me about the spares order."

"It's screwy. Some of the stuff seems legit. Almost all the highest-priced items might actually fit here, but then there are the things like those emitter bus couplings. I don't think they'd even fit in the inspection port, let alone into the gap between the bus bars."

"Tell me about the Zeta drives."

She raised her eyebrows. "Really?"

Trask grimaced. "I don't get out as much as I used to."

"Zeta is the next generation after Origami. More efficient in terms of power use and reach. They're useless on small ships, but rumor around the academy was that Manchester is coming out with a new class of mega-hauler. Maybe a thousand metric kilotons."

"So basically the same as five Barbells?"

"That's the theory. Lots of speculation. Not much in the way of hard data."

"Legs?"

"They've got to have something better than the stock Barbells or they'd not be worth doing."

Trask pursed his lips and stared at the desk. "Yeah. Logic isn't always the best predictor of human behavior, but businesses tend to be a little more hard-nosed about ROI. How many of these parts are like the bus couplers?"

"Some. They're hard to spot because most heavy haulers use a lot of the same components." She shrugged a shoulder. "Fusactor readout panels look the same regardless if the unit is one megawatt or a hundred gigawatts."

Trask nodded. "How long will it take you to get the inventory back in line?"

She sighed and ground her teeth. "Weeks. Probably. I need to find out what we're using now rather than what the system says we need for spares. Even then, I'm not sure I'd trust it."

Trask's head settled back on his neck and his eyes grew a little wider. "Is that even possible? There are a million parts on this ship."

"Probably more like twenty million but a lot of them can't be spares. We're not going to stock spare hull plates or ribs. It's not something we could fix outside of a yard. We have some replacement parts for the bigger pieces—like fusactor readout panels and spare boards for the Burleson drives and the field projection generators—but if we lose a whole generator, it's going to take a yard to put it back in."

"Good point." He shook his head. "That's still a lot of parts."

"Which is why I really need Lyons."

Trask looked at her. "You mentioned him before. Why do you need him?"

She shrugged. "He's the inventory specialist. He knows cargoes but he also knows logistics. I need somebody I can trust to go through this with me and set up a new inventory structure."

"Makes sense. Where is he, by the way?"

"I asked the brow watch. Wolk said he was ashore and would be back before dinner. But he didn't come back."

Trask made a dismissive gesture with his hand. "No real reason for him to, is there? He's not on watch. Has no duties aboard now that the Customs people are happy we have a can of white oil from Moe's."

"Wolk said he usually comes back drunk with a spare case."

"Something to tide him over for the trip home, I bet."

"That's the thing, Captain. He's not drinking."

"He wasn't drinking, you mean," Trask said. "How do you know he didn't start again now that we're docked?"

Natalya looked into her glass and swirled the heavy liquid around the bottom. "I guess I don't."

"What do we need to do about getting parts ordered?"

"You know any real chief engineers who've worked on Barbells?"

He shook his head. "Not here in Siren. Why?"

"Somebody who knows Barbells better would probably be able to look at this list and tell what's legit and what's bogus." She shrugged. "We could probably get a legit parts-order database from any other Barbell docked here, for that matter."

"You think the whole database is corrupted?"

"I know it is. We shouldn't have been ordering parts for other ships as part of our replenishment. That's why we have a spares database."

Trask nodded and drained the last drops out of his glass. "Granted," he said, and snapped the glass back onto his desk. "A stock Barbell wouldn't have the right parts either, would they?"

"Not completely, no. We'd still have to review it and upgrade the basic Burleson parts for the Origami T's." She shrugged. "I didn't notice anything else that wasn't stock."

"What about the fusactors?"

"Yeah, they're beasts, but the parts we can service without a yard are common across all the various sizes. We'd have to check the main breaker switches to make sure we got ones rated for the ship, but after we get the power out of them, it's all stepped down to standard fittings except where they drive the Burlesons' capacitors."

Trask smiled at her. "You talk like you know your way around an engine room."

She felt a blush rising and hid behind her glass, rolling the last sip around on her tongue before sliding it empty back onto Trask's desk. "I feel like I only know enough to be dangerous."

He chuckled. "I know that feeling," he said. "It doesn't get any better as you climb the ladder." He bit his lip and squinted at his desktop for a few heartbeats. "Can the chandlery help?"

Natalya thought about that. "They know all the parts but getting a database we could use isn't exactly trivial since they supply the parts for everybody." She shook her head. "No, the chandlery probably couldn't but ..." Her voice trailed off and she looked across the desk at him.

"But?"

"TIC might."

Trask blinked and then laughed. "TIC? How? All this time we've been trying to keep them at arm's length."

"Yeah, but think about it. TIC inspection teams have to know what every ship needs for spares. How do they know that if they don't know themselves?"

"So you just waltz into the TIC inspection office and ask for a copy of the spares database for a Barbell?"

"Not exactly. We'd need to know the precise model. Unwin's been making Barbells for decades and they're not all identical."

Trask frowned at her. "Tell me what I don't know, kid," he growled, but he started hammering on his keyboard. "Model 2345.4," he said. "Fourth flight in 2345."

"So the ship's almost twenty stanyers old?"

Trask frowned again. "Maybe. Kondur must have gotten it practically new."

"So, TIC has to have a list, if not the exact database," Natalya said.

"You think they'll give it to you for asking?"

"What can they say? No?" Natalya asked.

"They could ask what happened to the old one." Trask's mouth turned down at the corners. "I can't really see telling them somebody broke into it and changed all the values."

Natalya saw his point. "Lemme go ask Zoya. She's the real systems expert."

"If Charlie were here, we could ask him."

Natalya froze, halfway out of her chair. "Charlie."

Trask looked at her. "What about him?"

"That's the answer."

"Charlie is the answer?"

"Something Mr. Blanchard said a couple weeks back while we were coming in from Moe's. The ship's systems get infected when everybody upgrades their tablets here and they start plugging in new chips."

Trask nodded. "Half of them are infected. Doesn't matter how many times you tell them—" His voice cut off and a smile spread slowly across his face. "Of course."

"Permission to leave the ship, Captain?" Natalya stood.

"Go, go." Trask waved a hand.

She went.

Chapter Forty-one
Siren Orbital: 2363, August 1

Natalya made her way off the ship and made a beeline for the lifts. She thanked her Orbital Maintenance rotations for having taught her exactly where she needed to go. It was already closing in on 2000 hours, but all the ship services offices on the oh-one deck ran around the clock.

She made it to the lift just as the doors opened and disgorged a rowdy troop of spacers in civvies. She stepped aside as they passed and slipped into the lift behind them. The doors closed before she could press the button. She cursed to herself but pushed the oh-one button anyway. The deck sank out from under her, but her hopes were dashed when the car went past oh-one and opened on the oh-two deck.

She sighed and stepped back. With any luck she'd catch the oh-one on the way back up.

Two med-techs got on, followed by a pair of beefy individuals wearing orbital security jumpsuits and flashes. They all nodded at Natalya and one of the techs punched the door-close. They rode up in silence and everybody got off on the oh-one. The security people followed the techs around to starboard while Natalya consulted the office directory on the bulkhead opposite the lift. TIC Inspection and Certification lay just three doors to port on the outboard side.

She stopped outside the door and smoothed her tunic down, checking her gig line and taking a deep breath. She reached for the door handle but stopped. She purposely twisted the waistband of her slacks and ruffled both hands through her cropped hair. It was too short to muss up much, but it gave her the feeling of being mussed up. She took another deep breath, blew it out, and breezed into the office, opening her eyes wide and rushing up to the counter.

The agent behind the counter stood up quickly as she rushed toward him. "Can I help you?"

"Oh, I hope so. I need help and you're the only people I can think of that can."

She watched him check out her name tag and collar pips. "Ms. Regyri. What is it you need?"

"Well, this is embarrassing but somebody plugged in some fool virus-laden chip into the ship's system."

She saw his eyes widen. "Direct?"

"Watch stander. You know how port-side watches can be."

"And?"

"She decided she would just watch a little holo while waiting for the next VSI."

He frowned. "That shouldn't have affected the ship's operational systems."

Natalya sighed. "No. It's not the ship's main systems. That would be easy. Flush it out and restart everything."

"Then what?"

"Spares inventory."

"What about it?"

Natalya clenched her jaw and bit out. "It renamed every damn item to something different."

"Different?"

"Obscene, all right? Obscene."

She saw him bite his lips together but his eyes gave away the laughter he tried to suppress. "It renamed every item in your spares database?"

She closed her eyes and nodded. "Every. Damn. One."

He did well and she heard only one slightly choked laugh. "Can't you recover it from backup?"

"Normally, yes," she said. "We keep two versions of backup for all the systems in the ship's safe and another at our office on Newmar Orbital."

"So the problem?"

"We discovered it as we were rotating the backups and I spotted it on the logs."

"And ...?" he asked. His eyes grew wide. "Wait. You backed up the obscene database."

"Twice."

The man's expression lay somewhere between stifled laughter and sympathetic horror. He might have shown a little gratitude, too. "How can we help?" he asked.

"I just need a list of what we're supposed to have in spares. A fresh database with the items and recommended stores levels would be ideal. Failing that, just a list of what we're supposed to have. I've got a massive replenishment order coming in tomorrow and I've got no database to receive them into."

The man clapped the palm of one hand against his mouth and drew a deep breath through his nose before blowing it out again. Natalya didn't blame him. The picture must have been hysterical. It was all she could do to keep a straight face herself. If he started laughing, she'd probably join him.

"What ship?" He crossed back to his desk and started hitting keys on his console.

"Unwin Barbell."

"Model?"

"2345.4."

He looked up at her, eyebrows raised. "You just happen to know that?"

Natalya weighed her options and shook her head, biting the inside of her cheek. "I had to ask the captain."

She watched his eyes drift upward and his lips twitch as he must have pictured that meeting in his mind. He shook himself and addressed the keyboard again. The smile kept trying to break out around his lips. Natalya had to put her head down on the counter so she wouldn't lose it herself.

"How do you want it?" he asked.

"You've got it?" She lifted her head and beamed at him.

"Oh, yes."

"Hallelujah." She pulled out her tablet and placed it on the counter. "Can you send it to my tablet?"

He flipped a couple of screens and tapped. "I'm pinging you."

The ping showed up and Natalya accepted it.

"You're not afraid of getting your tablet infected?" he asked, a small smirk on his face.

She laughed. "Honestly, if I get infected from Inspections and Certifications, then there's no hope for us."

He appeared to recognize the compliment. "Sending now."

The database file slithered through the connection and dropped into her tablet's storage.

"Thank you. You've saved my ass."

He gave her a bigger smirk. "We're here to help." He crossed to the counter and leaned forward. "Is there anything else I can help you with?"

Natalya shook her head and turned for the door. "No, you've been great. I need to get this back and get it all integrated before that replenishment order hits tomorrow." She rolled her eyes and flounced out of the office. When the door latched behind her, she heard the peal of laughter from inside.

She chuckled all the way back to the ship.

Chapter Forty-two
Siren Orbital: 2363, August 1

Natalya bounded up the ladder to officer country and knocked on the cabin door. Trask opened it and peered out. She held up her tablet. "Got it. We'll have it done by tomorrow."

"What about the current one?" he asked.

"What about it?"

"Can you make a copy before you overlay it with that?" He nodded at her tablet.

His meaning became clear. "Yes. Of course." She wanted to believe she'd have done that anyway. "I'll get Zoya to flash it to nonvolatile media."

"Nonvolatile?"

"Glass. Once it's down, nobody will be able to change it."

"It won't have to stand up in a court of law," Trask said, lowering his voice and glancing down the passage.

"No, but it has to survive the trip back so we can give it to Kondur."

He grinned. "Excellent point. Carry on. Let me know if you need anything."

She paused. "Has Mr. Lyons come back yet?"

The captain frowned and shook his head. "Neither has Charlie."

"Think they're related?"

He shrugged. "Not like either of them, but I've got no reason to think there's trouble. Charlie has OD in the morning. If he misses that, then we have a problem."

Natalya nodded and waved the tablet. "If you'll excuse me, Skipper, I need to get this moving."

He grinned and waved her away. "Go, go."

Natalya strode down the passage and knocked on Zoya's door.

"Who is it?"

"Nats, Zee. Got a tick?"

Natalya heard the lock thrown before Zoya opened the door. "Sure, come on in."

Natalya scooted in past Zoya and waited while she rebolted the door. "You having problems?"

Zoya shook her head. "Not as such, no. Mr. Pritchard seems to be a regular in the passageway. It makes me a little nervous."

Natalya shrugged. "Can't blame you there. I spend so little time in my stateroom, I'm not sure I've noticed." She held up her tablet. "I got a blank spares list from TIC."

Zoya tilted her head to port a few degrees. "You what?"

"I got a blank spares list from TIC." Natalya paused. "How much do you know about the spares problem?"

"You've got a lot of junk instead of the spares you need."

"Right. We pushed a replenishment order to the chandlery from Moe's."

"I remember that. The skipper initialed it and it went through Moe's relay."

"Right. Then it gets weird."

Zoya's laugh carried more than a hint of desperation. "Really? I'm shocked. Shocked." She sat on her bunk and nodded at the fold-out chair. "Fill me in."

Natalya took the seat and perched on the edge of it. "I got the faulty emitter bus coupling out of the bus array in the spine. Checked the part number on it and it's different from the one we ordered."

"Uh oh. What did you order?"

"An emitter bus coupling rated for the new Burleson Kyoryokuna drives."

Zoya sat up at that and her eyes all but bugged out of her head. "A Zeta? They're real? I thought they were just academy scuttlebutt."

"Nobody's seen one yet, but the spares are already in circulation, apparently."

"Manchester must be close to shipping one of the new megas."

"Or already has," Natalya said.

Zoya grinned. "That's not possible. If they had, it would have been on every newsie in Confederation space."

Natalya pursed her lips and waited for Zoya.

"What?" Zoya asked.

Natalya waited.

Zoya's eyes got even bigger. "No."

Natalya shrugged. "Makes an odd kind of sense."

"Somebody in Toe-Hold space has a mega?"

"Somebody in Toe-Hold space has had a mega for rather a long time. Months, maybe."

Zoya frowned. "No, that makes zero sense. Why?"

"Prototype? They needed someplace to shake out the bugs in the design before they rolled it out to the big guns?"

"Why would they do that? I'd think the PR they got from putting a few of them out in the public eye would be huge."

"What if the design's not solid?" Natalya asked. "This is new stuff. The Kyoryokunas are completely new technology. Manchester's been trying to beat that five-hundred-metric-kiloton threshold for decades. They develop a new tech that does it but they keep the lid on it."

"Not a very tight lid."

Natalya shook her head. "We don't know that. We don't know when they might have developed it and if there's a working prototype out there? That kind of work takes a lot of time and a massive yard. Manchester's yards are all very public. Where would you build these?"

Zoya started to shake her head but stopped and stared at Natalya. "Toe-Hold."

"Right, and you'd have to keep it quiet there. You'd almost need a new Toe-Hold to do it in to keep the chatter down."

"You think that's where those clowns that kept stinking up Odin's Outpost came from?"

"I don't know. That's certainly a possibility. You'd think an outfit like Manchester wouldn't be flying faulty ships around running errands."

"Cobbler's children?" Zoya asked.

"That's possible. Even probable, now that I think of it."

"But why issue the parts if the ships aren't available yet?"

"I'd bet they're trying to roll one out in the next few months. Much fanfare. Many oohs. Lots of noise."

"So they're seeding the spares early for a ship they're confident will be sailing in Dunsany Roads?"

"That would be my guess. Can't fly without spares. Uncle TIC gets all fussy over it."

Zoya shook her head. "I never really thought about what it would take for a completely new class of vessel."

"We also don't know they'd actually fill the order for us, but that's beside the point," Natalya said. "When I started comparing parts, a lot of them were not for a Barbell. Like the emitter bus coupling. I pulled it out of the spares database and checked inventory when I found the nearly toasted unit."

"Right. That's how you found the junk."

"So, Lyons and I did the inventory."

"Good job on him, by the way."

"He's missing at the moment, but thanks."

"Missing?"

"Focus. We did the inventory and placed a replenishment order based on the stock numbers in the spares inventory."

Zoya's eyes blinked several times. "Wait."

Natalya nodded. "Yes. Our spares inventory lists the Kyoryokuna emitter bus couplers, and Kyoryokuna emitter arrays and a ton of other stuff for equipment we don't even have aboard."

"Would that coupling even fit?"

Natalya shook her head. "I don't think it'll even go through the inspection hatch."

Zoya stared at Natalya's tablet for several long moments. "So you got a corrected parts database from TIC. Inspections and Certifications office?"

"Right. Told them we'd gotten corrupted by a stray virus from an entertainment chip that got plugged directly into the console in engineering."

"They bought it?"

Natalya held up the tablet.

Zoya lifted a hand and laughed behind it. "You amaze me."

"I need you. I need to get this database installed, but I'm afraid it'll obscure the existing installation."

Zoya nodded, her lips pursed. "Probably would."

"I want to save that database in its current state to see if we can figure out who modified it."

"Be kinda dumb to leave digital fingerprints, wouldn't it?" Zoya asked.

"Most engineering officers aren't really conversant on the inner workings of ships' systems." Natalya shook her head. "Doesn't matter. Maybe we'll find something. Maybe we won't. If we don't safeguard it now, we'll never know."

Zoya nodded. "Sold. You want this on glass?"

"Yes. I assume we can burn glass?"

"Of course. Most of the official ship's logs go directly to glass but we've got a couple of spare drives for stuff we want to preserve as read-only." She grinned. "Even *Peregrine* had a couple."

"Yes, I know *Peregrine* had some, but I thought it was just because my father is a paranoid, anti-social psychopath."

"I thought you liked him."

"Love him. Those are his good qualities."

Zoya laughed behind her hand again.

270

"How soon can you get the current database burned?"

Zoya pulled out her tablet and began flipping through screens with her index finger. "We have a full system backup at Dark Knight," she said. "You only need the spares inventory data?"

"And any related maintenance logs."

Zoya nodded, flipping down through the system menus while Natalya watched. She isolated one section of the system and routed it to a backup drive in the systems' closet. "Lemme run up and toss a fresh chip in." She unbolted the door and left the stateroom.

Natalya heard Pritchard's voice in the passageway, but not what he said. She opened the door and stuck her head out.

Pritchard stood half blocking the passageway. His gaze tracked to stare at Natalya and his eyes widened. "My goodness, Ms. Usoko. Such company you keep."

"If you'd excuse me, Mr. Pritchard. I need to get by."

He looked at Zoya and stepped aside after glancing in Natalya's direction. "Of course." He held a hand out, palm flat as if in invitation. "Be my guest."

Zoya glanced over her shoulder and grimaced at Natalya before striding along the passageway to the data closet tucked under the ladder up to the bridge.

Natalya stepped into the passage and leaned against the bulkhead, her arms crossed.

"How is your evening, Ms. Regyri?" Pritchard asked. He had a half nervous twitch with his hands as if he didn't know what to do with them. Even his voice sounded shaky.

"I've had better. It's not over yet."

Pritchard nodded. "Tell me, have you found Mr. Lyons?"

Natalya shook her head. "No. The captain will start looking for him soon."

The news seemed to take Pritchard by surprise and he stepped back as if slapped. "Soon? Surely not before morning."

Natalya shrugged, watching him. "Captain doesn't answer to me. He seems to think it's not normal for Mr. Lyons to be out so long."

Pritchard began fiddling with the zipper on his shipsuit. "Surely a drunk like Lyons isn't reliable when there's booze to be had so close at hand."

Natalya shrugged again. "Not my call."

Pritchard nodded. "Of course. Of course. We still have a couple of days for him to drag himself back aboard." He made it sound like Lyons might soil the ship somehow by returning.

Natalya sighed but Zoya's reappearance saved her from additional discussion with Pritchard.

They slipped back into Zoya's stateroom. Natalya had no problem with Zoya taking extra time with the bolts.

"I see what you mean," Natalya said. "About Pritchard."

"He's normally not so pushy," Zoya said. "That was a new low for him."

"Gotta admire a person who lives down to his potential."

Zoya's eyes danced a little and she smiled. "Backup done in five ticks. I didn't feel like waiting in the closet while you parried Pritchard."

"He seems to have it in for Josh Lyons."

"I heard him saying some nasty things. I didn't realize they were at odds."

"They share a bulkhead." Natalya shrugged. "Remember when we had Sales and Promotion next door second term?"

Zoya's face went blank for a minute and then brightened. "What were their names? Seles and Pemberton?"

Natalya nodded. "If there was an award for headboard banging, I'd have nominated them."

Zoya smiled. "They were bad, but I don't think Mr. Lyons has been entertaining in his stateroom, do you?"

The thought gave Natalya an odd pang but she shook her head. "No. He's been too busy with his bottle to fraternize."

"Until recently," Zoya said with a sly side-eyed glance.

Natalya sighed and shook her head. "Not my type. Is that backup glassed yet?"

Zoya snorted and pulled up her tablet. "Yeah. You want to merge those or just start over?"

Natalya considered for a moment, staring at her tablet's blank face. "Most of the existing records show zero on hand. I think the safest course is to delete those and then merge what's there with what should be there. The non-zero records should be easy enough to reconcile by hand."

Zoya flipped her displays with her finger and frowned. "Yes," she said. "That would work. There are fewer than a hundred records with a valid on-hand count."

Natalya nodded. "What I figured."

"You want me to load the records for you? I can do it right from here." She held up her tablet and wiggled it in the air.

Natalya found the TIC files and tossed them to Zoya. "Thanks," she said. "I'll go get a cuppa and head back to engineering."

"You want help?"

"Don't you have OD watch or something?"

"I'm on it," Zoya said.

"In here?"

Zoya shrugged. "As good as the office. As long as I'm not drinking, sleeping, or otherwise unavailable to the brow watch, I'm fine."

Natalya thought about it but shook her head. "Thanks, Zee, but you've done enough. This will only take a couple of stans to reconcile. If that." She headed out the door but stopped to look back. "You could see if you can find a valid maintenance trace on those glassed records. If we know who changed them, we might know who replaced all those spares with scrap."

Zoya grinned and laced her fingers together, pushing her palms out in a stretch before firing up the terminal on her desk. "Something to do to keep me awake," she said.

Chapter Forty-three
Siren Orbital: 2363, August 2

Natalya swiped her burning eyes with her fingers and drank the last of her cold coffee before standing up from the console. With hands in the small of her back, she rotated her shoulders and leaned back to try to relieve the burning between her shoulders. At least it was done.

The chrono clicked over to 0214. She blinked her eyes and tried to stretch them open a bit. Everything felt gummy.

She checked her tablet. Lyons hadn't checked in. He might have come aboard late—or drunk, she had to admit—and hadn't seen the message. Not knowing where he was bugged her. Something just felt off. She leaned over the keyboard to kick off the spares replenishment compilation. It only took a few heartbeats. She noted that the total was only about a third of what it had been on the original. That should make the captain happy. She forwarded it to his box for approval before closing down the console.

On the long walk back down the spine, she zoned out—and blinked, standing in front of her stateroom door with no recollection of how she got there. She snorted and let herself in. When the door clicked shut, she stopped and flipped the deadbolt. Zoya had never been nervous about doors in the dorm. Given the shenanigans that had happened outside their room on a regular basis there, it said something that Pritchard bothered her.

She slipped off her top and went into the head to rinse off her face and hands. She tried to be quiet but as soon as she shut off the water, Zoya tapped on the door.

"You decent?"

Natalya opened the door and grinned. "After living with me for four stanyers? Now's a hell of a time to ask."

Zoya shrugged. She had bags under her eyes that looked like bruises. "I've been trying to find an audit trail on this glassed data all evening."

"Anything?"

"Oddities but no smoking gun."

"How odd?" Natalya asked.

"Well, Pritchard's fingers have been all over it."

"Not too surprising."

Zoya squinted as if she had a headache. "If he were an engineer, not surprising at all."

Natalya paused. "What are you getting at?"

"I'm not sure. I've got him signing parts in and out of inventory. All kinds of parts." Zoya gave her head a little shake. "I'm saying this badly."

"If you're as tired as I am, that you're saying anything at all is a miracle."

Zoya grinned and plopped down on her bunk. "Knowles and his crew in environmental. They signed out filters, spare parts, something called phen—phen something."

"Phenol red."

"That's it."

"Water-testing chemical," Natalya said.

"Whatever. They sign stuff out. The database is full of them signing stuff out."

"Sounds normal."

"Nobody signed it in."

Natalya leaned against the sink. "What do you mean, nobody signed it in?"

"I've got no receiving record against any of it. The parts are just there."

"How far back did you go?"

"That's the thing. The parts database doesn't have any records before June first."

Natalya blinked her eyes and stretched her face. "How is that possible?"

Zoya shook her head. "It shouldn't be possible, but somebody cleared that database. Wiped everything older than that right out."

"What about logs?"

"Navigation logs, stores logs, even tankage logs. All there on the main system. We didn't copy those to glass but I went in and looked to see if the ship had been sanitized. It hasn't. Records there go back stanyers."

"Anything in the system logs about maintenance to the spares database?"

"I don't even know when to look."

Natalya sighed and shook her head. "Sleep. Nothing makes sense. Maybe fresh brains can find something in the morning."

Zoya nodded. "Yeah. I've still got the OD watch, but I can't keep my mind from spinning around chasing its tail."

Natalya chuckled. "Yeah. I know the feeling. You didn't hear Lyons come in, by any chance?"

Zoya shook her head. "I've had my head in the systems. He'd have had to come into my stateroom and shouted for me to notice. Sorry."

"Not your problem. Just wondered."

"What do you think happened to him?" Zoya asked.

"Call me naÃ¯ve but I thought he'd found something beyond booze." Natalya shrugged. "Having him out makes me think I was wrong."

Zoya sighed and nodded. "Hang in. Sleep well. I've still got four stans to go but you can bet I'm crashing right after breakfast mess." She swung the door closed on her side.

Natalya stared at herself in the mirror for a few heartbeats trying to figure out who was looking back at her.

With a snort, she clicked off the light and found her bunk.

Chapter Forty-four
Siren Orbital: 2363, August 2

Natalya met Zoya on the way to the wardroom. "I checked with the brow watch at 0530," Zoya said. "Both Blanchard and Lyons were still ashore."

"Isn't Blanchard supposed to take the OD watch about now?"

Zoya nodded. "I've been on since 1800 yesterday so he better show up."

They stepped into the wardroom to find both Captain Trask and Mr. Pritchard looking up at them from their meals. Trask's face fell, but Pritchard looked oddly pleased with himself.

"Sorry we're late," Zoya said.

Trask shook his head. "You're not late. We're unfashionably early." He lifted his coffee mug in salute. "I wanted coffee and being the captain? I generally get what I want."

"Any word from our wayward colleagues?" Natalya asked, sliding into her place beside Pritchard.

Trask sighed and bit his lips together, shaking his head for a moment before replying. "No, and I'm officially worried. Charlie's never missed a watch change as long as I've known him."

"What about Mr. Lyons?" Natalya asked, helping herself to a short stack of the pancakes waiting on the platter. She pushed the platter in Zoya's direction while the captain passed the syrup to Natalya.

"He's a wild card," Trask said. "Never known him to stay ashore longer than it took to ..." His voice petered out.

Pritchard said, "Longer than it took to get drunk again and buy a case for the ride home." He seemed to take inordinate pleasure in his pronouncement.

Natalya took a deep breath and let it out slowly, counting to ten. The urge to slap the self-righteous smirk off the man's face nearly overwhelmed her.

Zoya helped herself to pancakes and dug in. "Do you need me to keep the OD watch, Captain?" she asked.

He shook his head. "Log it over to me. I got a bit of sleep last night." He glanced at her. "More than I can say for you."

She smiled. "I had to make a couple circuits of the ship to stay awake, but I managed."

"Well, we can't undock without them," Trask said. "I've notified station security to look for them both."

"Because we need Mr. Blanchard to navigate?" Zoya asked.

"Because we don't leave people behind, Ms. Usoko."

A wash of red came up Zoya's neck and spread over her ears. "Of course. Sorry. I wasn't thinking."

"You're barely awake. I'm surprised you're sitting up and taking nourishment," Trask said. His smile reached all the way to the creases at the corners of his eyes.

Zoya nodded and focused on her breakfast.

Pritchard scoffed. "All these rules and regulations. These High Liner ports are all the same."

Trask looked at Pritchard. "That's why you're a Toe-Holder, isn't it, Steven?"

"Well, yes." Pritchard's smirk disappeared like a soap bubble bursting. "Of course."

Natalya glanced at Pritchard, who focused on cutting his pancakes into tiny pieces before lifting them with his fork. She wondered if he'd always been in Toe-Hold space. Something about the captain's comment had soured Pritchard's good mood, and the captain knew it.

Trask looked at Natalya. "You get any sleep last night? You're looking almost as tired as Ms. Usoko here."

"A bit. Had things buttoned up by 0230. There's a new order in your inbox."

Trask glanced at Pritchard, whose attention seemed to be riveted on shredding a pancake. "See me after breakfast and we'll go over it, if you would?"

Natalya nodded. "Aye, aye, Captain."

Trask chuckled and tilted his coffee cup up. "Mr. Bray?" he said.

Bray stuck his head in from the pantry. "Yes, sar?"

"Our carafe has mysteriously developed a leak."

Bray bustled in with a towel. "I'm sorry, Captain. Where—?" His gaze swept the table before he looked at Trask.

Trask shook his cup. "Somewhere around the top, I think. It seems to have all drained away." He winked at the rating.

Bray grinned. "I think I can fix that, sar."

"Thank you, Mr. Bray," Trask said with a small nod.

Pritchard clattered his cutlery into his plate, giving up his assault on breakfast food. "If I might be excused, Captain?"

"Of course, Steven."

Pritchard rose and left the wardroom, closing the door behind him with a solid thump in the door frame.

The captain watched him go with the slightest of frowns furrowing his forehead. "I hope it wasn't something I said."

"He seemed a bit perturbed," Natalya said.

Trask shrugged. "He's sometimes a bit moody. I'm never really sure with him." He sighed. "But beggars can't be choosers, I suppose. We sail with the crew Mr. Kondur provides."

Zoya finished her breakfast and pushed her plate away from the edge of the table. "With your permission, Captain? I think I need to find my rack."

Trask nodded. "Of course. Get some sleep. We may be pulling back-to-back watches for a time until we find Mr. Blanchard."

"Thank you, Captain." Zoya rose and followed Pritchard out of the wardroom.

"She doesn't like Pritchard," the captain said when she was gone.

"More like doesn't trust him."

Trask held his cup in the fingertips of both hands and tilted it to take a slurping sip off the top. "Do you?" he asked without looking at her.

"I don't know him well enough."

"But you don't like him."

"He makes me uneasy. He's too friendly. He's always in the passageway outside our staterooms. I didn't notice until Zee mentioned it the other day. Then I remembered all the times I ran into him there." Natalya shrugged and finished the last of her pancake. "He is what he is and we just need to get back to Dark Knight."

"What'll you do when we get back?" Trask asked.

"Repair the *Peregrine*, I hope. Then we'll see. Worst case we'll do a little gas mining for docking fees."

"What's wrong with her?"

"Fuel coupling. The engines got overhauled just before I jumped to Newmar, but the throat in the fuel coupling took a bit of abuse when we were leaving."

Trask nodded. "Need to replace it?"

"Just relining it would do, but there's no place I know of in Toe-Hold that can do the ceramic work."

Trask shook his head. "Cheap part. Better off getting a new one."

Natalya stared at him. "I would if I could. Renfrew down at the yards wanted two hundred thousand to replace it."

"Abe Renfrew? Dark Knight Station? Sweaty guy? Always flashing a bandana around?"

"That's him."

Trask snorted and took another slurp of coffee. "Pirate," he said.

"I know, but what can I do?"

"That fuel coupling is the same one every fast packet from here to the Core Worlds uses. Probably could get one from the chandlery here for a grand. Charge it to the ship. You know how to install it?"

Natalya nodded. "I could figure it out. Those scouts weren't exactly precision machines."

Trask's chuckle rumbled in his chest. "No, but that's why so many of them kept flying for so long. Simple machines. Simple repairs. Computer systems on them weren't worth a damn, but they were cheap as water." He glanced at her. "You upgraded your systems, didn't you?"

She grinned. "First thing Dad did, according to my mother."

"Sounds like him." He glanced over his shoulder at the open pantry door. "Mr. Bray, I'm taking my cup and this carafe up to the cabin. Would you come pick it up in a bit?"

Bray stuck his head in. "Of course, Captain. Would you like me to top it off for you?"

Trask shook his head and levered himself up from the table. "Come along, Ms. Regyri. We have a replenishment order to review."

Trask lumbered up the ladder toward the cabin like he carried a full can of ore on his shoulders.

"You all right, Skipper?" Natalya asked.

He snorted. "Well as can be expected of a man of my age and general disposition, Ms. Regyri." He glanced over his shoulder at her. "Half my officers are missing, most of my friends are dead. We're docked in a Confederation port with a load of milk after swapping a load of illegal ore for it. The Burlesons are out of commission until we get those parts in, and the spares inventory has been boogered by person or persons unknown to the point where we don't know what we have or what we need." He grinned at her as he topped the ladder. "Did I miss anything?"

She laughed. "You're almost right. We know what we have for spares. Damn near nothing. We know what we need. Pretty much everything." She shrugged. "The good news is it'll cost about a third of what we thought it would."

They crossed the passageway to the cabin just in time to see Pritchard step out of his stateroom. He glanced at the captain and nodded.

"Feeling better, Steven?" the captain asked.

"I am, yes. Something didn't agree with me." He placed a hand on his stomach and grimaced.

"Carry on," the captain said, leading Natalya into the cabin and closing the door behind them. "I never noticed that before," he said.

"Zee keeps her stateroom door locked when she's there." She shrugged. "So do I. Now."

Trask crossed to his desk and slumped into the chair. "Don't blame you." He settled the carafe on the table where they could both reach it and fired up his console. "Sit, sit. You're making me nervous standing around." He shot her a grin but focused back on his screen.

Natalya took a seat and helped herself to the coffee, topping off the mug she'd brought from the wardroom.

Trask's mouth worked like he was chewing his tongue while he stared at the screen. "These numbers right?" he asked after several ticks. "That total's just a fraction of what we ordered before."

"What we ordered before was a bunch of stuff we couldn't use."

Trask nodded but didn't look up. "I didn't believe it till I double-checked."

"We got the old database backed up to glass last night. Zoya was working through the audit logs all night trying to see who changed the part numbers."

"You were up late to get this ready by this morning." He glanced at her. "Well done."

She shrugged. "Just doin' my job."

He glanced at her again and grinned. "You're doing more than your job. And more than Pritchard's, too. You know the part number for your fuel coupling?"

"For the *Peregrine*?" she asked.

Trask just looked at her.

She rattled the part number off.

"I'm impressed," he said.

"As much trouble as it's been? It's engraved in my brain beside that burned-out emitter."

He chuckled, keyed a few entries, and slapped the enter key. "There. Replacement order sent to the chandlery. With any luck they'll get that back to us by this afternoon."

"Maybe we'll have found Mr. Blanchard and Mr. Lyons by then."

Trask sat back in his chair and lifted his mug. He peered at Natalya over the top of it. "You have any ideas?"

"About where they might be?"

Trask nodded.

"No, Captain. My first time here."

"You've been on Confederation orbitals enough. They still do an Orbital Maintenance rotation at Port Newmar?"

"Oh, yeah. Spent a couple weeks lubricating docking clamps."

He snickered. "I pity all the orbitals that don't have cadets as slave labor." His jovial tone slipped away. "You went ashore to get that database copy. I won't ask how you got it, but thanks for doing it. Did you see anything odd? Out of place?"

Natalya blew a breath out between her lips. "How would I know? Only thing even remotely odd was the clerk in the TIC office tried to pick me up."

"Nothing odd about that, Ms. Regyri. The clerk showed good taste."

Natalya felt the heat rise up her neck. Compliments always made her squirm.

"Did Ms. Usoko find anything in the database maintenance records?"

"Oh, I should have asked. Last night she said the stores database had no records before the first of June. Is that normal?"

Trask frowned. "I came aboard June 1. Took over from the caretaker crew."

"Zee said all the other logs are intact back as far as she looked. Just the spares database."

"That's not normal," Trask said and turned to his console. He flipped through pages for several ticks, occasionally stopping to look at something before resuming his search. "Nice. You managed to keep the spare parts consumption records linked to the correct items."

"All of them were environmental and they had the correct IDs on them to begin with."

"Right," Trask said, nodding. "Cheap items, used often. They had to be solid in the system."

"What I don't get is how they changed or what the game is."

Trask pushed back from his keyboard. "Talk it out."

"It appears that the database got munged up before you took over in June. I don't know how that was even possible. It must have taken weeks to cross-load all these parts so they looked right."

Trask nodded. "Days, anyway. You corrected it in a matter of stans."

"Yes, but I had a blank template to work from."

"So maybe whoever did this spent the time to build the template and just did what you did. It could have been done just as quickly."

Natalya sipped her coffee and thought about that. "If all they had to do was change out the part numbers and they knew the record IDs for the existing ones?" She nodded. "Yeah, fast update. Probably fractions of a second. I hadn't thought of that."

"So why scrub the database from before June?"

"No idea. Would make more sense if they did nothing."

"What about the scrap metal?" Trask asked, leaning his forearms on his desk.

"Yeah, I don't know. There's no connection between the scrap metal and the database. Spares updates are basically on an honor system. There's no system check to require you to sign stuff out."

"Nobody in their right mind would skip that step," Trask said. "Getting caught a billion kilometers from the nearest parts store isn't something anybody wants to do."

Natalya thought of Bjorn Gunderson and nodded.

Trask filled his cup from the carafe and sat back, cradling the mug on his chest. "We know what?"

"We know we have—or had—a corrupted spares inventory database."

"Not corrupted," Trask said. "Purposefully modified to contain high-cost items."

Natalya nodded. "Not just any high-cost items, either."

"The Zeta drive components?" Trask shook his head. "I still don't get that."

"Would it make more sense if we suppose that there's at least one prototype of Manchester's new mega-hauler in Toe-Hold space?"

Trask froze. "Is that even possible?"

"I'm the new kid. You tell me. Four stanyers at the academy and the rumors of the Kyoryokuna drives only began surfacing in the last few months."

"Those are the Zetas?"

"Yeah. Burleson has a thing for oriental names. Origami drives fold space. The Kyoryokunas are the next generation. They got nicknamed Zeta because all the Origamis have letter designators for their jump rating."

"And nobody could pronounce that other thing."

Natalya grinned. "Probably."

"Back to what we know," Trask said.

"The physical inventory was stripped of anything of value that's not a regularly consumed item."

"Like the water filters."

"Yeah. Even the phenol red Knowles uses. Whoever did this knew how many they could take and get away with." Natalya shook her head. "I don't get what the motive is, if it's not to pad somebody's credit balance."

"What makes you think it's not?"

"The firewalled readers," Natalya said.

"What about them?"

"There's a rack of them in the pantry. Probably ten or fifteen thousand credits' worth that nobody ever uses. It makes no sense that somebody pilfering everything not nailed down in the spares locker would leave credits on the table like that."

Trask nodded. "So we know they weren't touched. We don't know why."

Natalya thought about that for a moment. "Fair statement."

"So why change the items in the spares database?" Trask asked.

"We're going into speculation now," Natalya said.

"So stipulated. By keeping the parts inventory full—even though the parts there amounted to junk—what's the incentive for anybody to order expensive parts? The replenishment order needs a manual process. Without an engineering officer to notice, who'd have ordered the parts?"

Natalya felt her forehead puckering as she thought about it. "We had to order here. Not at Dark Knight."

"Explain," Trask said.

"The parts wouldn't be available at Dark Knight. They're probably only available this quadrant. I'd go further and speculate they're only available in Siren and Dunsany Roads."

"Why?"

"If Manchester is about to release the new line of megas—and we don't know that they are, because nobody's even seen a prototype that I know of—but if they are? They need parts in the field. Distributing them to the Confederation systems makes sense and helps keep the lid screwed down."

"But all orbitals are controlled by the CPJCT," Trask said.

"Yes, but every new person who knows the secret raises the odds of discovery. Better to keep them in the Confederation systems."

"Why keep it secret?"

"Because it's still an untested prototype. Zoya and I talked about this a bit."

"Which is where the speculation that there's one in the wild in Toe-Hold space came from."

Natalya shrugged. "Makes sense. If it flops, it never happened."

"How do they keep it under wraps? Only thing that moves faster than light is rumor."

"I hear there's a lot of space in the Deep Dark," Natalya said.

"You're thinking somebody could established a new Toe-Hold?"

"I'm thinking somebody's already done it."

Trask sat forward. "What makes you say that?"

"Zoya and I made a run over to Odin's for Mr. Kondur just before we signed up with you. Nancy said they'd been having trouble with a bunch of amateurs with shoddy equipment using the Outpost as a staging area."

"Nancy Gunderson?"

Natalya shrugged. "I think that was her name, yeah. Introduced herself as Bjorn's first mate."

Trask leaned back in his chair and looked up at the overhead. "So, logical inferences. Whoever's done this knew we'd be at a Confederation port and that we'd discover the junk in the spares locker."

"Otherwise we wouldn't order the more expensive pieces to take back to Dark Knight Station," Natalya said.

"Seems logical."

"They couldn't have anticipated we'd discover the error," Trask said.

"Who would have placed the order if I hadn't come aboard?"

Trask stared at her for a moment. "Pritchard would have been the only logical one."

"Agreed but there's a breakdown there."

Trask nodded. "How would he have known? I don't think he's ever been in the spares locker."

Natalya sighed. "Do we have enough to posit that the spares were stripped to make room for the more expensive parts? Or are these two separate issues?"

Trask bit his bottom lip and stared up at the overhead again. "Without the spares being stripped down, there'd be no reason to order a big raft of parts. Good catch on that emitter bus coupling," Trask said.

Natalya nodded once in thanks. "Whoever received the order would have had to check them into the spares inventory."

"Right, but as long as the parts numbers matched, anybody doing it would have no way of realizing that the parts weren't for this ship unless they knew what they were doing." Trask looked at her. "Mel Solomon, for example. If Pritchard asked her to check them in, would she have known?"

"I don't know, Captain. Probably not."

Trask sighed. "Where the hell is Charlie Blanchard?" he asked, then shook his head. "Sorry. Rhetorical question." He pulled his tablet out and checked it. He sighed again and reholstered it.

"Mr. Lyons hasn't returned either," Natalya said.

Trask's face relaxed around his eyes. "Mr. Lyons has a problem, Ms. Regyri. He really needs help. Help we're not exactly set up to administer."

His voice reminded her of her mother's breaking-the-news-gently voice. "Yeah. I understand that, Captain, but just because he's an alcoholic doesn't mean he doesn't need our help now."

Trask nodded. "Rather the opposite, I suspect, but we can't help him if he doesn't want to be helped."

"If we got the parts into the spares locker, who'd have benefitted?"

"We'd have sailed back to Dark Knight Station and whoever took the first parts could get the next batch."

"So, this is a one-off job," Natalya said.

"Of course."

She flopped back in her chair closed her eyes. "I'm tired. Not thinking straight, but there's something not right here."

"Only one?" Trask asked.

She grinned without opening her eyes. "If this is a legit mega prototype, they've no reason to smuggle parts out of Siren."

Trask didn't say anything.

Natalya opened her eyes to look at him. He simply stared at her.

"What?"

"What if it's not a legit prototype?" he asked.

Natalya shook her head. It didn't help. "What else would it be?"

"Stolen?"

"No, it's got to have been built out here. Manchester yards are all in the middle of highly populated systems. They have to be. They need miners and asteroids to feed their refineries."

"Yeah, I didn't say it wasn't built out there. Only that it's no longer in Manchester's control."

The implications hit Natalya in the gut. "Who has that kind of resources?"

Trask held up a hand in a fist. "Iron Mountain." He held up his index finger. "They've got the knowledge and opportunity. They'd steal their own mothers and sell them into slavery for a fat pile of fresh credits." He raised a second finger. "High Tortuga. They have to know what's going on and where. Nobody spends a single credit unless they know about it. Having the first of these megas would give them a mobile platform to run banking from."

"They're already the banking system. They don't need a ship to keep track of. They've already got fleets out doing due diligence."

Trask shook his head. "Don't count them out too soon." He held up another finger. "Mel's Place. They're not exactly hijackers in the normal sense but getting this ship would simplify their logistical operation."

Natalya leaned forward. "We may be overthinking it."

"How so?"

"What if it's not a mega? What if there's somebody who got their hands on a Kyoryokuna drive and are trying to retrofit it onto—say—a Barbell?"

Trask's jaw opened and closed without making a sound. "How far could that ship jump?" he asked after more than a few heartbeats.

Natalya shook her head. "Too many dependencies. The power requirements alone beggar my imagination. It would have to be all but gutted and rebuilt—but a long, long way." She bit her lip for a moment, then said, "All the way to Iron Mountain from Dark Knight with a full load of stolen ore, probably."

Trask's eyes widened just a bit. "That's not good."

Natalya shook her head. "I don't know the full distribution of all the Toe-Hold operations but from the northern edge of the Western Annex, a ship like that could probably cover anything within twenty or thirty Burleson units."

Trask laid his hands palms-down on his desk and stared at them for several long moments. "Did Ms. Usoko find anything on the maintenance logs?"

"For the glassed drive?"

"Yes."

"She said the environmental team had drawn out stores but the inventory levels never showed the receiving records for any parts."

"That's all?"

"Well, she said something about Pritchard's fingers being in it, but that would be normal for an engineering chief." The reality of what she'd just said smacked her like a punch in the gut. "Wait." She looked up at Trask. He had a wolfish grin on his face and his eyes were anything but amused.

"Pritchard isn't an engineering chief," he said. "He's barely competent to dress himself. Did she say what kind of maintenance?"

"Only that he was moving inventory in and out. I think. I don't really remember. It was late and I was toasted."

"You're still not quite tracking, Ms. Regyri. Did she say *when* Mr. Pritchard manipulated the inventory?"

"Well, it had to be after June first. No records exist from before that, including backups."

"Not aboard," Trask said. "But I bet there are backups in Kondur's vaults that we can check when we get back."

"Doesn't help us now."

"No, but if any of the records are dated after you came aboard, that would be a very troubling finding."

Natalya's brain finally connected the dots. "I locked him out of the system."

"You did. Do you remember the date?"

"No, but Zoya should know. She created his guest account and it'll have a date-time stamp on it."

Trask started pounding on his keyboard. "I may be just the captain, but I think I can still find my way around the systems in my own boat," he said, a maniacal grin on his face.

After a few moments, he said, "June seventh."

"The glassed records are still mounted," Natalya said. "She burned them in the data closet."

He tapped some more, paused, and scowled. "That's odd. There's nothing there."

"Nothing there?" Natalya asked. "What kind of nothing?"

"No media mounted on the drive." Trask looked across the desk. "Would you be kind enough to go look and if there's nothing there, wake Ms. Usoko?"

Chapter Forty-six
Siren Orbital: 2363, August 2

Natalya took the three steps down the passageway into the data closet. The glass burner showed an empty carriage. She turned on her heel and was at Zoya's door in a matter of heartbeats. She knocked a couple of times. "Zee. It's Nat."

When she got no response, she tried again. "Zee?" She knocked a bit louder.

"What?" The voice was muffled and understandably grumpy.

"We need to talk."

Natalya heard some indistinct muttering and then the deadbolt clicked. "This better be good."

"Sorry, Zee." Natalya shrugged and cast a glance over her shoulder at Pritchard's door.

"What's wrong?"

Natalya lowered her voice and leaned in. "The glass drive is empty."

Zoya's eyebrows shot up. "Is it?"

"Skipper would like to see you."

Zoya nodded. "Lemme find a shipsuit. I'll be right there." She closed the door and Natalya heard the deadbolt snap into place.

She returned to the cabin and found the captain staring into his console with a perplexed look.

"The drive is empty, Captain. I woke Zoya. She'll be right along."

He grunted and looked up. "Our order was delivered yesterday."

"What?"

"I got a delivery notice for the new order we placed today. Apparently they delivered our old order yesterday afternoon."

Natalya shook her head. "I didn't receive it."

"I'm trying to contact the chandlery now. The new order should be here midafternoon."

"What the—?" Natalya heard a couple of quick raps on the door and opened it to see Zoya standing in the passage. "Come on in. It's getting weird out."

"Sorry to get you up again so soon, Ms. Usoko," the captain said.

Zoya walked in and plunked into one of the visitors' chairs. Natalya closed the door behind her.

"It's all right, Skipper. Nats says the glass drive is empty?"

"I checked twice," Natalya said. "Nothing on the tray at all."

"I take it you tried to access it?" Zoya asked.

"We were trying to look at the date-time stamps for Pritchard's maintenance on that database," the captain said.

Zoya pulled a disk out of her pocket and slipped it onto Trask's desk. "There's the glass."

"Whew," Natalya said. "I was afraid somebody took it."

"Somebody did," Zoya said. "I was worried about it too, so I swapped it out with a blank disk."

Trask looked up at that. "A blank?"

"Unless you know what to look for, it's hard to tell a blank from one that's not." She shrugged. "Somebody took the one in the drive. I'd look to Mr. Pritchard."

"Why him?" Trask asked.

"Deduction. I'm relatively sure it wasn't you, Captain. I've known Natalya a long time and she had no motive to take it. The only other officer aboard is Mr. Pritchard."

"Why an officer?"

"Ease of access, potential motive, and he knew we had something on the glass."

Natalya remembered standing in the passage with Pritchard. "He did see us last night."

The captain picked up the chip and slotted it into his desk console. "What am I looking at here?" he asked.

"There's a copy of the spares database along with an ancillary set of tables from the maintenance database. They're labeled. There's also a quick-and-dirty data analyzer there. It'll let you open the database records and scroll through them along with any maintenance activity."

"I see it," the captain said. "Got it." The captain scrolled through the records for several ticks while Natalya and Zoya looked at each other and waited. "This says Pritchard was in the maintenance database on the twelfth of July."

"Yes, Captain."

"Amazing work, Ms. Usoko. Don't let anybody tell you any different. His fingers are in the maintenance database. The question at the moment is how?"

"Not what?" Natalya asked.

"We'll get to that but you locked him out of the system on the eighth of June." He scrolled down the screen and pointed to records showing Pritchard logging in, setting up Natalya's account, and then changing his password. "I assume you did that, Ms. Regyri?"

Natalya looked at the screen and nodded. "Yeah. I had Zoya set him up with a guest account tied to his name."

"Shoulda been about four or five stans after those entries," Zoya said.

Trask scrolled up and found the record. "Neat job," he said.

"Thank you, Captain," Zoya said.

He sat back and looked back and forth between the two of them. "I'll ask again. How?"

Zoya and Natalya returned to their chairs.

Natalya shook her head. "I don't see how it's possible."

Zoya held her face in both hands and massaged her forehead with her fingertips. "Can you check to see what rights his account has now?"

Trask clicked a few keys. "Basically guest access."

Zoya and Natalya both looked up at the same time. "Backdoor." They spoke almost at the same time.

"How would Pritchard have a backdoor in this system?" the captain asked. "And why?" He pointed to his screen. "And what is he doing with these spares records? Checking things in as if we've just received them. Here's one on July twenty-third. We were in space that day."

"Moe's."

"Yes, but we got underway right after lunch mess. This is time stamped for 2150."

"He picked something up and wanted to hide it in the spares inventory?"

"He could have just tucked it under his bunk," the captain said. "Why the record?"

"We'd have to ask him," Zoya said. "Maybe it's not actually a thing. Maybe the updated record is a message to somebody."

Natalya shook her head. "Who else can see the spares inventory?"

"Almost everybody. Certainly every engineer," Zoya said. "Think about it. Who can check out a spare part?"

Natalya sat back. "Of course. I've spent too much time flying solo, I guess."

"We have a more pressing problem," Trask said, looking up from his screen. "Where's that half-a-million-credit parts shipment gone?"

"Did the chandlery get back to you?" Natalya asked.

"They've added the bill to our account. Somebody signed for it. I'm trying to find out who." He paused. "And how."

Zoya looked up. "Blanchard."

"What about him?" Trask asked.

"He signed for the order."

Natalya felt her eyes practically bug out of her head as she stared at Zoya.

Trask's forehead wrinkled but he didn't explode. "Spell it out for me, Ms. Usoko."

"Those maintenance records aren't Pritchard," she said.

Trask's eyebrows jerked upward. "How do you know?"

"Hunch." She nodded at the console. "Log in as Pritchard, Captain."

"I don't know his password."

"It's 'welcome aboard.' He never changed it from the default."

He shrugged but logged in. "I'm in."

"Try to edit something. Even grab a spare lightbulb from the spares system."

He frowned at the system. "I don't have anything but messages and entertainment options."

"Can you open a command window?"

Trask punched the hot keys. "No."

"He could have some kind of hot-key backdoor, but does he strike you as the brilliant but bumbling system geek?"

Trask pursed his lips and shook his head. "Steven's always been a bit of a cypher, but why Blanchard?"

"He's the only one not in this room who could spoof Pritchard's access. He's a system admin and can do anything. Including editing the logs after the fact to make it look like Pritchard did maintenance to files he didn't have access to."

Trask frowned. "Why would he do that?"

"Good question, but he wasn't aboard yesterday afternoon."

"Josh Lyons was off, too," Natalya said.

Trask's console bipped and he tapped a few keys. His face went slack. "Chandlery says Pritchard signed off on the order."

"I don't know. Perhaps ask him?" Zoya asked.

Trask nodded. "If you two would please wait here?"

They both nodded. "Of course, Captain," Zoya said.

Trask rose from his chair like it hurt him to stand. He straightened and left the cabin, closing the door behind him.

They didn't hear anything for a few moments, then a quick knock on a door, followed by a brief conversation, too low to hear— Trask and Pritchard's voices muffled by the distance and intervening bulkheads.

The captain returned, sat heavily in his chair, and tossed a chip onto the desk. "He claims Blanchard told him to get it and keep it safe."

"What about the spares?" Natalya asked.

"Claims he has no idea what I'm talking about." Trask looked at Zoya. "Could Charlie have spoofed the receipt?"

Zoya's eyes squinted for a moment. "Only if he could cross-load his thumbprint to Pritchard's record." She shook her head. "Depends a lot on where they pull the ident from."

"Explain," Trask said.

"Logically, they'd pull it from the CPJCT profile data, but sometimes these systems do stuff like pull from the ship's database because the ships provide authorization for signoffs."

"So you think they queried the ship and got Charlie's thumb but Pritchard's ident?"

Zoya shrugged. "Only explanation I could give for how Mr. Blanchard could have signed for an order with Mr. Pritchard's thumb."

Trask looked at Natalya. "Possible?"

Natalya thought about what would be required for a few heartbeats. "Not supposed to be possible," she said. "But neither is jiggering the auto-doc logs."

"So you couldn't rule it out?"

"Not with what we believe at the moment, no," she said. "If we can spoof ship transponders, swapping thumbprints in our own systems would seem pretty straightforward."

The captain's tablet bipped.

"I'm almost afraid to look," he said with a half-smile directed at Zoya and Natalya. He pulled up his tablet and flipped through a few screens with one stabbing index finger. "Interesting. Orbital security officers at the brow." He looked up at them. "They have Mr. Lyons."

Chapter Forty-seven
Siren Orbital: 2363, August 2

Natalya followed the captain down to the brow where two uniformed orbital security officers waited with Lyons just inside the lock. Lyons stood steadily enough but kept his head down, looking at his boots as nearly as Natalya could tell. The man's hair had a few cowlicks, but his uniform seemed clean enough, if rumpled. The alcohol sting in the air fairly watered her eyes.

"I'm Captain Trask. How can I help you?"

The female officer jerked a thumb at Lyons. "Morning shift found him sacked out in a shipping crate down on oh-six with a couple of empty hooch bottles. Won't say how he got there or how long he'd been there."

"Any charges?" Trask asked.

The male officer shook his head. "Nope. We kinda hoped he'd talk to you since he wouldn't talk to us."

"I dunno how I got there," Lyons said. His speech had a bit of a slur, like he didn't have complete control of his tongue. He bit his lips together, his head turning this way and that, looking anywhere but at Trask or Natalya.

Natalya stepped forward and touched his arm. "Are you being a mope?"

The frantic head movements stopped and he looked up at her. His face had a heavy stubble, and his eyes looked pouchy but clear. His lips tried for a smile and almost made it. "I don't remember. Last thing I remember was going ashore. Headed down the docks."

"That's the story he's been giving us all morning, Captain," the female officer said. "Nobody's pressing charges. Nobody's said boo about him. When we got him, he was a lot more confused. Rambling about cargo and spare parts. When we got his ident and found out he was your cargo master, we figured we might as well bring him along. He can sober up here as well as in our lockup."

"Not drunk," Lyons said.

The two officers rolled their eyes.

"Thank you, officers," Trask said. "I appreciate the consideration."

The male officer gave a jaunty wave. "You're more than welcome, Captain. Saves us a ton of reporting."

Trask chuckled at that. "I know how that works."

The officers left and the spacer behind the desk keyed the lock closed.

"Thank you, Mr. Lamparty," the captain said. He turned to Lyons. "Let's head up, shall we?"

Lyons nodded, his head moving in an exaggerated arc up and down. "Coffee?"

"I'll grab a mug on the way past the mess deck, if that's all right, Mr. Lyons," Natalya said.

Lyons looked around, one eye slightly squinting like the eyeball hurt. "Not drunk," he said again.

The captain looped an arm through Lyons's. "Come on, old son. Let's find someplace comfy and dark to chat, shall we?" He gave Natalya a nod and she scooted ahead.

Scuttlebutt traveled faster than Natalya. By the time she got to the mess deck, Chef Marah already had a tray ready with a carafe of coffee and a small plate of pastries. She thrust it into Natalya's hands almost before Natalya got into the galley. "Here you go, sar."

"Thanks, Ms. Marah. Appreciated."

The captain and Mr. Lyons had only barely cleared the ladder from the brow, so Natalya scooted up the ladder to the cabin and pushed through the door, balancing the tray precariously as she navigated the doorknob.

By the time she got the tray settled on Trask's desk, the two of them loomed through the doorway, Lyons all but stumbling and the captain's bulk turned sideways to get them both through the door. Natalya took Lyons's arm and helped him to a chair.

The captain closed the door behind him and blocked the curious glances of too many spacers walking past. He crossed to his desk and took a seat while Natalya poured half a cup of coffee from the carafe, handing it to Lyons, who took it in two rather shaky hands.

"Thank you," Lyons said with a jerky nod. "Thank you."

"Yes, thank you, Ms. Regyri," Trask said. "I think we can handle it from here."

Natalya felt a stab of frustration but nodded. "Of course, Captain." She started for the door when Lyons spoke again.

"Stay. Please." Lyons looked at the captain. "She can stay."

The captain glanced at Natalya and shrugged before nodding at the empty chair. She sat.

"When you're ready, Mr. Lyons," the captain said, sitting back in his chair and folding his hands over his chest.

Lyons gave another jerky nod and took a sip of the coffee. "I'm not drunk." He opened his eyes wide and then closed them tightly as if trying to exercise his face muscles. "Somebody slipped me something." He took another, longer, sip, then worked his nose and lips back and forth. "Feeling's coming back."

"What do you remember?" Trask asked.

"I signed off the ship and headed down the dock."

"Do you remember where you were going?"

Lyons squinted. "Burger," he said. "I wanted a burger. With onions."

Natalya watched the amusement flit across the captain's face. She felt herself grinning.

"Did you have any place in mind?"

"No. Figured I'd find one on the oh-two."

"Lots of bars on the oh-two," Trask said. His words carried no more weight than your average observation about a pleasant day.

Lyons stiffened as if he'd been stabbed. "No," he said, staring into his mug. He glanced sideways at Natalya. "No," he said again, quieter this time. "I wanted a burger. No booze. No beer. I hate beer." He shuddered. He stretched his mouth open and closed. "It's wearing off." He lifted the mug a bit. "This helps."

"You're not drunk," Natalya said. "I've seen you drunk."

"You've smelled me drunk," Lyons said with a crooked grin. "Do I smell drunk?"

She laughed and leaned over to give him a good sniff. She sat back, and frowned. "No, you don't smell drunk," she said, looking at the captain. "He smells like somebody spilled booze on him and left him. There's something else there, too. A mouthwash smell." The scent tickled her memory. "Pritchard. He smells like Pritchard."

"Pritchard?" Trask asked, his face slack. "Are you sure?"

"He uses that god-awful aftershave or cologne or whatever it is. Seems like he must bathe in it some days."

Trask stood and crossed to Lyons. "Nothing personal."

Lyons gave a short laugh that sounded more like a cough. "No problem, Captain."

Trask leaned over and took a snootful. "That fruity smell?" he asked, looking at Natalya.

"Yeah. That's not Mr. Lyons," she said. "He's got a milder, musky smell." She realized what she had said and felt the heat rising over her face. "Sorry, Mr. Lyons."

He laughed again. "It's all right," he said. "I do smell funny, even to me."

Trask took his seat again. "The officers said you were talking about spare parts and cargo when they found you."

Lyons frowned, his gaze centered on his coffee mug but his focus somewhere else. "Feels like a dream. Funny dream. Walking down the docks. There's a cargo train. Tug and a few wagons full of stuff."

"That's not unusual on the docks," Trask said.

"It's slippery. Like the harder I try to remember, the more it slips away." Lyons shook his head and closed his eyes. "It stops at our lock. Somebody comes out. I keep walking. Why did I keep walking?" He sighed and opened his eyes. "It's like I'm not really there. It's something happening to somebody else. Not real."

"You're getting more coherent as you go, Mr. Lyons," Natalya said.

"Can you see who comes out in your dream?" Trask asked.

Lyons sips his coffee. "It's gone again. I know I saw it. I remember seeing it, but I can't pull it together." He grimaces. "This is maddening. Like it's on the tip of my tongue but I can't think of it."

The captain nodded. "Take a little break. Have a pastry. You're probably hungry."

Lyons looked at the plate of dainties and swallowed hard. "I— uh—I'm not ready for food right now."

Trask sighed and ran a hand over his cropped hair. "I wish I knew where Charlie was," he said, a mutter barely audible over the blowers.

"Blanchard? He's dead," Lyons said. His eyes widened in surprise. "Did I just say that?"

Trask sat forward, leaning over his desk, his eyes practically bulging. "Dead?"

Lyons's eyes started darting left and right; even his head turned in tiny jerking arcs. "I don't know. It just came to me. I don't know."

"Auto-doc. Now." Trask stood and picked the cup out of Lyons's hands. "Come quick. There's probably still enough drug in your system for the auto-doc to identify."

The cargo master stood, considerably more stable on his feet after only a few ticks of sitting. "Of course. Yes," he said. He still stumbled and Trask took an arm to steady him.

"Damn me for being a fool. We should have started there. Can you make it?" the captain asked.

"I made it up here," Lyons said, a bit of spark showing. "I can probably make it down."

In a matter of moments they had him buttoned up in the auto-doc. After a quick scan, the machine closed down the lid and diagnostic processes scrolled along the readouts.

"What the hell?" Trask asked nobody in particular as he leaned in to watch the data from a few centimeters away, like that would make the process work better or faster or something.

After nearly a quarter stan, the auto-doc beeped and the lid drew back again, exposing Joshua Lyons lying on the diagnostic bed, his eyes closed and breathing regularly.

Trask looked at Lyons and then at Natalya. "Auto-doc says he's sleeping."

"That was more of a response than I expected," Natalya said. "Did it detect any kind of drugs in his system?"

"Some kind of benzodiazepine derivative according to this." Trask's finger pointed to a line on the monitor. "And something else I don't recognize. Auto-doc says it's a soporific."

Natalya read the line and nodded. "Knock him out and keep him out."

Trask looked at her.

"My mother had issues with insomnia. She took that for a few stanyers." Natalya shrugged. "Better living through chemistry."

Lyons stirred in the pod. His eyes blinked open and he looked at Trask, then Natalya. "This can't be good," he said after running his tongue over his lips and stretching his mouth a little.

"Have a headache?" Trask asked, his voice low.

Lyons considered the question. "A little. Nothing serious."

"The auto-doc flushed your system," Trask said. "You've been asleep for the last quarter stan or so."

The cargo master yawned. "Clearly not long enough. Am I injured?"

"Drugged," the captain said.

Lyons pursed his lips for a moment and blinked his eyes. "Sorry I missed it," he said.

"You remember anything?"

"I left the ship. Don't remember coming back, but I had the oddest dream." He looked back and forth between Trask and Natalya. "It wasn't a dream, was it?"

"Start from the beginning, you left the ship. Wolk had the duty. You must have checked out with him," Trask said.

Lyons closed his eyes and, for a moment, Natalya thought he'd drifted off to sleep again.

"Wolk, yes. Left the ship, turned to starboard. Headed for the lift. Met a cargo tug with three or four trailers full of stuff. I had to step out of the way. They practically hit me. They stopped at the lock and Wolk came out to talk to them. I kept going."

"Then what?"

"I woke up here."

"You don't remember coming back to the ship with Orbital Security?" Trask asked.

Lyons squinted a little but shook his head. "No. Not really. Maybe?" He shrugged. "Everything's a bit hazy and ... did I have coffee in the cabin?"

Trask nodded. "Yeah. You made some pretty astonishing claims."

"Like what?"

"You talked about Charlie Blanchard, for one," the captain said.

The cargo master blinked several times. "I don't remember it."

"Do you like Charlie?" Trask asked.

"Well, sure," Lyons said. "Everybody likes Charlie."

"Will you miss him?" Trask asked.

"Miss him? Why? Has he gone somewhere?" Lyons looked from Trask to Natalya. "He's all right, isn't he?"

"Haven't seen him since he left the ship yesterday," Trask said.

"That's not good." Lyons glanced around. "Say, could I maybe get out of this thing? I need to find the head and don't relish what this devil box might decide it needs to do about that."

Trask pushed the release button and the auto-doc tilted up to let him step out on his own.

"Thanks," he said. He staggered a little as he took his first steps.

Natalya grabbed his arm to hold him up.

Lyons nodded to her. "I guess I'm not as steady as I thought."

"Up to your stateroom, if you please, Mr. Lyons," the captain said.

Lyons nodded. "That's my goal, Captain." He looked at where Natalya still held his arm.

She released him and felt a blush building across the back of her neck.

He smiled at her before taking his first tentative steps out of the medical closet and up the passageway.

Trask sighed and ran a hand across the back of his neck before looking over at Natalya. "You and Ms. Usoko are getting quite an introduction," he said.

"He's not drunk."

"I know. Do you think he was actually going out for a burger?"

"I wouldn't blame him if he were. Ms. Marah's meals are wonderful but if a burger is his comfort food? Sure."

"What's your comfort food?" Trask asked.

"Fried chicken. Hot and greasy with fresh biscuits and butter."

"Don't see that much on a scout, I bet."

She laughed. "Now you know why it's my comfort food." She paused for a moment, screwing up her courage. "What's yours, Skipper?"

He looked at her with a sheepish grin. "Ribs. Barbequed pork ribs. So tender they almost fall off the bone."

Natalya's stomach growled at the thought and she fought the urge to wipe her chin. "Where do you find real barbeque in Toe-Hold space?"

He shook his head. "Haven't seen any since I left Dree. There was a joint just outside the shuttle port that made everything from scratch, including the charcoal. Raised his own pigs, even."

Natalya caught the wistful tone in the old man's voice. "That must have been amazing. You don't get back?"

He shook his head. "No."

The short answer made her bite back another question.

"What do you think about Charlie?" he asked.

"Me?"

"Yes, you. You and Ms. Usoko are about all I have left. I don't trust Pritchard as far as I can throw him at this point. Lyons—" He stopped mid-sentence and bit his lip, his eyes squinting a bit. "Well, I don't know about him." He shrugged and offered a sheepish smile. "He was easier as a drunk. At least I always knew where he was and what he was doing." He paused again. "I don't like that we haven't heard from Mr. Blanchard."

"He's either in on it—whatever it is—or he's dead?" Natalya asked.

"He could be hurt, lying in an auto-doc somewhere."

"Wouldn't the authorities have gotten in touch with you? They only need a thumb print."

"You'd think." He sighed. "Ms. Usoko seems to think he's in on it."

"That would be the simplest answer."

"Doesn't make it right," Trask said.

"No, but simplest answers often are."

Trask grunted and stood up from the stool, lumbering down the passageway after Lyons. "Cabin, Ms. Regyri."

"Aye, aye, Captain."

Trask stared at Natalya across the expanse of his desk. "You remember talking to me about recruiting a full-time crew?" he asked.

The question caught Natalya off-guard. "Yes."

"Think you can do it here?"

She felt like her eyes might bug out of her head before she got herself under control. "I've never been here before."

"Yes, but could you?" he asked. "How would you go about it?"

She sighed and let her brain work for a moment. "We need a couple of mates. We could use a real engineering chief. Engineers hang out at the pubs." She focused on Trask. "I assume there's a generic beer-and-finger food establishment here on the oh-two?"

Trask's shoulders twitched in a quick shrug. "I'd assume so."

"I'd start there. See if any engineering officer needed a berth."

"What about an astrogator?"

She met his gaze for a moment and then focused elsewhere. "Transient quarters on oh-nine. Put up a notice outside the lift."

"What? A sign?"

"Yeah. Old-school but there's always a community board down there. Wouldn't take much to add our own message to it." She shrugged. "Somebody between berths would be staying down there. We want somebody who's looking for an outfit like ours."

"Why not post on StationNet?"

"We could. We'd have to be a little careful about who we let aboard."

"That what your father would do? Post a sign?"

She felt a smile stealing across her mouth. "He'd just go hang out at the nearest breakfast joint and chat people up."

"That how he finds help?" Trask's eyebrows rose. He looked half amused and half intrigued.

"That's how he finds out what's happening on the station."

Trask sighed.

"You think we'll need an astrogator?" Natalya asked.

"Maybe."

"Zoya's pretty good."

"We'll need mates if we can find them. I'd put Ms. Usoko in as astrogator if she's willing, but we'd need a solid third and I'd feel more comfortable with a good first to cover her back."

"What about a chief engineer?" Natalya asked.

Trask chewed his cheek a bit before answering. "I'm going to restrict Pritchard to the ship until we get back to Dark Knight. You've done a good job so far. Any reason you couldn't keep doing it?"

"If we can get the emitter bus coupling replaced before we undock. I'm game. I'd feel better if we had a real engineer aboard in case something else goes pear-shaped on the ride home."

"Noted."

The chrono clicked over to 1145 with a snap in the sudden silence.

Trask eyed it. "Only lunch time? Seems like much later."

Natalya snorted. "Tell me about it, Skipper. I thought this was supposed to be a milk run."

He laughed and led the way out of the cabin. "We're not home yet, Ms. Regyri."

"That's what bothers me, Skipper."

Chapter Forty-nine
Siren Orbital: 2363, August 2

Lunch mess felt a bit lonely. With both Zoya and Lyons sleeping and Blanchard still missing, Natalya and the captain spent a strained—and virtually silent—half a stan with Pritchard carefully not looking at either of them. Even Bray knew enough to stay out except for those few moments he needed to serve.

As the meal ground to a close, Trask looked at Pritchard. "I don't have to ask you to stay aboard, do I, Steven?"

"I had no plans to go ashore." He didn't look up from his dessert plate. "If I might be excused, Captain?" Pritchard asked. "I'm not feeling very hungry at the moment."

"Please stay in your stateroom, Steven. I don't want any misunderstandings."

"Of course, Captain." He left the wardroom, moving slowly, and latched the door behind himself on the way out.

Natalya thought he made the perfect picture of a remorseful crewman.

She didn't trust it for a heartbeat, but there was little she could do. Looking at him set her teeth on edge. Even the scent of his too-minty cologne had her feeling slightly nauseated. She'd been aware of it before, but now the cloying scent stuck to the back of her throat.

She finished her meal and looked at Trask. "If we're done for now, Captain? I didn't get much sleep last night myself."

Trask nodded. "Grab a nap, Ms. Regyri. You've earned it."

Natalya made her way up the ladder to officer country. As she passed Lyons's door, she considered knocking to make sure he was all right, but thought better of it. After his ordeal, he wouldn't appreciate being awakened just for the social nicety.

That's what she told herself as she threw the deadbolt on her door and stripped off her tunic before sprawling on top of her bunk. She pulled out her tablet and set an alarm for 1430, just in case. The chandlery would deliver the real parts shipment around 1500. She wanted to be there for it.

It had been a long morning after a very short night but her brain kept trying to tell her something. She couldn't figure out what, but the ferrets in her head kept chasing the mice in her brain. Like the way Lyons had said Blanchard was dead. His apparent inability to remember even saying that had her baffled. Clearly something had happened but, try as she might, she couldn't figure out what it might have been.

Who was behind the theft of the parts? It seemed like a long-term plan, if the goal was to order more expensive parts from Siren. Who would have known they were there? Yet, without those parts having been stripped out, there would have been no reason to order more spares. Without that order, the Zeta parts wouldn't get onto the ship. When did the database get reloaded? And why was it zeroed out before the first of June?

Her exhausted brain went around the loop again.

Her alarm twittered her awake without her actually believing she'd been asleep. Maybe she hadn't. She took a moment to rinse off her face, then slipped into a fresh tunic and headed for the brow.

She found her old friend Helms at the desk, feet up and reading something on his tablet. "Good afternoon, Mr. Helms. I haven't seen much of you this trip."

He grinned at her. "Howdy, Ms. Regyri. You've obviously not been spending much time with deckies."

"It's been a bit hectic back in the rumbly bits."

"I heard you took out Town on the first day."

She felt herself blushing. "Are people still talking about that?"

"Only deckies, I think." He laughed. "You and Ms. Usoko have certainly livened things up around here."

"What's she done?" Natalya asked. "She doesn't talk much about what happens in her world."

Helms shrugged. "Not so much actually what she's done. It's that she's taken Albee's place." He rolled his eyes. "You have no idea how much difference it's made on this trip."

"Well, true. I've never been on one of these trips before, so I've nothing to compare it to."

He shrugged. "There's that." He shut off his tablet and pulled his feet down, leaning on the desk toward Natalya. "Can I ask a question?"

"You can ask," she said. "I won't guarantee I'll answer."

He smirked. "Fair enough." He wiped a hand across his mouth. "Scuttlebutt says you kicked Albee's ass after he attacked the Skipper. That's why he got booted."

"What's the question there?"

"Did you?"

"That's one I can't answer, I'm afraid." She shrugged.

"But you know what happened?"

"I was there, yes."

"I knew it," he said, his eyes alight with the excitement. "He had it coming, the old fraud."

Natalya held up a hand. "Hold it right there, Mr. Helms. I can't tell you what to think but I don't take well to talking about people behind their backs. If you want to speculate around deck berthing, I can't stop you, but not in my hearing, yeah?"

Helms sat back a bit, his uncertainty plain on his face but he nodded. Slowly at first, then more vigorously. "Aye, aye, sar. Understood."

"Thank you, Mr. Helms."

"Is there anything I can do for you, sar?" he asked.

"I'm just looking for a chandlery order. They said they'd deliver around 1500."

Helms nodded. "Busy day for stores. Chef Marah got a food shipment earlier. We getting underway soon?"

"I'm not sure, Mr. Helms. The brow watches getting old?"

He rolled his eyes. "Bad enough at Dark Knight. Here? Every few ticks somebody wants something. Complete pain in the ... er ... that is ... butt."

"Have you gotten to go ashore yet?" she asked.

"Oh, yeah. Got off most of yesterday. Had a few beers with some people from another Barbell. Forget the name. They were taking off last night, I think. The gang we were with had to call it a night about 2100 and get back to their ship." He shrugged. "Don't get to hang out with real spacers that often."

"Well, Mr. Helms, you're as real a spacer as I've met."

His hand went to the able spacer pips on his collar. "Not exactly legit, though."

"You want to be?" she asked.

Helms's face lit up for a moment and then closed down so fast Natalya wasn't sure she'd seen it. "It's not exactly possible, sar."

Natalya considered that for a moment or two. "What if it was?"

He shook his head, an odd expression on his face like he thought she might be messing with his head but he didn't dare call her on it. "I don't know, sar."

Natalya nodded. "Fair enough." She pulled out her tablet and did a quick query on ShipNet. When she didn't find it there, she pulled in a StationNet node and found what she was looking for. She downloaded it and then sent it to Helms. "*Spacer's Handbook,*" she said.

He looked up at her with a blank look. "What?"

"I just sent you a copy of the *Spacer's Handbook.* Everything you need to know to be a spacer is in there. You want to be an actual able spacer, you just need to pass the test. It's in there."

"I'm a Toe-Holder. How can I take the test?"

Natalya thought about that for a moment. "I don't know, off hand. What I do know is that if you're ready to take the test—and the opportunity comes—you'll be able to jump on it right then." She shrugged. "If you know the job, doing the job is a lot easier. Who knows? You might decide you'd rather be a High Liner than a Toe-Holder."

He laughed. "As if. Why would I want to be one of them?"

She grinned at him. "Careful, Mr. Helms. I'm one of them." She sighed. At least she had been. Once, not too long ago.

His eyes got wide and he pulled back a bit. "Sorry, sar. No offense."

"None taken." She smiled again. "Strange things happen between here and there, Mr. Helms. My father was a Toe-Holder and a certified High Liner engineer. I'm pretty sure you can be both."

He looked at his tablet and back at her. "Never thought of it that way."

"Never too late to start," she said.

The lock-call rang, startling them both.

"There's the chandlery," Helms said, pointing to the lock display.

A dark-skinned woman in a station jumpsuit peered into the pickup outside the lock.

Helms keyed the lock and Natalya stepped forward to meet her.

"Got parts for *Melbourne Maru,*" the woman said, even before the lock fully extended.

Natalya nodded and held out her hand for the manifest. "I'm Natalya Regyri, Engineering Third officer. I can sign for them."

The woman pulled the tablet back. "Sorry, sar. I'm only allowed to deliver to a Chief Pritchard."

Natalya stepped out of the lock and looked at the cargo tug with two wagons behind it. "Really?"

She held up the tablet and pointed to a line on the manifest. "I'm just the messenger, sar."

"Did you happen to deliver a shipment here yesterday sometime early afternoon?"

She shook her head. "No, sar. I was off yesterday. Can you get Chief Pritchard or should I bring these back when he's available?"

"Unfortunately, that might be a problem. Would the captain do in his stead?"

She frowned at the manifest then at the open lock. "Lemme check with the boss." She stepped away and hit a few keys on her tablet. With a glance over her shoulder, she hunched over the device and started speaking quietly.

Natalya pulled her own tablet out and sent a bip to Captain Trask.

Trask shambled out of the lock about the same time the chandlery worker—a Ms. Deunk, according to her name badge—turned back to Natalya. "Trouble, Ms. Regyri?" he asked.

"Interesting development. Seems the chandlery can't accept receipt from anybody but Mr. Pritchard."

Trask's eyes opened in surprise. "Is that so?" He turned to the delivery worker. "I trust your boss will accept my thumb for this delivery?"

"Yes, Captain. Of course." She seemed quite amenable. "You'll understand that I just needed to clear it with the office?"

"Prudent," Trask said. "You didn't happen to deliver here yesterday, did you?"

She shook her head. "No, as I told Ms. Reg ..."

"Regyri," Natalya said.

"Thank you, yes. As I said before. I had yesterday off."

"Would those instructions have been in force yesterday?" Trask asked.

She shrugged. "You'd have to check with the chandlery. I have no idea what might have happened yesterday."

"Can you give me a name? Somebody who might know?" Trask asked.

"See Labreque. He runs the fulfillment center on day shift."

"He'd know about yesterday?"

"If not, he'll know who does. Can I get you to sign off on this?" She held out her manifest.

"Let's wheel it on board and get it checked in, shall we?" Trask said.

She looked at the piles of goods and back at the captain. "Of course, Captain."

For the next two stans, they compared the parts coming in with the parts they'd ordered. Natalya double-checked the actual part specifications to make sure they were the parts needed for the ship.

Helms helped by providing muscle and reading off package labels while Deunk and the captain handled the manifest. When the last package came aboard, everybody breathed a sigh of relief.

"Thank you, Ms. Deunk," the captain said as he finished signing off on the receipt.

"Glad to be of service, Captain." She didn't waste any time getting off the ship and turning her little train of cargo wagons around. In just a few heartbeats she'd disappeared into the traffic on the dock, with only the tinny beep-beep of her proximity alarms to mark her passage.

"Halfway home," Natalya said, eyeing the stack of parts and packaging.

"Halfway?" the captain asked.

"We'll need to get this stuff all down to the other end of the ship and then log it into the spares inventory."

He shook his head. "Seems like your job is just beginning."

"Yeah, well, for this I can get help. A couple of grav-pallets, a few of my engineering crew. We'll have this stuff aft in a lot less time than it took to check in here."

"What about checking it into spares?"

Natalya grimaced. "That will take a bit longer but I learned a few tricks from Mr. Lyons on that score. Shouldn't be too bad."

Trask looked at Helms. "Button us up, Mr. Helms. No sense in letting all the heat out."

Helms snickered but keyed the lock closed.

"I'll leave this in your capable hands, Ms. Regyri. I need to see a man about a shipment." His expression had clouded over. Natalya didn't want to be Pritchard when the storm broke.

"Aye, aye, Skipper," she said.

CHAPTER FIFTY
SIREN ORBITAL: 2363, AUGUST 2

Natalya had just gotten started organizing the transfer of goods when Trask stormed back to the brow. "Helms," he snapped. "Tell me Pritchard's still on the ship."

Helms face went blank. "I'd be lying if I did, Captain. He went ashore while I was getting my lunch. Wazu was covering while I ate and logged him out."

Natalya watched Trask's jaw clench and his hands fold into huge fists. He nodded, slowly. "Very well, Mr. Helms. Thank you. If he comes back aboard, would you bip me?"

Helms nodded. "You bet, Captain. I'll pass the word to the next watch, too."

"Thank you, Mr. Helms. Carry on." Trask looked at Natalya. "Our little band keeps shrinking. Would you see me in the cabin when you've finished here?"

"Of course, Captain," she said.

Trask left the brow without another word.

"He doesn't seem pleased," Helms said.

"No, he doesn't."

"Is Mr. Pritchard in trouble, Ms. Regyri?"

Natalya looked at Helms. "Might be. The captain thinks Mr. Pritchard is restricted to the ship. Apparently Mr. Pritchard doesn't agree."

"Do you think he'll come back before we leave?" Helms asked.

"Who? Pritchard?"

He nodded.

"I don't know. I'd have to guess, and I've not had a lot of luck guessing lately."

Solomon and Town arrived with Sheddon and Reisine pulling grav-pallets. "We have spare parts now, eh?" Solomon said, surveying the pile on the deck with a certain glee.

"If you could help me get them down to engineering?" Natalya asked. "Just haul them back and stack them outside the spares locker."

Solomon nodded, and between the six of them they had most of the parts piled high on the two grav-pallets in short order.

"Anything fragile in this mound?" Solomon asked, eyeing the collection.

"Heck of a time to ask, but no. Everything should be packed solidly enough that a little bumping around won't hurt it," Natalya said.

Within a stan, she had everything stacked where she wanted it and felt confident that none of it had gone astray between the lock and engineering. She'd need to add everything to the spares inventory and stow it in the appropriate bins, but that would have to wait until she saw the captain.

She found him in the cabin, staring at his console. He looked up and offered a feeble smile. "So, we're down to you, me, Usoko, and Lyons," he said. "It's enough to get us home, but we'll get screamed at by TIC if we leave so shorthanded."

"There's also the matter of the emitter bus coupling," Natalya said.

Trask nodded. "I hadn't forgotten that. I assume you've got what you need to make it right?"

"Should have. Assuming the test and alignment tools work the way I remember."

"If they don't?" he asked. "Or do I not want to know?"

"Probably don't want to know."

He looked at her with a hard flat stare.

"Probably burn out the bus bars. Might wreck the channels."

"You make me feel so much more confident," he said, but his eyes took on a bit of life. "I saw your part came in safely. Stash that in your grav-trunk."

"I will. Thank you, Captain."

"Good, but that's not why I asked you here." Trask squinted at her across his desk.

"What do you need, Skipper?"

"At this point I have to assume I've lost both Blanchard and Pritchard. I don't know where Blanchard might have gone to, but after Mr. Lyons's pronouncement, I fear the worst. If Charlie were able, he'd have been in contact."

"You think Mr. Pritchard has fled?"

"Yeah. I have no idea what the hell he was thinking." Trask shook his head. "I don't even know him anymore."

"The alternative of going back to face Verkol Kondur wouldn't appear to have a long-term positive return on investment," Natalya said.

"If he didn't do anything, Kondur wouldn't do anything. He's a fair man."

"Not the kind that would scapegoat the nearest warm body?" Natalya asked.

Trask took a deep breath and blew it out. "I can't say never, but I've never known him to."

"Half a million credits might make a man see things in a harsher light."

Trask nodded. "I'm trying to get to this Labreque fellow at the chandlery."

"Why don't you go down there and roust him out?"

"I would, but I've got OD," Trask asked. "I'm not waking Ms. Usoko up unless I absolutely need to."

"Mr. Lyons?"

"I thought of him. In a pinch, sure, but with his reputation with the crew, it would be a last resort."

Natalya's eyes felt like they were bugging out when she realized where the Captain was heading. "You're not thinking of making me OD."

The small smile playing around his lips scared Natalya. "You've got a great reputation with the crew. Not just engineering."

"I don't even know the crew outside of engineering."

He chuckled. "They know you. You're the one who took Town without hitting him and kicked Albee's ass. You made a lot of friends that day."

"I didn't know Town was that unpopular."

"He wasn't. He's not." Trask shrugged. "He can have a temper and a lot of his shippies have felt it. You not only took him down, you picked him up after." Trask paused. "Albee was icing on the cake."

"What do I know about being OD?"

"More than pretty much anybody else on the ship, with the possible exceptions of Usoko and me." He tilted his head and squinted an eye at her. "You're not going to sit there and tell me Usoko knows more about running a ship than you, are you?"

"At least she's in the right division."

"Evasion doesn't become you, Ms. Regyri. What would your father do?"

Natalya chuckled in spite of herself.

"Good. Now, I'm going to make you OD for a couple of stans while I go track down this Labreque in the chandlery." He glanced at the chronometer. It clicked over to 1612. "I want to get him before the day shift goes off and I'm afraid I might already be too late."

"Any orders for me?"

He stood and thought for a moment. "Don't burn the place down while I'm gone."

"What if Mr. Pritchard or Mr. Blanchard returns?"

"Bip me. I won't be gone long."

"What if—"

Trask leveled a stare at her. "Bip. Me." He shrugged. "Or deal with it. Whatever it is. You're the OD. Maude knows you can't make any worse decisions than I have lately." He sighed and stomped out of the cabin. She heard him clatter down the ladder.

Realizing what had happened, Natalya jumped to her feet and followed him down. She wanted to check in with Helms and make sure the lines of communication were open and untangled.

At least until Zoya woke up or the captain returned.

CHAPTER FIFTY-ONE
SIREN ORBITAL: 2363, AUGUST 2

The grin Helms gave her when she stepped onto the brow could have lit up the entire engine room. "You're the OD," he said.

"He told you?"

"On his way out." He lowered his voice and stuck out his chest. "Regyri has the conn. Don't give her any grief."

"Is there anybody still aboard?" she asked.

"Ms. Marah is working on dinner, I hope. I think Bray has the duty today. Both the Solomons took off a few ticks ago. Deck gang is almost all ashore except for the watch section and Ms. Usoko." He consulted his console. "You want a list?"

She shook her head. "No. Just trying to get a feel for who's here and who's not."

"Mostly not," Helms said. "Actually, I think most of engineering is still aboard. Knowles left this morning but his people are still aboard."

Natalya nodded. "Figured most people would be off the ship."

The lock-call rang.

"Now who?" Helms asked, peering into the pickup.

Natalya looked over his shoulder but only saw the top of a cap with the station logo on it. A cargo tug and trailers waited at the foot of the ramp.

"We're not expecting another shipment are we, Ms. Regyri?" Helms asked.

"Not that I know of, but we should probably see what they want. Maybe they found our lost shipment."

Helms keyed the lock open and crossed the brow to see. Natalya started to follow him but nearly bumped into him as he backed up, his hands raised, and the barrel of a vicious-looking needler stuck in his nose.

"Ah, good. Ms. Troublemaker. He left you in charge?" Pritchard stood just inside the lock, his weapon pressed into Helms's nose and his eyes fixed on Natalya. "Would you like to try your ninja skills on me? I'm sure Helms here wouldn't mind getting a brain full of needles." He glanced at Helms out of the corner of his eye. "Would you, Helms?"

Natalya lifted her hands, palm out and backed away from the lock. "We thought you'd scarpered with the loot," she said.

"We?"

"Captain Trask and I."

"In a matter of speaking, I did." He nodded at the cargo train behind him. "I just brought it back again."

"So what's your plan?" Natalya asked.

"Well, since the captain so conveniently left the ship, it would be a good time for me to load up and head out." He smiled at Natalya. "You and Ms. Usoko won't give me any trouble about that, will you?" He pressed the needler into Helms's face.

"You know we can't leave the system, right?"

"Yes. Although, I understand you got the parts you needed this afternoon so you might be able to fix it before we hit the Burleson limit." He nodded at the cargo tug outside. "We just need to get those parts loaded up and we'll be on our way."

"The captain will be back before we could load that all up, right?"

"Just you? Certainly. Luckily, I'm not relying on your muscles." He nodded at the watchstander's desk. "If you'd be so good as to have a seat back there. Hands on the desk?"

Natalya took the watchstander's seat as Pritchard backed Helms against the bulkhead. "I've seen you in action, Ms. Regyri. Very exciting. I had no idea people could move that fast. Please don't move like that here. No matter how fast you are, you can't beat my trigger finger. That's a good girl."

"So how are you going to get that stuff aboard?" Natalya asked.

Pritchard whistled. "Wolk? Town? Come along, gentlemen. Time to earn your keep."

Wolk and Town strolled out of the passageway and smirked at Natalya.

"If you'd be so good as to fetch that cargo from the dock, gentlemen? We can end this farce and get underway," Pritchard said.

The two started dragging the parts in and stacking them against the bulkhead. Some of the packages were so large, it took both men to carry them. The loading took almost no time; Natalya had to give them credit. Not having to verify the shipment against a manifest sped up the process greatly.

Natalya glanced at Helms. Sweat coated his face and his eyes were screwed shut.

"How do you expect to get away with this, Mr. Pritchard?"

He shook his head. "Uh-uh. That would be telling."

"We can't jump. Do you think you can just dodge around outrunning TIC interceptors until—what? I fix the drives and we scamper off into the Deep Dark?"

"Seriously, Ms. Regyri. Have you been reading adventure novels?" He tsked. "I've been working on this for ... well ... a very long time. At first I thought your arrival was a disaster. Then I realized you were the perfect patsy. And no, I'm not going to share the plan with you." He shrugged. "Sorry."

"Captain Trask will have something to say about this."

Pritchard laughed. "Well, mostly he'll say 'where the hell's my ship?' because we won't be here when he gets back."

"Last ones, boss," Wolk said, adding a package to the stack.

Town joined him and tossed the last package on top before keying the lock closed. "Ready, boss."

"We can't leave without filing a flight plan. We need a tug to get out of here," Natalya said.

"Oh, stuff and nonsense," Pritchard said. "You think I'm going to hang around here waiting for permission?" He laughed. "Mr. Wolk, would you get up to the helm? We'll need a little assistance to get moving quickly."

Wolk disappeared up the passageway. Town lounged against the pile of packaging.

"How is this even going to work? You can't just blast out of a CJPCT dock."

"Don't be foolish, my girl. Of course we can." He spoke over his shoulder without taking his eyes off Natalya. "Get ready on the emergency release, if you would, Mike. We need to be ready to move when Aaron has the helm."

Town pulled the cover off the emergency release lever and tossed it to the deck with a clatter. "Ready, boss."

"You see, Ms. Regyri. You've been around High Liner docks long enough to know that, occasionally, vessels need to leave in a hurry. We can't be waiting around tied to an orbital that's ruptured and bleeding atmosphere. Perhaps on fire. Now can we?"

His words sent a chill into the pit of Natalya's stomach. "You wouldn't."

"Oh, wrong word. I think you're looking for 'didn't' but yes, I did. We've plenty of time yet, but by the time Mr. Wolk has secured the bridge, we'll be able to slip away in the confusion with few people being the wiser, I think."

They waited for several ticks. Helms opened his eyes and cast a sidelong glance at Natalya.

Natalya shrugged. "Seems like it's taking him a long time to get to the bridge," she said. "Suppose Zoya caught him?"

Pritchard shrugged. "I'm sure he can dispose of one jumped-up green third mate."

"What about Charlie? Blanchard is a big guy. I suspect he's won his share of fights."

Pritchard dug the needler into Helms's face a little deeper. "Nice try. Charlie Blanchard won't be bothering us any time soon. By now he's probably halfway to a re-entry burn." He shrugged. "Too bad he's not in a shuttle."

They waited some more. Town started to fidget. "Want me to go check on him, Boss? Maybe he ran into trouble."

"Patience, Mr. Town. Time has a funny way of slowing down. It hasn't been as long as we think."

After another two solid ticks, Pritchard nodded. "Go. Find him."

Town ran down the passageway into the ship.

"You know, Captain Trask is going to be back soon," Natalya said.

Pritchard's gaze flicked to the chronometer on the bulkhead above the desk. "He's probably still trying to locate Labreque." He shrugged. "Won't matter. He can't open the lock from that side."

Natalya tilted her head to the side. "No?"

Pritchard smirked. "You thought you were so clever to lock me out of the system. Silly girl."

She sighed. "I knew we should have looked for a backdoor."

"Yes, but even if you had found it, the system security on this bucket is dreadful. I'd have just co-opted Lyons's login and kept going."

"Looks like it's just you and me," Natalya said after another tick had passed.

"Well, and my pointy friend here, for the moment." He twisted his needler against Helms's face. "Have a little faith."

"How did you jigger the emitter bus coupling?" she asked.

"Easy. After we jumped into Albert, I ran a jumper across the terminals of the coupler. Next time we sent juice through it, the jumper fried but shunted enough of the power to the coupler itself to cook it."

"Ballsy. What made you think that would work?"

"Trade secret. Worked perfectly though, didn't it?"

"Until I pulled the coupling out and cross-checked the part number."

"Yes." Pritchard sighed. "You've been a bit tedious but very easy to lead into ordering the parts. I thought I was going to have to do that myself. When Kondur sent you and Ms. Usoko, I admit I wasn't sure how that would all work out." He smiled. "Turned out, it worked beautifully."

Natalya's tablet bipped and she started to reach for it.

"Uh-uh," Pritchard said. "Hands on the desk."

She flattened her hands on the desk and shifted her weight on the stool, gathering her legs under her.

"Easy, Ms. Regyri," Pritchard said. "Rash actions could be fatal for Mr. Helms."

She heard some scuffling in the passageway into the ship.

Pritchard heard it, too, but he only glanced that way before smiling at Natalya. "Won't be long now."

"Natalya?" Zoya's voice sounded loud, echoing down the passageway, as her footsteps came closer.

Pritchard looked over his shoulder, swinging his gun hand toward the sound.

Natalya dove for Helms, shoving him to the deck before Pritchard could turn back. The sprangity-sprang of high-speed needles crunching against the bulkhead followed only a heartbeat later. Natalya kicked Pritchard's left knee backward, felling him like a tree. A second kick caught him in the side of the head, leaving him dazed.

The lock beeped and then started to lever open as black-suited figures swarmed through the opening.

Natalya was never so glad to see TIC agents in her life.

One agent rushed Pritchard and stuck an ugly short-barreled weapon against the side of his head. "Please don't move. This would make a hell of a mess."

Pritchard said nothing beyond a high-pitched keening as he tried to cradle his broken knee.

Shouts of "clear" echoed around the lock and one more officer strode up the ramp and into the ship. He stripped off his balaclava and grinned at Natalya. "Nice work, Ms. Regyri."

It felt like the deck shifted under her as she stared up into the grinning face of the man she knew as Charlie Blanchard.

"Town and Wolk were in on it. They're somewhere aboard."

"We have them, Nats," Zoya said, looking down over the desk.

Blanchard looked at the pile of goods in the corner of the brow. "And we have our parts back. Excellent." He leaned over to Pritchard. "Just so you know, Vagrant's ship has already left the system and the little presents you left down on the oh-six deck aren't going to surprise anybody."

Pritchard's face, already a pale, waxy mask filmed in sweat, turned red. "I don't know what you're talking about."

"You hold onto that story, Pritchard. I'm sure the magistrate will love to hear it." Blanchard looked at Helms and Natalya, still tangled on the deck. "Sorry. Are you two all right?"

Helms nodded. "Banged my shoulder on the way down, but better than a face full of needles."

"Nats? You've got blood on your neck," Zoya said.

Natalya reached back and found only one stinging spot on the back of her neck. "I got creased, I think." She reached up and brought back bloody fingers. "Yeah."

"Morrison, Cross. Get Pritchard out of here. Velotta, go with Usoko and retrieve Town and Wolk. Waters, check Regyri's neck." He held a hand down to Helms. "Mr. Helms? Can you untangle enough to get up?"

Two of the black-clad agents hustled Pritchard off the ship. One agent—Waters—cleaned Natalya's wound and slapped a field dressing on it. Helms stood against the bulkhead, rubbing his cheek where Pritchard had ground the barrel of his needler into it. A couple of ticks later, Velotta brought Town and Wolk down in handcuffs and took them off the ship. Zoya and Josh Lyons peeked around the corner.

"What the hell is going on here?" Captain Trask bulled up the ramp from the dock, a black-suited agent attached to his bicep.

"Sorry, sir, he got by me," the agent said.

"Let him go, Wallace. It's his ship."

"Charlie?" Trask blinked several times. "My gods, Charlie? We thought you were dead."

"Not yet, Skipper. Sorry, I couldn't get in touch with you. I was a bit tied up."

Trask looked at Natalya, still sitting on the deck. "You all right, Ms. Regyri?"

"Caught a ricochet. Stings a bit, but yeah. I think Pritchard is the only one injured."

"Pritchard? Where is he?"

"Skipper? We probably should have this conversation in the cabin?" Blanchard said. He gave a nod to the multitude of wide-eyed crew who had joined Zoya and Lyons at the end of the passage.

Trask pulled himself together and nodded. "Yeah. Of course." He started for the passageway and most of the lookers vanished back into the ship, the buzz of conversation already building as they went.

"Waters, Cross. Get Orbital to send up a team to collect these parts and get them into evidence. Get a receipt to the chandlery so they don't charge the ship. Secure the dock. I'll be a few ticks with Captain Trask. Make sure Pritchard gets medical treatment for his knee."

"Yes, sirs" popped around the deck and agents streamed off the ship.

"Are you all right to finish your watch, Mr. Helms?" Blanchard asked.

Helms nodded. "Yeah. I think so." He rubbed his cheek again. "Yeah."

Blanchard put a hand down for Natalya and she grabbed it. He pulled her to her feet and held onto her hand for a moment. "You're all right?"

She nodded. "Yeah. Just a little shaky."

"After-action nerves," Blanchard said with a grin.

She laughed. "Yeah. Right."

With all of them in the cabin, Natalya felt a little hemmed in. Trask sat at his desk while Lyons and Zoya took two of the visitors' chairs. Natalya found herself propped against a corner of the bulkhead while Blanchard stood in front of the closed cabin door. In his black body armor and uniform, he looked huge.

Trask looked around the cabin once, then nodded. "How bad is it?" he asked Blanchard.

Blanchard shook his head. "You're not under arrest. The ship is free to go, but you might want to finish the repairs on that emitter bus coupling and maybe hire a couple of crew before you leave."

Trask's eyes widened. "You're not coming back with us?"

"Sorry, Skipper. I've been recalled."

Trask chuckled a little. "I knew we had TIC aboard. I never thought it was you."

"What was that all about?" Zoya asked.

"I can't tell you most of it. Pritchard is a pawn in a larger game. Unfortunately, he got greedy and stupid at the last, forcing us to step in. There's enough evidence to put him away for a very long time, but we lost a chance at cracking the larger problem."

"There's a mega out there, isn't there," Natalya said.

"We don't know. We believe there may be." He shrugged. "You've already put the pieces together. We'll have to do some more legwork, but it'll be up to different agents now."

"They're already in place, aren't they?" Trask asked.

Blanchard grinned. "No comment."

"Who'm I going to going to get to replace you, Charlie?"

Blanchard lifted his chin in Zoya's direction. "She can do it."

Zoya's jaw dropped. "You've got to be kidding."

Blanchard shook his head. "Not in the least. Boot third maybe but I watched you step up when it mattered."

Trask nodded. "I can see that." He looked at Natalya. "You and I need to chat about staffing levels."

"Me?" Natalya said.

"It was your idea."

Blanchard grinned. "Josh?"

Lyons shrank a little into the seat. "Yeah?"

"Good going," he said. "When you get back to Dark Knight, think about seeing somebody."

"About the booze?"

He shook his head. "About the other thing."

Lyons started and stared at Blanchard. "You know?"

Blanchard shrugged. "My job."

Lyons frowned and glanced at Trask, then Natalya. He nodded. "Yeah. Will do."

Blanchard's tablet bipped. He pulled it up and looked at it. "Time," he said. "Thanks, Skipper. It's been an honor sailing with you. Ms. Regyri, Ms. Usoko. Keep doing what you're doing."

"Wait," Natalya said. "What did Pritchard think he was going to accomplish by taking the parts out in a ship that can't jump?"

"A fast packet has been hanging around the L2 point. It's registered to a shell company over in Tellicheri. It jumped out of the system just after we grabbed Pritchard."

"That was dumb," Zoya said. "Coming back with the goods."

Blanchard smiled. "Yes. It was. He had a shuttle ready to take him and his goods off last night, but the shuttle pilot got cold feet at the last minute. He had to improvise. Lucky for us he picked the wrong people to mess with." He nodded to the captain. "I'll show myself out." He slipped out of the cabin and latched the door behind him.

Trask looked around. "Well, this is awkward," he said. "Not enough crew to actually get underway and we can't stay very much longer."

Zoya grinned. "I think we just got carte blanche from TIC."

"At least Enforcement," Natalya said. "Inspection and Certification might still give us trouble."

"Mr. Lyons, how are you feeling?" Trask asked.

Lyons blinked several times and rotated his head around on his neck a bit. "A bit boggled, Captain."

"Can I lean on you a bit?" Trask looked at Natalya and Zoya in turn. "All of you, actually. I need you to take OD watches while we get the crew established and the repairs done." He smiled at Zoya. "Ms. Usoko here gets them by virtue of being in Deck

Division and Ms. Regyri has had her trial by fire." He looked at Lyons again. "Normally I wouldn't ask a Cargo officer to stand OD because we'd have enough Deck officers to cover." He spread his hands to indicate the small group gathered. "We're a bit short at the moment."

Lyons nodded. "If you think I can do it, Captain? Sure." He paused and looked at his hands. "I think I'd like that, actually."

"No pressure, Mr. Lyons. You're the senior officer here behind me and I've seen you rise to the occasion helping Ms. Regyri."

"You'd trust a drunk?" Lyons asked, a red flush climbing up his neck.

Trask pressed his palms against the top of his desk and stared at the backs of his hands for several long moments before looking up. "No, Mr. Lyons, but I trust *you*."

Lyons swallowed hard and nodded. "Yeah, sure."

Trask looked at Zoya. "Would you run up a watch schedule for OD and brow watches? Put the four of us on rotation, eight on, twenty-four off?"

"Of course, Captain."

"Take anybody you have left in Deck Division for brow watch. Same schedule. I think we still have four people?" His grin looked a bit grim.

Zoya nodded. "We'll have to move up an ordinary spacer, I think."

"We just need a warm body at the front door," Trask said.

"Will do, Captain."

Trask looked at Natalya. "You've got Knowles and his team on environmental. They're not standing watches, as I understand it?"

"That's my understanding as well, Captain," Natalya said.

"Don't mess with success, but I need engineering to take over the fire-watch details."

Natalya nodded. "I'll get some of the gang to run them every couple of hours. We've got a few wipers who can contribute. We should have been doing it all along."

"Thanks, Ms. Regyri. We've had a rather loose organization aboard and the transition may be a bit rough, but I think we need to tighten this up so we don't wind up with people who feel like they're not important." He looked at Lyons with a sad smile. "Or people who feel like they're carrying the whole load."

Zoya said, "I think we can balance that out a bit, Captain."

"I know we can, Ms. Usoko." He looked around at each of them. "Anything else?"

"Can we start training some of the crew to actually have the ratings we're pretending they do?" Natalya asked. "I don't doubt they're capable with what they know, but getting them up to speed with what the CPJCT thinks they should know will help all of us."

"You're not thinking we're going legit, I hope?" Trask asked.

"I wouldn't dream of it, Skipper."

"Then sure. If they want to. You can be training officer." His grin bordered on evil.

Zoya chuckled. "You know better, Nats."

Natalya sighed. "Outsmarted myself," she said.

"If there's nothing else?" Trask looked around and paused for a heartbeat. "Then let's get this ship ready to go. Mr. Kondur needs this can of milk and I, for one, want to get home."

Chapter Fifty-three
Dark Knight Station: 2363, September 15

Natalya's tablet bipped with a summons to the wardroom. She'd barely secured from docking and still had to finish packing her grav-trunk. With the voyage over and the new crew settling in, she really just wanted to get back to the *Peregrine* to make sure the ship was still there.

She sighed and tossed a roll of boxers into her trunk before heading out. She met Zoya in the passageway outside. "You, too?" She held up her tablet and gave it a little shake.

"Wardroom? Yeah. Any idea what it's about?" Zoya asked.

"You were on the bridge with the skipper. I haven't seen him since breakfast."

Zoya laughed. "You know Trask."

"Never use two words when a grunt will do," Natalya said.

Zoya laughed again.

The passages seemed deserted after the six weeks of having a nearly full crew aboard. Natalya wondered if she'd miss the give-and-take of shipboard life with a full crew when she got back to her scout. She smiled, remembering the recruiting effort to bring the ship's complement up to snuff. She still couldn't believe she'd found a chief engineer who wanted a berth on a Toe-Hold ship. The woman's name still tickled her brain. She knew it from somewhere, but couldn't remember where.

Zoya opened the wardroom door and stopped short just inside for a moment before stepping aside to let Natalya in.

The room was packed and everybody was clapping.

The new mates—a first and a third—looked a little out of place but smiled and clapped along with everybody else. Trask beamed from the head of the table and Josh Lyons whistled and stamped his feet.

A huge cake held pride of place on the wardroom table, with "Thank you! Zee and Nats!" picked out in green icing across its surface. Natalya felt a prickle at the back of her eyes and swallowed hard to try to push the lump down.

Verkol Kondur stepped out from behind the captain—clapping along with everybody else, a broad grin on his face.

Zoya had her hands clasped together in front of her lips and turned to look at Natalya, her eyes gleaming in the overhead lights.

The ovation died down eventually. "What? Why?" Zoya asked.

"You two, probably more than anybody else this voyage, brought this run to a successful conclusion." Trask waved his hands around to encompass the officers gathered. "The whole crew decided that we owed you a big send-off." He paused. "You haven't changed your minds, have you?" His eyes were wide.

Zoya looked at Natalya.

Natalya swallowed again and looked around at the faces of her new friends. She didn't trust herself to speak, but gave her head a small shake.

"Ah, well. Can't blame a guy for asking," Trask said. "Anyway. Thanks. I'll miss you. We'll all miss you." He clapped his hands together once. "All right, then. Sappy sentimental moment over, who wants cake?"

Everybody laughed and began queuing up. They pushed Zoya and Natalya to the head of the line to accept the ceremonial first slices from the captain.

Nobody sat but Bray circulated through the room, pouring coffee and tea as he went. Everyone got their slice of cake and the wardroom felt a bit too small and too warm for Natalya. The whole exercise felt more than a little overwhelming so she stepped back to lean against the bulkhead and give herself some breathing room.

She found herself next to Kondur. He had frosting on his upper lip, which he dabbed off with a napkin. "You did well out there," he said.

"Thank you, Mr. Kondur."

"Not exactly what you expected, was it?"

She shook her head. "I don't think anybody expected that."

Kondur's eyebrows twitched a little and he forked another bite of cake from the plate.

"Thanks for the opportunity," Natalya said, feeling like she needed to say something.

"Margaret Newmar hasn't sent me a ringer yet," he said. "It behooves me to take advantage of the people she sends."

"Thanks." Natalya stared at her plate. She had a hard time with praise and just wanted to get back to her packing.

"Trask has something for you, I think," Kondur said after a moment.

Natalya looked up to find Trask crossing through the throng, a box under his arm.

"Before you get too far along in packing, you'll want to allow space for this," he said, thrusting the box at Natalya.

She juggled her cake and the box for a moment before Trask helped her out by taking the plate out of her hand and placing it on the table. Everybody in the room watched her and she wondered if, with any luck, the deck might open up and swallow her so they'd stop.

"Thank you," she said, wondering what to do with it.

"Open it," Trask said.

"What? Now?"

Trask nodded. "Of course."

Natalya peeled back the wrapping to find a standard fleet parts box. She flipped it over and saw it contained the fuel coupling she needed to repair the *Peregrine*. She looked at it, confusion washing over her. She'd stashed hers in her grav-trunk, hadn't she? An envelope fell out of the wrapping and she stooped to pick it up off the deck. The note inside held only one line.

"Always keep a spare. Charlie."

The Golden Age of the Solar Clipper

Quarter Share
Half Share
Full Share
Double Share
Captains Share
Owners Share

In Ashes Born
To Fire Called
By Darkness Forged *

Milk Run
Suicide Run
Home Run

South Coast
Cape Grace*

Tanyth Fairport Adventures

Ravenwood
Zypherias Call
The Hermit Of Lammas Wood

* Forthcoming

Awards

2011 Parsec Award Winner for Best Speculative Fiction
(Long Form) for *Owners Share*

2010 Parsec Award Winner for Best Speculative Fiction
(Long Form) for *Captains Share*

2009 Podiobooks Founders Choice Award for Captains Share

2009 Parsec Award Finalist for Best Speculative Fiction
(Long Form) for *Double Share*

2008 Podiobooks Founders Choice Award for *Double Share*

2008 Parsec Award Finalist for Best Speculative Fiction
(Long Form) for *Full Share*

2008 Parsec Award Finalist for Best Speculative Fiction
(Long Form) for *South Coast*

Contact

Website: nathanlowell.com
Twitter: twitter.com/nlowell
Email: nathan.lowell@gmail.com

About The Author

Nathan Lowell first entered the literary world by podcasting his novels. The Golden Age of the Solar Clipper grew from his life-long fascination with space opera and his own experiences shipboard in the United States Coast Guard. Unlike most works which focus on a larger-than-life hero, Nathan centers on the people behind the scenes—ordinary men and women trying to make a living in the depths of interstellar space. In his novels, there are no bug-eyed monsters, or galactic space battles, instead he paints a richly vivid and realistic world where the hero uses hard work and his own innate talents to improve his station and the lives of those of his community.

Dr. Nathan Lowell holds a Ph.D. in Educational Technology with specializations in Distance Education and Instructional Design. He also holds an M.A. in Educational Technology and a BS in Business Administration. He grew up on the south coast of Maine and is strongly rooted in the maritime heritage of the sea-farer. He served in the USCG from 1970 to 1975, seeing duty aboard a cutter on hurricane patrol in the North Atlantic and at a communications station in Kodiak, Alaska. He currently lives on the plains east of the Rocky Mountains with his wife and two daughters.

Made in the USA
Middletown, DE
04 December 2018